SUICIDE SONS

SUICIDE SONS
First Edition

This book is a work of fiction. All characters and events portrayed in it are fictitious, except where specific historical events are mentioned or cited in context. Any resemblance to real people or events is coincidental.

Printed in the United States of America

Published by Silverthought Press
www.silverthought.com

ISBN: 978-0-9841738-8-4

SUICIDE SONS

A NOVEL BY

MICHAEL GOLD

PHILADELPHIA | NEW YORK

This book is dedicated to the memory of my father, Harold Gold—Eagle Scout, United States Navy reservist, and walking companion.

He told me this story a few times—walking home from school once, he was set upon by a group of boys who tried to fight him because of his religion. He then threw a rock and hit one of them, ending the argument. He didn't think anyone should have to get hurt on account of religion—his or anybody else's.

"…Mr. Headley's description of a simple text message he received on November 26th: 'Turn on your television.' He spent the next three days glued to it, watching the siege in Mumbai that he had helped to plan take the lives of at least 163 people, including six Americans… When a prosecutor, Daniel Collins, asked Mr. Headley how the scenes made him feel, he said dryly, 'I was pleased.'"

—The New York Times, 5/29/2011

A Suicide Bomber's Statement of Intent

I am the bringer of life and a warrior for God.

God sent me to kill you.

You think you know God. You think God is on your side.

I know the mind of God. He has plans.

I will blow you up, as many of you as possible, and you will be killed. The carpenter's nails and ball bearings will pierce your skin and organs with the speed of bullets. Sacred nails. Sacred ball bearings. Sacred bomb.

There won't be much of my body left either. But I will go to God. I will cleanse my soul with your blood.

That will be God's revenge for your crimes against our people. God wants our tribe to rise again. That's why I'm here, at your doorstep. The filthy gates of your temple. Your money, your books, your very thoughts—all excrement. You're all just dirty little pigs to God.

My father taught me that.

And so the war will begin.

Part I

The Dry Run

(Akeyde Kletser)

The Manhattan heat pushed me down on the sidewalk until there was nowhere else to go but against the wall of a bank branch. Even at nine o'clock at night, sweat poured out of me. My shirt was soaked, my pants blotched. My black frame glasses slid down my nose.

Across 79th Street, the temple rose up, a stone wall four stories high. The wall had no decoration on it. There was small lettering near the entrance that told you the building's purpose. It didn't matter that the marquee said "Upper East Side Kawidtodian Center." To me, every word meant death.

A man and a woman walked by me sitting on the sidewalk, next to the bank. The woman, black-haired, leggy in a short red skirt, tittered as she passed, clung to her companion. I didn't notice what the man was wearing.

"Is he drunk?"

"I don't know. Just walk faster."

"Why is he wearing a blue and white windbreaker? In this heat?"

Wasn't it just like a woman to notice the details that don't matter? I was wearing a blue windbreaker with white stripes to match the favored colors of God's enemies.

"Don't know, hon. Let's keep moving."

They swept by. I hated the two, especially the girl, wished I could kill them also, right there.

I could have. Underneath the windbreaker was enough bomb to take out a good chunk of a city block. But the temple was empty and killing just two people who were clearly not my target would be an empty, pathetic gesture. The moment was not right.

My name is Akeyde. For a time, I didn't want it to be. I didn't want to face up to what I was.

My namesake is inscribed in our tribe's holy book. I am the beginning and the end.

Or so I thought.

Book of Heylik Shetyn, chapter XXXII:

A gray mountain stood over Akeyde. Clouds surrounded the sky, yet there was no rain. Most of the ground was like sand. God looked down.

Huts smoked with cooking fires coming through holes in the roofs. Animal hides were beaten into roofs for the huts.

Akeyde was walking in sandals. He was seven years old. Akeyde's father was ahead on the path.

"Akeyde, come now," he said, speaking the sacred language of the forefathers. His name was Zan, but Akeyde did not dare call him that. He was an elder of the tribe. Akeyde followed him on a path up the mountain.

"Where are we going?" Akeyde asked his father.

"Up the Heylik Shetyn Mountain."

"Why?"

"It is a holy place."

"What will we do there?"

"God will let me know."

Akeyde and Zan walked for many hours. The sunlight grew strong. The clouds went away. The heat from the sun was like that of God Himself.

"Father, I am tired."

Father carried Akeyde for a time. He found a cave on the path. There he set Akeyde down, in the cool of the dark place.

Akeyde drank water from his pouch. He slept in the cave. Zan went away. He found a lamb in a thicket. He drew a knife from the folds of his robe. With it, he cut the throat of the lamb and carried the dead beast to the cave.

A wolf came to the cave. It was a giant wolf. The animal was hungry. Akeyde awoke and hurried to the back of the cave.

Zan talked to the wolf.

"I offer you a lamb I have killed," Zan said. "We were to eat this lamb, but I give it to you."

Zan removed the lamb from the cooking place in the cave. He set it down before the wolf.

The wolf ate the lamb. Zan said that was good.

"This is the way of things," he said.

The next day, Zan and Akeyde came out of the cave. The wolf was there. He followed the two, Father and Son, as they walked up the stone path.

Akeyde did not want the wolf to be with them. Zan said "You walk ahead. I will walk between you and the wolf."

The heat of the sun fell on their faces. There were no trees on the mountain.

"There is no place to hide from God," Zan said.

They walked until the end of the day. Akeyde fell down on the path of rock.

Zan picked Akeyde up. He took the boy to a high place on the mountain. Then the son was set down on a plain of grass. There was a single tree in the middle of the grass.

The wolf was with them. Akeyde was afraid.

Akeyde's father said, "Do not worry. The wolf will not hurt you. God is with me."

In the evening, Zan stood up. From the sky came a point of light. The night was black, yet the point of light grew into a knife. The knife grew down and touched Father in the chest.

Then the knife withdrew back into the sky.

"I will do as you say," Zan said. Then the man and the boy slept.

The next day, the wolf knocked over the tree in the middle of the grass. Zan cut the tree into strips of wood.

"Why are you cutting the tree?" Akeyde asked.

Zan did not look at Akeyde. "We are going to make an offering to God."

"Should it please Father that I help?"

"No. You can rest, Akeyde."

Zan cut the wood into four cubits of beams, two for the arms, two for the legs. He bound Akeyde to the beams with rope on the wood. Then Zan drew a long knife out of the folds of his garment. The blood from the lamb was still on it.

"Father, why are you doing this?"

"God said we must honor His Word."

"I do not understand."

"God said that just as we gave the lamb to the wolf, so must we give ourselves to Him. He asked for a sign that I have faith in Him. You are the sign, Akeyde."

Akeyde looked at the wolf. It had sad eyes.

"Will it please God that I die?"

"Yes, son. It will please God."

Then Akeyde saw a tear come to his father.

"Do not be sad, Father. If God wants this, I will do it, with great gladness in my heart."

With hands clasped as one over the handle, Zan raised the knife over his head.

"You are truly pure, Akeyde. I hope God is pleased with my gift to him."

Akeyde looked at his Father. "You are a great man, Father. You will be a great leader of our people."

"It will be quick and merciful, Akeyde."

The knife came swiftly into the boy's chest. Akeyde went to God. And Zan and his people were blessed by their faith in Him.

The Blood Enemy

(Razvarr Abatut)

The sheet was made of polyester. Tacky as hell. It didn't breathe.

So typical of my mother. I had just gotten an associate's degree from community college and Mom couldn't even get me new sheets. This one was about 12 years old, I could feel it. It had bright yellow suns on a field of blue.

There was a part of me that wanted to throw it off. But, then, I was so tired. All I wanted to do was lie down.

Sleep made the time pass.

Every day was a prison. I used to mark them like the days on a calendar in a cell. Each day got a big black magic marker "X" on the calendar, each month featuring an illustrated event in the life of King Kawidtod. What a freaking bore.

I wished the old Soviet Union was still in business. They could make calendars with pictures of the gray apartment blocks they used to throw up. That I could relate to.

My father picked up about 800 of these pieces of crap for 10 dollars total at a garage sale in the neighborhood, to sell in his store. The things were made in the homeland by workers making about one dollar a day. The calendars were cheap, and it showed.

Each "X" meant one less day I had to spend here. I hated everybody.

The room was painted yellow too. That was my mother working on me. She thought yellow would brighten my mood. I hate yellow. Paint it black, the Rolling Stones said, and they were right.

I suddenly felt the urge to urinate. Thirteen straight hours in bed and my bladder was bubbling at me with urgency. How prosaic.

I fought the need. Even if I did get up to go to the bathroom, I was likely to end up pissing on my own feet. I couldn't even aim right. And I hated mopping up the wet tile with toilet paper. I wished my conscience would let my mother take care of it, but even I had minimal standards.

"Razvarr, come downstairs! We got you a gift!"

My mother was calling me in that sing-song, hopeful voice. She's such a bloody phony.

My parents didn't know me at all. One time in elementary school, shortly after we came here, they bought me a baseball cap and a mitt. Like I would care about something as stupid as baseball. Last year I got an iPod. I hate the music out there today. What am I going to play on it? Lady Gaga?

Suddenly, the polyester sheet looked a lot more appealing. I threw it over my head to make my mother disappear.

The Unwanted Meeting

(Akeyde Kletser)

I was a walking bomb and it felt good. Mostly. I just wished I could detonate myself, but I knew the time wasn't right. I came here on a dry run. Just to see how I would be able to walk around with the explosives strapped to my chest, and how the windbreaker would work with everything.

The test had worked out well. But why was my chest so heavy? The bombs, of course. But there was something else, too. Way inside me, trying to get out. I pushed it down and away from me. I didn't want to think about anything else but the job at hand.

I got up off the sidewalk, pushing off the hot concrete with both hands. The detonator button was bouncing around in the pocket of my windbreaker. I dusted off the bottom of my khakis, removed a pigeon feather attached to my pants. This town was so disgusting.

It was time to get on the subway. As I walked to 86th Street and the Lexington Avenue line, a young Upper East Side boy, rich, who couldn't have been more than 16 years old, walked right into me.

He was wearing gym shorts and a black tee-shirt with gold lettering that screamed *The Zan Clan—Mess You Up So Damn Good!* They're a heavy metal band from Stockholm. No kidding. Making fun of the tribe.

The boy had on running shoes that must have cost several hundred dollars, aqua blue. He was sweating heavily.

Him: "Ahhh!"

He smelled of liquor.

I tried to remove him from the delicate front of my jacket.

But having made contact, he was only all too eager to do it again.

"Hello, sailor. What bar did you roll out of?"

The son of a cow hugged me.

"Got a rocket in your pocket?"

I didn't say anything, didn't know what to say. There were 12 polyvinyl chloride pipes of TATP explosive packed in the pockets of the fishing vest underneath the windbreaker. My nerves shot through the roof.

I tried to unclasp his arms from around my neck. His breath was on me, the smell like being dunked in a punchbowl filled with vodka. The boy was a shark with its jaws open ready to eat.

"Come on, don't push me away. Don't be like that." He was acting and he knew it and I knew it. Then his mood turned quickly.

"Gonna whacko my Jacko? Or is it the other way around?"

Through my thick glasses, I gave him the most evil look I know.

"You're quite the little puppy, trying to look so mean."

I tried to push him away, but he was drunk and therefore unafraid. He patted my face and smiled.

Three other boys swarmed around me, like sparrows. His friends. They were blond and white and unblemished. Rich.

I realized I was openly naked. I wished I had brought a gun, but I had left it back in the apartment. Stupid. Idiot.

"James, are you trying to kiss this man?"

"He thinks I'm gay."

"Well, you hugged him. A man you don't even know. Shame, shame."

"Oh, like you know about shame, Armand."

"Come on, James. The ladies are waiting for us at Ginny's."

James was unmoved. He felt up my chest, surprised by what was in there.

"But he's so hard."

"God, you're such a whore," piped up one of James's little friends in the pack of sparrows.

James shot back: "And damn proud of it."

If he weren't so drunk, he might have realized what I really had packed inside the windbreaker. "Jimmy, let's go. He's such a freak, he looks like he might be a merd. A bullet dodger. Not worth the trouble."

Merd was a term of general insult for the tribe. It had the advantage of a double meaning. It meant "a pile of excrement," and was short for murderer, referring to Zan people as killers of Akeyde, the first sacrificial son. Bullet dodger meant something far worse—a reference to a century-old genocide of our people.

The comments stung, but I was too anxious to get away to reply. They were idiots of course—they didn't even know that the blue and white colors I was wearing were the colors of our blood enemies—the Kawidtodians, the Squids. And how would they know that I was a Zan? Did I have some sort of tattoo on my forehead announcing my faith?

Although I didn't know what I would have said anyway. When I heard this stuff, my tongue felt as if it was empanelled with cotton.

The boy stepped back, looked me over, from ankle to glasses, like I was the most beautiful thing he'd ever seen. He must have been really drunk.

"Let's go, bud."

Another boy, taller, maybe the leader, swept his arm around Jimmy and they hustled up the sidewalk to the corner and the white walk sign to cross 93rd Street.

I watched them leave. Jimmy turned to me as his friends guided him uptown, waved and smiled like we were old friends.

"Have a nice life, Goofy Glasses!"

Their tennis backs moved slowly on Third Avenue as they waded and disappeared into the knots of Upper East Siders walking to the movie theatres, the bars and the restaurants on a Friday night. These were what normal people look like. They had friends and jobs and conversations and trivial problems, mostly.

I could have killed them all.

I had never felt so alone.

The Visitor

(Razvarr Abatut)

"Raz, come downstairs now!"

It was my mother again. Talking to me like a child. I burrowed deeper into the polyester. It was quiet and comfortable and safe for what seemed like several minutes.

"RAZ!"

"Binele, go get your son."

You could hear even the quietest conversation in this cheap little house. The contractor must have made an extra special effort to build walls this thin. And my mother was not quiet.

"He doesn't want to come, Matca, leave him alone."

"You always say that, Binele. You have left him alone for 20 years!"

I could hear my father's head sink slowly toward his chest and breathe heavily. He had been given another job he didn't want to do. I saw my parents' lives and I wanted to run out of this house for all time.

Next came the predictable trudging up the warped wooden stairs that didn't even have carpeting to soften the blows.

He opened the door to my room.

"Razvarr, we bought you a gift. For your graduation."

There was no movement under the sheet. I was a glacier.

My father pulled a chair from the desk. It was an old wood chair you might find at a garage sale. It was flimsy and I thought how awful it would be if my old dignified father fell through the seat while talking to me. But also a little amusing.

"Razvarr, your mother wants you to come downstairs." His grammar was perfect. He was highly educated. But the voice carried a certain lilt, a left-over from our country, an unwanted immigrant sucking up all the air in the room.

I gave him nothing.

He sighed in the way that only a defeated man can.

"Do I have to pull back the sheet myself?"

Yes.

The sheet was peeled back. I tried to make myself into a fetus.

"Don't do this, Razvarr."

From a turtle crouch, I looked at his freshly shaved head for the first time that day. The sunlight striking the stretched-out skin on the skull made it shine like a flesh-colored bowling ball. That creeped me out.

"Why not?"

"You're a man now. You want to go back to being four years old?"

Not really. The prospect of having to live through all those days again was chilling. I decided to change the subject.

"Why do you still shave your head?"

"Because I still believe in God."

"After all they've done to you."

"After all they have done to me."

Our first prophet and king, Kawidtod, shaved his head. And he made all his followers shave their heads. For 2,800 years, Kawidtodians have been shaving their heads, in imitation of our founding father. Idiotic.

"It's a tradition. A way to be faithful to the tradition."

I stared at the ceiling. "What if the tradition isn't worth carrying on? Why follow a tradition just for the sake of tradition?"

He whispered out, "I don't believe that," as if he was not quite sure he really knew what he felt. "It's all we have."

"Maybe you should find something else."

"Like what?"

"I don't know. Something better."

"Where am I going to find that?"

Then his attention naturally turned to the stone on the top of my drawers. The drawers themselves were white and peeling paint and made of cheap particleboard. The stone was thousands of years old. It wasn't the only thing we'd taken with us to the New World, but it was the most obvious.

He looked at the stone for what seemed like a few minutes. I felt compelled to look at it too. It was mocking me, telling me, "This is only a small piece of what you are missing—your homeland."

We couldn't carry much with us when we left our country. The army and the police were after us. My mother had a backpack of freeze-dried food. My father and uncle too. We had to hike through rock mountains with very little grass or vegetable life. My father carried about 50 pounds of food.

With all that weight on him, he decided that the one other thing he absolutely needed to have was a rock from our homeland. Its edges were very sharp. The thing was about the size of a man's fist, but the stone was very dense with iron and its weight surprised everyone who had ever tried to pick it up.

My father walked with this super heavy rock in his backpack, this completely unnecessary thing, for hundreds of miles through steep gray mountain passes, winds that screamed with fevered anger, rain that whipped your face with little bullets, and wet, heavy snow that made your muscles stretch to the point of burning with every single step, all to deliver it to the top of a set of drawers in flat and boring Queens County, New York. He was a mailman.

The Subway Ride

(Akeyde Kletser)

I stumbled up Third Avenue. The heat enveloped my nostrils, ingesting me with every step. The valve above my stomach felt raw. It burned, a phantom punch in the solar plexus. A blood vessel in my brain tried to crawl out through my ear.

A herd of girls approached on the street, wearing linen shorts and light cotton tops with wedge shoes. I noticed these things.

A girl in the middle of the group had brown eyes shaped liked sugared almonds. Her hair was black and it glistened under the street lights. I wanted to touch that face and look into those eyes.

Almond Eyes took one look at me and steered her girls to the far left of me. A few even stepped off the sidewalk into the street to avoid getting too close.

After they passed, I pressed my forearms onto an apartment building's wall face, to try to get away from the heat that was swallowing me bit by bit. The girls talked about me in the distance. I couldn't hear them, but I knew. I was a minor freak show in this island of freaks.

I oozed slowly into the subway station, down the stairs, waited for a Number Six train on the platform. Sweat had soaked my hair completely. It dripped into my eyes, stinging. Salt.

The train came. I stepped in. We had to go five stops to Grand Central, where I was to transfer to the Seven train for the long ride out to eastern Queens. The air in the car was so cool that it made me calm down a little.

For the first time I realized that my right hand, my index finger, had been on the detonator the whole time I had been out looking at the Kawidtodian Temple and the passage back to the train. That thought made me start to shudder again. I tried to keep from falling apart. I had a long journey back home.

I transferred to the Seven at Grand Central, walking through the tunnels under the Lexington Avenue line. The police were out in force. Maybe there was another terror alert. A dozen uniforms stood in an array at key entry and exit points to the train lines. Their guns were little black coffins. Death stood all around.

I wanted to retch.

With the way I looked, I could have easily imagined one of those officers, with huge biceps sticking out of his short sleeve uniform, coming over to me and saying most politely, "Are you okay, sir? Do you need assistance? Would you like me to take you to a hospital? Get medical help?"

Where was God?

One stumble and I would have blown the whole thing. I had to keep moving, so I looked at the floor.

I made it to the escalator that took me down to the Seven line. The air kept getting hotter.

The train pushed through the heat and rode under the arches of the station. The doors opened, the cold air came at me. Thank you, God.

Opposite me was an advertisement. It said "Attack Life." A golfer, famous for his aggressiveness, was featured, his nose a triangular mountain, his cheeks valleys sown with wrinkles. The golfer was trying to sell me a low-brimmed hat with a shark on it, the kind he wore. The shark had its jaws wide open as if it was ready to eat.

I thought a lot about that phrase, "Attack Life." With my suicide vest strapped around my ribcage, I thought the golfer was right. Too many of us let things slide. We fell into sinful habits like drinking too much liquor or engaging in sex. We wallowed in ourselves. We bought things. Lots of things. We thought we were special and that we deserved a big SUV and a big house. We were so spoiled. We didn't deserve to live.

Some weeks before, I saw a young man throw an empty bottle of water from a Cadillac Escalade SUV on a little street near where I lived. So careless in my home. I wanted to run after the vehicle and smash my fist through the window like a sledge hammer. I wanted to drag that boy out of the Escalade and beat his face to a bloody pulp. I wished I could kill him.

The subway car was almost empty. A couple kissed in a tight clench at the end of the car. The boy, probably Spanish, was wearing a white tee-shirt with no sleeves out of the shoulder and jeans pulled down to the middle of his buttocks to expose his white underwear. The girl, painted into a pair of shorts, had the face of warm coffee. The boy stuck his tongue in the girl's mouth. Her full, round breast hugged the boy's chest. He puts his hand on her bare thigh.

It was awful. It was arousing. I didn't know what to do with myself.

The boy stopped kissing his girl suddenly, stared at me hard. He was crazy mad that I had intruded on his privacy. I got the same look from the girl. I brought my eyes to the floor, ashamed.

There was a hunger in me. A force. I felt women all around. I looked at them. I drank them in. I liked to hear them talk. Their voices were like music, even when they talked about the things they usually liked to talk about.

Their faces, their bodies were magnets, but not one had the least bit of seriousness to them. They took calls from girlfriends. They furiously clicked out text messages on their BlackBerrys. They sniffed cocaine out in the Hamptons.

The men they wanted had money. Lots of money. They ran hedge funds. There were houses with circular driveways. SUVs. Summer nights lived under tent parties and apple martinis. Nannies. Conversations about real estate. An easy life.

Who wanted what Akeyde Kletser was selling? God. My father. And my uncles.

My father and uncles ran my life. My father had four brothers. One, Lhokem, used to press on me books about the history of our people.

As if I did not know the whole history of bloodletting and pain. I felt the suffering in my bones.

Back when I was 12 years old, I lapped it up.

"Here, Akeyde, take a look at this."

I looked up at Lhokem. His jet-black beard flowed from chin to chest. He wore his hair long in the old style of our people.

He handed me a thick book. It was called "Ancient History of Zandria." The author was British—a man named James Dale.

"Why do you want me to read this?"

"When you read it, you will understand."

"But this man is from England. What does he know about us?"

"He has gone to our land. He has studied us for many years."

"I have learned all about our history in school, Uncle."

"This book is different."

He thrust the book in my hands. I took it without any further argument, because that is what I did. I was supposed to listen to my uncles. My father wasn't around much because he was running the affairs of the community.

The early part of the book focused on whether the sacrifice of Akeyde actually happened in history. I wondered why Lhokem would give me a book questioning the moment of the giving of the gifts we received from God.

But as I read, I saw that Professor Dale was not one of those people who denigrated us constantly. There were many. They ridiculed us for our primitive beliefs. They cursed us for our involvement in low-class businesses, from money lending to arms trafficking. There were countless numbers of people, from the lower classes to the most-decorated writers, who disparaged our tribe for our different customs and beliefs. They made fun of us for getting killed in great numbers by angry mobs, or told us it didn't happen.

Mr. Dale had headed an archeological team that went to the Heylik Shetyn Mountains. This was not an easy thing to do. The Kawidtodian government, those whores and thieves and dogs, did not usually allow outsiders—let alone a professor from a university—to enter the country.

He walked through the mountains, looking for evidence of the original sacrifice of Akeyde. It was extremely difficult to hike through those mountains. The heights were made of heavy rock long ago and scarred by the winds and they had never given anybody anything. The name Heylik Shetyn itself means "God's Knives."

Plants and flowers and vegetables had once grown in the valleys between the mountains, according to the legends of the ancients. But a millennium ago, things stopped growing there. A sign from God? Perhaps.

Through thousands of years, the Kawidtodians had stripped the land, so it was bare of sustenance. Northern Africa was once the breadbasket of the Roman Empire. It had fertile soil, a natural home for grain. Now, it was mostly sand. Similarly, the Kawidtodians had turned our land into an alien place for crops.

The ancient land was a place of extremes. At either edge of the day, the cold wind sliced up your chest. By 11 o'clock in the morning the sun took you in its eye and blasted you with heat like that from a tea kettle. When it rained or snowed, the water ran down the mountains to the east, feeding crops in the next country, not Kawidtodia, or Zandria, as it was once called. This much I've read.

After several seasons of searching through the harsh landscape, Professor Dale wrote that he had found an ancient skeleton in a cave, a child's small bones, with no legs, no arms and no head. The skeleton consisted of a breast bone with eroded stumps of ribs. The breast bone had a tear in the middle of its chest, about three inches long. This, Professor Dale concluded, must have been the knife wound Akeyde took from his father.

This, Mr. Dale said, was proof of the founding of the Zan religion, and that it really happened.

Lhokem had been impressed by this. So was I.

The Kawidtodian government condemned the result. The religious authority governing the country said the existence of the skeleton proved nothing. The bones could have come from any child. The Kawidtodians said the filthy Zans killed children all the time, so why should it be surprising that the professor had found the remains of one?

Professor Dale said that was true. But the skeleton was analyzed by a team of scientists hired by the professor. They established that the bones were at least 5,800 years old. And the wound was the exact type made by hunting knives used in that period.

That's why Lhokem wanted me to read the book. The professor was an outside authority, not a Zan, who had established a real proof for our religion. Lhokem expounded on Professor Dale's divine mission and said to me it was a mystery why the Kawidtodians had even allowed Mr. Dale into the country—a mystery that God had wrought. God must have helped persuade the Kawidtodians to let Mr. Dale in. God was helping us in our struggles.

I wished I had some of that young hope and strength. Because I felt that God had asked me to do something so difficult. I needed to be strong, like I was when our tribe was born.

The Storm Crashes In

(Razvarr Abatut)

My father walked down the creaking wooden stairs without me. The heaviness in that walk! I suddenly felt bad for the old man. He had too many burdens. I didn't understand why he needed to take me on as a responsibility as well.

There was a whispering between Binele and Matca. The kitchen fell silent, finally, thankfully.

Sleep pulled me into its sweet embrace. I started to dream that I was alone, finally, lying under a sheet on a bed and no one was talking.

"Razvarr!"

The door blew open and the savage hurricane that was my mother poisoned my sleep. I jerked from my scrunched-up position under the polyester.

"Get up now! You lazy sack of horse pookie!"

My mother could not bring herself to curse. These were her words for excrement.

I wouldn't go.

My mother ripped off the sheet and grabbed my cheek in her right hand and started to pull. I kept my eyes shut tight.

I thought her next move would be to try to rip off my underwear. That was a popular tactic, because it worked.

But no, she did something unexpected and poked me in the eyelids.

"Ow!"

"Open your eyes!"

"No!"

So she took an index finger and lifted one eyelid up.

The sight of her shiny bald head made me roll my eyes in pain.

I curled up even tighter.

Into my ribcage came a fist, no bigger than an 11-year-old girl's. It felt like I had been struck by a small meteor. Boom.

"Oh my God. Mom!"

"We sent you to school. You graduated from one of the best community colleges in the state. For what? So you can sleep all day?"

Before I could answer, another fist landed in my chest.

"We bought you a gift. Now you are coming downstairs to see it. Get dressed."

Baldy didn't even wait for an answer. Combination punches started beating me from all directions.

I covered up, but it was useless.

"Okay, okay! I'll get dressed and come downstairs!"

"You better, or I will hit you again."

She wouldn't even let me alone while I pulled on a pair of American Levi's. I hit back in the only way I can.

"What about justice for the oppressed? You're breaking Kawidtodian law."

"That is for people who are really oppressed. You are not poor. You are not suffering. God will judge you as a lazy, unkind son."

"You know how God judges me?"

"In this house, I am God. And I say you better get downstairs."

"What if I don't believe in God?"

"Don't you dare say that in this house! You must have faith. There is no other way."

"Did God torture Dad? Was that his will?"

"Is that what we sent you to college for? To question and disobey your parents?"

I grabbed a tee-shirt from the floor. It said *Zan Ran With A Can.* Just to have a little fun with those freaks. Merds.

I smiled, even though my ribs still hurt. "Yes. Of course, that's what you did."

"We wanted you to have a better future than running a newsstand like your father. And your uncle. Thinking about religion has nothing to do with college."

"Oh, no? I learned how to think for myself."

My mother shook her head. "Then you are in bigger trouble than we thought."

Getting Closer to the Bomb

(Akeyde Kletser)

I was lying in bed, the explosives vest strapped to my body, the detonator trailing wires to the bombs attached firmly inside my fist. The blue and white windbreaker had come off; there was nobody around to hide anything from.

One quick downward push from my thumb and the bombs would go off. Easy.

But I knew Vehktre would be disappointed.

I thought about the bomb. The bomb and I had gotten very close. I talked to it. Her name was Tina. That was the name of my first girlfriend.

"Tina, I want to love you. With all your little powders, your ball bearings, your nails, we need to be close. Let's get close."

I took my finger off the detonator and wrapped my arms around my ribs, where Tina was. I longed to feel her.

If Vehktre were here, he wouldn't have liked what I'm doing. But he had left. He trusted me. Now I was violating that trust.

A true man of God, Vehktre was. He trained me for the mission. He wouldn't want me to lie in bed with this bomb strapped around my body.

I was being bad. There was something in my heart, a little ping that was talking to me. I just wasn't sure of the message.

"Tina, don't leave. We just started."

I was 14 years old, in 10th grade, before the tire iron incident. The bad thing.

Tina and I were friends in junior high school the year before. We had been in social studies class together, in ninth grade. I was a good student. Sometimes Tina used to look at me whenever I talked in class, which was a lot. I could see her out of the corner of my eye. We both sat in the last row, separated by a few columns of chairs.

She wasn't a Zan, but a real blonde, with magnificent hair the color of yellow corn that swept down from the middle of her scalp toward each side of her face. I think the haircut was called a shag.

Our social studies teacher, Mr. Truman, arranged for the class to go to a state facility way out on Long Island on a Saturday, to entertain mentally handicapped people as part of a carnival. I dressed as a clown and walked around trying to make the residents smile.

It was easy with a painted-on grin. The boys and girls and men and women, mouths half-open, eyes wide, walked up to me. I extended my arms, did a little dance, took my giant orange clown hat off my head and bared my teeth. Some of my front teeth were red. Tina had put on my clown makeup and she slipped a few times with the red paint that was supposed to be my wide smile. I could feel that thick red goop on my incisors.

I begged her to wipe it off.

"Oh, it doesn't matter, Akeyde. They'll laugh at you anyway."

"But it looks bad."

"Well, you could wipe it off yourself. I'm not cleaning your teeth!"

I couldn't find a bathroom and the carnival was about to start. So I didn't do anything about it. She was right. It didn't matter. I walked around the giant hall where the carnival was set up, trying to find a resident or two to amuse. It wasn't hard. The residents laughed from the bottom of their guts and pointed at me. Some of them followed me around.

One man, very tall, about six foot two inches, walked up to me and pulled a chocolate chip cookie out of the chest pocket of his shirt. He offered it to me, with his arm fully extended. Before I could even react, the man would retract the arm, put the cookie in his mouth and lick it like an ice cream cone. Then, satisfied, he would put the cookie back in his pocket. He performed this little trick several times for me during the day.

Tina dressed like herself, which was just fine with me. I loved looking at her hair and her soft brown eyes, with her fleshy cheeks rising up from under that abundant hair.

She worked at a booth where you had to throw a rubber ball through a hole. The ball was about the size of a softball. The hole was as big as a basketball hoop. Everybody won a prize.

I had a headache at the end of the day. Mr. Truman said to expect that. It was a strain to spend the day with people who were impaired. But Tina and I sat next to each other on the bus ride back to Queens.

When 10th grade started, in a new school, Tina and I used to find each other out by the football bleachers. She was there to smoke cigarettes. In my usual way, I was wandering around, trying to figure out things.

So we talked. One day she was sad. It was October. The air was cool and pleasant. She was crying. She was complaining about being treated badly by one of her teachers. The story was disjointed and mumbled and I couldn't understand what she was talking about.

But I petted the top of her blonde head as she cried. And she let me.

That was the start of it.

My friends and I had a Zan social club and we wanted to raise money for our activities for the year, things like renting a basketball court at the local high school so we could play in the winter or paying for soda for Saturday night socials with the Zan girl group in our little part of Queens. So we sold hard-boiled eggs house to house.

It was a gimmick. We would go around the neighborhood, ringing doorbells and offering to sell an egg to them for a dollar for the Zan Action Network (ZAN). Most people laughed and gave us a dollar.

I went outside our little neighborhood, where the Zan families lived. I walked to Tina's house. It was three miles away from mine, but I was motivated.

She was there, with some of her friends. They were just hanging out, smoking cigarettes.

I knocked on her door. She welcomed me in. Tina's parents weren't around. The girlfriends were in the living room and they took a look at me like I was nothing. I was suddenly very self-conscious about my glasses. They were very thick and black even then. I needed strong frames to hold the heavy lenses.

Tina led me upstairs to a sitting room. She was wearing a sloppy old tee-shirt and expensive jeans.

"You had a long walk."

"Yeah."

"Want some pistachio nuts?"

"Yeah."

"Let me run downstairs."

When she left, my chest fluttered a little. She was back in a minute with the jar.

"Can you open them?"

The cover was very tight. I couldn't. I strained. I pulled. I twisted. Nothing happened.

"Let me see it."

She loosened the cap ever so slightly.

"Try it again."

I opened the jar. She smiled. That's when I knew I had her.

We sat there and ate pistachio nuts for about a half hour and didn't talk much.

"My parents are going to be home soon, Akeyde. You have to leave."

"Can I get your phone number?"

She didn't say yes or no, just scribbled it down in pencil on a piece of scrap paper I was carrying in my pocket for just this purpose.

I called her a few days later and asked her to meet me at our old junior high school near her house. It would be an easy walk for her, about 10 minutes at the most.

I was there first. Tina arrived, moving slowly, wearing a heavy brown coat that cascaded to her knees. It was November, a little chilly. The leaves had fallen, sunk in the beds of the gutters lining the roads.

She sat down on the cold ground. I kissed her and my head exploded. Her lips were electric.

Tina lay down on the ground and brought me with her. We kissed, not moving, just kissing for minutes.

Every minute or so, she pulled her arm over my head so she could look at her watch. I knew what she was doing, but I didn't say anything. She was trying to get home by curfew. I just wanted to keep kissing her. Eventually she broke off. I let her.

I saw her walk off into the darkness beyond the school to the houses on the street where she lived.

I walked home three miles, back to my Zan neighborhood, my face glowing despite the chill.

A few days later it was all over.

The Thing at the Bottom of the Stairs

(Razvarr Abatut)

As I walked down the stairs, I realized I should have told Old Baldy, "If you really wanted me to succeed, you would have paid for me to go to a private university, where I could meet rich people and make important contacts."

What did Gore Vidal call it? The wit of the staircase. You figured out the exact cutting response to your rival after the conversation was over as you were walking down the steps to leave the party.

Well, I already knew the response. My parents didn't have that kind of money and didn't want to take out loans for a private school. The tuition was breathtaking. And a newsstand business just didn't generate that kind of serious cash.

As I hit the bottom of the stairs, my Mom screamed, "Surprise!" Dad was quietly smiling.

They got me a personal computer. Powered up, it was sitting on a table in the living room, wires spilling out everywhere to connect to a surge protector strip hugging the wall outlet. You could actually hear the wheezing of the central processing unit.

"Isn't this great, Raz! We wanted to give you something special for your graduation. Your father saved so much money from the newsstand."

It was a real stinker of a product. It had a 21-inch monitor, with a central processing unit, your standard computer from, oh, I don't know, about 2004. The tower was a black block of plastic, sitting there dumbly like some kind of robot from the past.

I knew they were working hard, especially my father, and trying to make me happy, but I felt an emptiness inside me, a hollowness. I missed my home. What gift could they give me that would fill up all that space? This beast certainly wasn't going to do it.

"Oh, you're going to love it! Think of all the things you'll be able to do."

I nodded my head and mumbled, "Thanks, Mom. Thanks, Dad."

Why couldn't they at least have gotten me an Apple? Or a laptop, which I could have carried around from room to room? I mean, didn't they read? Didn't they study the products in the computer guides? There were only hundreds of them.

In front of me I could have had a Mac with great graphics, a wireless keyboard and mouse, and multi-tasking abilities up the wazoo.

Instead, I got this crude beast.

"Go on, sit at the monitor!"

I obeyed with all the excitement of a kid with cavities who had to go to the dentist. I stared at the monitor. It had a photograph of the Blue and White Temple, the central worshipping place in Kawidtodia, my parents' homeland. My homeland. I don't know how they got ahold of that. Maybe Uncle Arak. He was involved in a lot of businesses all across the neighborhood.

The doors were open and you could see the four pillars of the temple from the outside, representing the four tenets of my parents' faith.

I stared at the computer.

"Do something with it."

I opened up Word. My mother was standing beside me. She was beaming.

I typed: "This computer sucks."

"What does 'sucks' mean, Raz?"

"It's a good thing, Mom."

"Oh, good."

My father knew I was playing my mother. I caught a glimpse of him standing next to her. His face dropped and he looked like he was going to cry. I felt a little ashamed for a moment.

The poor man, always suffering in silence. He turned away and went to the kitchen.

I checked out Web access. Dial-up. That's when I lost my patience.

"What am I going to do with dial-up access? What is this, the Stone Age?"

"You don't like it?"

"You don't understand, Mom! I need cable to make this thing work at all."

"Well, you know better than us. You can fix it."

"Yeah, I can fix it. But that costs money."

My mother sniffed. "Then you can get a job. I would love to see you do some actual work."

She walked away into the kitchen, her head held high, but I knew she was hurt.

"He doesn't like it, Binele."

"We tried."

"Trying isn't good enough! How are we going to live with him like this?"

For a moment, I thought she was going to cry. That might be one of the only things that would get to me—old stone face cracking.

I headed up the stairs, back to my room, leaving the computer behind, alone in the living room. The heat in the house was suffocating. The weak air conditioner couldn't cover the whole room.

At the top of the stairs, I sagged a little holding the wooden hand rail. I looked around the top floor of the house. It was coming apart. The wallpaper was peeling. Little splinters of dried wood poked out from the wallpaper.

The houses in this neighborhood were all made of old wood. They could catch on fire and be gone in a matter of minutes. If we were still in my homeland, the houses wouldn't be made of wood. We would have concrete or rock walls. Something solid, something you could hold onto.

Here everything could be taken from you in a matter of minutes. And if it could, what exactly were you losing?

I was exhausted after climbing the steps, but I pressed on, back toward my room and the bed.

The Detonator

(Akeyde Kletser)

I liked pressing the detonator. It had a plastic plunger that sank into a plastic casing. What a great toy.

Up and down, up and down I pressed the button.

BOOM!

Now that would have been something.

Tina was sitting upright on the flaming orange carpet, a suicide vest without a body, the wires without the detonator. I had detached the wires from the trigger so I could play with my toy. I imagined blowing myself up right there and taking down half the building.

There was a big part of me that wanted to. Just end it all. Too much pain for one body.

I remembered Tina. The girl, not the bomb.

After the first kiss, I wanted more. I called her one Friday night from my father's office downstairs after school, in the darkness of the night.

"Want to meet at the school tonight?"

She sighed. "I'm going to Glen Garber's house. Bunch of people."

"Want me to go with you?"

"I don't care if you come or not."

My eyes went wide and my mouth slackened. Didn't we just have great kissing three days ago?

"Okay."

"Bye, Akeyde."

That's wasn't even the worst part. No, that came later. In school, and I didn't know how this happened, but if I was walking to my locker or a classroom, whether the halls were empty or crowded, I would almost always see her, looking straight ahead, like I didn't exist. Like I wasn't even there. The Man Who Never Was.

A lot of times I would see her from the other end of the hall when it was totally empty. She and I would both move slowly. No need to rush. We were two gunfighters approaching each other from opposite sides of a dusty Western street.

We walked by each other and BAM! Every time she stared beyond me to the vanishing point my heart would be shot through with lead.

After a month of this, I was finished.

I was going to ask my parents to take me out of public school and put me in the Zan school.

The public high school was big and intimidating and the kids came from everywhere. It was a great big pot of a New York City public high school, with 3,000 kids thrown together, boys challenging each other to fights in the hallways over nothing, tough girls tripping people who walked by and thinking it was funny.

I saw one boy get beaten up in a field after school as I got on the bus to go home. The loser was down on the ground, on his knees, and the winner was smashing his fist into the boy's rib cage over and over.

The elementary and middle schools weren't like this. At least a third of the kids in those schools were Zans. I could walk to the schools from my home. I knew most of the kids there. I was comfortable there. In sixth grade I was the head safety monitor for the school. I had a little silver badge on an orange vest. Mostly I told the other kids before school that they couldn't lounge around on the bicycle racks at the back of the school. I liked the authority, liked being a little policeman.

My parents had debated whether I should go on to the public high school. My father said it was time for me to learn more about our people. He wanted me in the Zan religious school. Mom said no. She wanted me to go to the public high school. I would become more worldly, more well-rounded.

I remembered the fight well. I sat at a kitchen table and watched them as they stood like boxers in the ring. Except they separated themselves by standing at exact opposite sides of our rectangular wood table.

"That's exactly what I don't want!" Dad screamed through the walls themselves. "He'll forget where he's from! Who he is! What the Squids have done to us!"

"How can he forget who he is? You remind him every day!"

My father's eyes scrunched up in anger.

"This place is like a giant cesspool and it will swallow him up."

I wasn't sure if he was talking about the school, or Queens or the country. About 100 different languages are spoken in Queens. It is the world in microcosm.

"This place saved us. It saved me. And if I weren't here, he wouldn't be here."

"It's not home."

"Neither is the religious school!"

"It's the closest thing we can give him."

"Alter, you really want to bring all that pain to him on a daily basis? With all our people have been through? It's too much suffering. I can't stand it."

My mother brought her hands to the scarf on her head. Her eyes fell together.

Father took advantage and shot back: "Without religion, he won't have a sense of right and wrong. He needs to think about God to keep him on the right track."

"I'm not talking about religion. I'm talking about history. Akeyde is going to get the history pounded into him every day at the Zan school. And you and your brothers are already doing that. He needs something else. What will he be if he just knows about the Zans?"

"He'll be a good man, a righteous man. He'll know where he belongs."

"He already knows."

It was the only time I remember my Mom winning a fight with Dad. He said I could go to the public high school on a trial basis.

"If anything goes wrong, he's out of there."

I was filled with anxiety going there every day. My stomach tried to turn itself inside out on the bus to school. Too many awful kids, a great big streaming mass of humanity coming through the doors every day. We were all just numbers.

And now Tina, my great love, had shunned me. I wanted out.

My father smiled in triumph when he saw me at the kitchen table, heartsick. My mother folded her arms, but my sad sack face beat her on points.

Then came the bad thing.

Sitting on the bed with the detonator, making the little plastic clicks, wasn't enough for me after a while. Tina weighed heavily on my mind. I remembered the coldness in her pretty face too clearly as she passed me in the hallway. She may as well have broken up with me that very day.

So I went into the nice clean white bathroom in the apartment and tried to cut off all my toe nails down to the flesh.

Finding a Purpose in Life

(Razvarr Abatut)

I stared at the Blue and White Temple on my computer screen. I couldn't help myself. My parents didn't speak to me about the computer, which was strange. And then I started to think about it, all lonely in the little living room, and me upstairs, staring at my father's rock.

Then, just like that, I sneaked down the stairs and turned it on. My mother was in the kitchen, making breakfast. While she was busy, I thought I could turn on the machine and enjoy a moment of solitude with it.

But no. The PC made one of those roaring introductions when the operating system woke up and almost blasted me out of my chair. Why didn't I think to turn down the volume?

Baldy came running out of the kitchen.

"What was that?"

"The computer you bought me."

"It makes sounds?"

I waved at the screen. "Apparently!"

This confused her.

"Okay… Well, keep it down, okay, Raz?"

"Yes, Mom."

"And don't talk to me like that. With disrespect. Or I will hit you."

"I'm going to report you to child services."

"You're going to pick up a telephone? I would pay to see that."

Mercifully, she disappeared into the kitchen. I turned to look over the machine. The Blue and White Temple was in my face. I started to look for the menu for putting a new screen saver on the monitor.

But then, there was the Temple, the sky turning deep blue, the moon overhead, lights dug into the ground turned on to highlight the beauty of the stone architecture. The outside pillars were gray, but the four pillars inside the central square were white with blue triangle stones running up the columns, punctuating scenes from the founding of our religion.

The building was made of stone cut from the mountains in Kawidtodia, a land that doesn't grow much. Wheat or corn or oats? We don't have a lot of any of those things. But rocks? Those we've got. You can't eat them, but the Kawidtodians are damn proud of the stones anyway.

The Temple was the center of Kawidtodian worship. Inside the building the carvings and paintings of Kawidtod, our first king, were delicately and intricately painted and considered a treasure by the nation. Except for the small minority of Zans left in the country. They sold drugs, laundered money, and bred enormous dogs and sold them to the wealthy, underground businessmen and Yekmonveldter drug dealers, too, for protection and status. Nobody cared what they thought—they were just leftover debris. But that's another story.

Thousands of people worshipped in the Temple every day in the capital city of Shalhak. Shalhak was full of trash. The wind blew dust and animal dung and garbage through the streets, but the Temple was maintained as well as possible, with contributions coming from emigrant communities all over the world to keep the faith alive. Kawidtodians from other countries visited the country just to make a pilgrimage to the Blue and White Temple.

Outside the Temple were booksellers and trinket peddlers. The Temple site was a major area of commerce. But the intellectual product the Temple sold was far more dangerous than anything sold outside.

I went to the Temple dozens of times with my father when I was a boy, to worship. This was before the authorities took a dislike to him. We were part of the culture, happy to be part of this great people.

At school, we learned to recite the Dreptat, our holy book. I took it all in and got good grades in Kawidtodian history. My parents were proud. It didn't matter that our family was poor. Everybody I knew was poor. We were all the same. I knew who I was.

I played football in the streets with my friends—not American football, real football. We didn't care so much about the wind and the dust and the bits of torn paper and plastic bags flying by our heads. We had each other and a ragged round ball and that was enough.

The Temple had great vaulted arches with paintings on each section of the ceiling. The main roof in the central building was 100 feet high. The building was 200 feet wide and about 140 feet long. If you've ever been in the Lincoln Memorial, the effect on the visitor is very similar. The Temple and the Lincoln Memorial were about the same dimensions.

Other buildings, about a half dozen, were constructed around the Temple later to make allowances for the need for additional chapels for the throngs of worshippers streaming in. They were in the same style but not nearly as big. Taken together, the whole thing was a mess, but the central building, close to 3,000 years old, was still impressive.

In the middle of the main roof there was a glass circle to let in light from the sun.

The light illuminated the main altar, from which rose a sculpture of a giant arm, at the end of which was a closed fist. The arm rose 20 feet high. The work was so detailed that you could see folds of muscle fibers and giant veins running down the arm.

Growing up, I never questioned the prayer service reciting the legends and deeds of King Kawidtod. He conquered the filth of the Zans and founded our religion. Our devotion was to him and his ideals, and to the God who had blessed him with greatness.

He was the leader. He was the one who had a vision for our people, as bequeathed by God. After my father was tortured and I saw America, I started thinking about this religion.

The more I stared at the screen, the more I realized what had to be done. Blow up the Blue and White Temple. But first I had to get the computer out of the living room.

The Self-Mutilation Option

(Akeyde Kletser)

It was not easy to cut off my own toenails. I didn't know how they pulled them out in Kawidtodian torture cells, but I wanted to learn.

Ordinary nail clippers wouldn't do. They only took little quantities of nail. So I used a serrated knife, about a foot long, taken from my mother's kitchen. It was one of the few things I was allowed to bring to this apartment.

If Vehktre came back, he might see if I cut myself on the arm. But he wouldn't ever see my feet. I knew he was lurking around somewhere, so I had to be careful.

I bent down in the bathroom, the bright light all around me, like God's light, and started sawing at the nail on my big toe.

I worked the knife back and forth. It was like cutting through hard plastic. I managed to get about half the nail off. I was about to attack the rest of it when blood started to spurt out of the place where the lower part of the nail met the skin.

The very redness of it was beautiful. Lovely. It was a little fountain of pulp. I watched and worshiped the blood.

After the gusher stopped, I started on the other big toe, achieving the same effect. That was enough bloodshed for one night.

It was time for bed. I walked through the apartment. It didn't take long. Vehktre set me up here, to live modestly and alone. It was a tiny one-bedroom place, with a hallway that had closed-in walls. There was a bathroom and a single bed and orange string carpeting spread over the linoleum. That was the landlord's idea. Red mixed in with the orange, as well as yellow. The carpet needed more red.

I turned off the lights and stumbled to bed with my bloody toenails.

I couldn't sleep. Visions of Tina came back. And there was the other Tina, my bomb vest, my lovely, sitting on the floor.

For a moment, I couldn't remember where I put the detonator. Back came on the lights in a flash. I looked around the bed area, which is the last place I had it. I checked the night table, looked under the bed, but the trigger wasn't there. Just a lot of cockroaches. I had the urge to kill them, but I needed to set my priorities and focus. The detonator was more important than the roaches. The panic rose in me.

It couldn't be in the kitchen. I wouldn't have been in the kitchen. I hadn't bothered to eat for a few days.

It didn't take long to crawl up and down the hallway on my hands and knees. The hallway was black linoleum, so the detonator could have easily blended in.

I started to sweat. Oh, God. Where was the damn thing? What if I couldn't find the trigger? Where was I going to get another trigger? Vehktre would kill me.

I could throw myself into the East River. Its vicious currents would take me out to sea and drown me quite efficiently. No worries, then.

Or I could shoot myself with the gun Vehktre gave me, the one I forgot to bring with me earlier. The gun had a big black tunnel for the hot lead I could pour into my chest.

It was in the bathroom. I had put it on the lid of the toilet when I went to cut my nails. How could I have been so stupid?

I clutched at the black plastic, holding it as if I were going to press the button. Thank you, God, for helping me to find it. You're always there at the last minute.

I tried to go to sleep with the trigger in my hand. I didn't want to lose it again. But sleep eluded me. There was too much to do.

If I thought about the past, it would help me to sleep. The days with my uncles. My mom. And sometimes my father. I didn't see him much, because he was the Onfirer, the leader of the local Zan community.

Lhokem, Dreykop, and Narish were my companions. Sometimes I saw Uncle Cookie too. His name is really Shayhey, but somebody started calling him Cookie because he is extremely fat, and that became his name. I was an only child and the reincarnation of Akeyde, so they were appointed to spend time with me. But it seemed like they were happy to do so.

My father and uncles pooled their money together to buy a property in upstate New York, near the Adirondack Mountains. My father was the official owner, and he ran the camp for any Zans who could afford to pay. Most of the kids came from Zan assembly houses in Queens.

Lhokem would drive us to the property upstate each July first. I started going to the camp there when I was 12 years old.

I remember being so excited to get in a station wagon with my uncles. Lhokem had it painted glossy purple, a favorite Zan color. My uncles were all so young and mostly handsome, with their long black beards.

Dreykop would sit in the front passenger seat. I would sit in the back with Narish. We would sing Zan songs, trying to stay on-key with the help of the singer on the cassette tape playing in the front of the car.

The songs had titles like:

- "We Will Avenge the Blood of Our Zan Ancestors"
- "The Kawidtodians Are Dogs"
- "The Zans Will Rise Again"
- "We Curse the Hell of King Kawidtod"

We sang our hearts out merrily to each tune. I felt so close to my uncles when I was singing with them. Dreykop would turn from the passenger seat and smile at me with such love as we sang. Narish would too.

Each mile we put between ourselves and flat, hot and crowded Queens made me feel more and more happy. It was a long drive, but I had so much excited anticipation inside that I stared out the window and drank in the mountains, the trees, the grass, the open sky.

After the hours on the New York State Thruway, on the right-hand side of the road, hundreds of feet from the asphalt, there was a brown house with a windmill and a pond in front of it. I was so glad to see that house. It meant to me that we were now in magic land.

After the exit on the Thruway, we took a small, two-lane road that snaked through mountains that looked like giant green waves. Mists often rose over the tops of the mountains.

Lhokem drove us through a place where the road finally straightened in a valley between two mountains. We passed a graveyard, then an ice cream place. At the foot of the hill up to our property was a gas station. How I loved that gas station. It was a sign post that we were so close to magic land.

The road up the hill was curved with switchbacks and very steep on the final stretch to the property. The curved part of the road was lined with little cottages and simple A-framed houses. I almost cried when I imagined I could live in one of those houses, with the trees all around them and a brook flowing downhill in the back yard.

At a certain point, the road became unpaved. It was just rocks and dirt. Lhokem had to put the station wagon in second gear much of the time to push us forward.

With one last thrust of the gas pedal, we rose over the crest of the hill. And here was the biggest thrill. An oval shaped valley stretched out before us, with two lakes and two mountains in the distance, which formed a saddle to join themselves.

Cabins were assembled in straight lines on both sides of the lake, painted brown and white.

Hundreds of Zan boys and girls were pushing their trunks into cabins. Kids who had finished unpacking were playing on the baseball and football fields. There were basketball courts and clean lakes for swimming. Some kids would just be sitting around on round wooden fences lining the roads. The laughter and the shouting of children filled the valley.

This was Zan summer camp. My family had purchased the property fairly cheaply, I was told, from the United States Army. The cabins had been built during World War II for the training of soldiers. They were simple wooden structures, constructed of long logs, cut at the ends to cleave together.

My uncles pulled the car up to a football field. Lhokem and Dreykop would carry my trunk to my cabin. There we would meet my counselors and everybody would get introduced. The counselors were Zan teenagers, about 18 or 19 years old, young, wearing shorts and sneakers and tee-shirts. I would stay with about 10 other 12-year-old boys, who were mostly very polite to me, especially with my uncles around. No one else had the name Akeyde.

I was different from the other kids in a number of important ways, but also this: the parents or relatives of the other kids had to go home after they dropped their kids off. My uncles would stay, to work at the camp. They would all live in their own cabin at the top of the hill. I could go in their place anytime and read Superman or Captain America comic books or play music on their cassette players or even watch TV. I would eat dinner with them two or three nights a week at their special table in the dining room.

My father had a cabin there too. He came up once a week. His cabin sat about a third of the way up the hill toward the dining room. As my little bunk walked up to the mess hall for meals I would often see him, smoking a cigar or massaging his long beard and sitting on a little porch to look out over the baseball fields and basketball courts and the two lakes. I would wave to him, throwing my hand back and forth in huge sweeps to get his attention. From a distance he would look at me and nod his head. How I craved that nod. I wanted more of course, but I knew all I could hope for was a nod, that little acknowledgement that I existed.

But my uncles involved me in their lives. Often, whenever we were doing something like playing basketball or softball, badly, Narish, wearing a big gray backpack, as if he were going on a long hike in the mountains, might come around and take me to lunch at the town down the hill. After that, he bought me ice cream then took me to a small stream in the woods, where we could dip our feet in the cold water on a hot day. He put his backpack on the bank of the stream.

"Why did you bring that?" I asked.

"I have a few things I like to take with me, nothing special," he said.

A man would come around and talk to Narish. The man had a rough way about him. He looked like he worked with his hands. He had big arms and walked with a limp. They would talk about things I didn't understand while I kicked at the water.

"You have the cash?" Narish might say.

The man gave Narish a letter-sized envelope. Narish opened his backpack and handed the man a small package wrapped in brown paper.

I was too shy to ask any questions in front of the man. When he shuffled off, I said, "Who was that man?"

"An old friend."

"He's not a Zan?"

"No. Just a regular man."

"What did you give him?"

"Something to help him. He's sick."

"He can't get that up here?"

"No, only the city has it."

Other times, Lhokem or Dreykop might come by my bunk as we were preparing to go to the mess hall for dinner. With the green trees being swallowed up by the darkness, they made me put on a button-down shirt and long pants to take me away from my little friends for a dinner at a local restaurant. The counselors could do nothing about it. I saw them quietly protest with their eyes this temporary loss of authority over me, but they wouldn't say anything. My uncles were gods in the camp.

We would bounce down the rocky hill to a restaurant with a lighted deck and a view of the mountains. Men I didn't know would come by our table and sit for a few minutes. I didn't understand their conversations, but the word "money" came up a lot, and the words "your interest rate." I could not bring myself to look at the men, but concentrated on my plate, usually a hamburger or steak, cooked rare, with lots of red in it.

Sometimes my mom visited me too. She didn't work at the camp, because she had to stay home to take care of my father. But if my dad came up, she traveled with him. Even if my father didn't acknowledge me much, my mom did.

She invited me to her cabin (she and Dad had separate places to sleep) every time she was at camp. She'd make me a turkey sandwich and watch me eat. If I ate my sandwich, I got to eat cookies she had made in Queens and brought upstate for me.

Then we'd listen to classical music or draw on her porch. She liked art. We drew pictures of the mountains, of trees, of birds we had seen.

I wasn't very good, but she insisted I draw with her. She was a good artist, in my 12-year-old mind, even though she didn't have any formal training.

Sometimes she would stop drawing and just look at me. I would notice and look back at her.

Her face was heavy, but I still saw beauty in it. Her brown hair was held back by a kerchief, always, but she had a certain light in her face, especially when she wasn't around my father. Her cheeks were full and happy. She smiled like she and I were in on a joke. Her big brown eyes, often sad or set in a grim way, were open and full to the experiences of life during these few moments.

"You're a good kid, Akeyde."

"Thanks, Mom." But I didn't really believe her.

After she finished a drawing, she might have a cigarette.

I was surprised by that the first time I saw her do it.

"When did you start smoking, Mom?"

She laughed, embarrassed a little, the cigarette held high at the end of her hand, the smoke trailing off into vapor.

"I don't. I smoke when I'm happy. I'm a happy smoker."

"You don't smoke around Dad."

"No. Look, there goes a blue jay."

"I don't see him."

"He just flew into that tree."

"I think I see him now."

"He's so pretty."

"Did Grandpa smoke?"

"Who? My father? No, he didn't smoke. He was a Spaama, in Zandria."

A Spaama was the leader of a Zan congregation.

"What happened to him?"

"He was beaten up by a group of men in Kawidtodia. They killed him. That was more than 30 years ago. I was a young girl. We shouldn't talk about it."

"Were they Squids?"

"Don't use that word."

"Okay."

"But, yes, they were not our people. I don't want to talk about it."

"Okay."

Thinking about all that stuff in the past made me so happy and excited that I couldn't sleep anyway.

I took a warm shower, even though it was so hot in the apartment. I sat in the tub and let the water run in little streams over my back, neck, and head. That helped. I finally dropped off around two in the morning, Tina a few feet away on the floor, with the detonator next to me, under a thin sheet on the bed.

The Blue and White Temple— An Appraisal

(Razvarr Abatut)

Once I got the computer into my room, I started to think about the screen saver. And that made me think of Kawidtod, our first king and prophet, who built the Temple.

Kawidtod made everyone cut off their hair. Oh, he was a foxy smart barbarian.

He wasn't our only prophet, but he was the most important.

So all the paintings of the founding of our religion in the Blue and White Temple showed bald people. One of the most prominent paintings was of bald, bullet-headed Kawidtod running a sword through a Zan prince. The Zan prince had a blade in his stomach, with blood spurting out onto his shirt, but that wasn't the most important feature to focus your eyes upon.

Kawidtod's face was the most arresting feature of the painting, which stretched out across a wall for at least 15 feet. He was smiling, with rays of light from God flowing all around his head. Because he knew he's doing God's work.

But here was the thing about Kawidtod's face. It was not a saintly smile. It looked more like the grin of some demented criminal. The eyes were staring down on the bloodied prince like guns encased behind iron walls. The nose was pulled back by the force of the smile. The mouth itself was fierce and crooked and hot with blood lust.

It was not the most beautiful show in the world.

When I was a kid, I thought, *This is the way it is for everybody.* The Zans were monkeys and they deserved to die horrible deaths. Somebody had to conquer them and create a more just law, build a better nation.

And if building a new nation required everybody to shave their heads, even the children, then that's what we would do.

It was only on our move to America that I learned differently.

After our escape from the country, I was walking around an airport in eastern Europe and here were all these people with hair on their heads. *What is this all about? People can grow their hair? Why are they different than us? Something is wrong.*

Kawidtod didn't want any of his people thinking about sex. Most people, when they think about sex, consider the obvious things—the breasts, the buttocks, the legs, the arms, the muscles. But Kawidtod realized, thousands of years before real science, that hair is a great attractor for the sexes. Shiny, lustrous, gleaming hair. It was usually the first thing you noticed about a woman. Only then did your eyes lower to those other parts.

This man, the leader of our people, wanted the tribe to think about war. The psychologically damaged Zans had ruled the land for close to 3,000 years. But our tribe had grown large among them.

Kawidtod didn't like them. The Zans had grown fat and corrupt. They didn't believe in justice for all. They treated our tribe badly.

Kawidtod went alone up to the mountains, the Heylik Shetyn, to find God and listen to His advice on what to do. He had a meeting with God in one of the high places and God told him what to do.

God gave him a vision.

To get the people focused on the battles to come, Kawidtod had everybody cut off all their hair. God has willed it, Kawidtod told the tribe.

It was brilliant. This decision brought the people together. They fought the Zans viciously. They kept coming at their enemy and they didn't stop until the Zan tribe was utterly defeated and their King blinded and taken away in chains to live in some out-of-the-way cave.

A problem came after the Zan War ended. The King liked the results of his decision about taking off your hair, so this became the law of the land. He said God told him thought that without their hair, our tribe would be more focused on building, strengthening, and maintaining the country than on love and romance and wine. It got written into our holy books as a way to restrict our vanity. We were stuck with it. We've been cutting off our hair for 2,800 years.

And the hair had to be shaved because it was an act of worship for our original father and the way he did things. You were not supposed to take the easy way out and put hair remover gel on your head. Kawidtod shaved his head. To bring us back to that moment in time, to make us feel the sense of holiness when he had his revelations, we, his descendants, must copy his actions. Shaving your head every morning was a religious act. We were always supposed to say a little prayer right before we shaved our heads down to the flesh of the skull.

Nobody knew until much later that the King kept a stable of hundreds of mistresses in his palace who were allowed to keep their hair as long as they stayed in his houses, out of sight.

Some liberal religious authorities used this story to justify Kawidtodians who want to keep their hair. But that only works in Kawidtodian communities in America and Europe. In Kawidtodia itself, everybody has to shave their heads, or they will be punished. Only the few thousand Zans left in the country can keep their hair, because they're not part of our religion. They're punished for it every day.

The Kawidtodians survived in a harsh land. The ground wasn't very hospitable to planting crops. Water and food were precious. If a man stole from another, the victim's whole family could go hungry.

The King, in his compassion for the victims, ruled that the robber should have his right hand cut off. In the Kawidtodian religion, punishment is iron-hard. Why? Our holy book, the Dreptat, says that we must do all we can to prevent crime. Cutting off the robber's hand deters others from trying to take from somebody else.

What I want to know is, if you cut off a man's hand, how is he ever going to work again? The King could have made this man a slave and given him a job in a prison, so he could be productive.

Let's look at other, more serious crimes. Adultery? You could be stoned to death. They took the adulterer, whether you were a man or a woman—but usually it was a woman. They buried you up to your waist in the ground. One of the guards put a bag over your head and your hands were tied behind you.

Then people recruited from the neighborhood threw pieces of concrete at your head. They did this until the bag was soaked with blood and you were dead. It made me sick just to think about it.

For saying anything critical about the Dreptat and its teachings, you could be hanged in a public square. Or your head could be cut off with a traditional Kawidtodian sword. What an honor!

Do you think our concept of justice has been stretched a little too far?

This may have worked well 2,800 years ago. But today? Let's grow up, folks.

None of this might matter in a different world. Kawidtod's ideas about criminal law wouldn't mean anything if the Kawidtodians had been eliminated by other civilizations. America is mostly Christian. China is officially atheist. India is mostly Hindu. The Middle East? Let's not talk about that. Europe has moved on to secularism.

But in one little corner between continents, next to Yekmonveldt's northeast border, there is still a country called Kawidtodia. Our people survive as an ethno-national organism, like cancer.

The Bull

(Akeyde Kletser)

I woke up early the next morning, around 6:00. I had a dream that a giant bull was sitting on my chest and wouldn't let me get up.

The sunlight gave off a sharp blast. I had forgotten to close the heavy curtains to the two windows in the apartment. Vehktre had insisted on putting up the curtains, and I had forgotten to follow his instructions and close them.

The next day would be the big day. First day of August. The day of the Kawidtodians' most important holiday—their victory over the Zans. The Kawidtodians in the city would be going to the temple on 79th Street and 3rd Avenue in Manhattan to pray to God and celebrate. They would have their service, then drink cheap, unbearably sweet wine and eat long straight tubes of bread, more than three feet long, with a round knob on the end and laced with sweet raisins, called "Pumns," to represent the fist of Kawidtod.

A good day for a bomb.

Blow them up, all to Gock (our word for hell), where they will have little wooden pins stuck in their bodies for all eternity.

On the day after the Kawidtodians' holiday, the Zans would commemorate the loss of our nation with much sorrow and weeping and shaking of our bodies in our comparatively few assembly houses around the world. There were only six million Zans left on Earth, compared to about 30 million Kawidtodians.

To try to comfort our much diminished tribe about this terrible fact, my father would say to congregations in the assembly houses in our area, "That means there are millions more Zans in Heaven than Kawidtodians, all working to help the Zans left here. Our power is growing and we are going to help God make things right. Justice will prevail for the Zans because God has blessed us. We are a sacred people and always will be."

I heard my father lecture about this dozens of times.

Well, I would give the Zans something to celebrate after tomorrow, despite all their tears commemorating our almost three-millennia-old defeat at the hands of Kawidtod. I was ready to strike a blow for our pride as a people. I would win a victory for God.

My name is Akeyde for a reason. It was written in our holy books.

Akeyde is a warrior for God. He is the reincarnation of the very first Akeyde, who went willingly to his death because God asked him to do so, who offered himself up as a sacrifice to show that our people would be faithful to His rule.

I was supposed to be that man.

There were five reincarnations of Akeyde before me. I am the sixth.

Only one child of all the Zans was to be named Akeyde every 1,000 years. The first Akeyde made the great sacrifice to found our religion.

As our religion spread among the people, the legend grew that Akeyde would come back each millennium to help the people. It was written into scripture.

After the religion was established, the authority to name someone Akeyde was given to our holiest man, the head of the Spaama religious order, of all the assembly house priests around the country. He was called the Onfirer. The reincarnation of Akeyde could be a baby, a boy, or a grown man.

If this happened, there would be a big ceremony to re-name the person at our central assembly house in Sed, our first capital. It was a great stone cylinder and could hold thousands of people, according to the holy books. At the climax of the ceremony, the priests in the center of the *Basmadrosh* cylinder would light wood piles to build flames that would shoot to the ceiling. The flames signified that the spirit of Akeyde was descending into the chosen male. An iron poker was put in the flame. At the end of the poker was the shape of a knife, to symbolize the sacrifice of

Akeyde and what he was when he reincarnated—a warrior for the Zans.

The Onfirer would take the poker and place it on the right arm of the designated person. The knife was imprinted in heat on the person. Then they were proclaimed Akeyde by the Onfirer.

The first reincarnation of Akeyde helped the people deal with a famine. He planted a flower called the Toyre that sprayed seeds all over the land that people could eat. And so Akeyde saved the Zan tribe from starvation and death.

The second reincarnation fought against corruption in the ruling Zan monarchy. He led a revolt against the king, who had become greedy and stole food from the people for his own court. The revolt went on for two years. Akeyde stormed the king's fortress with 12,000 men, according to the writings in the holy books. He was slaughtered inside the fortress by the King's elite guard. The king said he wasn't really Akeyde. He cut off Akeyde's right arm and hung it upright on a pole to show the people that it had no knife imprinted on it.

But the Heylik Shetyn holy books say that the King was not a true Zan, because he had intermarried with our tribe. He was really from Yek (today's Yekmonveldt), our hostile neighbor in the west country. And he could have easily substituted the arm of a slave for that of Akeyde.

The third reincarnation came because of an invasion by the king of Yek into the lands of the Zan tribe. Yek's people invaded the capital and the Yek king took thousands of our people away to make them slaves in his mines. Akeyde came to make the king die just after the invasion. He appeared to the king's advisor in a vision and told him to tell the new king to let the Zans go back home. The new king did and the people worshipped Akeyde. Then Akeyde disappeared. In the story, he goes back to heaven to sit in God's court.

The fourth reincarnation was brought to life because of Kawidtod. After the Zans were decimated by Kawidtod's soldiers and the central *Basmadrosh* in Sed destroyed, the remaining Zans lived in small segregated towns, with houses built on top of one another. Lack of food and disease were killing off the remaining Zans. Akeyde led an emigration of the strongest men and women of the tribe, called the Nine Hundred, out of the new nation of Kawidtodia, to a land in the north that had no people, just green grass and trees and a great river. After a settlement was established, Akeyde was supposed to go back to Kawidtodia to try to help the remaining Zans living under the oppressive rule of Kawidtod.

But he never arrived back. The holy books said he was killed by a Kawidtodian squadron on the frontier of the country.

The fifth reincarnation came forth because of a war between Kawidtodia and Yek. The Yeks invaded the country and the Zans came to their side to fight the Kawidtodians. To us, the Yeks were now our friends because they were willing to fight the greater enemy.

Akeyde led the Zans in battle. The Kawidtodians fought the Yeks to a standstill, but they slaughtered the Zans. Akeyde was killed during the last battle of the war, on the dusty summer plains in front of the holy mountain, the Heylik Shetyn.

I was the sixth reincarnation.

However, I was 200 years early.

There were a number of controversies surrounding me. I was not supposed to reincarnate until the full end of the thousand year cycle. And Zans around the world questioned my father's authority to name me Akeyde.

But my father, with his power, was able to at least persuade the Zan community in Queens that I was really the sixth reincarnation. He organized a board of three Spaamas in the borough who certified my authenticity.

I didn't start out as Akeyde. My legal birth name was Joseph Wood. My father wasn't even an Onfirer then. After the central *Basmadrosh* was destroyed 2,800 years ago, Onfirers were no longer the highest priests—they were community leaders. Local

Onfirers could be selected from among each Zan community. It was a way to defend each little town, because there was no central authority left among the tribe after the Kawidtodian war.

My father's name was Alter Kletser. Kletser meant "wood" in the Zan language, a reference to Akeyde's sacrifice on strips of wood in the *Heylik Shetyn* holy books. A lot of Zans had Kletser as a last name. It's the equivalent to *Smith* in English.

His purpose in giving me my legal last name of Wood was to assimilate me. My mother agreed. She had emigrated from Kawidtodia as a young girl after her father, a Zan priest, a Spaama, was killed there. They were temporarily afraid of being Zans, even in America.

But when I was two years old, my father's tribal senses were awakened. He told me the story many times.

The events that set him off were called the Midnight Murders. In Kawidtodia, local groups of Squids, gangs really, would invade Zan homes and kill an entire household. The invasions always happened after midnight every Monday, the Zan Sabbath day.

Each week a Zan family was killed—the parents, the children, everybody in the house. In all, about 70 people were killed during the first four months of the slaughter.

The New York Times then published a story on the killings, but the murders continued. My father was incensed.

He drove around the Zan community in Queens with a petition he prepared to protest the killings and to arrest the perpetrators. After he collected 20,000 signatures on the petitions, he personally delivered them to the Kawidtodian embassy to the United Nations in Manhattan, as repugnant as that was for him to actually see and talk with Squids.

He walked into Amnesty International and asked for their help. They sent mailings to their members and collected signatures for a petition that went to the government in Kawidtodia. They made a protest to the Squid embassy in Washington. They sent out a press release.

Despite all the activity, nothing happened. Nothing. The murders went on for months. The Squid government never officially responded. My father wrote to his Congressman, Senator, even the President. He got back form letters. There were too many other pressing problems around the world.

Nobody cared about the Zans. So my father decided to deal with the problem with the old-fashioned American value of self-reliance. He campaigned to get himself elected the first Onfirer of the Zan immigrant community in Queens, about 30,000 people.

After he got elected, he made himself an even greater pain in the neck to everyone around him. He contacted the State Department. He led a delegation of Zans around Washington, personally visiting anybody he could. He got a meeting with an Assistant Secretary of State. He threatened to form the Zans into a bloc that would vote for politicians who supported the campaign to end the Midnight Murders.

After two years of his efforts, the Midnight Murders stopped. There was no explanation from the Squids and no further action. Kawidtodia is an opaque country, to say the least, but Amnesty International and the U.S. State Department made inquiries and determined that the government did not attempt to find any of the killers.

This knowledge burned within my father. A match had been lit and it did not burn out. He decided to name me Akeyde. He wanted a warrior to fight for our people. He wanted Akeyde to be born again.

My father had to persuade our local Spaama to perform the ceremony. I believe the man was threatened with the loss of his job.

The ceremony took place when I was almost five years old. I stood, without a shirt on, in front of the Spaama on the front platform of our local *Basmadrosh* in Forest Hills. My parents, uncles and cousins and the rest of the congregation were all there. The assembly house overflowed with attendees. There were about 500 people there. We violated the fire code.

The Spaama placed the poker in an iron pot that burned with fire.

He said a prayer. Then he took the rod out of the pot and stamped the shape of a knife on my right arm in fire for my entire life.

I tried to take it like a man. But the pain, the burning was so intense that I screamed and passed out.

The Spaama pressed a cold sponge on the area and this revived me. He gave me a sip of water. Then he said a prayer and declared that my name was now Akeyde Kletser. Akeyde means "Bound" and Kletser means "Wood" in the Zan language. Put the two words together in Zan and the phrase becomes "bound to wood."

The congregation cheered. From that moment, Joe Wood was dead. I was Akeyde Kletser, and I always would be.

The Trival Holiday

(Razvarr Abatut)

I was 20 years old and a community college graduate (with honors), who majored in political science with a few psychology and computer courses thrown in, and my mother made me go to Temple.

I didn't want to do it. Lying under the sheet of yellow suns on a field of blue, I was awake, but leaving my eyes closed against the sun attacking the room. I had visions of the Blue and White Temple in rubble, its giant pillars collapsed like Lego blocks a four-year-old kid has scattered around a living room carpet.

My mother threw open the door to my room like a cop busting in on a dealer with thousands of pounds worth of cocaine.

"Good morning, Raz!"

"GO AWAY."

At first she was pleasant in her fake polite way. She sat on my bed, near where my shoulders lay.

"Be nice. I thought you could come with us to the Temple today."

"Why would you think that?'

"Because it's Trival. It will be fun."

I groaned. "Fun? You want me to celebrate something that happened 3,000 years ago? We beat the crap out of a sick and rotting tribe that wouldn't have even been able to defend itself against the state of Vermont."

"It was 2,800 years ago. And it was a glorious victory for God. For justice."

"Why do you always think that if we win it's what God wants?"

"Because that's what I believe."

"You didn't answer the question."

"Oh, my son, my dearest love, questions like that are for college graduates. I am just your mother and I want you to come."

"What's the point?"

"To show that you care."

"But I don't care."

Then she got mean.

"You're coming. Get out of bed, take a shower, put on your clothes and then we will leave."

"What about breakfast?"

"There's no time. You can eat at the Temple. There will be plenty of food after the service."

"I don't want to go."

Mom shouted downstairs.

"Binele, our son doesn't want to come to Temple!"

The next sounds were of my father walking slowly up the stairs in a very resigned way. The long pause between each step was almost painful. Somebody could finish the 100-yard dash in the time it takes for my father to climb one step.

He arrived in the room and suddenly I was feeling very claustrophobic. The air, already warm, got hotter with every exhale of breath.

"Binele, please talk to him. It's the most important day of the year."

My father looked at me, still lying under the sheet. His bald head had little red cuts on it from shaving his skull. There was the usual grayness in his eyes and his shoulders were slumped as if he were in mourning. The religious police back home had done a thorough job on him. He really should have been dead.

I was very glad he wasn't, but every day I saw him like this, I could see that the tortures inflicted on him those many years ago had not gone away and never would. He was hanging on, pushing through every day, making a bare knuckle effort to stay alive.

"He doesn't have to come."

"What? Why do you always take his side? You are spoiling him beyond belief!"

A deep breath and the eyes got even sadder, if such a thing is possible.

"He's already spoiled. You can't force him to go. He's not a believer."

"What is it with you and this country? Back home, he would go without question!"

"We're not back home. Things are different here."

"Binele, please say something. This is something we can do as a family."

My mother was whimpering and I thought, *"I've got her."* What a mistake.

"Matca, I love you. But he's beyond saving. He'll have to figure out his own way. It's a long journey."

"What's the big deal? We're going to Manhattan. It's only seven miles away. The subway will take us there in 25 minutes."

"I'm not talking about distance in the sense of miles. I'm talking about what Raz will have to do spiritually if he has given up his faith. He will wander forever."

I didn't know why, but my father's thinking made me feel sad. Then I really wanted to go back to sleep.

"Matca, we're going to be late for the service. We must go. Leave the boy here."

My father walked out and went down the wooden stairs. It was quiet for a few moments. I could hear my mother draw in deep breaths, sucking all the oxygen out of the room.

"Matca, let's go! We have no time!" A sudden sign of life from the old man.

"You won't come?"

"No."

My mother turned toward me on the bed and threw her hands around my neck.

"I will choke you to death, you little piece of horse pookie!"

And she did. Her hands pushed in on my wind pipe.

I brought up my hands quickly to remove hers, but her grip was unnatural.

"Stop!" I managed to gutter out this one word.

Then she pulled my head up and threw it down on the bed repeatedly.

"I will not stop! Not stop! No!"

I tried to talk but all that came out of me was a baby's gurgle.

My mother's eyes were evil with anger. Her hands pressed down on my throat again. She was going to crush my windpipe. I was going to be dead. We were going to be on the six o'clock news.

Then, the thunderstorm was over. The six o'clock news would have to wait.

"Will you come?"

I recovered my breath, then whispered a little "no" because that's all I could manage. My mother sat on the bed for a moment. I relaxed.

A fist came roaring out of her small shoulder and hit me right in the eye.

"Holy Kawidtod, Mom! You punched me!"

"There will be more punches if you don't come with me RIGHT NOW!"

My eye was lit up like a street in Las Vegas. It burned with complaint. I could actually feel the broken blood vessels underneath the eye.

A series of punches hit me like exploding missiles in the rib cage, then one in the stomach, just to bring my body upward.

"Okay, okay! Stop!"

"Will you come now?"

"No. Yeah. Okay! Just stop hitting me."

And that's how I came to ride the subway all the way from Jackson Heights in Queens to the wealthy Upper East Side Kawidtodian Center on 79th Street and 3rd Avenue, with an eye smashed all to purple.

Last Day on Earth

(Akeyde Kletser)

The Squids went in to the Temple in bunches. Every time I saw them, I felt like shaking with anger and hatred. I wanted to jump on them and smash their heads into the concrete.

Most Zans couldn't bring themselves to call them Kawidtodians. A Zan somewhere in America came up with Kawids. Then it got modified to Kwids, but that sounded too close to the word "kids." So somebody came up with Squids. It conjured up just the right picture of alien slime.

The sidewalk was a mish-mash of dozens of these pigs. Very soon they would all be dead and in Gock. Hell.

If we were in Kawidtodia, the Temple wall might be decorated with a giant flat metal sculpture of a fist. But here in America, the Squids were less sure of their place, so the four-story-high wall fronting the Temple was blank.

The differences in architecture came down to population. In Kawidtodia, they were confident in their religion and their place in the country. There were 20 million of them in that mountain-scarred country, and just a few thousand Zans.

In America, there were just seven million of them in a nation of 300 million people.

They had to compete with a predominantly Christian culture, and they were extremely uncertain about winning that kind of fight. So they tried to fit in, not get too obvious. They had this kind of attitude like, *Hey, it's America, we have freedom of religion, but we're not here to try to displace your Christianity or make you feel uncomfortable.*

They made me uncomfortable, and if I didn't do anything about them, they would keep pushing the Zans around. Somebody had to put them in their place. Undermine their confidence even more.

It was 10 o'clock in the morning and the temperature felt like 90 degrees already. Of course, I had Tina strapped on me, as well as the covering blue and white windbreaker.

I was standing across the street and wondering how to get inside. Security was thick. Men with jackets and ties, bulky and sweating, were checking handbags and backpacks.

How could anyone get through those defenses? Vehktre didn't think of that.

I could just walk into the crowd. Press the detonator.

Everything seemed easier to pull off the day before.

When I woke up the day before, I thought about how I would like to spend my last full day on Earth. I placed the vest around me and slowly pulled the windbreaker on over it, like a funeral shroud.

I thought about going to the movies. I wanted to see the new action picture, with lots of guns and killing, where the bad guys are sliced up and discarded like rotten apples. The star played an international spy, a real man, loaded with muscles from his neck to his wrist to his chest, dark eyes and a fierceness nobody else could compete with. He was a real man. I didn't know what I was.

But there had been reports of bed bugs in the movie theaters in New York. Some were found in a lingerie store in Manhattan. And a movie theater near Federal Hall had them. That's the site where Washington was inaugurated as President, when New York was the capital of the country. The first United States Congress met there. They had to close down the movie theater and fumigate the whole place.

I was afraid to go to the movies because of the bed bugs. It seemed funny, because why would I have to worry about bedbugs? I was going to explode myself and, hopefully, many Kawidtodians.

But somehow I kept thinking I would be coming back to my apartment and I didn't want bedbugs in my couch or in my little bed. They are very difficult to kill.

So I didn't go. And I didn't want to do anything joyful, like go to a park or visit the East River. I briefly considered the idea of going to a strip club for one last thrill, but I didn't think it would make me feel good. Besides, it was sinful.

I wasn't allowed to see my family, either, especially my uncles. Vehktre made it very clear that I could no longer spend time with them. I was a warrior and I had a very difficult job to do. Akeyde must be alone for this mission.

Family and beautiful women aren't important. God is.

After I woke up, I walked around the neighborhood in Queens where Vehktre had set me up. It was a place of auto garages and warehouses and small factories that made wooden kitchen tables.

The sun was strong. The buildings looked as if they were burning from the heat.

There were also men on these streets that had nothing to do. They stared at me, all cold eyes. They knew I didn't belong there. These were big men. They had strong arms coming through the sleeves of their tee-shirts. Many of them smoked cigarettes and drank from small bottles in paper bags. A few played loud music off the stereo systems in their cars, using the battery to run the CD player.

I had my Tina and my gun, but I felt so weak in front of these men. They didn't like me. They wanted to rob me if they could figure out how to do it and get away with it.

They wanted to beat me up or kill me. I was just a piece of meat to them. A furry little rabbit who could be attacked at will. They were wolves. And they were hungry.

I couldn't take their eyes. I walked to the other side of the street when I saw them bunched up in groups of two or three.

I came to a new street where there was a sugar factory and warehouse. A dozen big tractor trailer trucks were parked in a lot. I walked on this street, the sun blowing up in my eyes.

Three teenage boys were walking toward me. I could see them coming from a quarter of a mile away. They saw me and smiled.

Now I began to panic. Should I keep walking? Should I try to find a turn-off? Where was the turn-off?

I turned around. The boys started running. I could hear their sneakers, pounding the pavement, sprinting. I started to run, full-out, but Tina held me back. The detonator was in the right pocket of my windbreaker. It kept hitting my hip. The gun was in the left and felt like a boat anchor in my windbreaker pocket.

The boys kept coming. They were closing quickly. What did they want with me? What would they do?

I pushed myself to run as hard as I could. The sugar warehouse ended with a street corner. I wheeled around it and kept running.

Another street pulled around a curve. I took it. Before I could even conceive it, a big street with stores and shops and newsstands came at me. This was Burns Street. Somehow, I had found Burns Street. Thank you, God, for guiding me. I ran into an open newsstand.

The man behind the counter jumped a little when I blew in. He had a shaved head. Must have been a Kawidtodian.

I didn't give myself time to think about that too much. I ran to the back of the store, to hide from the boys. There was an alcove there, a rectangle that bent away from the main aisle.

It was filled with magazines you're not supposed to see. There were naked women on the covers of these magazines. All this sin spilling out in front of me. I desperately wanted to look at the pictures, to see flesh, beautiful naked skin. Then I wondered if I should blow up the store.

No, no. I had to remain focused on the mission for tomorrow. I clapped my hands over my glasses like a child playing hide-and-go-seek. A second bald man was looking through the magazines. He took a look at me like I was an insane man.

To get away from him, I walked to the front of the store. I figured I would be safe from the boys by now.

The magazines became safer, but not as safe as I would have liked. An issue of *Rolling Stone* featured a 25-year-old singer who was so famous that even I had heard of her. She was wearing nothing on the cover but a brassiere and underwear. Her breasts looked like hillocks.

But the girl's face was interesting too. Not as interesting as the breasts, but beautiful. She had smooth, black, lustrous hair. Her eyes looked directly at me. They were blue, so blue. Her mouth was formed in a perfect little pout. Oh my God.

God. Right. I forced myself to turn away.

Farther up the aisle were women's' fashion magazines. One title had a 42-year-old actress on the cover, wearing a leotard with orange stripe patterns. The actress's breasts were bunched together within the leotard. Her hair in a ponytail flowed up and around her head like a whip.

On the cover the woman was quoted as saying, "There's still a tiger within me."

God entered my brain and told me to move on. Sin was here and I didn't belong.

The man behind the counter held both of his big meaty hands on the glass and looked at me as if I were a bad person. His eyes had narrowed to little wrinkles.

"Are you here to buy something? Or are you a bum?"

I looked at the rack of newspapers in front of the man and picked up a cheap tabloid.

"I'll take this."

"You need 50 cents."

I fished around my windbreaker pocket to find the money. The plastic detonator bounced around in there as my hands tried to grab some change.

I gave the man a quarter and two dimes and a nickel.

After the transaction, I asked the man, "Are you a Kawidtodian?"

"What the hell do you want to know for?"

"I just want to know."

"Are you a bullet dodger? I'll beat you to a bloody pulp."

The man brought a baseball bat out from the wall behind him. He held it tightly above his right shoulder.

"Get out of the store now."

I pushed the metal handle on the glass door, so hard I could have shattered the glass.

"I'm an American, you little freak! A goddamn American!"

From Burns Street I headed back to the apartment. Ahead, I saw a cheap women's clothing store that had been destroyed by fire. All of a sudden, I realized that God was trying to talk to me.

Metal beams stood in a cluster in the middle of the wreckage, charred black. The fire had burned very hot. Most of the building materials were melted. In some places you could still see the outline of the aisles. Here and there some mannequins lay on the floor, still identifiable as mannequins, their pink or brown bodies burned, their plastic faces flaking off ashes. A few mannequin heads had been detached from the bodies, smooth and bald, their eyes still twinkling underneath their charred heads, absent of hair. Their eyebrows and eyelashes were still there, for the most part, but their wigs were gone. They looked like Kawidtodians. Dead ones. I felt a little rush of excitement.

It was a small sea of destruction. A little bit of the poetry of the Divine.

I stood in awe in front of the remains of the store. A few men with shaved heads walked by me, gesturing at me and talking in whispers. Squids.

Every time they went by, my eyes pinged and I wanted to kill them.

But I walked home. I had to wait for tomorrow. The Big Day. Their Trival. Our revenge.

In the apartment, I removed the gun from the windbreaker and took off Tina. I had been sweating horribly.

I put the newspaper on the small kitchen table and took a long shower. When I got out of the shower, I was hungry. But there wasn't much in the refrigerator.

I ate a whole box of square crackers, low sodium (because I had high blood pressure), with water to wash them down. I read the paper. On page 12, deep inside, was a small article. A suicide bomber had blown up 27 people in a restaurant in a small mountain town in Kawidtodia called Sputten Dovil. The report said that the bomber was from a small terrorist group made up of Kawidtodians protesting the government's policies. The government blamed "extremist groups."

That could mean Zans, although I considered the likelihood of this pretty small. Most Zans left in the country were too fearful to organize something like that. They'd rather stay hidden in the underground economy, and do things the Kawidtodians consider filthy or low-class but necessary, like importing and exporting opiates for U.S. currency (giving government officials a big cut) and moving money around for various wealthy families.

The Zans would provide other services for the rich and willing in Kawidtodia, such as selling guns for security for their fortress-like mansions, securing prostitutes, smuggling drugs into the country, and dog breeding, hard as that may be to believe. A number of Kawidtodian men had friendly competitions to see who could breed the biggest, most vicious dogs. Sometimes they had the dogs fight each other, to see who had the toughest dog.

The Zans had made it clear by their choices that they were willing to serve the Kawidtod nation in whatever capacity, as long as they were allowed to live.

I didn't think any Zans had done it, but the bombing made me glad. I slept well.

The Prayer Service

(Razvarr Abatut)

The priest droned on about why we should be thankful for God's blessings. We are just humble little beings, he intoned in a monotone that wouldn't be out of place as medication for insomniacs. *We need to come to God as little more than ants, as insects, if we want to gain His blessings. That's what He thinks of us. And we owe Him our little ant lives.*

"*God is watching us, all the time.*" I had heard this sort of thing thousands of times. "*God is always judging. We must prepare ourselves to repent our sins 10 days from now, after the festival of Trival is over. This is the time to cleanse ourselves, to purify our souls of our sins.*"

It is only then that we can pursue true justice for the oppressed and convert the unbelievers, by force if necessary.

I thought about what the Kawidtodian religious police had done to my father and felt like a hypocrite being there. So I looked around the enormous prayer hall to check out everyone else. At least that was somewhat entertaining. There were many bald heads. A few looked at me with scorn because of my own long black hair. (I sometimes had a little trouble with the security guards when entering a temple because of my hair. They might have given me the bad eye, or an upraised brow. Or they would have fun with it. *"Hey, look at the rock and roll geek-head!"* Which I'm not.)

But far more of the worshippers had hair. In America, people have tried to find ways to grow their hair. They've succeeded.

While it's considered sacred to shave your head, in imitation of the Kawidtodians who crushed the Zans 2,800 years ago, there's an interpretation of the aftermath of the Zan War in a book of commentary that was written about 400 or 500 years after the Dreptat, our first holy book, was completed. No one knows for sure when it was finished.

The book, called the Dragostpa, stated that Kawidtod kept hundreds of mistresses in his palace, who all were allowed to keep their hair as long as they stayed in his houses, out of sight. As he was the king, and the conqueror of the awful Zans, this was his right and no one else's.

It's interesting that something so contradictory about something so fundamental was allowed to be printed. How could the king violate his own law? But the Kawidtodians have not always been monolithically observant. There was a strain of Kawidtodian thought less strict than the orthodox way.

That was all the commentary said about Kawidtod's deviance from the law. There was nothing else written but some liberal religious authorities had used this commentary to justify Kawidtodians who wanted to keep their hair.

In the home country, virtually everybody had a shaved head. The religious authorities didn't allow you to grow your hair. But in America, hey, we could party.

The prayer leader's deep voice carried through the vast auditorium, with steady blows. I wondered if anyone was buying the priest's message. A few looked on with fervor, but a lot of people seemed to have their eyes glued open, straining to look reverent.

I nodded off a few times, until mother shoved an elbow into my ribs.

To stay awake, I imagined Zan terrorists leaping over the pews with machine guns and raking the assembly with bullets. The thought struck fear and fascination in me at the same time. The chaos of the ultimate scum invading and killing.

I could see the Zans, wearing masks over their faces, running into the balcony and spraying bullets at the crowd, blood spurting and people screaming, dying, wounded, running. Then, from the main floor, jumping onto people and standing on their victims, shooting anyone in sight. The mass of quivering people stampeding for the exits. Dozens wounded or dying. Blood flowing like spilled milk.

There weren't too many Zan terrorists running around. Most of them were so cowardly they wouldn't have dared to do something like that. But maybe there was one guy running around out there who would be insane enough to try.

The Back Door

(Akeyde Kletser)

The best thing to do would have been to just walk into the crowd and press the detonator. I could kill at least a dozen people, maybe more. Get it over with quickly.

Then meet God in heaven.

When the light changed, I walked across the wide avenue. People were milling around, talking. The main hall must have been very crowded. The Squids had all come to celebrate the destruction of the Zandrian kingdom eons ago. I hated them for that.

Kawidtodians shuffled around in the heat, pressing to get through the funnel of security guards. Long rectangular tables flanked the guards on two sides. That's where the backpacks and handbags were to be placed for examination.

I didn't know why there was so much security. Maybe it was the bombing the day before in Kawidtodia.

I let myself get moved along slowly like a pig being herded to slaughter. Sweat paddled my face. We were so bunched together that Tina was getting jostled. I didn't like it. I had to get out of there.

I turned around and put my arms up in front of me, then walked out of the crowd.

"Excuse me. Sorry. So sorry."

Squids raised their eyes at me, but said nothing. My politeness had disarmed them.

I walked around the whole temple, to try to find another way in. There was a towering black iron fence on 79th Street, about 10 feet high. I thought I could climb it, but of course anyone could see me.

On the 79th Street side, beyond the entrance, there was an alley. Maybe there was a way to get in there. I walked across the street, east on Third Avenue, so I wouldn't have to go through the crowd again. That was too dangerous.

Then I made it down to 78th Street and crossed Third Avenue going toward the Temple. I approached the Temple from the south this time.

On the south side of the Temple, the alley presented itself. It had a high metal fence as well. A gate stood in the middle of the fence. This was the janitor's gate, to take garbage out of the building, and to take deliveries.

The gate was closed.

I tried the door anyway. When I pulled at the knob, the gate opened. The janitor either forgot to lock it or he didn't want to deal with constantly locking and unlocking the gate in order to take out the massive amount of garbage that would have to be removed after the service and celebration in the hall. There would be leftover food and wine glasses, paper plates and plastic cups, the residue of hundreds of Squids eating and celebrating.

In the alley, I walked by dozens of plastic garbage cans and bags. They were overflowing with pastry paper and wine bottles and empty bags of bread. Rats flew from can to can as I walked through the alley. This is where I belonged.

The heavy metal door to the building was open and it was lined with garbage cans as well. But these were empty. This was the janitor's preparation for the trash to come.

I came in through the kitchen. A man in a white jacket saw me.

"Hey! You! You're very late. Get a jacket on. The service is about to end, and we need to get to work."

I was afraid to walk by him. He wouldn't let me go. I knew it.

I grabbed for the gun in the left pocket of the windbreaker.

My hand reached for nothing but the folds of the pocket. How could I have forgotten the gun on a day like today? This day!

Before I could do anything else, a white jacket slapped me in the face.

"Come on, let's get moving. There's no time to take off your jacket. Why are you wearing that anyway? It's so goddamn hot out there."

"Okay."

"What's your name?"

"Joe."

"Who the hell is named Joe these days?"

"Nobody."

"Well, get your jacket on. It's time to serve."

I put on the jacket. With the windbreaker under it, I looked very broad.

The jacket cut off access to the detonator in the right-hand pocket of the windbreaker, if I buttoned it all the way down.

So I decided to leave the bottom button unbuttoned. I reached into the windbreaker and found the little plastic tube. Oh, heaven.

"What are you looking for? Come on!"

I followed the man in the white jacket.

"Grab a plate and let's go!"

With a large plate full of bread, he shoved open the double doors of the kitchen. He walked briskly to a long table and set down his tray. He gestured for me to follow him.

"Now, stand here and smile. You don't even have to serve. The people will serve themselves. I'll get the rest of the plates."

The plates had long loaves of bread punctuated at the end by a knot. It was supposed to resemble the fist of Kawidtod. It did.

I shook with panic. It was like throwing a swastika in front of a Jew. And there were dozens of these things on the plate in front of me. I wanted to blow myself up right there.

Then the hungry Squids came on, in a massive dumb buffalo herd trying to run toward a cliff. So many of them, crowding around, grabbing for the loaves, like animals, then holding them up in triumph. It's part of their religion. They've gotten a symbol of Kawidtod's fist. The pigs. Some were bald, some had hair, it didn't matter. They were gross in their desires.

I was in a room full of cannibals. Revulsion flooded my chest, and anger. Who were these people? Why were they so awful?

It would be easy to kill at least two dozen of these pigs right here. One press of the button. I would become a little sun. An explosion of light and fire, nails and ball bearings flying out of the vest like missiles. Flesh would be pierced, organs ripped, faces blown off. Blood exploding out of veins and arteries. Lungs split open by daggers. Heads ripped open with ball bearings.

I fingered the detonator. I rubbed my thumb on the button back and forth.

More of them were coming on to grab the loaves of bread. The pulsing, grasping mass of Kawidtod animals. Squids. Apes with the brains of birds.

This was the moment. Time for Tina and me to unite. I put my finger down an eighth of an inch.

"Mr. Wood, what are you doing here?"

I took my finger off the button to look through the crowd of Squids. Somebody was talking to me, calling me by my legal name, a name I could barely remember at the time, but I couldn't place the voice.

"That's Mr. Wood! Hey, Dad!" It was a male's voice. But I didn't see where it was coming from. I put my finger on the detonator. Hello, Tina.

A kid, maybe 19 or 20, shoved his way through to the front of the table.

"Mr. Wood, what are you doing here?"

I removed my finger from the button and stared at the kid.

My throat was dry and unsure. "Do I know you?"

The noise from the crowd was rushing everywhere and it was very difficult to hear the answer.

"I'm sorry, could you say that again?"

"You've gained some weight. Wow."

"Who are you?"

"Razvarr Abatut."

"Okay."

"You were my teacher! You don't remember?"

"Uh, I had a lot of students. When were you in my class?"

"Twelve, 13 years ago. Second grade. You know me."

"Okay."

"I didn't speak much English, remember? You drew me superhero pictures. Superman, Batman. As a reward to me for learning."

"I'm trying to think."

"You had to take a second job, huh? Man, they don't pay public school teachers much."

I didn't want to tell this boy that I hadn't been a public school teacher for close to 10 years. Since I quit the public school system I had been a teacher in the Zan religious school.

"Uh, no."

"Hey, can you get us some more bread! Your plate is all empty. Or didn't you notice? More Pumns! Come on, get on the job here!" Somebody from behind the boy was yelling at me.

I lifted the plate.

"I'm sorry. I've got to get more bread. Excuse me."

I took off for the kitchen. Out of the corner of my eye I could see the boy, gesturing to somebody else at me. I was glad to be out of there.

My job for the afternoon became serving fists of bread to these animals celebrating their destruction of my people thousands of years ago.

The detonator beckoned. I kept coming to it, wanting to meet with Tina. But something held me back. The kid.

At the end of the shift, when all the Squids and all the Pumn breads were gone, I took off my white jacket and went home on the subway. I unlocked the metal door to my apartment and walked to the bathroom mirror with my windbreaker still on, the detonator still in the pocket.

I looked at myself in the mirror, my hair matted and soaked with sweat, my whole face slick with moisture. I looked down at the blue and white windbreaker. Inside was the unexploded Tina.

Then I looked in the mirror again. What was this face all about? So I took my fingernails and clawed my cheeks until they bled.

Part II

Fire, Memory

(Akeyde Kletser)

The sun was a harsh mistress. It invaded every corner of my eyes with failure. The heavy curtains beckoned. I pulled them together and changed the room completely. It was now a dark chamber, a small theater for me to reenact my failure.

The scabs that had formed on my face stretched and broke as I closed the curtains. Blood ran down my cheeks, the only blood I had shed for the mission.

My history, with all its complications, had shrunk itself into one decision, which I had failed to make. There was only one task left for me on this Earth and I couldn't perform it.

The curtains were black and the linoleum floor was black as well. They seemed to swallow up everything, like a coffin encasing a body.

I remembered a dinner with my uncles once, at our summer camp, so long ago. What else did I have at that moment but old memories?

Narish, Dreykop, and Lhokem. We sat at a round table in my uncle's cabin, which was attached to the kitchen for the mess hall, up a long sloping hill from my father's cabin. Narish was cooking a dinner of chicken cutlets and spaghetti. My favorite. Two bottles sat on the table. Red wine for the uncles. Grape juice for a 12-year-old.

Dreykop and Lhokem were arguing. The uncles were laughing at Lhokem, something which eluded my 12-year-old brain. It didn't matter. When I was with them, I felt like I belonged.

"Lhokem, that's a ridiculous idea."

"No, no Dreykop. We've got to do something. Poison the water supply. Flood their neighborhoods with counterfeit money."

"The war is over, Lhokie. We lost. Three thousand years ago. You can't change history."

"And that's okay with you?"

"As long as we have our businesses, we'll be all right."

Narish had his back to us, busy at the stove top.

"And the camp."

"We can't live like this forever. What happens when we get older?"

"We're already old, Lhokie," Narish said, coming to the table with chicken cutlets, steaming in the pan.

"Forty isn't so bad. We're in good shape," Dreykop said.

"Think about Alter. Now he's OLD."

Alter, my father.

Lhokem protested. "Forty-five isn't so old."

"He's the Onfirer. That makes him old," Narish said, cutting up his chicken.

"And he smokes cigars like a fiend," Dreykop pointed out.

"The Onfirer job makes you old," Narish said loudly. "What else can he do but smoke?"

"Cookie's old too," I said.

The uncles laughed at me. I was embarrassed.

"Your Uncle Cookie, he's on the outs with the family."

I was hurt. "Why? He's your brother."

"Should we tell him?" Narish asked.

"He's old enough," Dreykop said.

Lhokem shook his head. "We haven't seen him in a while. Your father talks to him a little bit on the phone. About what I don't know. But I would like to find out."

I didn't understand all this adult maneuvering and my eyebrows were raised and my mouth open with unasked questions.

"He bought a strip club," said Dreykop, as if that would put the matter to rest.

"What's a strip club?"

I got laughed at again.

"Flesh, Akeyde. Naked women. Flashing their boobs."

"I don't get it."

"Oh, he's old enough, Drey," Narish roared. "He's old enough to not understand!"

"Let's not talk about it," Lhokem said. "He's a disgrace to the community. We're supposed to be modest about these things."

"What things?" I said, terribly interested.

"SEX!" Dreykop shouted.

I turned a massive shade of red.

Lhokem took a long swallow of the wine and decided to change the subject. "Alter has got a lot of decisions to make. He has to worry about the whole community."

"Well, he needs to worry less and live more."

Narish deliberately thrust his long beard into his wine glass.

"You can drink my beard now!"

Everybody laughed at the sight of Narish's beard swimming around in the wine.

Dreykop did it too. I couldn't help myself. I almost spit out a piece of chicken, I laughed so hard.

Lhokem wouldn't join in. "Get serious. You know the Squids have done some things in the neighborhood. More of them are moving in. Alter is trying to figure out what to do. We have to fight back."

Narish was mad that Lhokem wouldn't play along and shake his little mood.

"With what, Lhokie? We're a little group. There are a lot more of them than us."

"There's always Akeyde."

That got the other two uncles quiet. I didn't quite get what was going on.

"Leave the boy out of this," Narish said, firmly.

"He's got to know sometime."

I knew about the knife brand on my arm and why it was there, but didn't have any idea about anybody's plans for me.

"He doesn't even know what a strip club is!"

Lhokem turned to me. "You want to go to heaven, Akeyde?"

"Yeah, sure."

"Don't do this, Lhokem."

He turned to me. "You're the one."

"The one?"

"You were chosen to be the defender."

"Defend what?"

"That's all in old books," Narish said. "Almost 6,000 years old."

"Those books are holy. Alter has been thinking about this for a long time," Lhokem said. "That's why Akeyde has the name."

"Come on, Lhokie, don't throw all that stuff at the kid."

"What about the songs we sing? That's all just old stuff too, right?"

"They're just words. They don't mean anything."

"You can turn words into action. That's why we say them."

A splash of red blew up on Lhokem's white tee-shirt. Narish had thrown a glass of wine at his brother.

"Hey!"

"Stop taking yourself so seriously. We're in summer camp, for God's sake!"

So Lhokem threw a glass of wine on Narish's beard. That's how it started. Dreykop struck with flying wine at Lhokie. Lhokem laughed loudly, grabbed the mostly full bottle and swung it so the wine came out in an arc at all of us.

Narish grabbed a bottle of red wine and doused Lhokem on the head. Drey took an uncorked bottle out of the little refrigerator in the room and brought it around his body like a baseball bat.

Wine hit our faces and shirts. It was a blood bath. We were all laughing. I licked some of the wine off my shirt.

"No drinking wine, Akeyde. Not until you're 13!"

In a matter of minutes, the wine was gone. We all stood there, soaked. Laughing. Having fun. It was as if some giant had written on our shirts with a red magic marker the size of a garden hose.

There was so much happiness in me that day because I knew without being able to say it that we all belonged to each other.

When I look back on it, I remember us all as so young. Even my uncles. They were easier about things.

Everything turned around because of the tire iron. We all became harder on the Squids.

A few Kawidtodian kids moved into the neighborhood when I was 12. The Zans and the Kawidtodians became sort of friendly. We played a little football, baseball, and basketball, but we didn't really hang out together. No Zan kids ever went to a Squid kid's house to read comics or watch horror movies on TV.

One deep winter day, we all found ourselves in a snowball fight. There were about seven Zan kids and six Squids. The Zan kids decided to make the teams Zan versus Kawidtodians. We were throwing snowballs pretty hard at each other. Each kid tried to turn himself into a machine, scooping, packing, and zinging the balls off as quickly as possible.

The teams were pretty evenly matched. Then three of my older cousins walked by—Tsen, Eygene, and Hano. These were Dreykop's kids. Tsen was 15, Eygene 17, and Hano 18. They saw what was happening and joined in.

Tsen ran up to a Kawidtodian boy and stuffed snow in his mouth. Hano ambushed two other kids and dumped snow on their heads, then pushed the boys to the ground. Eygene tackled the rest.

The Squid kids were completely dazed. We pounded them with snowballs until they were beaten, lying in the snow, not moving. Then we walked off, noses in the air, proud.

I was excited when I got home. I told my mom and dad in the kitchen, over dinner. We were eating salad with Toyre seeds and chicken coated in Toyre oil. My mom, with a brown scarf tied around her head, blanched. My father was very angry.

My father told me what we had done was wrong.

"You shouldn't mix with these people!" he yelled. "What's wrong with you? They're killers and pigs!"

I put my head down and took it.

"Alter, he's young. A boy. He doesn't know," my mom said.

"Well, he should know! His name is Akeyde!"

He rose up out of his chair and punched me in the chest. Even though I was 12 years old, I was thrown out of my seat by the downward force of the punch and hit the kitchen floor.

I looked up at my father and he glared at me with hate. I didn't want to get hit again, so I stayed on the floor, looking at him with shame and fear.

"Where is your sense of survival! Don't you know anything?"

Mom came down to me, put her arms around my shoulders as my face collapsed into a pile of flesh, not a face at all, just a collection of skin molecules that happened to be situated close to one another.

"That's enough, Alter. You've made your point."

"You're always protecting him. How's he going to grow up when you're not there to save him?"

My mother brought me into her more fiercely. "I don't know. But hitting him isn't going to make him grow up faster."

My father's hands were curled into fists and he stood over the two of us with his hammer arms, ready to fight.

"I have plans for him. He's not an ordinary boy. He doesn't have the luxury of growing up like a regular child. I need him to be strong. Not like this! Not like this!"

My mom helped me get up, keeping her arms around my shoulders like a protective cordon.

Dad took an angry breath then pitched at me again. This one was a punch to the gut. The force of it tore me from my mother's arms and I fell on the floor again.

All the air came out of me. Dad was about to lower himself to the floor to do something more, maybe hit me again, when my mother threw herself on me and put a hand in the air, a traffic cop of a mom.

"Stop hitting my son," she said in a steely voice.

He started shouting at me. "When are you going to stand on your own?"

I had no reply.

"Now I have to go apologize to all those sons of bitches for what you did. I don't even like seeing them on the street, and now I have to find them and go over to their houses. We're not ready for this! You don't start a war if you're not prepared!"

"It was just a snowball fight, Alter."

"No, it wasn't. It was part of a war. And for war you need a strategy. Or you're dead."

He walked out of the kitchen, disgusted. Mom hugged me fiercely. "It's over, sweetie. It's over."

She was wrong.

Dad took me over to the Kawidtodian house where the fight started, to personally apologize, even though my cousins had been the bullies. From that house, he got the information about where all the other boys lived. We visited those houses too.

My father said he was sorry to the fathers of the boys and to the boys themselves. He had to swallow hard every time we walked up the concrete steps, grimacing as if he were going to meet the demons of Gock himself. His face looked like a death mask as he made his apologies.

I looked over at him. His eyes were set fiercely. I could see what he wanted to do. He wanted to kill everybody inside these houses, then blow them up. He had that much anger in him. All I felt was shame.

After we visited the last house, Father said, "You will never play with those boys again. Understand?"

"Okay."

"Do you *understand*?"

"Yeah."

"I want you to say, *I understand.*"

"I understand, Dad."

"You just made a promise. I'm going to hold you to that, you idiot."

A few weeks later, somebody threw a brick into the rear window of my father's station wagon. During the spring time we went to a tree planting festival at the *Basmadrosh*. We stayed at the assembly house most of the night for a party. When we came home, the front door was off its hinges.

"Stay here," my father commanded my mother and me. Then he walked inside the house. Blue and white paint was splattered on the yellow walls. My mother's jewelry was missing. Dad's holy books were torn from the bookshelves and several pages ripped out.

My mother looked around the house and put her hands over her mouth, but she didn't cry. My father did, a little. He looked as if someone had died.

After that, Dad looked a little different. He always got tense easily, but this was on a new level. His jaw was set up hard into his teeth. He squinted a lot, as if he expected to get hit again.

And we did get hit.

One night that November, I was out walking in the neighborhood. I found a small fire in the middle of the street, about three houses down from our house. It was a book, burning up. The Zans teach that all books are sacred, so I ran from the sidewalk to try to save it.

I started stamping on the fire-licked pages, but the flame was very stubborn. A car nosed up the block.

"Hey, kid."

A man on the passenger side flashed a badge. They were plainclothes police officers.

"Yeah?" I said.

"What are you doing?"

"Trying to put out this fire."

"I'm thinking maybe you set it."

I was scared and I didn't know what to say. The cop got out of the car and stamped the fire out with his foot.

"I'm taking you home, kid. Where do you live?"

I pointed and said, "Over there. Down the block."

So the cops took me home and explained what had happened. My mother was very embarrassed.

My father was angry.

"Did you do this?" I thought he wanted to hit me again, but the police were there.

My mouth was frozen, but I managed to unhinge my jaw and say in a quiet voice, "No."

"Let's go see," he said.

All the men left the house, the cops, my father and me. We walked to the burned book, which was still sparking a little.

Dad put his foot in the embers. He kneeled down and looked at the book. Then he took a handkerchief out of his pocket and grabbed the spine. The book was still hot. He dropped the book on the ground. Then Dad got down on his two knees and blew on the pages like it was a too-hot hamburger. The cops looked at each other, and I imagined them thinking, "What kind of nut do we have here?" I was ashamed.

After a few minutes, my father picked up the book again. He studied it.

"My son didn't do this."

"How do you know?" one of the cops said.

"Because this is a holy book from our tribe. My son wouldn't burn a Zan book, would you?"

I was terrified on several levels. I shook my head no. Burning a tribal book was like destroying pieces of me.

The cops were a little embarrassed now. They walked back to their car. To save face, one of them said to me, "Be careful when you walk in this neighborhood. You don't want to get pulled in for a robbery."

I thought the police officer was being ridiculous. At the time I was 12 years old. I was mad at the guy, but I didn't have the words to fight back. My father let them go without responding. He looked at the book with great sadness. The wind blew ashes off the pages. Dad read some of the sections, looking for the areas that were burned off. He kissed the book, two full lips planted on the damaged cover, bits of burnt paper blowing against his face like black snowflakes.

I helped him bury it in our back yard. You can't simply throw a book like that in the garbage.

Dad purchased four wooden poles about eight feet high. He stretched a black cloth over the poles and tied the cloth to the poles with black ribbons.

Once that was accomplished, we took prayer books under the tent. Father kissed the book, as did I. Then he placed the burned book in a gift box and closed the top. The box sat on the grass, crushing down the blades with its weight.

Hunched over and reading from our books, we said several prayers in the old language of our people. When the prayers were finished, I leaned down and touched the box. Pain and sorrow flowed through the dead book, into the box and filled up my nerves.

"It's time," Father said.

With a spade, Dad dug a small hole about two feet down into the grass, while I watched. The box went into the hole. Then Dad shoveled brown dirt on top of the box and covered over the burial place completely.

Dad patted down the dirt. I thought that was the end of the service. Then he looked up at me.

"This is what happens when you play with them. They're not people like you and I."

I nodded my head.

A few hours later, I placed an old toy soldier over the spot to mark it. That wasn't required. I did that on my own. After a few days, the wind had blown the soldier away.

More Kawidtodians moved into the neighborhood.

My father was the leading elder, the Onfirer. He proposed that he needed an advisory board, a group of elders, to help consult with him on important matters, like defending the community. He wanted to form a Zan defense committee as well and send men out on patrols to protect us.

All my uncles were selected to be on the advisory board and the defense committee, as well as many of my cousins.

Mom talked to Dad at dinner about it.

"Are you sure we should do this thing, Alter?"

She talked in a little soft voice to try to pacify him, but we all knew she was trying to stand up to my father.

"I don't want to talk about it."

"Why not go to the police?"

"This is beyond the police."

My mother pressed on, brave soul. Her voice firmed up.

"Have you talked to the police about this? They have a very good community relations department through the local station. They always have articles in the local newspapers about how to protect yourself from crime."

"Oh yeah? Did they protect us from getting our house broken into? Or from having a brick thrown through our car window?"

"Umm, what about the auxiliary police? A lot of people sign up for that to help protect the neighborhood."

"They're useless."

My mother took another tack.

"Are you sure you want to get your brothers involved in this? They're not the most trustworthy people. They're involved in some bad businesses."

I raised my ears to this news. I wasn't quite sure what she was talking about, but it did make me wonder what they were doing when I saw them around the neighborhood and on our little trips out of the camp during the summer.

"They're trustworthy to me."

"It's not you I'm worried about. I'm concerned about other people. How do you know they're going to protect the neighborhood instead of doing business in the stores and on the street corners they're supposed to be patrolling? And you know what I'm talking about."

"How do you know about this?"

"Do I not have eyes? Do I not see?"

My father dismissed her. "They're religious men. They are faithful to God. They're in the *Basmadrosh* virtually every day for prayers."

"That doesn't mean anything!"

"They'll do what I tell them to do."

"Why not talk to Cookie? He might be able to help. He knows politicians."

My father got even madder at that.

"He's a smut peddler. He's lost to God. Your father was a Spaama. You know the laws."

"But your other brothers, what they do is okay?"

"They're religious and they don't sell to Zans. They're just trying to take care of their families."

I had very little idea about what was going on, but I swerved my head back and forth for each verbal punch.

"This is not a good idea, Alter."

My father snorted.

"You keep saying the same thing over and over. Say something useful for once."

He threw his napkin on the table and walked out.

Then he yelled over his shoulder.

"We're out of toilet paper. Go buy some at the store."

I looked at my mom.

She looked down, picked up her half-finished dinner and emptied it into the garbage can below the sink.

Then she washed it off and placed the dish in the dishwasher.

"Akeyde, you finished?"

"Yeah, Mom."

"Give me your plate."

"Okay."

"Want to go out for ice cream?"

"Yeah."

We walked three blocks over to the main avenue. At the ice cream place, her face grew a little lighter.

"I may have a job."

"Oh yeah?" I said, barely interested as my chocolate ice cream was far more important at the moment.

"The *Basmadrosh* needs a part-time secretary."

"I thought the school already had a secretary."

I must have looked surprised, because she said immediately, "Your father has nothing to do with it. The Spaama wants to hire me."

"Why?"

Mom swallowed half a scoop of strawberry ice cream in one quick motion. I had to wait for her to get it down before she answered.

"He says he needs somebody to plan out his schedule. He's swamped with appointments."

"Really?"

"His job is becoming more demanding. He's not happy with the school secretary. She won't do his work. She says she was hired to take care of the school, not the congregation."

She leaned over the table and whispered to me conspiratorially. "And you know what else?"

"What?"

"She drinks."

"Who?"

"The school secretary. So the Spaama doesn't like her anyway. But he can't fire her. She's one of your father's cousins."

"How?"

"I can't figure it out. Your father has all these cousins. And so do you. But all the families are so tangled up, nobody wants to diagram the family trees."

While Mom and I ate ice cream, Dad started to look into the Zan holy books and decided to import a number of customs and traditions from the stone mountains. Some thousands of Zans were left there, the remnant of a population of millions, living in a collection of villages around the ancestral home.

My father told the men on the newly formed elder and defense committees to let their hair grow long and to grow long beards, as he and my uncles had done years ago. He said it was time to show that we were all Zans, to show solidarity, that we would not be cowed. Growing our beards and hair long was a revolutionary act, he declared.

"We will not hide anymore. We need to show we are a proud people."

All the elders followed his lead, as did most of the men in the assembly house. The defense patrols went out in the neighborhood, armed with reflecting strips on their jackets, but the men saw very little action, much to my father's disappointment.

He also purchased new license plates for his car. They said: OBEY GOD.

Well, I wanted to obey God, but in my young mind, I wanted to play with other boys, whether they were Zans or Squids.

In my social studies class, I observed a bald Kawidtodian boy, new to the neighborhood, all alone. Not even the other Squids spent time with him. I saw he had a cover on his composition notebook of Captain America. Captain America was fighting a French super villain called Batroc.

After a few months, I went up to him after class.

"What's your name?"

He just looked at me.

"You like Captain America?"

"Yeah."

"I have, like, a hundred Captain America comic books."

"Yeah?"

"Want to see them?"

"I can't go over your house. You're a Zan."

"How do you know?"

"I see the kids you're friends with."

"You have any comics?"

"Yeah."

"Can I see 'em?"

"How?"

I knew we couldn't go over to my house. My father might explode. I could visualize his whole body rumbling with anger, then see his skin turn red. His arms would begin to shake, and his legs. The body would come to a boil, then fire would start to come out of his neck, licking his head in flames. Finally, the head would ignite. The pressure from the boil would push his skull outward. The explosion rained down on me.

I was pretty sure I didn't want to see that.

"We can meet in the library on Saturday."

"I don't know."

"C'mon. Nobody goes to the library."

"Alright."

"I'll meet you at 11."

"Okay."

"Bring your comics!"

He had about 25 comics, mostly Captain America, a few Avengers, some Superman. I had about 200 comics, from the Silver Surfer to the Fantastic Four and all kinds of DC comics, like Batman, Hawkman, and the Justice League.

His name was Palash. We shared comics. Mostly I shared mine. I had most of his. We traded on Saturdays, then traded them back the next weekend.

After a few months, we got tired of this. There was a movie out about the police fighting crime in Los Angeles. Two cops, one white, one black, were fighting a drug smuggling ring. You could walk to the movie theatre from your house in our neighborhood. It was only 15 minutes away. I met Palash at the show.

In one scene one of the cops was tortured with electric shocks by the leader of the drug ring. Somehow he escaped and saved the other cop's daughter and killed the bad guys.

We both really liked it. We saw it again together the next weekend.

I had my regular Zan friends, too, like Advo Kluger and Redner Brkna, but Palash was like my secret friend.

He couldn't come over my house, but he invited me to his house one Sunday. His parents didn't seem too happy about it, but they let me in. I was a little uncomfortable with their bald heads, but Palash's own bald head had sort of prepared me for this.

Anyway, we didn't spend much time with them. He and I went to his room and played army with his soldiers. He had whole armies that could fight. We played Monopoly and Risk. We watched TV.

My father found out about it. We had another argument at the kitchen table. My mother was out shopping.

"Why did you go over that boy's house?"

"He's my friend."

"You can't be friends with him. You know the history."

"He's not history. He's just a kid."

My father batted his eyes and looked at me like I was the dumbest little pigeon in the world.

"You know how many millions they've killed. They're animals."

"He's not."

"I'm not worried about him! I'm worried about the grown-ups! Somebody is going to see you playing with him and they're going to hurt you."

"Who?"

"I don't know. One of them. They think we're monkeys. They think they can do whatever they want to us."

I was confused. "Even here?"

"Especially here."

Palash's parents had lectured him too about me.

This made no sense to me. I liked the kid.

So, despite our parents' rules, we kept up the friendship. We played catch in the schoolyard. We threw a football back and forth, pretended to be New York Jets. He had a strong arm. He played quarterback. I was a wide receiver. We threw a softball around too, and played basketball at the courts in the schoolyard. One-on-one.

My father was right. Somebody saw us. Of course they would. We weren't hiding.

But it took two years for anybody to do anything about it.

My one-night relationship with Tina had ended a few weeks before. After that, I sought out Palash as much as possible, to drown myself in physical activity, to run around, to try to forget.

I was even more interested in finding distractions and trying to have fun, trying to forget about this girl.

Around 5:30 in the afternoon one Sunday in October, we had finished playing one-on-one. I had played fiercely, not because of Palash, but because I was so angry with Tina that I wanted to burn out my feelings for her by playing as hard as I could. I beat Palash five times in one-on-one.

He tried to keep up with me, but he couldn't. We didn't speak about it. He looked at me a couple of times, as if to say, "Why are you beating the crap out of me?" I knew he was wondering why I was playing so competitively. It was not like me.

I was holding my basketball at my hip. We were walking to the road where he turned left and I turned right, to get home for dinner

Two men drove by in a car.

I wouldn't have noticed this at all, except the passenger was pointing at us and gesturing wildly as they passed us.

I looked at the car as it went down the street. I could see the passenger in the front yelling at the driver and jerking his arm backwards at Palash and me. The car stopped about 100 feet away. The driver made a three-point turn and came back down the street, gaining speed.

I told Palash, "Another stupid Queens driver."

Palash ran off. He knew. Somehow he knew.

The car screeched to a stop at the curb.

The driver and passenger jumped out of the car. They had shaved heads.

"Shame on you, you little piece of Zan monkey shit, for polluting that boy's mind!"

The driver swore at me in Kawidtodian language. He slapped me. My glasses flew off my head onto somebody's lawn. My head got twisted backwards then whipped to the other side so he could slap me again on the other side of my face.

I stood there, humiliated, hurt and sad, and I took uncounted numbers of slaps without fighting back. I thought, "There is a debt that must be paid. I have hurt Palash."

Despite all the slaps, I held onto the basketball. It was my basketball and I didn't want anyone else to get it.

That wasn't enough pain and suffering for these two men. The passenger took out a tire iron from the well of the trunk of the car.

I don't know why I didn't run. Maybe I thought I deserved to be punished.

I saw the man raise it above his head. I put my hands up to ward off the blow, and the basketball bounced away down the street, all alone. The driver grabbed my arms and held them down. I can still see the tire iron there, poised like a sword high up in the air, then slicing down. It came fast and hard.

My father, coincidentally, was walking down the same street with my uncles at the time, and he saw me get slammed from a distance of about 200 feet away. He and my uncles came running and yelled at the men. The Squid threw themselves in the car, along with the tire iron, and drove off.

I was on the ground and my head felt as if it were trying to lift itself away from my neck. My father leaned over me and cradled my head. My uncles were up there too, in the sky. Dad looked so worried that I felt bad for him.

I blacked out. My father drove me to the hospital in his car. I was diagnosed with a concussion. The hospital did some tests and had me on observation for three days, determined I was in okay shape, then released me.

The doctors were sloppy, though. My right eye, never particularly strong, was even weaker after that. The tire iron seemed to change my brain wiring. The optic nerve sent out tears whenever it felt like it, independently of whatever was going on in the environment. My right eye might flood with water at anytime. I became more excitable and prone to great anxieties.

The Squid tire iron was the final bullet my father needed to get me into the Zan religious school. First Tina, and now this. It was a safe haven, he argued. And, he said, it was where my education could really begin.

After I got out of the hospital from the tire iron, my mother retreated more into herself. She had whispered conversations with somebody on the phone, a number of times. For months she barely spoke to my father. Or me.

My father put me in the Zan school. And he arranged for me to become part of the Zan religious prayer services on a weekly basis.

According to our ancient calendar, Akeyde was sacrificed to God by his father on a day that worked out to Monday in the modern Christian year. That became the Zan Sabbath. In America, celebrating the Sabbath on a Monday was another thing that set us apart from the rest of the population and it got us into trouble with the majority. If you were a Zan and had a job, good luck asking your boss for a Monday off every week so you could celebrate your Sabbath.

So most Zans didn't. They worked and sloughed off the rituals of the faith. If anybody kept our compact with God, they would go to the assembly house on Monday night.

For 50 Monday nights a year I was appointed to read a portion from the Heylik Shetyn, the blessed holy book of our people. It had to be read in our ancient language. The portion usually lasted about 20 minutes.

I memorized the piece each week. I knew how to read most of the words and I was learning more Zan words every day in my new religious school.

But I was nervous reading in front of more than the 20 to 30 people who came to the assembly house, mostly old ladies, but a few young Orthodox Zan couples too. So I memorized the whole portion. The Spaama had arranged to give me recordings of each reading and I would listen to the words and say them at home, after my school work, until I could recite the piece by heart.

It was hard work, but my father was smart to give me the job. At least I thought so, until recently. It took my mind off Tina and the tire iron smashing down on my head.

One Monday of the year was different though. I didn't read from the Heylik Shetyn. I became the boy who told his father to kill him for God, the saint of our religion. We had a pageant at assembly houses all over the county.

Since I was considered the reincarnation of Akeyde, this was applauded as a natural move by the Spaama and the congregation.

My father played the part of Zan. I was Akeyde. Or I am Akeyde. I got confused about it. It was not straight in my head. I was reincarnated. And yet I didn't remember anything that happened to me 5,800 years ago. I had to learn it by reading the books.

I visualized the entire pageant in my head standing there on the sidewalk outside the Squid temple.

The entire assembly house was dark. There was a spotlight on my father and me, which moved as we moved.

My father and I walked up the aisle, holding hands as Zan and Akeyde originally did almost six millennia ago. We were wearing long robes and sandals in the fashion of the time and the place. We climbed up the steps to the stage, as if to ascend the mountain where the sacrifice would take place.

On stage, my father slaughtered a stuffed lamb. He grabbed it by the neck and sliced its throat. A balloon on the throat was filled with red paint. It poured out onto the lamb's neck. My father offered the lamb to a wolf, usually played by one of my uncles. The wolf pretended to eat the lamb, then looked at me with pity.

We stepped to the side of the stage for the moment of God's revelation to Zan.

The man at the light board switched on a new spot for the stage, with a shadow on the light in the form of a knife.

Then my father led me to the center of the stage. He guided me gently down to the floor of the stage. He bound me up with rope on wood planks—two cubits long for the arms and two for the legs.

A single stage lamp shone down on us.

He took out a sacred knife from the folds of his robe. He hesitated.

I said the words from the holy book:

"Will it please God that I die?"

My father said, "Yes, son. It will please God."

My father pretended to cry.

Then I said, "Will it please God that I die?"

My father, playing Zan said, "Yes, son. It will please God."

I said, "Do not be sad, Father. If God wants this, I will do it, with great gladness in my heart."

My father raised the knife over his head and said: "You are truly pure, Akeyde. I hope God is pleased with my gift to him."

I looked at my father and made the prophecy. 'You are a great man, Father. You will be a great leader of our people."

"It will be quick and merciful, Akeyde."

My father took the knife and brought it to my chest, with the point just touching my breastbone.

I died. I could always make a good death. My head slumped backward, my arms went limp, my right leg twitched.

The stage lamp quickly switched to a red gel light, then yellow, to signify God's light.

My father got down on his knees and I rose up on my knees, so I could get ready to ascend to God's side. We lifted our arms up to the sky, to heaven.

From the left side of the stage, the Spaama read from the holy book these lines:

"The knife came swiftly into the boy's chest. Akeyde went to God. And Zan and his people were blessed by their faith in Him."

The house lights came on and the assembly house said a prayer of thanks to God. Then we all ate baked goods made with Toyre seeds and oils, the holy plant of our people, along with grape juice, or wine.

I very rarely got to eat them. My father and I wore our stage robes at the reception. People mobbed us to shake our hands and hug us and gush over what a great job we did.

And of course we didn't have much time for the reception. Since the first one at our assembly house had become so popular, other assembly houses in Queens heard about it and asked us to do it for their congregations.

On stage once, I thought I saw Uncle Cookie at one of our pageants. During one of my deaths, I looked out at the crowd and I could swear he was there, in one of the front rows. He was pretty big. He stood out, even among the masses plunged together in the assembly house. He looked at me, shook his head, and looked down at the floor. When I went to look for him after the show, he was gone.

We ended up doing seven of these pageants on this one day of the year. It was exhausting, dying so many times. So, after a few years, we cut it down to five each year and rotated among the congregations so as many people as possible could experience it.

Now it was time for me to die for real and I was having a little difficulty.

The Upgrade

(Razvarr Abatut)

Through my Internet searching on underground anti-government blogs, I had found a new friend. His name was Necu. He was 18 years old, which was very good. He was young and strong. He was interested in helping me. I didn't ask him why he was getting involved, but I thought it that it wasn't important.

I had stolen Mom's credit card number to buy a new, more powerful disk drive for the computer, as well as expanded memory. Then, instead of using the centuries-old dial-up service we had, I contracted with a cable company to connect my computer with a state-of-the-art (for Queens) network pipe that was as fat and fast as possible.

Finally, I purchased a backup power unit and generator that would run the computer for several hours in case the electricity went out. During the summer, with the terribly wicked heat that New York is punished with, we had brown-outs about every two weeks. I didn't want to be interrupted by anything as silly as climate change.

I had to arrange for deliveries and installations around Mom and Dad's visits to the local Temple for weekly services. That was a little harrowing (I was constantly afraid they might come home in the middle of a delivery and ask me what I was doing).

But compared to all that, the hard part was having to figure out how to bring the Temple down.

I wasn't that good at logistics and I didn't have much experience in destroying sacred ancient temples, but I was willing to try.

For my father. For all the other poor meatheads in Divinnot Prison. For me too. Actually, especially me. Kawidtodia is my home– my true country. And I wanted to go home, yet I could not, as long as the regime was in power.

My father was a religious teacher. He was arrested by the religious police. Ironic, no?

These men beat my father's feet with police batons so his feet swelled up. They stuck his head in filthy toilets. He was hung from the ceiling upside down. His cell had the light on all the time. If my father somehow fell asleep despite that, thugs rushed in and beat him.

After two weeks of this, he was dumped at our doorstep in the middle of the night, barely alive.

He ended up running a newsstand on Burns Street in Queens. In our country, he had respect. A teacher of the Kawidtodian religion was esteemed by the neighborhood. And feared. Now… nothing. He was a two-cent businessman swallowed up by the whale that is America.

Nobody can stand out here unless you're an incredibly good looking woman with large breasts. Everything is about style. If you can sing and get on television, you're on the way to fame. I'm still stunned that people are willing to watch talent shows to see if some poor fool can entertain you. If they can't, you're encouraged to laugh at them.

And the music has become more and more of a freak show. I mean, like, what's the point? Singers pose half-naked in music videos dedicated to finding a man or losing a man or hating a man. A group of African American men fronted by a white lead singer with extremely large breasts sing about wanting to have a night on the town and smashing things up. They're happy because they have a car with a full tank of gas. It was a very popular song.

A young blonde singer walks around wearing cow meat on her body and this is considered revolutionary? She ought to be locked up in a mental institution, not showered with money.

Let's consider the male singers. They wear gold-encrusted baseball caps sideways on their heads and shout about putting their things in lots of women and having boat loads of money, all over a monotonous backbeat. They want to shoot other men.

They want to wear lots of big, loud jewelry. They drive around in big trucks that shoot dirty fumes through giant pipes that stink up the planet.

The films aren't much better. What important subjects do they address? Finding love. Losing love. Having a baby. Robbing a bank. Men with big guns shooting at each other. How earth-shaking.

Then you have sports like auto racing. Cars go around a track at high speed. Thousands of fans watch them, drinking soda and beer and hoping for a crash, where the cars get mangled and the drivers are injured, some fatally.

America depressed me. Kawidtodia depressed me even more. America was free, but shallow. Kawidtodia was un-free and completely humorless. Isn't there some mid-point of a country out there where you can be free and yet serious? Don't talk to me about the French.

Since I got home from the community college upstate, I had been spending this pathetic life practicing for death. My mother was pushing me to apply to the four-year college near our house, a city school, and maybe I could get financial aid to pay for tuition, but I felt exactly zero inspiration about it. The only thing that got me excited was my Blue and White Temple project.

I came close to diving into the bed again after I saw Mr. Wood. I couldn't believe he didn't remember me. There he was, the poor man, in his thick black glasses, with so much book knowledge in that huge block of a head. A teacher, serving bread to the crowd after a religious ceremony.

Sometimes he used to teach us the Latin roots of some common English words, so we could see where the language came from. Most kids didn't get it. It wasn't really appropriate for second grade. Some kids got it, though. I got it. And with all those books he had read, he was forced to work for a catering company. It reminded me a little of my Dad.

That's how much America values teachers. And they get all the blame when the test scores don't go up. As if the poverty of the children and the culture of shallowness they grow up in doesn't matter in getting an education.

How is a kid supposed to respect school when he's hungry, or his dad comes home drunk and throws a half-empty can of beer at the kid? One girl in my class wrote a story about that when we were in Mr. Wood's room.

Why should a kid pay attention to his teacher when his parents give him video games where wrestlers crush each other's heads? Why aren't they buying these kids books? What does a video game teach you but to flick your fingers around really fast on a keyboard?

One thing I'll give to America is the past. Taking on the Nazis, that took guts. Abraham Lincoln. Martin Luther King. Folk singers. Peter, Paul and Mary and Bob Dylan and Pete Seeger. They didn't sing about getting and spending while being fabulously good looking. They could sing about things that mattered.

That's why the Blue and White Temple project was so important to me. I wanted things to change. I thought everybody else wanted change too. They were just too scared to do anything about it. They needed somebody to lead them, to start something, to get the wheels turning in the right direction. My family was all twisted up because of what happened to us in Kawidtodia. Everyone was distorted. We were all perversions of our true selves, our better selves.

If I had to admit it, I would have said I cared about my parents. But in my college psychology course I learned to obtain the self-perception to know that I was strangled inside. There was a beast within me choking off the fresh air from getting to my lungs.

I had to get rid of this thing. The plan to hit the Temple was the only way to do it. I felt driven to do it. I was possessed by the idea. It was my only right course of action.

The project became my life, the one positive thing I could hold onto, the only reason to get out of bed.

The Reminder

(Akeyde Kletser)

I wanted to find Vehktre. He was the one who could help. My uncles assigned him to me, to teach me how to perform the mission. Orders from my father.

The first thing I remember about him is that he wore yellow and purple, the colors of our people, the colors of the Toyre plant, the food that saved us in the early days, the desperate times.

Nobody in our tribe wore those colors in public. The Zans are a sacred people, because we were the first to find the one God, 5,800 years ago, even before the Jews, at least five years before the Jews (although they get all the credit and publicity for it). But we're also a scared people. You can move around just one letter and turn sacred into scared.

I didn't feel sacred anymore. (But if I blew myself up, I knew I would be sacred again.) The Zans had suffered too many wounds. We didn't want to stand out too much. Most of our men didn't even wear beards for that reason. A Zan had to be brave to wear a beard. My uncles were brave.

Vehktre was brave too. The first time I met him he reminded me of the meaning of purple and yellow to our people. It was in the early chapters of our holy book, the Heylik Shetyn. It was the first book ever written. God wrote it with his finger.

Vehktre told the stories again, even though I knew them, of how God saved the Zans and had a special pact with us, to stir the spirit of God within me. According to one story, I once sprayed Toyre plants at our tribe to save them from hunger.

I wished I could spray flowers out into the world again. Instead, I had ball bearings and blood to spray.

I took Tina unto myself. She was the only companion left. It was beginning to feel like an old ritual, strapping on Tina, connecting the detonator to her, snaking the wire through the hole in the blue and white windbreaker, so the detonator sat warmly in the right pocket.

Summer was in high bloom. The sun burned in all directions. Heat made everything ugly. I wanted it to kill me right there on the sidewalk. Maybe the sun would get so hot that it would set off the explosives.

I walked from the neighborhood of warehouses and factories and bad men to where I grew up.

Memories flooded back, of my uncles, schools, playgrounds, and friends.

I remembered going to Narish's house once after school because my parents weren't around. I was about eight years old. He let me eat Oreo cookies with milk at his kitchen table while he counted out hundreds of twenty-dollar bills and bundled them in rubber bands. His wife helped him.

Her face was very beautiful, in a hard way, like a sculpture, but I never saw the rest of her body. She sat at the table wearing a tent of a dress that swallowed her, and tennis shoes. Her hair was bundled back in a kerchief. She was modest in attire, as all Zan women are supposed to be.

Narish's first wife, my aunt, had died, from a long, slow, wasting cancer. I was about four years old at the time, so I wasn't allowed to see her when she got sick. My mom just told me that Narish was very sad because his wife was ill.

Now he was happy again. He had a new wife. Her name was Aeterna. She was younger than Narish by about 15 years.

I ate the cookies and looked at this small city of bills growing out of the table.

"Where'd all this money come from?" I asked between bites of the cookies.

"Never you mind that," Aeterna said.

"It's no big deal, Akeyde," Narish said, glaring at her. "It's from my business. I do things on a cash basis."

"What kinds of things?"

"What are you, a newspaper reporter?" my new aunt said.

"I sell things. Pharmaceuticals, mostly."

"Medicine," Aeterna said. "Important medicine. Your uncle helps people."

"For people who really need it, right?"

He smiled at me.

"Yes, like that."

I used to spend time over at Dreykop's house too. He had older sons, but he also had a boy my age. We played together. On the outside his house looked like most of the other houses in the neighborhood— a little shabby. He said he didn't want to attract attention or upset the neighbors by painting the house. On the inside, everything was white and new. He had a six-foot marble sculpture of a Toyre plant in his living room.

"Come on, Akeyde, let's play!" shouted my cousin, Pozzo, the youngest of his sons. "Stop looking at the statue. I've got new trucks."

Dreykop, often reading the *Heylik Shetyn* in the living room where we were playing, used to laugh and shout to his wife, "Akeyde really loves the Toyre!"

"He's a good boy!" his wife used to shout from the kitchen. That's how they talked—they shouted at each other from other rooms.

So I would stop looking at the sculpture and play trucks on the carpet with Pozzo.

Another time, on a hot spring day, I ran into Lhokem at the newspaper store. The store sold the three New York papers, weekly ethnic group papers for the Italians and the Irish and the Jewish people, ladies' magazines, comic books, and lottery tickets. It had dusty brown and white tiles and not much business. Lhokem was with the owner, behind the counter, talking. I was looking at the rack of comics at the back of the store, and my uncle was at the front of the store, about forty or fifty feet away.

"You're having trouble with the other newsstand guy down the block?" Lhokem asked the owner, another Zan.

"I don't understand it. He's getting a better deal from the magazine distributors than I am."

"How do you know?"

"One of the truck drivers I'm friendly with, he told me. Why would they do that, Lhokie?"

"I don't know. Could be a kickback. I'll talk to the guy."

"You'll take care of it?"

"Don't worry about it. You have the money this month?"

"Yeah, here, let me get it."

I was really proud of my uncle at that moment. He was trying to help the poor man.

I don't know why, but after Lhokem stepped back from the counter, he turned to the back of the store and saw me.

"Hey, Akeyde! Come here. Bring your comic books."

I laid out my comic books on the glass counter. I had Batman, Captain America, Silver Surfer, and the Avengers.

Lhokem paid the owner for my comics with a broad flourish, then said, "You hungry? Want an ice cream soda?"

He took me to the ice cream place and bought me a chocolate ice cream soda. He looked at me with admiration, which I didn't understand. All I was doing was drinking the soda.

"You're a good boy, Akeyde."

"Okay."

"You must study and learn. Not just comic books, understand?"

"Okay."

"When you grow up, you're going to help our people. It's in our books."

Half the time I didn't know what he was talking about, and this was one of those times, so I just nodded my head like I understood, even as the chocolate ice cream hit my taste buds.

Some of the best times I ever had were during a few bad winters, when my uncles and my father gave out food to the neighborhood from the back of a big truck parked in the lot at the *Basmadrosh.* They handed out turkeys and chickens and cheese to poor Zans. I stood in the back of the truck with my father and uncles as they took food from the truck and put it into the hands of waiting, hungry people. People were cheering my family. I was so happy. We were famous!

Then there was Dexthor. He was the one friend from the neighborhood who went to camp with me.

I didn't know him from the neighborhood. He went to another school a few miles away. But he was in my bunk for the summer, the summer before I met Palash.

Saturday night was movie night at the camp. One July evening, five hundred Zan kids saw a movie on a projector purchased in the 1960s. The movie was housed in a large metal can and the picture clicked with almost every frame because of its age, or the projector's age.

In the movie, a beautiful, full-bosomed rich woman, with the help of a lover, faked her own death, to drive her husband insane so she could inherit his fortune. He ended up wondering if he had buried her alive. He kept hearing scratching sounds throughout the mansion as he walked. He went through the halls of the mansion and heard scratching sounds. He went down the stairs and he could hear faint scratching sounds. It pierced my heart to hear such things.

The wife's coffin was dug out of the ground. When the workmen of the house lifted up the lid of the coffin, you could see quite plainly that the woman was not dead when she was laid in the coffin. Her desiccated body's hands were frozen in place as she tried to scratch her way through the wooden coffin before she died. My impressionable 12-year-old mind was terrified.

But then later in the picture the man saw his beautiful wife come from out of the shadows on a landing. I remember well her heaving breasts. This drove the man over the edge.

I don't recall all the details of what happened after that. But I do remember that at the end, somehow the woman got locked in an iron maiden in a torture chamber. An iron maiden was a metal container large enough for a person to stand inside. You locked the person in. There were spikes on the inside to pierce the body.

The last scene of the movie was of the beautiful woman's eyes, frightened out of her wits, locked inside the iron maiden. And then you heard scratching. She was trying to get out.

I could not sleep that night. My bunk bed was next to a wooden wall. Somebody was scratching from behind the wall to get out. I lay there for two or three hours, listening to the scratching, terrified.

I had to get away from that wall. In the middle of the night, I woke up Dexthor, who had a bed in the middle of the bunk. I asked him if I could sleep on the end because something was scaring me.

He didn't ask why or what it was. He just pulled up his legs and let me sleep on the lower half of his bed.

We became friends. A few weeks after the night of the scratching incident, Dexthor said we should go rock-hopping down the stream that coursed down the hill to town. We could go get ice cream after that.

We sneaked away from our bunk to go rock-hopping. We went three miles, jumping from rock to rock as the water rushed around our feet. The rocks were as small as basketballs and as big and flat as tables. The sun came through the trees spreading out from the banks of both sides of the stream.

At the end of our trip down the stream, we tried to walk into the little local town, to buy ice cream. But a man from the camp was there, waiting for us. He had been sent to find us. Somehow we had been spotted. We were taken to my father.

We stood on the porch of his cabin. He sat in his favorite chair, stroked his long beard, and smoked his cigar for a long time, looking out at the fields of the camp. Dexthor and I were terrified of him.

He didn't yell. I thought he would yell. He just looked at us with a steady rage.

He said to Dexthor. "You, what's your name?" He didn't bother waiting for an answer.

"We'll call your parents. Do you want to go home?"

Dexthor shook his 12-year-old head no.

"Go back to your bunk."

Dexthor walked off the steps of the cabin and I followed him.

"Him, not you."

My breath turned heavy. With my father's words, I knew that not only would I be punished, but that Dexthor and I would not be so friendly again.

I turned around and faced him. He stood up.

"You know I have to hit you, right?"

I wanted to scream, "NO!" But I didn't. I just said, "Yes, sir."

My father's arms were once as solid as oak trees. He stood about nine inches away from me, taller than me by at least a foot. His fist rattled my chest like an iron wrecking ball. I felt as if my breast bone had been caved in.

"Now go back to your bunk."

I didn't even dare to put my hand over the place of impact. I just walked down the wooden steps of the cabin, my head sunk.

Dexthor was long gone, but my father's fist remained.

The Old Country

(Razvarr Abatut)

Necu was a very valuable man. His mother had been a high school teacher. She learned English and taught it to Necu. He spoke and wrote in both English and Kawidtodian. A bilingual person was a big plus to me. He knew how to lie in two languages.

Necu went to the Temple Architect's office, posing as a student. He asked the Architect if he could look at the blueprints for the Temple. Necu said he was writing an analysis of the structure for religious studies.

The Architect was not a busy man, but he was also not very well paid. Necu offered 75 dollars to the architect and he was able to get the blueprints in a few days.

Then Necu took digital photos of the blueprints and emailed them to me. I worked on analyzing the blueprints in order to find structural weaknesses in the building. The idea was to place explosive charges at those points. Then we would see what we could do to the Temple.

Necu was using Internet servers piped through from Yekmonveldt. Kawidtodia is a police state, but it's also poor. The police can't be everywhere. It's not an oil-based economy, with lots of money. I'm not even sure what the economy is based on these days. They could sell stone and sand, if anyone might want them. China could buy the whole country with one day's worth of work.

Through Necu we also found a half a dozen men who were willing to help with the project. Some lived in Shalhak. Some had the advantage of being Kawidtodians who lived in the country next door, Yekmonveldt. We could communicate through Internet servers in Yekmonveldt.

The long border between the countries was not well patrolled. There were a few police checkpoints dotted along the border, but people who wanted to could slip back and forth between countries if they were willing to hike through the mountains. The mountains were a terrible iron beast, of course, but it was possible to do this. My family did.

When I think of the mountains, I think of how they rise up out of the sand and dust, overwhelming any human presence. To stand in front of them and look up is to appreciate how small you are in the scheme of things. It's a good place to think about religion.

People come and go, live and die, but the mountains keep pushing upward.

Despite the harshness of life there, things used to be better. My father told me stories of living under a King. The Kings were alternatively authoritarian and progressive, whichever style of rule best fit them.

The last king, who somehow managed to reign for 30 years, was a slacker at heart. His father had been a strict king, even with his own family. When the father died and the son took over, the son indulged himself. He enjoyed a number of girls and went off to gamble quite a bit in Europe. Late in his rule, he used tax money from the Treasury for the gambling.

This didn't sit well with most of us, but the only one who could do anything about it was the top general in the army. Of course.

So there was a coup. The King was easily overthrown by the general and a single brigade of soldiers. To show everyone he meant to be the number one pit bull in the neighborhood, the general took the name Pumn, an old religious name from our Dreptat, the first holy book, written more than 2,500 years ago.

When my father was a child, Pumn was the name for Kawidtod's methods of smashing the Zans to little pieces. It translates literally as "Fist," but it was primarily known as a piece of bread. A real fist had never been used so severely against Kawidtod's own descendants.

Now it would be. The Pumn's first act was to put the King on trial for stealing from the Treasury. The charges were real enough, but my father told his friends he thought the army would put the old King on a plane and escort him out of the country.

We all should have known better. If a man calls himself a human fist, you should watch out.

At the end of the trial, the King was taken to a public square, the central place in the capital. He was stripped of his shirt and flogged with a whip. One hundred lashes. That took care of his back. It was whipsawed with bloody tracks. He fainted. The torturers revived him by throwing water on his face numerous times. Then they burned his chest with a poker over the heart, the iron from the poker mined from the local mountains.

My father was there, in the crowd watching. People were cheering. Not my father. He was torn apart inside by the mob's lust for revenge.

The King's arms were tied behind his back. He was bleeding badly and crying. He pleaded to be killed. Nothing doing. A Kawidtodian priest, a holy man who was a prominent artist, came up to the King and painted his forehead with a knife, sketching a fist on his tightly knotted skull. The crowd cheered. Photographers were directed to come forward and take pictures of the outline of the bloody fist on the King's head. Light bulbs flashed as the photographers jammed around the King, on his knees. The crowd was laughing.

Finally, the Pumn came, with a force of 20 guards with submachine guns and wearing blue and white masks, the colors of our country. He took a pistol from his holster, unlatched the safety, pressed the gun to the King's head, right on the fist on the forehead, and fired the gun.

The explosion blew open the king's head and his brains and blood shot out all over the Pumn. The king's body fell. The Pumn faced the crowd and raised his pistol, blood all over his military uniform.

The crowd went wild. My friends and I were at school at the time. A television was set up in our classroom so we could see the King's head explode. I was seven years old.

Now I'm 20. The King was killed a long time ago, in my book. And a long time ago doesn't count for much in the world, even when you can't forget it.

The Phantom Mountains

(Akeyde Kletser)

The apartment towers, mostly brick and concrete, sat around doing nothing, saying nothing. They were a poor substitute for the mountains I remembered from reading the *Heylik Shetyn.*

Those mountains spoke. I missed the mountains in Zandria, even though I had never seen them with my own eyes. Such is the power of the holy book over the reader. The poetry of the book is that while you are reading the words, it makes you feel transported to another place.

Paradise.

You lived in a tribe of people that knows just one thing—that despite all the pain and suffering coming at them throughout the seasons, the long years of struggle, they had a special relationship with God. Our people found him first and he had us in His thoughts, always.

Living beneath the mountains may have been a harsh existence. We struggled for food. But we did it together. Our tribe consisted of hundreds of thousands of people who were all related by blood. We were strong that way. It gave us great comfort, especially when facing the trials of living. God was part of us too, which made us even stronger. In a way, it was paradise. This was Zandria the way it used to be, 5,800 years ago, before Kawidtod came.

Walking on the main shopping district with Tina, the stores had the same monotonous look, but the people looked different. As I walked, if anyone noticed me at all, they steered clear. Maybe it was the scabs of the claw marks on my face, about four inches long apiece. Or it was the blue and white windbreaker, Kawidtodian colors, worn in heat sufficient to turn the top of the asphalt into gum.

I opened up the glass door to a pastry shop. I thought I could use something sweet for breakfast. A baked scone laced with Toyre seeds would be good, with orange juice.

Toyre could still be found in the old country, but only in a few places. The seeds of this purple and yellow wildflower were carried to America when most of the Zans fled the country, during the Kawidtodian persecutions more than 100 years ago. It wasn't enough for the Squids to kill us; they had to wipe out our sacred plant too.

Idiots. They didn't know the value of anything but killing Zans and our culture. You could eat the seeds. They provided some sustenance in a land that wasn't fertile, that couldn't grow much.

The plant is life itself.

I could almost taste those seeds while waiting on the long line. It was a popular place and you had to wait.

Behind me a man pushed something hard into the middle of my back, just above Tina. I twitched and turned around to see who would be so rude.

The rude man had his finger pointed in the air at my mid-section, like a gun.

"People are looking for you, Akeyde Kletser."

"My name is Joe Wood."

He was much taller than me, a full head above. He wore a purple and yellow shirt, the colors of our people. I wondered what it would be like to be that tall, to see the world from that great perspective. Like a redwood tree.

The redwood tree man smirked. "Yeah, right."

At that moment, I knew I wouldn't be getting my scone.

"I want to talk about this outside," I said in a dry, toneless voice.

So we walked out of the store, my mouth craving the seeds. On the street, I stood in front of the man. He was angry.

"You shouldn't be here," he said.

"What do you mean?"

"I'm one of your cousins, you know."

"Are you sure?"

"You're an idiot."

Suddenly, with Tina astride me, I got some courage. "I could blow up the whole street."

Redwood man smirked again. "Yeah, but you won't. You were supposed to do that yesterday and you blew the deal."

I was suddenly conscious of my status among all these people. If this man knew what I was doing, maybe others around me did too.

"Why don't we go to the assembly house?

"Why?"

"We can talk there."

So we walked to the *Basmadrosh*. In the Zan language it means literally "prayer house." It was a few blocks off the main street, standing humbly among a row of houses. The exterior of the building was made of a simple wood and painted white. In Spanish, the word for white is "blanca." That's how the building is supposed to look—like a blank. As you're walking by, you're not supposed to think about this building. It's supposed to blend in to the lower-middle-class surroundings of small homes with small lawns off the main boulevard. Underneath the eaves of the roof was painted a small emblem of a Toyre, a little sign, about a foot long, indicating who was responsible for this building.

The door was locked. Why were the doors to our assembly houses always locked? You can go up to any church and walk right in and sit in a pew.

"We can sit on the steps," I said, like a robot.

I used to come to this place as a boy, to worship, to read from the Heylik Shetyn in front of the congregation, and to act out our founding story, in the pageants. I grew up here. This was like home. I ached at the memory of it.

The redwood tree sat down immediately at the place where the front porch met the steps. It took me a little more time to do so. I had to calculate the nature of Tina into this simple act. I looked like an old man easing into a chair.

Before I got the chance to fully place my buttocks on the porch, the redwood tree blurted out: "There's nothing really to talk about."

"Yes. That's true."

"You didn't do the mission."

"Okay."

"If you didn't do it, maybe you're not the real Akeyde."

That taunt hurt. I felt my ribs heave against Tina.

"There's another Squid holiday in 10 days. The Cainta." Cainta means repentance.

After celebrating the victory over the Zans, the Kawidtods try to humble themselves before God by repenting their sins. They have 10 days to consider all the bad things they've done that year. Then on Cainta, they go ask God for forgiveness.

It was a pointless exercise. God would never forgive them for what they had done to us. Yet they still tried. Every year.

Redwood man looked out at the empty street. The sun blasted away at the houses mounted on both sides of the road. Even the grass itself seemed to be melting.

I looked at him. He reminded me of a writer who was famous in the 1950s. That man played football in high school. He had big shoulders and interesting friends and he wrote one great book. He drove all over the country in a car with his friends. Then he wrote about it on a long scroll, as if he had a religious experience. All he had to do to be a man was get in a car. Why did I have to blow myself up to prove that I'm a man?

Because I am a Zan. And I am Akeyde.

"Have you seen a man named Vehktre around?"

"Who the hell is Vehktre?"

"Never mind."

"You better do it, or I'll come looking for you."

He lifted himself off the wooden steps and walked off with a confident air. I suddenly wished I could have his life.

Exhaustion crawled around me like worms through soil. I carefully lowered myself onto the floor of the porch of the assembly house and my eyes shut with the suddenness of a bomb going off.

I had a dream that I couldn't speak, but the vest of bombs could. I was standing in front of thousands of people, at a podium. The vest was discussing something important into a microphone, but it didn't matter to the audience. The people were drinking liquor in tall thin glasses and talking, as if the vest weren't there. I was angry. The vest didn't seem to care. It droned on.

Then the dream changed. I was kissing a girl on a bed in the dark, but my arms were wrapped around nothing. Nobody was there. I was hugging air.

A kick in the bombs laid out on the left side of the vest shook me to the core. If somebody was trying to hurt me, they would be very surprised.

From the floor of the porch I saw him. His face was way up high above me, like a giant's. It was twisted with anger.

"Get up."

I propped myself up on my elbows, then pushed off the floor to stand next to him. He was slightly taller than me, with a long black beard. His eyes were ripping mad.

It didn't matter if he was angry with me. I couldn't help myself. I was so happy to see him. I tried to hug him.

"Stop it." He threw my arms off.

"I missed you."

"Let's go inside." He had a key to the prayer house. Just like that, the door was opened. I wanted that key.

He directed me to sit in one of the back pews. The entire building was made of wood. Wood was considered the most sacred building material for Zan prayer houses because Akeyde was sacrificed to God on strips of wood. Sprinkled every 20 feet or so, along the lines of the walls, by windows, are pots growing Toyre flowers, so lovely in their bunches of yellow and purple.

They even came with their own little lamps, to project light onto the plants when the sun was weak or blocked by clouds.

Also, on each of the side walls were murals of the origin story, with Akeyde and Zan walking in the mountains, the encounter with the wolf, and the sacrifice.

In front of the prayer space, on the front stage, to punctuate the meaning of the murals, a statue was hung over the room, looking down. A statue of me as a little boy, with my arms reaching up to God, a long rip in the middle of my chest to signify my father's knife.

So many feelings struck me then, little bullets slicing through my skin. The pain of Akeyde's sacrifice. An overwhelming love for God. The desire to be with Him. And yet, so much emptiness inside. I felt hollowed out.

Vehktre seemed to know. "You have a responsibility. To God. We must be avenged."

"I understand."

"You failed in that responsibility."

"I made it into the Temple. I saw a kid. I used to be his teacher."

It was true. I knew the boy. I didn't want to admit I knew him when I saw him. His name was Razvarr. How I met him involved fighting with my father.

After four years of doing the pageants of sacrifice and death with my father, I got tired of it. I didn't want to do it. I wanted to go to college.

This started another fight with my father. My father wanted me to train to become a teacher in the Zan religious schools in the city. There was one small college in America that offered this training. Of course it was in Queens.

My father wanted me to visit the campus with him. We did. It was in an industrial section of northwest Queens. The streets were lined with factory buildings and auto body shops. One factory made staples. Its neighbor was a slaughterhouse.

The college consisted of three yellow brick buildings stained with decades of soot. There was no campus. Just three buildings that looked like offices. That's what you get when rents are high in New York. The property had been abandoned, the landlord went into foreclosure and the city gave it to us for one dollar.

The president of the college took us on a tour. My father was the chairman of the board of directors of the college, so the president himself decided to take the time from his busy schedule to take us around. He was a highly regarded Spaama who had written several books on Zan religious practices and history.

The president introduced us to several teachers. There were about 100 boys going to school there and about 25 or 26 girls. Every boy had a beard. These were the brave souls who announced themselves as Zans when just about everybody else was trying to blend in.

The halls were gray, as were the classrooms. The president told me in a grave voice that I would be taking on a great responsibility. Because of my name, because of who I was, I would be fulfilling the role God had laid out for me – my proper destiny.

My father and the Zan college president discussed whether I should train to become a Spaama.

Ironically, because of my name, the president said that would not be a good idea. Akeyde was the first teacher in our religion, because of his great sacrifice. But he was also a fighter for the Zans. A Spaama had to be an interpreter of the holy books, a spiritual leader. Because Akeyde was a savior of our people and faith, he could not interpret his own actions. No, no, it would be more appropriate for me to teach the history. I was good at history.

I knew the holy books inside and out and I was sick of them.

In the president's office, my father signed my enrollment papers as the Spaama looked on with approval. I wanted to throw my father down on the floor and tear up the papers.

But I didn't. I just glared at him through my thick glasses.

When we got home and had dinner that night, as my father waxed poetic about my great future, I spat out, "I'm not going."

"What?"

"I can't do it."

"Why?"

"I'm not ready."

He roared. "Of course you're ready. I've trained you for this. Four years! Four years of reading the Heylik Shetyn portions and playing the role in the pageants and you're not ready."

"That's not what I mean."

"Well, what in the name of Gock do you mean?"

Mother spoke up. "I think, Alter, that Akeyde has been surrounded by Zans his whole life and he wants to see some of what it's like outside the bubble you've created for him. "He's been in the Zan religious school for four years. He needs to see the world. He's a young man now."

"So you're both against me."

"Why does everything have to be a confrontation, Alter? Why can't you just let the boy have some room to breathe?"

"Your father was a Spaama. And look what happened. The Squids killed him. How can you say this?"

"I hate that word. They're Kawidtodians. Don't reduce them to animals."

"They do it to us! Look how they treat us!"

"There's more to the world than our tribal fighting. It's exhausting."

"You're both in denial. It's a very cold world. What happened when Akeyde met the Squids? They took a tire iron to his face. The Zans are the only ones who will be there if he needs help. Like we were there when he got hit."

I didn't know how to articulate arguments like my mother and father. I could only say one thing over and over.

"I don't care what you say. I'm not going."

My father stood up and slapped my glasses off. The tire iron scar flamed up like a bee sting. The knife brand on my arm ached. It does that when I'm stressed out.

I wanted to hit him back. But I was afraid. Instead I retrieved my glasses from the floor.

Mother went to hit my Dad, but he caught her arm and punched her in the jaw. Her head was knocked backwards, but she recovered fast and stood tall.

I had seen enough.

"I'm gone."

I packed two duffel bags. My mother cried and my father shouted over and over, "Don't come back! Don't you dare come back!"

I shouted out from my room, "No problem!"

As I was walking out the door with my duffel bags, Dad grabbed me from behind. One of the duffel bags fell to the floor. I took the other one and swung it at his mid-section.

He got hit. "Good," I thought. "Now you know what it feels like."

"I'll fucking kill you," he said, his eyes and mouth tight.

That helped me find my voice.

"You already have," I said. "Many times."

The State University of New York teacher's college in upstate New York was my savior and refuge. My mother had helped me apply. I qualified for tuition assistance. Plus, I won a New York State Regents Scholarship, which helped a little with the tuition. I had done a lot of reading outside the Zan scriptures when Dad was busy with his Onfirer duties, in the neighborhoods and assembly houses where the Zans lived.

As for the rest of the money, I got a job in the school library, which suited me well. I liked to be surrounded by books. There were no Kawidtodians around that I could see and very few Zans.

I was a Zan who dreamed of being a public school elementary teacher and became one.

But I screwed up my career. After graduation, a public school in Corona, a grit-filled neighborhood in Queens, offered me a job. I had another offer for a job in a small town in the Adirondack Mountains. It didn't pay well. Neither did the job in Corona, but it paid better.

The school in Corona was five miles from my parents' house. I should have stayed far away. But there was another, smaller voice in me, buzzing in my ear to go back home.

Vehktre cut me off.

"I'm not interested. The Cainta is in 10 days. That's your last chance. There aren't any additional Kawidtodian festivals for two more months after that. We can't wait that long. Your father can't wait that long. It has to be now."

At the mention of my father, I felt a large lump in my throat. The Onfirer.

"You weren't at your apartment."

"I wanted to go for a walk."

"I spent half the morning looking for you."

"I'm sorry."

"That's not good enough."

"Okay."

"You walk around here, the whole elder council will know. You're not supposed to come back to this neighborhood. Ever."

My uncles were on the council. Their beards, now long and scraggly, gray, their hearts now white with age. Narish, Lhokem, and Dreykop. I felt like the statue in front of the hall. I wanted to reach out to them. They were gods to me, so distant. I could not bridge the gap that had grown between us.

I looked at the statue of me. There was a rustling, and then he was gone, leaving me there in the assembly house, alone.

I wished he would have stayed, like during the weeks of my training. He taught me how to assemble the bombs and the nails and the ball bearings. He bought the vest for me, a fishing vest, with lots of pockets for placing the explosives.

We ate meals together, lit the candles for our own little prayer services, at night in my apartment, with all the lights turned off. He made little jokes then, about his thinning brown hair, and smiled with his eyes, much like a doll's, and put his hands on my shoulders and looked at me, his little protégé, with admiration and warmth.

Looking around at the place where I had spent so many days in worship, I saw the assembly of pews as silent sentinels guarding the house. They were my companions now. Sculptures of wood. I wondered if they felt anything when you sat on them.

I looked up at the statue at the front of the hall. The statue of me had a complete look of bliss. That must be what it is like to know you will be with God. For minutes on end I tried to feel God but fell asleep in the pew.

Digital Blueprint

(Razvarr Abatut)

Looking through the digital blueprints was exhausting work. The pillars in the Temple were made of a type of granite that was very thick and strong. After three hours on the computer, I gave up and fell onto the bed for a rest.

I had a dream about Mr. Wood, of all people. I was sitting in his second grade class, but I was all grown up.

He was talking to the class about making sure we did our work, one of his usual lectures. I tried to get out of my seat, but it was glued to me. Whenever I stood up, the seat came with me.

"What are you trying to do, Raz?" Mr. Wood asked.

I tried to speak, but no words came out. Mr. Wood told me to sit down but I wouldn't. He told me to give myself a reminder to improve my behavior. It was a blue index card. You got three reminders each day, then you got a note home to your parents.

The computer woke me with a buzz. I looked at my email. Necu had appointed two men to buy half a dozen cell phones so we could try to communicate better, so I didn't have to go through Necu all the time. Their names were Debyl and Mintal. Debyl and Mintal bought the cell phones from a dealer and stored them in Debyl's house.

Debyl also found a man who got us explosives. We obtained C4, just like that. C4 can be molded into any shape. It can fit into just about any kind of container.

It was amazing to me how fast and easy it was to acquire bombs in a police state. Perhaps I had underestimated the level of dissent in the country. I was ecstatic.

Debyl stored the explosives in his house too. The next step was to find some electronic medium to set off the explosives—a detonator.

My new big problem became where to place the C4. How could we get the explosives into the building?

My first idea was that we somehow place a metal container in the Temple square. We would explain to the guards that we were bringing in extra copies of the Dreptat, our holy book, for worshipers. We could hollow out dozens of copies of the Dreptat and put the C4 in them.

I went through this idea in my mind many times. I ran through the scenario. And the more I thought of it, the more impractical it seemed. A metal container in the Temple? Somebody, a guard, would notice it. They would ask questions about what it was doing there. They would want to inspect it. And what if they opened up a copy of the Dreptat?

No, it was stupid. I needed a far better plan.

I kept thinking of ideas to bomb the Temple, then shooting them down, which depressed me all the more. I thought of filling a small plane with the C4 and flying it into the roof of the Temple. But you can't just get in a plane and start flying it around. In a centralized state like Kawidtodia, you need permission and a reason to go up in the air. Otherwise, if you somehow managed to get a small airplane up, the air force would come looking for that plane and blow it out of the sky.

I considered a truck bomb. But a truck requires a driver. And the driver could easily be shot driving right into the Temple gates. And if he succeeded in detonating, what damage could he really do to the pillars from the outside of the Temple?

A commando assault was also very tricky. We needed top men, real soldiers, and they would have to be highly trained to get inside the Temple and set off a bomb. A gunfight at the Temple gates would arouse the security forces. What if the security people shot them? We would have publicity, but little else. The Temple itself would be virtually unharmed. And I didn't have military expertise.

The only way to do it was to get the bombs inside and set them off. We needed to fool the Temple authorities, to disguise what we were doing.

Now things were in motion. It all depended on me coming up with a solid plan. I went through periods in which I was faint of heart.

Sleep helped get me through the day. There were times when I thought we should abandon the whole project.

What difference would it make if the Temple was destroyed? And could I really do it? Was I capable of bringing the house down? I was buffeted by anxieties when I read Necu's emails, or when my mother screamed at me to come eat something.

Suddenly, I had intense feelings for the cozy little world I lived in. Why get political? It was a lot easier to hide in my bedroom than step out in the world and get mud on my shoes.

Then I thought of my father, the beaten man. I looked occasionally upon his great wasted face as he went off to work or returned home, and I thought of my home country and what they did to him, what they did to me. They took away my homeland. It got me motivated.

It was hard for my parents and me to leave. We loved the stone mountains, as hard as they could be in making a life. Our people had been there for thousands of years. We were one with the land. The people could not be separated from the country. It was like removing your head from your neck.

I was a boy, so I had only that partial understanding of why things happened. But my mind was full of questions. My father was a religious teacher. Why would the police torture him? He was a righteous man. He was a teacher because he believed in the sacred stories. He followed God. We just got by on the salary the state paid him to work in the neighborhood school teaching the religious laws written by Kawidtod and his followers in the Dreptat books.

After my father was tortured, our family stayed quiet. Mother did her best to help Father get better. It took seven months for him to recover some measure of his previous good health.

But my mother's Binele was never the same. His once-proud head was pointed down, his shoulders permanently slumped. He shuffled when he walked. This was not the father I had known before. I didn't understand what had brought him so low.

At the time, I couldn't make the connection that the ascent of the Pumn as ruler had something to do with my father.

After I became a teenager, I started to see the perversions of the government. All kinds of people were thrown in jail. You never saw them again. Writers caught it a lot. Under the king, there was censorship of the newspapers. A few times, here and there, the government got sloppy. Occasionally, the authorities would let something critical of a key ministry come through on the page.

Then the newspaper might be shut down, but the King didn't throw people in jail. Usually. People felt a little more freedom. The old King let things slide. People were allowed to talk in their homes and in the restaurants or bars.

Under the Pumn, it was much worse. Everyone was afraid. There were neighborhood networks of spies. You could be reported for just about anything.

A newspaper could be shut down, sure, but more than that, if one of their writers published work that the Pumn's government didn't like, they gave him the lash and threw him in jail. Mortred Prison in the mountains was the worst. The writer would often have to sleep in an open air cell, unless he had enough money to bribe someone for better confinement. (Corruption is rife throughout the police corps and Army.) In the open air, you could easily die of pneumonia.

Unless you have had pneumonia, you don't know how horrible it is. I got it when I was seven, in Queens of all places, after we first got to America. First I got the flu, then pneumonia. The flu helped bring on the pneumonia. Every breath is a labor. All you want to do is sleep because breathing takes so much effort. Then there is the coughing. It's not a little polite cough like when you try to clear your throat. It's a cough that takes over your whole body. You dance like a puppet as the roar of a lion working independently of you tries to escape your fragile puny human body.

A typical statement from the Pumn's state apparatus about a writer's imprisonment would go something like this: "The writer is a spy working with foreign agencies to defame the state. As a paid propagandist for other governments, (name here) has compromised national security and has committed treason against the people."

Notice how the state and the people were linked together in that statement. Who presumed to speak for the people?

Another popular one went like this: "(Name here) has committed crimes against the God of Kawidtod." That's more serious. That meant a bullet to the head or a hanging was going to come.

Shakespeare said, "Let's kill all the lawyers!" In Kawidtodia, it was the writers.

About 10 journalists a year were thrown into either the Divinnot or Mortred mountain prisons. Some were never seen again. It was enough to scare the rest. Usually.

But the bloggers had become an underground force. They were anonymous, so they were braver about standing up to the regime. An arms race started between the government and the bloggers. The government would find an Internet pipe that was leaking real news and they moved to shut it down. So the bloggers had to find a way to get the word out. They discovered a way to connect to the cable networks Yekmonveldt's less efficient authorities had next door. Or they smuggled in cell phones and smart phones. Cell phones and iPhones were driving the regime crazy.

It was either blog or bomb. Every few months, somebody went completely crazy from the absence of a serious public conversation about what was really going on in the country and decided they couldn't take it anymore. So they blew up a café or a small temple around the country. Usually, it was in a rural area or a small city.

Every once in awhile, a Zan was brought up on spying charges, almost certainly a farce. It didn't happen often. There were only four or five thousand of them left, in a country of 20 million. Don't get me wrong, I had very little sympathy for them. Their religion was based on human sacrifice, after all. They scurried around fast on the streets as if someone was going to see them and kick them.

But they were a convenient scapegoat for the Pumn. It helped divert the peoples' attention from the literal and cultural poverty of the nation.

To get back to the main subject at hand, nobody had tried to bomb something in Shalhak, the capital city. And nobody had even thought of taking down the Blue and White Temple, the center of it all.

So, yeah, I wanted to quit this project every day, but I forced myself to get up and do this work. Because if I didn't find a way to get those fuckers thinking differently, I thought I would just die.

Animal Terror

(Akeyde Kletser)

I wished I had an atomic bomb strapped to me. A Tina with super powers. Or a bomb planted inside my body, surgically inserted under the skin. The government put out a report in the newspapers that it was now possible to do that, to evade detection by body scanners. That might have made it easier to push the trigger.

I probably would not have felt any pain. Poof, gone in an instant. I could have done it right in the central shopping district for the Kawidtodians.

That was where I had wandered after the long nap at the assembly house. Night time came on, the sun fading west, leaving long tentacles of purple and orange and pink light trails in the sky.

The Kawidtodian families walked around me like a river avoiding a rock. Many of them were carrying their evil fist breads. They were pushing along the boulevard with their children. There were a number of infants in strollers with their older brothers and sisters wearing fancy clothes, skipping along the street in their little shiny black shoes. It must have been another of their holidays, a minor one.

Even though I was wearing blue and white, their tribe's colors, I was too wild looking to be among them. My hair was matted to my head with sweat. My eyes felt like they wanted to break out of my face.

It seemed like there were thousands of them. Their home country—our home country, which was stolen from us, the greatest crime of all time—is so tyrannical that millions of them have fled. They run as fast as they can to get out of Kawidtodia. They come to Europe, America, Australia, South America. And wherever they settle, what do they do? They create little

Kawidtodian towns all over the place. They don't mix with anyone else.

These Kawidtodians, they looked at me like I was a space alien. I didn't like the way they looked at me. I wanted to kill them. They made me sick.

On the sidewalk were sellers of cheap paperback books. Their titles sucked up my eyes, like ink to paper:

- "The Filthy Zans"
- "The Dirty Zans"
- "God Does Not Hear the Prayers of Zans"
- "The Many Lies of the Zan People"
- "The Mind of the Zan—Brains of a Bird"
- "The Dogs of Zan"
- "The Zans' War Against God"
- "God Hates the Zans"
- "How to Fight Back Against the Zans"
- "We Will Eat the Zans"
- "God's Light—Kawidtod"
- "Kawidtod's Plan for Your Personal Salvation"

Blood was ready to shoot out of my eyes. I had Tina. Here was my opportunity. If I did it, I wouldn't have to worry about Vehktre ever coming after me again.

I fingered the detonator. God, I'm so tired. Just let it go.

What the hell. Push it down. Push it. Do it. It will be over fast.

A man, a very tall man, wearing his bald head like a crown, walked toward me, a basket of bread in his arms.

I hoped the kid from the Squid service wasn't around, but I pressed the detonator anyway.

Nothing happened. No explosion. No boom. No head flying off my body. No ripping apart of my lungs. No Kawidtodians blown apart.

I stood there, looking at myself, unbelieving. Why did I still exist?

Too much energy inside me and I couldn't contain it. So I put my fist through the window of a Kawidtodian grocery store.

The window was cheap and thin and it shattered easily as my arm went through it. A wall of glass fell on my arm and cut through the sleeve of the windbreaker. Blood, finally.

People shouted at me. Parents scurried away with their children. Glass lay on the floor in little diamond pieces, sharp edges gleaming like knives.

I looked at the results and smiled a crooked smile. Good work, Akeyde.

A cashier came running out. She stood a few feet away from me, wanting to shout but seemingly unable to do it. Instead her mouth formed a perfect expression of dread.

Her bald head gleamed under the street lights. I wanted to punch her right in the hole that her mouth made.

"I'm calling the police," a Squid a few feet away announced to the crowd. Blood drizzled from the knuckles of my fist and out from under the windbreaker.

"Don't bother," I said.

A few men moved to restrain me by grabbing my shoulders. Raw terror of the idea of Tina being discovered underneath the blue and white windbreaker animated my arms. I hit anybody who touched me. I punched the underside of their jaws with uppercuts. I hit them in the throat. I kicked somebody in the testicles. The warrior Akeyde had taken possession.

The men reeled back. I ran down an alleyway next to the wounded storefront and a number of Squids bleated into the night, but nobody tried to stop me.

I ran and ran, blood flying behind me in gobs of red.

Hours later, the heat was my best companion, showering itself all around me. I sat in a corner of the train station, the Long Island Railroad, on the westbound side of the tracks. Sweat continued to pour off my head. Rats picked through a garbage can next to me and ran over my feet as they filled their night with comings and goings. Two-inch-long cockroaches competed with the rats for the trash.

I looked at the blood drying on my arm. Scabs had formed on my fists. They felt right. I had done something good. A little thing.

But I kept thinking bad thoughts. The bomb didn't go off. I hadn't killed even one Squid.

Progress

(Razvarr Abatut)

I made a huge effort to look over the blueprints yet again and again. The blueprints didn't yield much useful information. That was very discouraging. I turned to reading about the Temple's construction in a book my father had.

The rock in the four pillars of the central square had granite in it, but the walls in the square had some limestone mixed in. The limestone was added because it was quicker and cheaper to mine than the granite. That was the first real good news we found out about the Temple. Limestone was not as strong as granite. It was more susceptible than granite to shifting and fragmenting and crumbling.

If we could place a bomb near a limestone wall, the central square in the Temple Complex could be greatly damaged, if not destroyed. If a wall collapsed on the pillars, perhaps we could make one or two of the pillars come down, like rotted trees. We would make a statement, strike a blow against the legitimacy, the very foundation, of the state.

The 12-Step Program

(Akeyde Kletser)

A rat tapped my shoulder. I was dreaming that I was sitting in a service in the *Basmadrosh*, our assembly house, attending the Khurbm memorial service to commemorate the day Kawidtod conquered the Zans. It was the saddest day on our religious calendar. My father was giving a speech on the stage. I sat in a pew, quietly, but weeds kept sprouting out of my body. I couldn't stop them. They thrust through my suit, kept up through my chest, grew out of my ears.

I started to hit myself to beat back the plants, but they ended up covering my whole body, except for a tiny slit at the eyes to let me see my father's gestures.

The rat touched me again.

I pushed him away, so I could fight the weeds overtaking me.

Then the rat spoke.

"You okay?"

"They're everywhere!"

The rat pulled my chin up. I looked at him through the haze of the dream and the heat.

"You need some help?"

His head was shiny in the faint red light of the street lamps hanging over the train station. He wore a long blue and white shirt. Oh, God. A Squid.

I looked him over, but then I couldn't keep my eyes open.

"Are you sick?"

That made me open my eyes again.

"You want me to call the police, get you to a hospital or something?"

My head sank down between my knees. I mumbled something.

"What?"

I picked up my head. It felt like a piece of raw iron. I managed to eke out a hoarse whisper in the dense air.

"Stop trying to make me feel good."

"What do you mean?"

"Go. Get out of here. Leave me alone."

"Maybe you need a 12-step program, friend."

I tried to make my speech sharper.

"I'm not your friend. You don't know what I need."

He rose slowly, sighed. Then he kissed me on the top of my head.

"Go with God, my friend."

He padded off.

Then I laughed to myself. If only they had a 12-step program for suicide bombers. That might be something I could have used.

The Early Setback

(Razvarr Abatut)

The bomb that killed 27 in Sputten Dovil, in the north of the country had serious implications that continued to shake the country. The Pumn and the Corif (the judiciary) increased repressive measures, closed down more newspapers, arrested scores of people and ordered more people into the temples for reeducation rallies. And they blamed the influence of the Zans left in the country, arresting some of them too. Not that there was anything wrong with that. Their weird, archaic religion deserved nothing but contempt.

But I still thought my plan could have made a difference. The bomber's mistake was to strike in a small town of no consequence. We needed to strike at the heart of the country's power. That would send a message that the people strongly opposed the nation's rulers. Perhaps others would join the fight. We needed a revolution, violent if necessary.

I surfed away from the Net news and went to my email account. Necu sent me an email saying that with the provincial bombing he wanted to lay low for an indeterminate amount of time.

My depression came back. We were just getting the project going. I couldn't wait. We had to press the attack. It was either that or get under the covers. For a long time.

I wasn't always like that. When I was a boy, in Kawidtodia, I remember when my father registered me for religious school for the first time. I was about five years old.

We walked into a small temple in Shalhak. It was January, the traditional start for classes. There were no religion classes for boys at the Blue and White Temple. Only scholars with degrees from the major religious colleges studied at the Blue and White Temple's school.

The little temple had a school in the basement, with a long corridor containing classrooms for the children.

My father was signing me up for the school's kindergarten program. He and the head of the school talked about things I didn't want to think about, like the starting day for classes, and the hours for the kindergarten class, and fees for tuition, blah, blah, blah.

I was bored by their conversation, so I looked down the corridor. It went in a straight line to the west. One classroom door was open. The winter sun came through the windows of the classroom and lit up the dark, dull blue tiles of the floor in the hallway.

I looked at the light.

I thought to myself, "There is God."

On the wall behind my father and the religious school principal was a painting of Kawidtod. Our first king. He stood with his fists on his hips, a sword on his belt, on top of a mountain of rock and sand, overlooking thousands of his warriors with their swords raised to the sky. In the painting, the sun stood behind Kawidtod, a big light, illuminating the mountain and the outline of his head. The light was shining on him like it was shining on me.

The Fanatic

(Akeyde Kletser)

I wanted to go back home and look at the vest, find out what went wrong with the detonator, but the heat was up all around me and all my body would let me do was sleep, even though I was at the train station.

I had a dream that I became famous for something; it wasn't clear what. A slim, fresh-faced reporter with beautiful flaming orange hair and wearing a black leather jacket wanted to take my picture for her newspaper. Before she could arrange for the photographer to shoot, my Uncle Narish stomped up to me and told me how much he despised me.

There he was, back in my life, with his now-gray and white beard, long hair and tall, thin frame, his arms still firm from working out. I was glad to see him, until he started talking, telling me I was a disgrace and that he didn't respect me.

"You're out of the family." Then he turned away and walked off.

The reporter said she was sorry but asked if we could take the picture anyway.

"Sure."

She directed the photographer to take a picture of the two of us together. She put her delicious cheek next to mine for the picture and held me close. I glowed in that wonderful moment I had with Tina so many years ago, when I was kid, when things were easier.

The photographer snapped several pictures of us, although none of them could have looked like a news photo. The way the girl held me around the shoulder, breathing on me, enjoying being with me, this moment felt like we were taking engagement pictures.

"Isn't it great how two Zans can get together and just be happy? Would you like to take me out to dinner?"

Yes I would. Very much. And look at you with moon-wide eyes the whole time.

But then a thought came to me. My responsibilities to God and the tribe. What could I do about them? I had to make a choice.

"I have to tell you something."

"Yes?" She looked at me expectantly.

"I'm a suicide bomber. Can I still take you out to dinner?"

Her good mood clicked off like an alarm clock.

"No."

She turned away.

I shook off the dream.

I thought of Raz for some reason. No, there was a reason. He and I had a connection, despite all the troubles between our tribes.

I had gotten a job at an old battleship of a public school. The place had been built in 1925. It held 700 students. The floors were made of gray tile. The walls were painted gray. It was depressing. But there were no Zans working or going to school there. No Squids either. Just miles and miles of Spanish-speaking kids, which was just fine with me.

The neighborhood was falling apart. The apartment buildings were stained with air pollution. Auto body shops and car washes seemed to be the main businesses. There were a few construction supply stores too.

I got an apartment down the block from the school. Almost everybody spoke Spanish. There was some crime. A 19-year-old man was killed at three o'clock in the morning over a drug deal. A 22-year-old man threatened the police with a knife a few blocks from the school. They shot him. Another man was shot in front of a deli by a street gang.

These killings upset me, yet I felt safer here than in my old Zan neighborhood. Nobody cared about my religion. I was just another Anglo to the people living here.

During my third year, I was assigned to teach second grade. I enjoyed it. In October, the newspapers reported that the Kawidtodian government was cracking down on the population. The year before, the king had been replaced by a military dictator. The king had been shot in a public square by the dictator himself. This was very rough stuff and I hoped no Zans would be pulled into this horror.

This dictator, who called himself the Pumn, started closing down the newspapers. Some people protested. The new government arrested hundreds of people. They just disappeared. The New York Times protested. The U.S. government debated withdrawing its ambassador.

Squids trickled away over the border to Yekmonveldt, then to Europe. Some came to the United States.

In December, one came into my classroom, feeble and weak. I met his parents in the office before school. They wanted to introduce themselves and their child to me. The principal asked me to come downstairs from my classroom as I was preparing my lessons for the day.

I was annoyed. I had a lot of preparation work to do for the school day and now I was interrupted.

They were sitting in the office when I came in, the mother, the father, the boy slumped in a chair holding two black and white composition notebooks. No hair on any of their heads, which was startling enough. The small mother almost leaped on me in excitement, started talking to me in Kawidtodian and gesturing wildly.

I whipped my head back in response to this little meteor, an echo of tire iron digging a line through my skull. The knife brand on my arm flamed up.

The father placed himself in front of the mother slowly, yet firmly. He looked exhausted. His eyes were crushed seeds.

The father spoke in broken English. The boy's name was Razvarr. He had just gotten over pneumonia, which he contracted when he left the country, or after, I couldn't tell which.

They were new to the neighborhood, new to America. The boy spoke no English.

As the father spoke, the son looked at me and I looked at him. Despite the effects of the pneumonia, the kid's face was angry.

I hated their bald heads.

All the time the father was talking I was acting polite because I was a public school teacher and public schools accept anybody who walked in the door. But various thoughts were colliding inside my head.

If they find out I'm a Zan, are they going to hate me? Are they going to try to kill me?

How can I work with this kid after all the Squids had done to the Zans? Do I hate this kid? Should I hate this kid?

After the war inside me, I decided to steel myself for this child and get through the year with him. I swallowed it all and nodded as the father talked to me. I didn't understand most of his conversation.

It was about 10 minutes before school was supposed to start. I stopped the father by saying to Razvarr, "Okay, Razvarr, let's go to the cafeteria."

He just looked at me. He had no idea what I was talking about. The boy glared at me.

I pointed the way out of the office. The father started to guide the son to the hallway and the cafeteria.

At that point, the mother swept down on the son and pulled him to her. The boy grimaced.

The father separated the two. He spoke to the boy softly and the boy started to move his little feet. The boy was wearing little jeans, midget sneakers and a button down shirt and he looked like he wanted to rip off everything and go running through the streets.

We all walked stiffly to the cafeteria. At the doors I told the father and mother they could go no further. I opened one of the double doors and walked Razvarr inside to where most of our class was sitting for a free breakfast for the kids officially under the poverty line.

A few of my students saw me and yelled out, "Mr. Wood!"

I took Razvarr over to the table and introduced him.

"This is Razvarr and he's joining our class."

The kids looked at him with his bald head and decided he was from another planet.

"Be nice," I told them. "Remember the rules. We are polite to everybody."

The first couple of weeks were difficult. The boy didn't understand what was going on. I tried to use hand directions for the bathroom, when to open your composition book, when to close it.

He couldn't read any English at all, so I taught him basic phonics—the sounds of the language.

Every day in those first days, his bald head looked like a light bulb to me. And the kids were tough on him. They pointed at his skull and laughed. I had to scold them several times a day about it.

Eduardo Jimenez, one of our classroom comedians, went into the class bathroom one day and put water on his thick hair. He molded it into a Mohawk and went over to Razvarr and started whooping. Despite Razvarr's fragile health, he hit Eduardo in the stomach.

Eduardo hit him back, in the chest. The class started yelling. I had to call security to remove them both from class. They were suspended for three days and had to talk to a counselor.

After that, everybody settled down about it. Nobody wanted another fight. Razvarr was a kid, just like them. Eduardo decided he liked Razvarr and pulled him into his orbit.

After a month, Razvarr could read books with one sentence on each page. I rewarded him by giving him stickers after he did even one little thing well. That he understood.

Sometimes I would draw him Batman and Superman pictures at the end of the day, as a special reward. He had no idea who they were, but he seemed to like them. The kids showed Razvarr how to color in their costumes.

The boy's math skills were good; he knew the numeric system, which needed no translation.

In the springtime, his reading took off. By the end of the year he had caught up to the class. His writing needed work, but he was getting to where he needed to go.

The school promoted him to third grade. His parents were grateful to me.

"I'd like to take credit for what he's done, but he did the work," I told the father. He shook my hand and put his other hand on my shoulder.

They gave me a gift on the last day of school—a flimsy green tie with Santa Claus holding a sack of presents in the middle, snow falling all around him. It didn't make sense in terms of the season, but I knew they were poor and they had tried to find something that would make me happy.

So they didn't know what I was. I had escaped!

He was the first Kawidtodian child I would have in my class and I survived it.

There would be more.

A heavy breath, hot, fell on me. It broke into my thoughts.

Where was I? The train station. Something animal was in my face.

A man crouched down to look in my face. His face was very lean. He was wearing a New York City police officer's uniform, complete with a blue cap.

"Hey, wake up."

"Huh?"

"Wake up. I need to ask you something."

"Yeah?"

"Is your name Akeyde?"

"Are you a cop?"

The man looked away for a minute, down the train line.

"Look at me. I'm wearing the uniform. Got the cap."

"So, how do you know my name?"

"Your father called the station house."

"My father doesn't usually call the police about tribal matters. It doesn't make any sense."

"No? Then maybe this will."

He reached for something in his sock. I thought it would be a gun.

"Die, Akeyde! Fulfill the prophecy!"

A flash of steel reflected from the orange light of a tower on the station told me I was wrong. The blade ripped into the meat of my shoulder, then came out.

For a long, slow moment, as if in a dream, I thought, this is it. Sweet release. I get to die and go up to God. I will finally have some rest.

Then the knife went for my throat. I don't know what it was, but my body wasn't ready to die yet. So I thrust my right arm up and it met the knife.

A razor dug into the muscle and it argued the point. Despite the fire in the arm, I told my left hand to move. It reached for the detachable top of the metal garbage can standing next to me and brought it down on the man's head as hard as I could. Vehktre's training had been good for something.

The man fell over onto his side and let go of the knife. He was a little dazed. I pushed up off the floor with my left hand. My right arm was burning.

I grabbed the garbage can top again and slammed it into the man's head, even though my right shoulder and arm made enormous complaints.

I went to hit him again when he put up his hands. The metal top hit his hands and pushed them backwards.

I took the garbage can top and shoved it into his face with everything I had. This time the top flew over his hands and met the skull with a satisfying thump. I hit him again and again, until his nose was flaring with blood.

Then he was still. I briefly considered the possibility of throwing him onto the railroad track. I knew he wasn't a police officer because of the knife, because of what he said. He was one of my kinsmen, one of my tribal brothers. What a joke.

But then I thought that he would be dead. And I was clearly having a hard time with the whole idea of killing somebody, even this delusional creep.

So I left him there, slumped against the concrete platform, unconscious.

My arm and shoulder were screaming with blood. I could go to the hospital. But I had Tina with me, so we had the obvious possibility of arrest. I ruled that out.

There was the option of going to the apartment and cleaning out the wound and resting under a cold shower in the tub. The tears in my arm and shoulder were too long and I might bleed to death right there.

My father's house. My house until he sent me to live in that apartment. I couldn't. I didn't think he would let me in.

There was only one option and that was Uncle Cookie, the owner of a strip club. The black sheep. He had been shunned by the tribe and now so was I. I didn't even know if he would remember me, but I didn't know what to do and I didn't have one friend left among the Zans. Plus the Kawidtodians might be out looking for me too.

I dragged myself away.

The Pick-Up

(Razvarr Abatut)

Debyl and Mintal were picked up by the police. Necu said they had been careful, but the police were on edge. There had been rumors of a bomb attack coming, but nobody knew where. I hoped Debyl and Mintal would keep their mouths quiet. I hoped they didn't get tortured. Necu wrote me that we should go completely dark and suspend our plans until it was safer. The news was a real buzz-kill.

I went to bed and pulled the polyester sheet all the way up over my head. The blankness of it helped with the necessary escape to another place.

But I got screwed. The doorbell rang. My mother opened it, which I of course heard. Ordinarily, I wouldn't care about this, but my mother shouted out, "Raz, somebody is here to see you!"

I didn't get up. Who the hell would be coming over?

There was talking between my mother and the visitor, this cretin mass of zombie flesh, and then they went to the kitchen to drink tea.

I fell asleep.

Then BOOM! Knocking on the door with the force of a small wrecking ball was my mother's fist.

"Raz, wake up! It's Amic. Your friend."

I didn't get up. The knocks kept coming. I peeked out from under the sheet and I swore I could actually see the door moving with each blow.

"He's not getting out of bed," Mom said. "So we will barge in on him."

"Are you sure?"

"I'm sure. He never sees his old friends."

The door flew open and there stood my mother with a sick little smile on her face.

"Raz, wake up!" she shouted, even though she saw quite plainly that I was already awake.

"Hi, Raz."

"Hi, Amic."

"Get out of bed and say hello to your friend."

Then she left.

Amic looked at me and shook his head. "Moms."

A friend from intermediate school. We were never really that close, but he lived down the block. He sat down on a wooden chair near my father's rock.

"Tell me about it."

"Haven't seen you since you got back from school."

"I'm busy."

He made a gesture with his hand curled up and moving back and forth vigorously.

"Jerking off?"

"Hah."

"Your Mom said you got a computer."

I propped my head up on an elbow. "Yeah."

"Why do you have a generator?"

"In case the power goes out."

"Right. So what are you working on?"

I changed the subject. "What are you doing?"

"Well, you know I got the scholarship to NYU for engineering."

I was annoyed that he was reminding me. "You told me before."

"I finished up my second year."

"Yeah."

"It's really hard, man. I study like six hours a day when I'm not in class."

I lifted myself out of my bed with the greatest of efforts.

"Yeah."

I didn't want to talk about his "great" life or anything. I nodded my head and wondered how I could end the conversation and then get him out of the house.

"Hey, I heard you graduated with honors. Congratulations."

"Thanks."

"What are you going to do now?"

"You're looking at it."

"You going to start your own tech company?"

"Something like that, maybe."

"Did you hear that Tevengi is majoring in finance at Columbia?"

"No. Who cares?"

"Who cares? After he graduates he's going to try to get hired by one of the big firms. He's got an in. His cousin works down there already."

"So?"

"Wall Street, man! Money, women, a Porsche!"

"Wall Street isn't doing *that* well these days., as I recall."

"There's still a lot of money there."

"It's not that interesting, really."

"You're so crazy, Raz. He's going to make the big money while I slave away for 40K at some industrial company in Ohio or Connecticut or something boring like that."

"So, if you're bored, why do it?"

"I dunno. I understand this stuff. It's scary."

"You *scare* me, you big doof."

"Hey, how about we go get lunch or something?"

"Nah. I got things to do."

"C'mon."

"I'm busy."

"Doing what?"

"Thinking."

Amic shook his head. "Thinking never does much good."

"You think all the time."

"Yeah, but I'm thinking about how to make machines work. Once you get beyond that, it's a crazy-ass world." He got up off the chair. "Call me or text me or something. Let's do something."

"Okay." I would have said anything to get him out of the room. He scrambled down the stairs. Ah, relief.

Wandering

(Akeyde Kletser)

A train rammed down the line, going east. I could have taken that train. But I kept thinking that Vehktre would come and find me and return me here.

The main street of the neighborhood was filled with people going to restaurants and bars on a summer night. I avoided that, even though it was the most direct route to where I thought Uncle Cookie might be.

The back streets always seemed to be where I ended up, dark and silent. No people. My arm throbbed and the streams of blood flowing down my blue and white windbreaker started to dry out.

I walked by a small Kawidtodian Temple. Even in my hazy state, I wanted to destroy the place. There were more and more of these temples in the neighborhood every year. Kawidtodia was too much for them. They slaughtered millions of us over the centuries, and they didn't even have the decency to stay in their own homeland?

As I briefly considered the idea of blowing myself up here, I realized there was no one there to kill, and second, destroying this little temple—or any one of the other Kawidtodian anthill, Mickey Mouse temples in Queens—would not be very big news. It was maybe one day worth of news. Vehktre wanted to target the big Manhattan temple. It was where all the rich Kawidtodians lived and blowing up the Manhattan temple would have gotten us the worldwide attention we needed. A bombing in Manhattan could get at least one week's worth of media coverage, and maybe more, depending how many Squids were killed.

Several blocks away, I passed the *Basmadrosh*, our prayer house. I wished I could go in and fall asleep in a pew in front of Akeyde raising his arms to God.

After stumbling through the winding back streets, I found what I was looking for. There was a street that turned north and eventually emptied onto the boulevard.

The boulevard to the west was very different from the main shopping district. It was filled with car rental businesses operating out of temporary trailers, a few pawn brokers sitting between empty asphalt lots, pornography shops and a strip club.

The strip club had a neon sign with bright wavy letters on a background of midnight black paint.

The bouncer, all beefy arms and stout belly, took a look at me and almost turned me away.

"You're bleeding."

"Yes."

"You'll get blood on the floor and the tablecloths."

"If I give you 20 dollars, will you let me in?"

He waved his head back and forth and rolled his eyes.

"I'll take it. Go pay. Sit at a back table. Don't let the owners see you."

"Okay."

I paid the bouncer and the admission requirement at the counter. Another 20 dollars. The voluptuous young lady sitting at the booth didn't look me over too carefully, which was lucky.

I didn't want to sit at a back table. I wanted to find Cookie.

The redwood tree man was the bartender. I was surprised to see him and very unhappy about it. He saw me walk by and put a beer down in front of a customer. Then he took his finger and drew it across his throat.

I kept walking, passing the main stage, where enormous globules of flesh were thrust out at men who looked like children being presented with lollipops as big as their heads.

The stage was shaped like a "T," with the upper part of the "T" jutting into the audience area. Poles that were twisted like spirals so girls could writhe through the gray metal had been built into the stage. A cage was suspended from the ceiling. It could be lowered down to the audience floor in front of the stage so an especially attractive girl could entice the customers.

Two girls wearing white thong bikini bottoms and no tops gyrated aggressively in front of dozens of men. One of them wore her hair in a blonde shag. Her feathery hair fell around her shoulders. I thought of Tina. The men were silent as they sipped their beers, wrapped up in a private world, like they were watching a movie.

I found the blood rushing to my face in spite of myself. I was embarrassed and fascinated at the same time. I tried to think about God. It didn't work.

Through a back hallway I found an office. A huge man with a shaved head, tall and with arms as thick as oil pipelines, stood in front of it.

"Hey, what do you think you're doing?"

"I need to see Cookie."

"You can't go in there."

"I have to."

"You look like you belong in a police station. You're getting blood on my carpet."

"I'm his nephew."

The guard took a walkie-talkie out of his pocket and called the bouncer.

"Hey, fatboy, why'd you let this guy in?"

"He paid. So I let him in. And don't call me that. I told you."

"He's a mess."

I was starting to lose hope. My knees sagged. Tina gripped me tighter. My breath came in little short gasps.

"He just fell on the floor. Get back here, idiot face, and take this guy out of here."

"I have to cover the front. You take him."

"I'll kill you, fats, I swear to God."

Sunk on the floor, somehow a roar came out of me.

"He's MY UNCLE!"

The door opened slowly, as if it were reluctant to find out what was there.

He was about five foot six, weighing at least 225 pounds, even heavier than when I saw him just a handful of times more than 20 years ago. I could sketch out the remains of the face I remembered under all that flesh.

"Hi, Cookie," I croaked out.

"Get him in here," he said to the bodyguard.

The bodyguard picked me up by my string cheese arms and lifted me over his shoulder.

"Why is he so heavy? He's a little guy."

"Put him down on the couch."

A black leather couch looked like it might be my final resting place. I admired Cookie for not caring about getting blood on the leather.

I was beginning to fall apart mentally and lots of disjointed thoughts came out of my mouth. Blood loss had me drunk.

"Think I can get a date with one of those girls out front?"

"Jesus Christ, kid, what the hell happened to you?"

"Is the blonde named Tina?"

"You're bleeding."

"Still? What about that girl?"

Cookie talked to the bodyguard. "Arak, get his jacket off."

"It's good to be home."

The bodyguard was less than delicate in removing the blue and white windbreaker. The blood had acted to adhere it to the skin on my arms.

"The zipper's stuck," he said.

So he worked on the rips the fake policeman had made, pulling the jacket apart by using the tears already there.

After he finished getting the jacket off, he laid me down on the couch. I was half conscious and ready to have a good time.

The guard saw the vest. "What the hell is that?"

I laughed. "Be nice. Her name is Tina."

"Jesus Christ, Akeyde!" Cookie shouted.

"Isn't it just like you to leave the fold? No Zan god for you anymore. Very classy."

The bodyguard was panicked. "There's enough explosive here to take out the whole block!"

"Don't worry."

Cookie slapped my face. "What do you mean, don't worry?"

"I want to sleep. Please let me sleep."

"He's off his nut. Arak, call Karen."

"This guy needs to go to the hospital."

"Then he'll be arrested. You want the cops around here?"

"She just got off her shift, Cookie."

"I don't give a damn! We need an emergency room nurse, or we're going to lose him."

Arak quickly whipped out a cell phone and dialed.

Everything went black.

"Mr. Kletser, try to focus. Look at me."

She had raven-black hair, each strand curled to a tight wave and chocolate brown eyes each the size of a small lake. Warm eyes. Giving eyes.

"Is your name Tina?"

"I've cleaned out your wounds and put bandages on them."

"Knife."

"They look like they were made by a knife, a very large one. Now I'm going to use a very sharp knife to cut the vest away from you."

"Don't touch the bombs." Cookie was nervous. He was standing behind Karen.

"I'm going to work on the place in the front where the two sides of the vest meet. There's nothing there but cloth."

"Okay, okay, just be mighty goddamn careful."

The knife edge pushed easily into the vest then sliced down its entire length.

"Okay, now, Mr. Kletser, I want you to try to sit up."

"Do you drink, young lady?"

"Only after work. Now stay with me."

Enchanted, I did what she asked.

"Cookie, Arak, grab one side of the vest and pull it away from him."

The vest was placed delicately onto the couch.

I felt somehow diminished.

"Can I lie down now?"

"No! You'll set off the bombs!"

"Arak, he can't do that. You can't set off explosives by just sitting on them. You need a trigger."

"Yeah, we took that away from him. I found it in his jacket."

Just to be safe, Karen held me in her arms while Arak took the vest very carefully from the couch and placed it on the floor of the office.

"I love you, Karen."

"Thank you, Mr. Kletser."

"Did you know that God wants me to be President of the United States?"

No response.

"Can I sleep now?'

"Yes, Mr. Kletser."

"Can I have my vest back?"

A very long pause.

"No, Mr. Kletser."

The Big Risk-Taker

(Razvarr Abatut)

I sent an email to Necu. I couldn't help it. I wanted to share the good news about the limestone.

Necu emailed me that we must not talk about the project. The police were combing through the Internet traffic for mail that was "dangerous to the stability of society."

He wrote that he was emailing me from an underground Net café with a pipe through Yekmonveldt. This seemed safe, as long as we didn't talk about the project, although he didn't say how he knew that. He couldn't use his own computer.

I had to be more patient, Necu said. My boys Debyl and Mintal were still in police custody.

The cell phone store owner reported the sale. Why did he do that? And why did he get to keep the money from the transaction? My money.

The cell phone purchases were like a trip wire going off to the police. The cell phone store owner wondered why anyone would buy six phones at the same time. So did the police. He still sold Debyl and Mintal the phones, though, then reported them. The store owner's call made the police aware of the two. Then they contacted Debyl and Mintal's community leader, who everyone knew was a spy for the government.

He told the police that Debyl and Mintal hadn't been seen in their local temple in several months. That was enough to get you put in jail. They weren't sufficiently religious. And there were questions about the cell phones.

We had freedom of religion in Kawidtodia, as long as you worshiped Kawidtod. What about freedom from religion?

Patience! I was so tired of waiting around for other people, especially when this repression went on each day, every day, for decades.

This wasn't easy work. What did Necu expect? Yes, I hoped Mintal and Debyl weren't tortured. But we had to go on. We had to do something or the state would swallow us all.

"You don't really know what it's like here," he wrote. "You are safe in America."

Yeah. Sugar cake America. Home of American Idol. World center for celebrity gossip. Isn't that sick and repressive enough in its own way?

I wrote him back.

"MY FATHER WAS TORTURED BY THE RELIGIOUS POLICE. AND HE WAS A RELIGIOUS TEACHER. Where was the sense in that?"

I didn't hear from Necu for several days. When I wasn't fuming at the computer, I slept. I was very depressed. If I couldn't make this happen, what would be left for me?

My mother barged in on me several times. We had 13 conversations about one thing.

They usually went like this:

First she poked me in the ribs. I hated that.

"Why don't you get up? We are worried about you."

"Get a job, baldy."

A fist would strike my chest.

I laughed.

Then silence.

"Well, I wanted to talk to you about a job. You can work at your father's newsstand. He needs help. He'll pay you."

I peeked out from under the polyester sheet and stared at her.

"Why don't you hire somebody from the neighborhood?"

"He wants a person he can trust."

"Why would he trust me?"

"Why? You are his son!"

"What about Arak?"

"That's crazy. You know your uncle owns half of the newsstand."

"That's why he's perfect."

"Arak has another job. He's working two jobs, maybe three. I've lost count."

"I've heard about his other job. He works for a strip club. That's noble."

"He's got a five-percent interest in the club. That is big money."

"He's a perv."

My mother sighed. "That's what they taught you in college? To judge your family all the time? You would be the worst religious policeman back home, always going after people for trying to survive."

This was a terrible blow, but I didn't know how to talk back to it.

"We do what we have to do. We are trying to make things better for ourselves. Not live day to day in fear that we won't have any money."

"What if Arak was a hit man? What if he killed people? Would you draw the line there?"

"Perhaps, perhaps not."

"Mother, you are over the border, way out there crazy."

"I was joking, Razvarr."

"It's not very funny."

"I am sorry."

"I'd rather be dead than work at the newsstand."

"I hope it doesn't come to that."

"Don't threaten me, old woman."

"You threaten me all the time, lying in bed here. Working on the computer by yourself, never coming out of your room."

"How is that a threat to you?"

"You are hurting my heart."

"Give me a break."

"And what are all these new machines doing in here with the computer? Where did you get the money for all this?"

"Oh, well, hmmm, Amic down the block let me borrow this stuff. He wanted me to help him with advice on some software installs, so this is my payback."

"You lie in bed, give him some of your thoughts, and he gives you all this?"

"I did graduate with honors, you know."

She pointed to the power backup unit.

"What is that?"

"It keeps the power on for the computer, in case the electricity goes out."

"I don't like it. I don't like any of this. It will drive up our electricity bills. They are already too high. Give the machines back to him."

I didn't want to point out the small generator, sitting next to the uninterruptible power supply (UPC), with five gallons of gasoline sitting inside it, to keep the power going in case of an extended outage.

Mother sniffed the air, as if she could sense my thoughts.

"And what's that smell?"

"It's probably coming up from the garage. You know, the cars leave little drops of gasoline on the floor."

"That's a big smell for not so much gasoline."

"What can I say?"

"Maybe you should go downstairs and clean it up."

"That's funny."

She didn't like my sarcasm: "Go do it now!"

"Sorry, old witch. No way."

She rushed at me one time and for a moment I thought she was going to choke my neck. But she stopped herself a few feet from me and bared her teeth at me like a wolf and held her fingernails out like claws. She actually growled.

"I would rip you to shreds if I could. Such a lazy son. So disrespectful."

"Stop it, already! You don't want me to lie around, so now I'm doing something, and you're giving me a hard time about it!"

She actually listened to me then and left the room with a quick push of her feet and slam of the door for dramatic effect.

With the sound of the slammed door trailing after her, I considered the gasoline in the generator. If my project failed, I supposed I could always open up the unit and throw a match in. Blow up the house. I would finally be able to get more sleep.

Maybe that's what I deserved. Suicide. Get rid of the pain of waking up in the morning.

After that particularly wonderful conversation, I got up and checked my email. Nothing but spam trying to sell me shoes, real estate, chats with girls sporting big breasts. Depression hit me like a weight to the head.

Two weeks into Internet silence, I got an email from an address I didn't recognize. It was a string of nonsensical letters, which was always a bad sign. Probably a virus.

But the final three letters in the string said "Yek." If this email were coming from Yekmonveldt, maybe it was from someone I knew.

I opened it. It was Necu. He wrote a short strand.

"I traveled by bus to Yekmonveldt to write you. I cannot be arrested. Then all will be lost."

Now here was something I could grab on to. It fed my anger at him, at the country, at everybody. Two weeks of nothing and all I got was this? Where was the action? Where was the progress?

Like I didn't know what Necu was going through. I knew he walked the streets of Shalhak every day. He smelled the slaughtered chickens hanging on hooks by their necks in the open air markets and heard the buzzing of the people in their shops and temples.

I considered the possibility that the boy may not have had enough heart to work with me. I needed strong men! We had to take big risks. If he was not willing to do that, then I had no use for him.

Besides, I wasn't even sure he was still in, based on his email.

The Delights of the Old Country

(Necu Brav)

I couldn't chance writing Raz from Kawidtodia.

It took me several days to go 100 miles to the border. The bus service was very bad. I brought my own food, which ran out. I had to beg from people on the side of the road for a scrap here and there.

Raz hadn't been in the country for 12 or 13 years. He didn't know the land. He didn't know me.

The mountains sat all around us, silent soldiers. They protected us from the outside world, but they also kept us in. We were in a fortress and prison.

I was too poor to go to the university. I lived in Shalhak, the capital. My mother was my greatest teacher. The best thing she taught me was how to read and write in English.

It was a great skill, and I wished I could use it more. If I could get to the United States somehow, I could start out from day one teaching English to Kawidtodian immigrants.

My mother was dead. The police took her one day five years ago because she said something to her class. We were not allowed to find out what it was. Her words were considered blasphemy against Kawidtod.

A Corif judge told us she died during questioning, of natural causes. We were not allowed to see Mother's body. The judge said she was buried in a corner of a cemetery near our home. You could go and see her there. There was a small marker with her name.

The marker was tagged with a ribbon of purple, which indicated to the world that my mother was an infidel, is an infidel, will always be an infidel, even in death, like the Zans, and will go to Zgmoto—hell. We were not allowed to remove the ribbon. Even in death, for all eternity, my mother would be stricken with disgrace, and so was our family.

My father was an engineer, but he lost his job five years ago because of the situation with my mother. He ended up working in a little booth in the main market in Shalhak, fixing watches and clocks and anything else mechanical that people could carry to the market. He died suddenly last year. Natural causes, the police said.

My job prospects were not good. I could have joined the Army, but that was a hard life. My best chance for advancement was to take religious training and become a temple priest or scholar of the scriptures. It cost a great deal of money, but it could be done if you got jobs on the side to help see you through. Once you got a position as a priest, the pay was generally good.

I didn't know if I could bring myself to enlist in this service. But if I didn't, it would be hard for me to find a girl and marry. I didn't have the money to start a business. And business was hard here, unless you were connected. And I was clearly not.

Food was cheap, especially bread, because the state provided subsidies to the producers, creating large government deficits. In this way, the state made sure we had a basic level of survival so the people didn't rebel.

Our religion and the state could not be separated. In the name of our beliefs, the state had laws where the people chafed. There was a core of true believers who ran the religion-state. But for many, we were dissatisfied.

Almost everyone had to shave their heads every day, men and women. If you did not shave for a few days, your hair would start to sprout and the religious police would stop you on the street and give you a hard time. They walked in groups of four to six men. These men had bright blue triangles on their white blouses. They carried wooden batons to hit you if you were disrespectful or failed to follow the rules.

If the religious police said you were disrespectful to the religion, or blasphemed against Kawidtod or God, they might very well say you are a Zan. That was the worst thing you could say about anybody. It was the lowest insult. There were only four or five thousand Zans left in the country, but their barbarian history was so much part of ours that everyone knew they were the enemies of the Kawidtodians, forever.

We were required to go to temple two times a day, in the morning and at night. On Thursdays, our holy day of rest, we were required to go four times. We carried paper pocket calendars so the men at the temple could stamp the number of times we attended prayers.

I thought about girls all the time. Their bodies may have been hidden under long robes and their heads may have been shaved, but I knew the curves were inside, waiting for someone. A husband.

I had seen pictures in magazines smuggled in from Europe. The girls were either in little swimsuits or they were naked. The flesh was bursting out everywhere. And they had beautiful hair—blonde, brown, red, black. The hairs sprang out from their heads like flowers, like the manes of horses. It was art that they carried around on those heads.

I could not stop my lust for them. If you were caught with one of these magazines, you were beaten by the religious police. Sometimes they conducted a spot check of houses and they could come in to your rooms with no warning.

Sometimes the government allowed newspapers that were a little off the center to publish, but the editors had to be very careful. If they expressed opinions that the government did not like, the national security ministry would shut them down and maybe send the editors to jail. On one day you could publish an opinion about the poor state of the economy and the government wouldn't touch you. On another day, you could write the same thing, and the police would come to visit you. The line of tolerance always changed, and God help you if you were beyond the line on the wrong day.

You could not write anything bad about the Corif or the Pumn. That would land you in Divinnot Prison. Or Mortred. Or if somebody powerful really didn't like you, they would just drag you out to the central square in the city and hang you until you were dead.

Unlike Raz, I did not have the time to be depressed. I was too busy trying to survive.

People left, if they could. There was an underground railroad, but you had to be careful. The religious police sometimes posed as dissidents and offered to take you out of the country. If you were receptive to them, they would accuse you of betraying the nation. Then you would go to prison. You did not come out.

If you had relatives in America, you could sometimes get out. The relatives might appeal to the U.S. government to help them get out of our country, and they used to do so quite a lot before all the immigration fears took hold in America.

Raz's plan gave me something positive to work for. If we succeeded, it was possible the Zans would be blamed for the bombs. But I couldn't worry about that. I could only hope other people would take up opposition to the government and try to overthrow the existing order.

Refuge

(Akeyde Kletser)

I woke up on another black leather couch. A lady with shiny, curly black hair was sleeping in a sitting-up position on the other couch, perpendicular to mine, facing a huge flat screen television fixed to the wall. It was about as long as the sleeping lady.

The television was on in the dark, casting blue light on the woman.

My glasses were off and I was a little groggy, yet I could see her face, dressed with curls, sliding off a pillow propped behind the top of the couch. Her cheeks were blue from the television. She had a pert little nose and fleshy lips.

Her eyes opened. "What are you doing?" she asked me, her voice flavored with smoke.

I didn't want to say the obvious thing. "Thinking."

She sat up. "You should go back to sleep."

"I don't know. Where are you from?"

"Out east. Long Island."

"What's it like?"

She rubbed her eyes, yawned without covering her mouth.

"You've never been out there?"

"I don't travel much."

The TV was showing an old movie with two stars kissing in the dark under a street light.

"Not even 20 miles away?"

"I used to go to summer camp upstate. In the mountains."

"Well, I guess Long Island isn't that interesting. It's flat."

"So, what town are you from?"

"It's not important, just another small town."

"Why'd you leave?"

"It's boring. All houses and shopping malls. I guess the most interesting thing about the town is that the county jail is across the street from the high school. Isn't that strange? I wanted to get away from my parents, like everybody."

"What are your parents like?"

She started to nod off.

"Hey."

"Yeah."

"You're falling asleep."

She looked at her watch. "It's 2:45 in the morning. I should be asleep."

"I asked you about your parents."

"You ask a lot of questions for a suicide bomber," she said in a dreamy voice. "Go to sleep."

"I have another question."

"So many questions," she said, her voice heavy with sleep.

"Why don't you turn me in to the police?"

She picked up her head for a few seconds.

"Do you want to be turned in?"

I didn't want to answer the question.

"Why don't you call the police on me?'

"Cookie."

There were dozens of threads in that name and I wanted to pursue them. I wanted to know more. How much money did Cookie pay her? Why did she take it? There were so many worlds far beyond my meager education. Once I started asking questions and getting a few answers, I had many more. I couldn't stop thinking.

Sleep was the only way to put a halt to it. I managed to keep my eyes open for a little while longer, until the movie soundtrack played violins melting into endless happiness for the couple on the street.

I woke up again at 10 in the morning. The house was air-conditioned cool. Thick oak trees hung over the house, which was made of brick. Finally, some relief from the heat of August.

We were in Cookie's house in the Gardens neighborhood, near my neighborhood. Or what had been mine. I pushed myself up with my left hand, as my right was shredded and bandaged.

The lady was watching television and eating a bagel with cream cheese with coffee. The television was showing another movie, about a girl who couldn't stop shopping. The colors on the screen were bright orange with pink, lots of pink.

"You're awake."

"Who are you again?"

"Karen. Karen Rogers. I patched you up last night."

"Right. You don't watch the news?"

"Too depressing. My job is tough enough. You woke up in the middle of the night. We had a conversation."

"Yes, I think I remember now."

"You wanted to talk, I guess. You've been through a lot. You lost some blood. I fed you a pint of blood to replace what you lost."

"How?"

Karen gestured to an IV stand and an empty bag with red streaks standing behind the couch.

"None of this seems very legal."

"Cookie didn't want to take you to the hospital."

"How did you get all these things in here?"

She just looked at me, said nothing.

Cookie walked into the living room, holding a large mug of coffee. His eyes were a bit smudged from sleep.

"Our patient is up?"

"Yes, Cookie. And now that I see he's okay, I'm leaving."

"I owe you, sweetie."

"Yes, you do. A lot. He should go to Parkway Hospital, to see if he's okay. He needs real medical care."

"That's not gonna happen, baby. There are too many people who know him."

Karen walked up to Cookie, so she was barely a foot away. Then she pointed at him.

"I don't want to get involved in ethnic politics. All I know is he's been injured and he should be monitored properly."

"Well, I'm worried about the boy's health too. You don't know his father."

"Let's not talk about it anymore. We'll just argue. I don't understand all this tribal conflict."

Cookie put up his hands in mock surrender, forgetting he had the coffee cup. Some of it spilled on the hand-woven carpet.

"You win, Karen. I'll think about it."

Karen sighed, then pivoted to the right. I ached at seeing her curly black hair vanish just like that. For one more look at her brown eyes.

"Goodbye, Cookie!" she shouted from the foyer. Then the door clicked open and shut.

From the window in the living room I could see her noble form carry off to parts unknown.

"Well, kid, here's breakfast."

"You know I'm 35 years old."

"I don't care how old you are. You're still a kid."

A blonde woman in a long purple nightgown, which barely contained the curve of her skin, walked into the living room and yelled out.

"Come to the kitchen!"

We ate cheese omelets and cream cheese on toast. A pitcher of orange juice sat in the middle of the table.

"Here, sweetie, let me pour you some."

I almost died when she called me sweetie.

"This is Barbara."

"Hello."

I couldn't say hello back. I just stared at her face atop that slip of a nightgown. Blonde hair, streaked with even more blonde hair. She may have been 40 years old to Cookie's 60-something. She reminded me a little of Tina, except she had a charming uneven smile under big lips. Her brown eyes actually sang.

"He's shy," Cookie explained.

"I've met boys like him. Usually too serious."

We ate in silence, mostly. I noticed Cookie occasionally looking over and smiling at Barbara and her smiling back. They had an intimacy.

After breakfast, I went to brush my teeth in the bathroom. A toothbrush was laid out for me, in plastic wrap, like in a hotel. The bathroom had a marble toilet and a green marble floor. The shower walls were made from granite.

I showered with plastic bags over my right arm and shoulder. I dried myself off with monogrammed towels.

New clothes had been purchased for me somehow. A new pair of shorts, an Old Navy tee-shirt with a U.S. flag imprint, and white tennis sneakers. I felt as if I were back in summer camp.

I took a tour through the house. I hadn't been in this house for almost 30 years. Every room was carpeted with rugs from India or some other exotic place. Antique clocks decorated the walls, and sprawling paintings of the green English countryside and paintings of mountain views, which I thought must be of the Adirondack Mountains – Hudson River school.

There were also a few paintings of recumbent naked women, in gilt frames. They attracted me so much that I forced myself to look away.

Large windows divided by metal squares fronted the living room. The first floor had high ceilings, at least 20 feet. Most of the walls were painted in a light blue.

"Federal Blue."

"I'm sorry?"

"You were wondering about the paint. The color is called Federal Blue."

"Oh."

The house itself was quite large—a brick structure that could have been at least 100 years old. Cookie's house was in the heart of the Gardens, a much wealthier neighborhood bordering my own. The noise and clash of central Queens here turned into an English style country village. This area was deliberately designed to copy the English. Two-hundred-year-old trees lined private streets. The houses were mostly Tudor. The streets were mostly free of people.

The house was very beautiful, but somehow it felt all so wrong to me. Part of me wanted to stay here forever. But then another thought would tag along and tell me I wouldn't be staying long and that I shouldn't even try.

I had unfinished business. There was a job to do. A very serious one.

Cookie made the house my house for a couple of days and he let me alone to wander through the place or watch movies on the huge screen TV.

On the third day I saw him. I was watching "Pirate Wenches of the Caribbean." Out of the corner of my eye, a flash of yellow and purple caught me. A bearded man standing out on the lawn, next to the hedges bordering the house, wearing a windbreaker in the rain.

The pirate wenches called out to me, but I had to tear myself away. I went to the front of the house to the metal-framed window and stared out beyond the hedges. He had his hands clasped behind the back because his eyes were the only weapon he needed.

We stared at each other for what seemed like a long time.

"Hey, what are you looking at?" Cookie had rumbled over to me.

"That man."

But as soon as Cookie had come over, all that was left of the man was a streak of yellow and purple.

"I didn't see anybody. What's wrong with you, kid? We fixed you up. At least we took care of your body. Your brain, that's something else entirely, isn't it?"

"Yes."

Cookie kept looking out the window, but focused his eyes north.

"Wait, now I see something. A man in a purple and yellow jacket way down the street, going toward the train station."

"Yeah. He was here."

"You sure?"

"Yeah."

"That's not good. What am I going to do with you?"

"Okay."

"Okay, what? You're still the same, Akeyde. You don't take action. You don't think."

"I read."

"Like that's going to help with anything. I haven't seen you in what, 25 years?"

"Twenty-one."

"Okay. Right. Whatever. Since your accident."

The tire iron. I didn't want to talk about the tire iron.

"You could have visited the house."

"I had a falling out with your father."

"Why?"

"We didn't agree on things."

"I don't understand."

"Your father thinks mostly about revenge. The things he did to you, I didn't agree with. And he's got our other brothers so brainwashed now, that's how they spend their lives. I can't do that."

"Right."

"Besides, my brothers are involved in some nasty businesses that I don't want to touch. They're angry with me because I own a strip club. What they do is far worse. But to them, sex is the worst thing. It's like you can do any terrible thing you want to make money, no matter if it hurts anybody. But sex? That's really bad!"

"Really? What are they doing?"

He waved his hand. "They're all nuts. It's not good for you to know. Just stay away from your uncles. Anyway, with more of them moving into his neighborhood, your father's got piss in him all the way up to his neck."

Cookie didn't need to say who was moving in. We both knew.

"Hey, aren't you a public school teacher? What are you doing mixed up in all this?

"I stopped doing that a long time ago, Cookie. I only did it for five or six years."

"Why'd you quit?"

My classroom started to flood with Squids. The Pumn nationalized every large business he could find in the country. The year after Razvarr arrived, the Pumn instituted a national security apparatus that strangled dissent in the cradle. Neighborhood patrols encouraged neighbors to spy on one another. You could increase your food rations if you turned in a neighbor. People didn't trust anybody.

The year after I had Razvarr, I got five Kawidtodian children in my second grade class. They had just sprung up there, like mushrooms.

People weren't allowed to get out. Yet they got out. The country may have been turned into a police state, but it was poor. The border wasn't well-patrolled. It was physically tough to cross, but it offered a way out.

Two years after Razvarr, I got eight Kawidtodians. He was in fourth grade by this time. He always stopped by my classroom after school to say hello and tell me how he was doing. I asked him to help me organize my students' work or put up a bulletin board. He and I talked about Batman and Superman or some new book he was reading. He liked to talk about how amazing America was.

My other Kawidtodian students were generally as dedicated to studying as Razvarr. They did their homework. They tried in class. They listened. I was impressed with their diligence. Their parents asked me weekly how their children were doing and how they could do better. These kids were driven. As a teacher, I loved it.

Three years after Raz was in my class, six Kawidtodian students entered my class. I was very happy to have them. The trouble came from somewhere else.

That year, the Pumn announced to the country that 13 Zan men had been caught spying. As a danger to the country, they were tried by a national security court and sentenced to hang in Shalhak, in a public square.

The United States lodged a protest with the United Nations. So did the French. The British had some business interests in the country, so they didn't say anything. Amnesty International put out a press release.

Anyway, none of that mattered. The whole thing was a scam. The Zans in the country, a tiny minority, were more like prisoners than actual citizens. Their power to spy on anything was about nil.

The New York Times suggested in an editorial that perhaps the government was trying to distract the country from the poor state of the economy. And, indeed, in conjunction with the spy story was the news that the Kawidtodian economy's gross national product had dropped for the fifth year in a row. The state increased subsidies for bread, putting the country further into debt.

The public hanging went through. A picture of the men's feet, cuffed at the ankles, hanging suspended several feet in the air, made it onto page seven of the Times.

I studied the picture over breakfast in my apartment in Corona. Kawidtodians stood all around, looking at them like dead animals. It made me sick.

My father showed up in my classroom after school two days later. Razvarr had come by to say hello. We were just getting into a conversation when my father walked in.

My father took one look at the boy's bald head and glared with eyes that threatened death. To say that Razvarr sprinted out of my classroom would be an understatement. He flew.

"How'd you get in here?"

"I told the security guard I was your father."

"And she let you in?"

"I showed her my driver's license, then I had to go to the office."

"Why are you here?"

I was trying to put up a new bulletin board. My father sat down in my chair at my desk.

"I want you to resign."

"What?"

"You read the news?"

"Of course. It was horrifying."

"I told you, these people will never leave us alone. They hate us. They'll always hate us."

"These kids in here, they have nothing to do with it. They're good kids."

"It's in their holy books, their blood. They'll turn on you. You'll see."

"The people who are here, they're trying to become something else."

"It's all an act. They're trying to take over this country. And when they do, we'll all be dead. They'll herd us into prison camps like sheep."

I didn't say anything.

My father walked over to me as I was stapling a border to the cork on the wall.

"Look at this."

It was a black and white picture, about five inches by seven inches, of an unsmiling man, set against the mountains, rising up high above the land, jagged and unforgiving. I knew the mountains. From the books. The man was squinting into the sun.

"Who is it?"

"This is one of your cousins. He was hanged with the other men. They said he was a spy. He didn't do anything. He was just a small business man."

I tested my father by asking: "What's his name?"

"Kiva."

This victim had a name. That froze me. He got to me. I should have run away then. But, just like with the tire iron, I didn't. I stayed.

"I've arranged a job for you at the Zan religious school. It pays the same as this job. You'll be the highest paid teacher in the school. And there's a good benefits package. You'll get the same health care and savings plan as the Spaama."

"I'm finishing out the year here. I have an obligation."

He stared at me. But he let the ice in his eyes melt a little.

"But then you'll go?"

I breathed in a huge amount of air. But I still felt like I was suffocating.

"Yeah."

"Okay. We want you to come home. Your mother misses you. We all do. It's been too many years. Your uncles ask about you all the time."

My uncles. My friends. Memories of the summer camp.

I surrendered.

I didn't tell Cookie the whole story. Just enough to get into an argument.

"Dad was upset about me teaching the Squids."

"Him again."

"He said it wasn't right. We shouldn't mix."

"There couldn't have been that many back then. Not like now."

"Most of the kids were Spanish. But there were always four or five Squid children in my classes."

"Well, how'd you feel about it?"

"I tried to do my job."

"Didn't you teach second grade or something like that? They're just kids. Kids are the same all over."

"Not when they hate you."

"C'mon, Akeyde. That's crazy."

"Their parents teach them. It's in their holy books, their blood."

"You should try being an American. It's easier."

"I tried. It didn't work out. I've got to go."

He took a deep breath.

"Akeyde, before you do that, just let me say that if you think you're doing something good or noble, reconsider. Your father is blinded by hate. And he's got your head so far up your ass that all you can see is shit."

That stung, badly, but I wasn't quite sure I understood.

"What do you mean?"

"Alright, you need to have it explained to you in clear terms. Blowing up other people and yourself isn't going to accomplish anything but a world of pain. Do you really want to do that?"

I looked away from him and out the window of this false world of silent trees and long, grassy lawns.

"It's not a question of what I want, Cookie."

"Jesus H. Christ. Don't be too sure about what God wants."

"You own a strip club."

"So what?"

"I have to go."

He took me by the shoulders and squeezed so hard that it hurt, then looked hard in my eyes to try to find an opening.

"Look at this another way. If you succeed— and I hope like hell you don't—this is going to be bad for the Zans. Just think about that. People are going to point their fingers at us. Not you, you'll be gone, but us, the whole fucking tribe. And we don't need that. We've already gone through a lot of crap."

That stopped me short for a minute.

"We have to fight back, or we will be like lambs going to the slaughter. It will be 1908 all over again."

"Oh, don't bring that up! That was another country, Akeyde, another world, more than a hundred years ago."

"Not to me, it's not. If you look at our history, you know they keep coming after us. They never stop. They won't stop unless we do something. We have to show them that their aggression has a cost. We can't lay down for them to cut our throats."

"I'd say don't bother coming back here ever again, but if you really do what you say you're going to do, you won't be coming back here or any other place."

Break-Through

(Razvarr Abatut)

I wrote an email back to Necu.

"Stop whining about getting arrested. Are you in or out? If you're in, you need to try to find the explosives and the phones that were purchased. They cost a lot of money. You have to find a way to get into Debyl's house and see if they're still there.

"If you can't do that, I don't ever want to talk to you again."

I didn't hear back for hours, despite constantly checking my email every 15 minutes.

Six hours later I finally got an email. Necu wrote a short, curt note:

"I will try."

I was a little dissatisfied that he didn't write, "I will do," but he was starting to show a little more guts. I thought I might have a real soldier.

Going Home

(Akeyde Kletser)

When I walked into the apartment, there was a strange book on the nightstand. I walked over immediately to pick it up.

The title stated, "The Akeyde Fraud," by some man I hadn't heard of. I looked at the back cover. The man was a professor at a university in Michigan. He had written a book whose main premise was that the book Lhokem had given me all those years ago contained a complete fabrication about the bones that were found by James Dale.

That book, "Ancient History of Zandria," discussed at length whether the sacrifice of Akeyde by his father 5,800 years ago had actually happened.

I read the summary on the back cover. The professor, a man named Finger, stated that the chest bone with the knife wound that Professor Dale found was not 5,800 years old. He was able to get the skeleton from a British museum after Dale had passed away.

Analyzing the skeleton through carbon dating, the skeleton was found to be about 400 years old, Professor Finger claimed. The skeleton was a fake. He was challenging the whole premise of our religion.

Finger also tried to debunk the Zan "little miracle" of how Professor Dale had gotten into Kawidtodia 30 years ago. There was no divine intervention, Finger said. Dale had bribed regional government officials with convincing amounts of British pound sterling, which he had conned from his senile old father, a very wealthy man.

I wondered how someone could have gotten into the apartment. Cookie must have had one of his people put the book here. He was like a shadow of my father, with people everywhere.

I wondered if Cookie would report me to the police. His disapproval of my plan was a little black bird fluttering inside my heart. Would he call the authorities? Was he going to try to stop me? Would he give me the freedom to do what I needed to do?

Or was he too afraid of my father to do anything about me?

Reading the back cover of "The Akeyde Fraud" for those few minutes was enough for me. I threw the book into the gray metal trash can next to the bed. I didn't need that kind of filth in my home.

I briefly considered how I could kill Professor Finger, but that would be a diversion from my main mission. I decided I would build a bomb vest for the Temple on 79th Street and 3rd Avenue, blow myself up, then find Professor Finger and blow him up too.

For my new jobs, I decided to build two new suicide vests. Each one would have a wireless connection. That way I could avoid the problem with the wire that I had on the streets of the neighborhood, when I was surrounded by all those Squids and pushed the detonator, with no result.

I could have been in heaven, right next to God, if the detonator had just worked. A faulty electrical wire had prevented my dream from occurring.

That wouldn't happen this time. Vests with a wireless connection would be the way to go. I would use a detonator that I could hold in my hand and push without any kind of wire connecting it to the vest.

There would be some research required, but Vehktre had given me web sites and links and a credit card to do the original blessed work. I would call on these sacred tools again to help me finish the job the right way this time.

When I started work at the Zan religious school, after leaving the public school system, I wasn't a believer. It took years for me to reestablish my faith.

Teaching our tribe's history to my little second and third grade Zan kids helped. And being surrounded by all these Zan religious teachers and the Spaama too.

I missed meeting all the different types of people you see in a public school, the mix of cultures that is this country, but my father was right in a way. The Zan school, the *Basmadrosh* were woven into me and everyone treated me like an old friend. I moved in with my parents, which was good. It felt familiar and comfortable. My Mom was in the front office every day.

But I couldn't get a date.

I tried. I did. Some of the teachers at the school were very attractive to me, despite their head scarves and brown dresses and tights.

They wore their head scarves back a little on their heads, so you could see about an inch of scalp but no more. The back of the head scarf was folded into a triangle, so you could see the fall of their hair reach down to their necks and shoulders.

I made friends with virtually all the teachers in our little school. There were about 20 in all. Most of them were female. We had grade meetings and faculty meetings. I stared at them, waved hello, talked about the school's curriculum, students' progress, the good kids and the troublesome ones.

Sometimes groups of us would go out together for coffee, or dinner, about once or twice a month.

There was one woman, her name was Michy. She was about 23 years old, just out of the Zan college I had rejected. At our dinners, I would look at her brown eyes, so deep, and her full, round lips. They were gorgeous even without lipstick. I didn't even listen to whatever she was talking about, just nodded my head and agreed with her so I could keep looking at her.

And I could see, even with a brown tent dress on her, swallowing her, that there was a nice, shapely body under all that fabric.

After several months in the new school, in March, I asked her out at the end of the week. Friday afternoon.

"You want to go get some coffee?"

"Sure. That sounds good. I'll ask the other girls."

"No, I mean. Just you."

"You want me to go alone?"

I wasn't prepared for her little joke and stammered out a reply. "No, I mean, you and me together. Alone together."

She looked at me, searching my face for several moments, even though it had no answers for her. I looked at her the wrong way. At least I think I did. I didn't smile, or give her any hint of warmth, just my own searching hunger. Her eyes were so beautiful.

"I can't, Akeyde." She looked away.

"Why?"

"I just can't." Then she walked down the hall, her brown head scarf marching away a little unsteadily. Just like Tina.

I spent all Friday night thinking about it, and for the next few weeks. I was able to teach my classes, but beyond that I lived in a fog of rejection, regret and confusion. I wondered if she didn't want me because of my thick glasses, or the scar on my forehead, or my sometimes-tearing eye.

Whenever I saw Michy in the hallways, I looked away. I tried to ignore her, and she me.

The worst part of it was that I felt I deserved to be in so much pain. I wasn't good enough to be happy.

My uncle Narish invited me over for dinner a month later and I took the invitation like a drowning man grabs onto a life preserver in a roiling sea.

He sat at the head of his long table and I sat next to him. He made chicken cutlets and spaghetti, my favorite. His wife, the new one after my aunt died, was not so new anymore. Lines ran down her face around the mouth. Her eyes looked tired. She told Narish she wanted to eat by herself and watch TV.

"Sure," said Narish. Which was just fine with me. I didn't like her much.

So the dinner was just me and my favorite uncle, the clown who had dipped his beard in a glass of wine during one of those idyllic summers at our camp in the Adirondacks, the land of mountains and morning mists and lakes and streams. Even to say the name "Adirondacks" is to transport yourself halfway to magic land.

We talked about the old times.

"Why don't you come back to camp this summer? You're a teacher, you have the summer off. You could be a counselor."

"Are you going to be there?"

"No. I have a lot of business in the city now. I'm too busy."

"I don't know, Narish. I feel like I need to grow up."

"What do you mean?"

"I want a girlfriend."

He sat back over the ruins of his meal and drank some wine.

"Ah, yes, I heard about that."

"Heard about what?"

"You asked out that girl, what was her name?"

"Michy."

"Yeah. She can't go out with you."

"That's what she said!"

"Look, nobody can, if they're a good Zan."

"Why not?"

"Because in the holy books, Akeyde never had a woman."

"What?"

"Come on, Akeyde, you should know this. If a girl wants to be an orthodox Zan, she can't date you. It's not sanctioned."

"Oh, my God."

"Exactly. Michy may actually like you, but she was just following the law."

He paused to look at my miserable face.

"You could date somebody who's not a Zan. That way you don't have to worry about the law."

"But what if I wanted to marry her?"

Narish smiled. "You know your father wouldn't accept that."

The trap that my father had set for me was now very plain. And it shook me.

I picked up a butter knife and smashed the butt-end into his table.

"Hey! Don't mess up my beautiful table!"

I ignored that.

"Then what am I going to do?"

"Your father has plans for you. You are Akeyde. That's a very special thing."

"I'm a person too. I want things."

"I know Akeyde. But you are a part of God. And you have a special role to play."

"I know about the reincarnations and all that. But I don't see what you all want me to do now."

"Your father will train you to do something good, something great for our people. To be something more than just a human being, with all the little wants and needs that come along with that."

I didn't like any of this.

"When is this supposed to happen?"

"When your father thinks the time is right."

"Great."

After my request to go out with Michy was turned down, the invitations to group dinners and coffees ended. It was clear she had put the word out that she was uncomfortable with me.

I felt the coldness around me and tried to get on. I briefly considered going back to the public school system.

Instead I threw myself into studying with the Spaama. I worked on reading through all the holy books and the commentaries on the holy books and the commentaries on the commentaries. After school, three nights a week, I took courses at the Zan college, even though the whole area still smelled of automobile grease and slaughtered animal parts.

The weekends were the toughest to get through. I would often go to Manhattan, by myself, to go to the movies.

My favorite types of pictures were romances. I saw a movie about a British girl who was attracted to a con man of sorts. She smoked and was overweight. From my seat in the back of the theatre, I studied her face, which seemed a mile high. It was puffy and her blonde hair was frazzled. And I wanted her. She ended up with a nice lawyer and they kissed on the street at the end.

Another one I liked was a movie about a man and a woman who got together, then were driven away from each other by her mother. Somehow they found each other again after seven years and kissed on the shore of a lake in a driving rainstorm. I was very moved.

There was another one where a woman was going to be killed by a car crossing a street. But her boyfriend traveled back in time to save her. After he saved her, he looked at her face like she was the most beautiful woman in the world. I agreed. I wanted to kiss her. He did.

After the movie was over, I wandered around Manhattan. I walked up and down the avenues, north and south and watched things happen around me. Couples walked hand in hand to dinner or to go home. Girls walked in groups to bars. I stared at them as they laughed, full-throated, on the street. I fell in love with not a few of them.

If I looked up, I could see the fourth or fifth floor windows of apartment buildings across the side of the avenue from which I was walking. They looked to be the size of postage stamps from where I was. But I looked into those little postage stamps and saw men and women kissing in somebody's bedroom. Sometimes the woman would have her back to the window, no shirt on, just a black brassiere. The man and the woman gripped each other with a passion that I had only known once, with Tina.

After hours of wandering and staring at women and looking at the love going on in those apartments, I would get on the subway and head home to Queens, to my room in my parents' house, stupefied by the life I had let my father choose for me.

The years spread out on me.

I was close to falling off a cliff and I knew it, but I didn't know how to stop myself. Every day I walked on the knife's edge.

I thought about seeing a psychologist, or just walking into the mental ward at the local hospital and asking to be committed. That was the more comforting choice actually. I wanted somebody to take care of me, tell me when to eat, when to go to sleep, when to take a walk.

Six months ago, a man came to meet my father in his house one night. I let him in. He studied me for a few seconds. I was uncomfortable and looked away.

The man asked where my father was. I walked him into the den. My father thanked me, then closed the double doors to the den.

I laid down on the couch in the living room and watched a medical show. The female doctors were talking about a particular male doctor who was very handsome and charming. I wished I were that man.

After an hour, my father opened the doors to his den. He called out, "Akeyde!"

"Yeah, Dad?"

"Come here."

"Okay."

I went to the room. My father sat down in his chair. The man was already sitting in a chair next to him. I stood in front of them.

They looked at me, as if in the process of appraising the dollar value of a statue.

"What?"

"Akeyde, you know how hard things have been for the Zans?"

"I know the history inside and out, Dad."

"Yes, yes, of course. The Squids are moving into America. And they won't tolerate us. Five years ago, they shot a Spaama in Los Angeles. The shooters were never found. I don't even think the police tried to find them."

I nodded my head.

"Then there was the firebombing of our small assembly house in Chicago last year. Thank God nobody got hurt. They blew out the doors, but that was it.

"And yesterday, a Zan woman was shot and killed in her home in Maryland, Bethesda. The man shot her through a window while she was making dinner for her family."

"Was it a Squid?"

"Of course it was."

"They arrested the man?"

"They're still looking for him."

I took in a deep breath. My father could have recited other stories about violence against the Zans. It was an all-too-familiar recitation. The pain of the years, the centuries of killings, was almost too much for me to bear.

"Listen, Akeyde. I have decided that you are ready for your mission."

This changed me.

"Yeah?"

"It's time. We need somebody to fight for us, to fight back."

"What do I do?"

My father gestured at our visitor. "This is Vehktre."

I went to shake his hand. "Hi."

He gave me a slight smile. "Hello."

"Vehktre is going to be your teacher. He's going to train you for something, something important."

At last I would have some guidance. Somebody would tell me what to do.

The Soldier

(Razvarr Abatut)

Necu emailed me a progress report.

He had walked through the tight little streets snaking over the hills of the city to find Debyl's house. The houses blocked out the sun most of the day. The country lived inside shadows.

Debyl's house was at the end of an alley. His parents were dead and he got the place. He might be dead too. No one could get in to look at him in the Divinnot detention center, so no one tried. Even to stand outside the place brought suspicion upon you. Bribes to the guards could buy off such suspicions, however, and maybe bring you word of your son, husband, wife, brother, sister, cousin.

The street was empty. Most people were in the main square or in the temples for religious celebrations leading up to Cainta.

The religious police walked around in the neighborhoods. They were looking for people not in temple. Or who hadn't shaved their head in four or five days. If they didn't find anybody, they might decide to break into someone's house. Either they said they thought someone wasn't displaying the proper number of pictures and statues of Kawidtod, or they thought someone was staying home when they should have been in temple.

They usually ended up turning over the house and stealing what little money or goods are there. Computers could be sold for a good price. Televisions were good too. Sometimes they took clothing and sold it to a dealer in the market.

The front door was plywood, painted blue and white, like all houses of faith. Necu tried to push it in. Stupid. The door was attached to the wall in some way. He could have tried to kick it in with his foot. That would be a lot of noise. The neighborhood was too silent. Necu walked around the corner. There the alley ended, giving out to a series of dusty hills that grew bigger and bigger, until they walked their way to those foreboding mountains of stone.

The house was very small, maybe perhaps the size of a tool shed in Bulgaria. There was a single window, standing at about the height of a man. Necu took a crate in the dusty field nearby and stood on it to get on the level of the window. In the folds of his shirt was a knife. Necu tried to trace the outline of the window with the knife, trying to find an opening.

Paint on the window sprinkled out and away; some crusted up on Necu's face. He was rained on with blue chips. This worried him, as the paint probably contained lead.

Then he hit gold. The hinge was very rusty and Necu was able to cut away a little part of it with the knife. He punched away the rest of the hinge with the butt of the knife. Then he did the same thing with the second hinge. Rust nuggets hit his face. He would have to clean himself up later.

Necu pulled at the frame of the window and the wood crumbled. The glass facing fell out when he took the frame off. This frightened him, but the glass hit the dust on the ground and the breakage wasn't loud.

The remains of the window scraped Necu's chest as he crawled into the house. The house had been ripped apart by the police already. And yet they were careful to put the door back in place to cover their little riot. They didn't want to arouse the interest of the neighborhood.

Necu went through everything they had torn up. My heart exploded in my chest as I read the terrible news.

Drawers, kitchen cabinets, beds, storage boxes had all been collapsed. Necu was trying to get in and get out, but he also wanted our goods. He did not want to attract people coming home from the temples.

His search turned up nothing. He took out all the dishes in the kitchen cabinets. Maybe Debyl had hid the phones behind them. He looked through a small city of tea cups.

He told me he was very crazy. "I wanted to throw all the dishes on the peeling kitchen floor, but that kind of noise might be bad. Attract attention," he wrote.

So Necu sat on the torn-up couch to try to think beyond his panicked thoughts. He wondered what he would tell me if he could not find the phones and the bombs. He wrote that he was afraid to make that kind of report to me. I liked his fear. I would need it.

Frustrated, Necu threw all the torn up pillows off the couch. Then he flipped over the skeleton of the couch so it was upside down.

That accomplished nothing. He pushed the couch away from the wall. He thought maybe Debyl had hidden the goods inside the frame of the house. The walls were made of a cheap paneling which covered over concrete. Once he ripped off the panels, he discovered there was no frame to rip into. The house was simply a concrete box.

Necu sat on the floor of the ravaged house. He scanned the room, desperate for any type of clue. He sat there for about a half hour and wondered if he would have to go to Mintal's house and look there too. Maybe he had misunderstood Debyl. Maybe they had hidden the goods in Mintal's house, about three streets away. He didn't want to have to break into two houses in the same neighborhood.

Then he went through the house again. He moved the oven away from the wall, with lots of sweat and grunting. Nothing. He unplugged the refrigerator, a cheap 1970s job from Russia, and put his weight behind it. The refrigerator wasn't hiding anything.

He went to through the closets again, trying to see if Debyl had hidden anything behind clothes or bins. It was entirely possible that the police had found the phones and the C4 and that we would have to start over. Or that Necu would quit because our project had been compromised. My heart kept sinking as I read his email.

He went to the bathroom. The light had been left on by the police. The toilet was open. It smelled badly and was full of dark yellow urine. Just another calling card from the police, in case Debyl ever returned.

Necu flushed the toilet. He was that polite.

With nothing else left to do, the boy got on his knees in front of the toilet and prayed that he would find our goods.

"Please, dear God, help me. Help me."

It was pretty pathetic.

He looked at the ceiling and noticed that the concrete above the toilet was a different color than the rest of the bathroom ceiling. He went through the closets to try to find something to break open the ceiling.

A broom might do the trick, he thought. But it didn't do much. He went searching again, and found a crowbar in another closet.

Necu battered the ceiling above the toilet with the crowbar. Chips and chunks of newly installed concrete rained down on his head and cut his bare skull. A few plopped into the toilet. A brick wrapped in tinfoil fell into the toilet.

Necu retrieved it, shook the water off the brick and set it to the side of the floor. Then he closed the lid of the toilet. He went back to jabbing at the ceiling. A chunk came down and hit the lid, followed by five bricks in tinfoil.

He opened up the tinfoil. Inside were several neat bricks, off-white in color, with the texture of modeling clay. Our explosives.

Necu didn't find the cell phones. But at least we had the C4.

He put the bricks in his backpack, adjusted his balance, and walked out the door, into the shadow of the street.

Now all we needed was to figure out where to put the bricks inside the Temple. Easy.

What if we made Necu into a suicide bomber? He could strap the C4 to his body and walk in to the Temple on a big religious day and just blow himself up.

He could kill dozens of people gathering for services in the Temple Square, which would make the revolutionary statement we needed. But all those bodies might block the impact of the explosion on the pillars. We wouldn't do as much damage to the state as I wanted.

I had a flash of inspiration. Necu seemed good at ingratiating himself with people. What if he continued to pose as a religious student who was studying the religious symbols in the Temple Square? He could go to the Temple managers and talk them into letting him do research on the pillars.

Perhaps he could photograph the pillars as part of a research project. Not with a digital camera, nothing small. It would have to be big. Really big.

The light in the Temple Square is unreliable. The Temple faces north, so the sun comes into that part of the building at a low angle in the morning. The light is fine for walking through the square, but the artwork on the upper parts of the pillars is hard to see. You have to squint to get a good look at the top half of the pillars at that time of day. It's bad light for taking photographs.

So, if you wanted to take good, quality photographs of the symbols on the pillars, perhaps you would need a lot of light. Big lights. Flood lights, for instance.

If you needed flood lights, you would also require tripods to hold up the lights. Flood lights are large, as big as somebody's face. Maybe Necu and his team could lay the C4 into the floods, with detonators.

We could explain why we needed the flood lights for the project, with a research proposal for the Temple authorities.

The New Girl

(Akeyde Kletser)

I had a dream that I was walking up a hill through dense and dark foliage. Then there was a path that opened to me. I came upon my old camp. Happy to be at my second home, I met a girl I didn't know but who said she knew me. She said, "Call me Tina." We ended up lying down together, with her on top of me. I struggled to hold on to her, because there was a hole under me and my buttocks were in constant danger of falling through it. We were discovered by some children playing. They arrested us and planned to take me to my father.

That dream stayed with me as I visited various underground weapons dealers over the next few days to purchase bomb materials to make a new Tina. I dismissed the idea of making two vests, the inspiration that came to me the other night because of Professor Finger's false accusations. I cannot kill myself twice, I realized, even though I would explode my little body thousands of times for Him.

I had to work quickly. The Kawidtodian festival of Cainta was coming up and I needed to be there.

The idea of falling through a hole seemed terrifying yet appealing at the same time. I was full of thoughts. Too many thoughts. Maybe the only way to get rid of them was to dive into a hole, like a rabbit.

It was much easier to find the explosives than to find the right kind of vest to hold them. Vehktre had purchased the first vest and he didn't tell me where he got it. But when my father introduced Vehktre to help train me, he told us about a man who dealt in explosives, a Zan. I went to his house and he was eager to sell to me.

I went all over central Queens and could not find the right kind of package for the charges.

Since I hated shopping, this was a particularly onerous piece of business. I visited half a dozen stores and came up empty. I tried on four or five vests in each store. None of them had the long, deep pockets I needed.

As distasteful as I found it, I forced myself to go to the Kawidtodian district in northern Queens and came up empty there as well. I did find a new blue and white windbreaker there but was unable to find a vest. So I decided to go to a street in lower Manhattan to see what I could find. Washington Street had dozens of clothing shops clustered together. If they didn't have the right kind of vest, no one would.

I hauled myself onto the subway and made the trip to Manhattan.

I had to remind myself that God requires many things from us. He was not here for our entertainment. We were here to serve Him.

Washington Street was a mix of many cultures, not as bad as Jackson Heights, but a little too crazy quilt for my taste. There were Zan, Chinese, Jewish, Italian, and Arab vendors, with a few Kawidtodian shops thrown in. I didn't discriminate. I went into any store that looked like it sold vests.

But nobody had the right kind of vest. It was very disheartening. I wasted an entire afternoon on this venture. And time was running short. Cainta was upon us. I bought some cigarettes, even though I didn't smoke. Why not start, right?

So I went home to my apartment and worked more on building and packing the explosives. They looked like fat candy bars. I slipped some C4 into the bomb packages. That would definitely help to kill more people.

After a few hours, I got tired. I ordered in some Chinese food then watched a rerun of a police procedural show where they liked to get into the bodies of dead people. You could see the inside of brains and hearts and other organs. I lit a cigarette and tried to smoke it. This time the tobacco blazed, but I couldn't figure out how to draw the smoke into my mouth.

Then I watched a cable show about commercial fishing in the Arctic. It was cool to see the men's arms or hands get speared with giant hooks. In one part, a man's ribs were crushed by a giant iron cage that swung across the deck. The danger the fishermen faced gave me a big adrenaline rush. I got so excited I couldn't go to sleep for hours. I spent most of the night pacing up and down my apartment.

After a few hours of sleep, I woke up. Sleep just didn't feel right with this mission I was set to do.

I thought more about the fishing show and it gave me an idea. I went online to see if I could find the right kind of vest. I looked at stores that sold vests for fly fishing.

An outdoor store on 19th Street and Broadway in Manhattan sold a fishing vest that might work. I was so excited, I got dressed and took the subway to the store at six o'clock in the morning.

The store didn't open until 10 o'clock. These people just didn't have any sense of urgency.

I went to a diner a few blocks down from the store. It was on University Place. I bought a newspaper and ordered French toast, scrambled eggs, and two glasses of orange juice. My eating was growing careless and I was gaining weight. I had a devil-may-care feeling about it. I mean, why not enjoy the little time I had left?

As I waited for my food to arrive, I read in the newspaper that the government in Kawidtodia was cracking down on dissident activity again. It upset me because the more they repress the people there, the more eager many are to leave. And most of these people come here, to New York. They are like little rats that infest everything they touch with disease.

When my food came, I tried to put aside my thoughts about the Kawidtodians. I read an article about the restoration of an old, 100-year old Zan assembly house on the Lower East Side, near Washington Street. That cheered me up and I was able to eat my whole breakfast, and an extra blueberry muffin I ordered later.

I thought about Uncle Cookie. He was here and gone from my life very quickly. He was a wicked man in many ways, the strip club and the pornography he had at home being the prime examples. I wondered if he would go to hell.

It made me sad. He was pretty much the only friend I'd had in a long time. I couldn't get it straight in my own mind—he was sinful, yet he was nice to me. Something didn't feel right.

After breakfast, I walked up to Broadway to the store. It still wasn't open. I looked at my watch. It was nine o'clock. I walked through the streets near the store. The buildings here used to be factories and printing shops and warehouses. They dated from early in the last century and were about six to ten stories tall.

The sun was beginning to burn through everything and the heat blazed through the sky like it was aiming for my head. But Manhattan had so many tall buildings that you could find shadows on every block. As I wandered, I crossed the streets away from the line of the sun to get to the shadows.

"I'm like Dracula," I joked to myself. "Always looking for darkness."

Dracula means "devil" in Romanian. That word would have been a good addition to the Zan language. We could have used it when we were talking about the Kawidtodians.

When 10 o'clock rolled around, I walked briskly to the store. On the main floor, I saw kayaks and hiking boots and fishing vests.

I tried on several. The vests all came in tan colors. I didn't like that, but the pockets were deep and wide and long.

I made the purchase of a vest and took the subway back to my apartment in Queens. I felt very good about accomplishing this part of the mission.

"I'm going fishing for Squid pigs," I joked to myself.

At home, I tested the trigger on the detonator with the wires that would be placed on the explosives. Each bomb would have a small wire that connected to a main wire. The main wire, a thick coil, ended at a square terminal, which had a plastic box with a tiny light bulb. This would theoretically light up when the detonator was pushed.

Once I had the baby wires looped into the mother wire, I pushed the trigger. The terminal on the mother wire lit up with hope. Here was a little piece of God shining through the night.

Next, the explosives, with their wiring, had to be inserted into the pockets of the vest, a precise task.

This was accomplished after several hours of work. The bomb was primed. Everything was ready. I had a new Tina.

Yet I felt a great disquiet. I looked out the window at the street. Bright orange lights burned in the night. Cars ripped through the neighborhood, running stop signs, playing obscenely loud music, yelling about guns and killing people and drinking and getting naked girls in bed.

They bothered me, but what disturbed me even more was the quiet when they tore off. No one was walking on the street. The asphalt just sat there under the orange light. It was a picture with no movement, no thought. I wondered if I would be like this when I was dead. I wondered if my life had mattered to anyone.

It was a sick feeling. I wanted to tear myself away from the window, but I had nowhere else to go.

The Building Manager

(Necu Brav)

Each of the four pillars in the Blue and White Temple display the primary elements of our religion:

- Humility before God
- Justice for the oppressed
- Judgment of your thoughts and deeds
- War forever against the Zan religion

The pillars have details illustrating these ideas of the Kawidtodian theology. The building manager of the temple showed me around. I thought this would not arouse any suspicion from the religious police, even though the tension in the city was so high. Summer and dust from the mountains was blowing in big winds through our old capital. The heat sagged on us.

People were keeping their heads and voices down. Nobody smiled. The newspapers without government backing were closed. The Pumn did not speak to the nation on TV. He did not need to.

The temple walls were white, laced with blue striped ceramic tiles running through the granite. The ceiling was a great dome. The walls were painted with pictures of Kawidtod's struggles and his victories. The temple paintings, along with the daily prayers, were designed to make you feel as if you were there when Kawidtod received the word of God and renew your feeling for his vision.

When I told the building manager that I wanted to write a paper on the temple, which I was hoping would get me into a religious college, he was impressed. The man's name was Bava Creder. He took me on a tour through the building.

I pulled him toward the four pillars and asked if my friends and I could set up tripods with flood lights placed near the pillars and the walls and take pictures of the details of the paintings on the pillars in the coming weeks, or even months, to allow for approvals from the Temple authorities. He said he would consider it. People had done it a few decades ago for academic studies. But no one had done this in recent times, he said.

A Visitor

(Akeyde Kletser)

There was a knock on the door. I didn't want to answer it. I had been standing at the window for many minutes and felt rooted to the spot.

Then three quick knocks. I turned from the window to face the door and looked at it.

Whoever was standing on the other side of the door decided to start slamming his fists into it. The door shook, which I didn't think was possible. It was metal and quite strong, like a rock.

A sense of fear rose up in me like stomach acid. I was frozen with anxiety.

The door banged and banged again.

Finally, I walked to it and asked, "Who's there?"

A dry, dead voice came from the other side.

"Open up."

I knew who it was then. I turned the lock and unbolted the spring.

Vehktre had come to visit. He was still wearing his purple and yellow windbreaker despite the heat clinging to the neighborhood like a parasite.

He stood next to the metal door. I didn't invite him to come any further and he didn't ask.

Vehktre didn't say anything, like he was waiting for me to speak.

"I want it to be over quickly. I want to be released from all my commitments."

"Tomorrow, Akeyde. I envy you. You will be in a better place, next to God."

I wasn't so sure.

"I'm scared."

He did nothing but nod his head slightly.

"Do you know a man attacked me at the train station?"

"I heard about it," he said dryly.

"My father sent him, I'm sure."

"You know who you are. You need to be sacrificed one way or the other."

I tried to absorb this. Swallowing hard I made myself say, "Can you find the man and tell him to not try to kill me so I can blow myself up?"

He changed the subject.

"I have decided to come with you to the Temple. We will go to the city together."

"Okay."

He pointed to a couch across the room from the bed, facing the television.

"I'll sleep over there."

He took off his purple and yellow windbreaker and button-down shirt. Underneath was a tee-shirt. His chest was all muscle. I wished I was that strong.

He put his body on the couch and kept his eyes open.

I turned off the lights.

Then he said, "Goodnight, brother."

"Goodnight."

The next and last word came out of my mouth somewhat slowly and unsteadily. "Brother."

Repentance Day

(Razvarr Abatut)

Cainta, our day of repentance, came with its boring predictability. We were supposed to humble ourselves before God. I didn't see the need to do this anymore.

My bald, skinny immigrant parents were planning to go to the temple at 3rd Avenue and 79th Street again.

"Why don't you go to the temple here in our neighborhood?" I asked mother.

"Because Queens isn't good enough for your father. He wants to sit with the rich people, the big shots."

Mom and Dad asked me to go. I begged off. They looked disappointed but said nothing.

Then my mother went to the bathroom. Mom took several minutes.

"Matca, let's go!" Dad shouted through the door of the bathroom.

"Holy Kawidtod! Can't you give your wife a little time, Binele?"

"We're going to be late for the service."

"They always start late anyway."

"The seats, Matca. We won't be able to get good seats."

"Why do you need to see anything? You're supposed to be talking to God."

"If we're closer to the Scena, I feel I'm closer to Him." The Scena is the front platform of the temple.

"You are an idiot husband."

"You are a double idiot."

All this was taking place through the bathroom door. This is what I had to put up with every day.

The bathroom door opened. My mother came out, her head in the air as if she were a queen.

"You shouldn't talk to your wife like that."

"You talk to me like that all the time."

"It's different if I do it. You need help. I don't."

She turned to me. "Razvarr, you want to go with us?"

"You asked me already."

"So, to ask again, it does not hurt."

I pointed to the bathroom. "I would be delighted to spend more time with you two, but I've got things to do."

"All you do is play on that computer."

"I'm working."

"On what? You graduated and you don't have a job." She turned on my father. "It's your fault. I told you to get him something else."

"I thought he would like a computer."

"He does. Too much!"

Since my father got tortured by the secret police, you would think Mom would be kinder to him. But she has gotten harder on him—she blames him for what happened.

"You're going to be late for the service," I said.

As they walked out the door, I said, "Goodbye, coneheads," but they didn't hear me.

I thought about my father's shuffling limp and the way his eyes seemed to pull down toward his cheeks like an unhappy dog.

He spent his days in a long but very narrow news store. One person can barely fit into the door. I'm not kidding. You would think he would have built a wider entrance, but it's as if he wanted to let America inside, but only a little bit at a time.

The store sold the New York Times, the Daily News, the New York Post, and a number of Kawidtodian language papers, which were published in the city. He also sold cigarettes, popular magazines, and lots of pornography. The Kawidtodian religious authorities back home would not too have been too happy about this, but my father had escaped their grasp. He had thrown over his spiritual feelings in this area for the sake of money.

There was candy, too, from Three Musketeers and Hershey Bars to Airheads and Starburst. Despite all that noise, the store made most of its money from selling lottery tickets.

My Uncle Arak helped set him up with the business. We borrowed money from our extended family. Immigrant Kawidtodian families often pooled their money to get started here. Once you had gotten a business up and running, you were asked to contribute cash to the family pot. There were also seemingly hundreds of family members who could and wanted to work for the businesses we started. Dad worked from 7 am to 8 pm, almost every night. On this day, he had one of our not very religious cousins filling in.

Just like Mom did, Dad asked if I would work in the store while I thought about what I wanted to do after I had graduated. I said I just wanted to relax for the summer and figure out what to do.

I thought about doing work on the project, but I was so exhausted from dealing with my parents that I decided to take a nap.

"Hey, wake up!"

My mother pinched my cheeks together like you would a baby. She had come back for me. How touching.

"What now?"

"Come with us, Razvarr."

"A 20-year-old man should not have to go to temple with his parents."

"We'll buy you ice cream." Talking to me like I'm a four-year-old.

"No. You gonna hit me now, like last time?"

"Maybe we will take your computer away. And those other machines sitting near it, doing God knows what."

My only weak spot. "How are you possibly going to do that?"

"Maybe I will ask your Uncle Arak to come and give it a virus."

I laughed. "You can't just walk up to a computer and give it a virus. Good thinking, Mom!'

"Then I will cut all the wires while you are sleeping. You sleep a lot. You cannot possibly protect your precious machines while you are sleeping."

I was tired of these games.

"You were on your way to Manhattan. What happened?"

"I cannot leave you alone, Razvarr."

I had to concede that was true.

"So?"

"It doesn't feel right going to temple without you."

"You managed during the two summers I worked at the college upstate."

Those two summers I had worked on a school economic development project for the county, which mostly consisted of gathering data on why nobody wanted to live there anymore.

"That was different. You were away. You were getting an education. Or so I was thinking."

"I got enough of an education to steer clear of you."

"You have been very much successful at it too."

"I'll move out."

"Hah! You would need to get a job. Please come with us." She was wheedling now and she knew it.

I got angry, kicked off my sheet. "This is IT! I'm coming with you and that's it, the final time. Then I'm moving out."

Mother actually giggled. "Good luck on that. Now, get dressed. Your underwear is dirty."

"How would you know?"

"I can see it from here."

I was exasperated beyond measure. "Can you leave the room then?"

She laughed. "I will wait outside the door to make sure you don't jump into bed again."

Preparations

(Akeyde Kletser)

The knife wounds in my arm and shoulder still had plenty of sting, but I tried to focus, to keep my mind on the job. The brand on my arm came to life with a slow, steady burn.

I tried to think of God.

He was all around us. He was very plain in our sights. I thought I could see Him in the black linoleum floor, the stucco walls, the gas range.

I looked around. God was in this one-room apartment with orange carpet draped on black linoleum. He was in the bed sitting in the corner, and the window fan. He was in the kitchen in the other corner, with a gas range and a sink. He was in the television.

I decided I would miss the television a lot.

And God was in the vest jacket lying on the floor. Maybe especially in the vest jacket.

It was 4 AM on a Thursday morning, the Kawidtodians' day of repentance. I couldn't sleep. I had a dream that a man with a small wood ax wanted to kill me. Cookie stepped in at the last second and took the ax in his arm. Then they both disappeared.

Vehktre appeared to be sound asleep on the couch. I briefly considered killing him.

The Kawidtodian Temple would open for services at 10 o'clock.

While I waited, I decided to talk to the vest.

"So, are you ready, Tina? Because I am ready. Are you my friend, Tina? You are! God is beating in your powerful heart."

The vest stayed silent. There must have been holiness in it. An astronomer named Brian Greene wrote, 'The language of God is silence.' Perhaps it is so for periods of time. But maybe God was just a quiet person and talked only sometimes, in little snatches of words. You had to listen carefully for them.

"Hey, Tina, you want to go to the movies?"

I showered and ate my last breakfast in the apartment while Vehktre slept.

"Tina, my little friend, how about a walk in the park? Do you need some air?"

I didn't want to get too decadent for my last meal, but I ate three kinds of cereal with whole milk—Lucky Charms, Cocoa Puffs, and Frosted Flakes. The manufacturers of these cereals in no way endorsed my activities.

"Does Tina want a bicycle ride? Do you want to see the mountains? Michigan, where that fuck-head Professor Finger lives? The Adirondacks?'

I couldn't keep up with my little joke. The vest wasn't laughing.

I ate two fried eggs with butter on toast and a tall glass of orange juice.

Afterward I flossed, brushed my teeth, and used an alcohol-based mouthwash to cleanse my mouth.

Vehktre woke up. His button-down shirt was on in a quick moment.

"Don't you want to wear your windbreaker?"

"Not today. I'll pick it up later."

When I would be gone.

"That reminds me, give me your keys to the apartment."

I handed them over like I was moving out and he was moving in. A new tenant.

Then came an important moment—putting on the vest. While Vehktre watched, I sat on the floor, like the vest was a baby with whom I was going to play. I drew it up to me and put the jacket on. It fit comfortably over my shoulders, but it was heavy. It felt like lifting boulders. I held the new wireless detonator with one hand and snapped the buttons closed with the other.

A voice whispered to me from the fan. I didn't hear it well.

The fan leaked words to me again.

"Malekhamoves."

I didn't understand the word. I remembered learning a word like that in religious school, but I forgot what it meant.

I put on a new Kawidtodian blue and white windbreaker over the vest. Then I took the detonator and placed it in the pocket of the windbreaker. Vehktre looked on, nodding, approving.

Paranoia was like a second nature to me, and especially so in this delicate situation. I took the jacket off and then unsnapped the vest.

Vehktre looked like he was about to scold me, but he merely looked on, impatiently.

I put the vest on the floor and checked the packs of explosives and nails and ball bearings again. Three times I checked to make sure everything was in place.

The word "Malekhamoves" danced around my ear.

I tried to ignore it, like a little black fly. I felt around the detonator. Then I remembered the gun. I quickly pulled it out of the bottom drawer in the bureau.

"Malekhamoves."

The word was very irritating, but I wasn't sure what it meant. I put the vest on again, for the last time. The new windbreaker came on. It had blue triangles and white racing stripes.

I put an unlit cigarette in my mouth. Vehktre looked at me a little strangely, but said nothing. The stick had a calming effect, but I had to throw it out when I passed through the gates to go underground.

The ride on the subway wasn't pleasant. The air conditioning was alright. It was about five o'clock in the morning. Early. Very few people. That wasn't the problem. Something just didn't feel right.

A funny thought came to me on the subway. Why did the vest not detonate on the street when I pushed the plunger a few days ago? Did God make that happen? Was it possible God did not want me to do this?

"Malekhamoves."

I sat down on an orange bucket seat. Vehktre was in the seat next to me, sitting very close, like he was guarding me.

I went over the logistics of the operation. God is often in the details.

A bum came up to me, wearing nothing but long rags, his face smeared with soot. He held onto a pole with both hands and looked as hard as he could into my face. The man had some kind of disease. His legs were bloated and the top layers of his skin had fallen away.

I tried to look anywhere but his face. I looked to the right. The bum mimicked the turn on my face. Next, I tried the other way. He turned in the same direction. I tried staring at the floor. This time he kept his eyes fixed at a spot on the top of my head.

I blinked and finally faced up to him. Vehktre looked as if he wanted to crush the man's skull into the floor of the train.

His voice was raw and raspy.

"Spare some change?"

"No."

"You can't give these bums anything," Vehktre said. "They'll take your arm if you let them."

"Hey, I know you."

"I doubt it."

"Aren't you on TV?"

"No."

"I thought I saw you on TV."

"You have a TV?"

"No, not now. Years ago. Can't you give me some money?"

I dug into my pocket.

Vehktre said with contempt, "Don't give him one nickel."

I took out a quarter and tossed it to the bum, not wanting to touch his hand.

"Hey, thanks. Got any more?"

"No."

"Don't you believe in charity?"

"I believe in justice."

Vehktre smiled at that.

The man in rags looked at me like he was sorry for me.

"Good luck with that, pal. Good luck with that."

He shuffled away to the other end of the car.

We had to transfer from the local train to the Number 7 elevated line. Then we would have to transfer again at Grand Central Station to take the Number 6 subway to the 77th Street Station.

We walked from three train levels below ground to the "7" train above ground. The line would take us out to Jackson Heights. There were about a dozen people in the "7" train car. It wasn't yet rush hour, so we had a small number of people in the car.

Across from us a teenage boy and his girlfriend kissed ostentatiously. Why were they here at 5 o'clock in the morning? She was wearing a tight tee-shirt and had a huge bust. The boy had a Puerto Rican flag spray-painted on his shirt. His biceps gripped the girl fiercely. The girl was panting furiously.

Even though I didn't want to, I looked away. Vehktre stared at them with intense hatreds.

Down the car, through the weave of poles, sat a young man, maybe 20, 22 years old. He sat with his girlfriend, or wife. The girl was holding the handle to a stroller. A baby girl was sitting in the stroller, but thrashing her legs and squalling. The mother gave her a bottle, but the girl threw it out of the carriage and the milk landed on the floor, squirting and leaking all over. The baby wanted something else.

The mother unfastened the straps holding the girl in place and picked her up. The train lurched to the right on the tracks. The baby almost went flying out of the mother's arms, but the Mom caught her and held her fast to her breast. The girl started to cry, but now close to her mother, she quieted down and looked at me in the most curious way.

The baby stared and smiled at me for no reason whatsoever

"What is it with people?" I thought to myself. "Life is messy, but God is not."

The Sermon

(Razvarr Abatut)

"There is unrest in our home. We should not, cannot deny it. We need to face it. I know it troubles many of you deeply. It troubles me. I cannot counsel you to take one position or the other. This temple is a spiritual refuge from the world. We must pray for our brothers and sisters in Kawidtodia. We must pray that the people find a solution that will not result in bloodshed."

The preacher was droning on in his predictable way, then changed his course.

"Of course, if the Zan people, who have always been a scourge upon our land, have caused this trouble, they should be dealt with appropriately. But that decision will be up to the government. We must pray that God will shed light on the situation and show the leadership the right way to deal with the problem."

Oh, this priest, he was good, getting the Zans involved with just a few little snake flicks of his tongue.

I wondered what he would have said about my father's case.

When the Pumn banned several newspapers from publishing, my father wrote an anonymous commentary disputing the right of the Pumn to do that, citing the Dreptat. He taped the commentary to a few street lights in our neighborhood. This was his big crime. He had challenged the government on one small, insignificant street.

The religious police sniffed around. A resident in our building ratted out my father. He was taken to the notorious Divinnot Prison.

If you have ever wondered what two weeks of torture will do to a man, look at my father. Two weeks may not sound like much. But how does a man live after he is beaten with police batons and hung upside down and not allowed to sleep? How does a man live after getting his head stuck in a filthy toilet?

The memories of all that must be like looking at yourself in a broken mirror, all jagged and disjointed. How do you ever put yourself back together?

Because the police didn't want the blame for killing a religious teacher, they left him on our doorstep.

They thought he would conveniently die at our house. But he didn't. He recovered, under the tenacious care of my mother, that bulldog. It took seven months for him to get better, to recover a measure of his health. But he was never really the same.

I could see that even though he made himself get out of bed and push himself to do things, his face was contorted with anguish. A big part of him wished he was dead. It was an effort for him just to get through the day. Even though I was only seven years old and didn't understand everything, I knew the look on his face was the shadow of a shattered soul.

Outwardly, he came back to some measure of health. Inside, he was broken by fear.

The better he got, the more the police became interested in him again. They were not happy. I only heard bits and pieces of the story. We got phone calls at the house. Mother and Father would pick up the phone. Men would yell at obscenities at them. Or threaten them. Or just say nothing. This was the most unnerving of all.

Men would visit us in the middle of the night, make us all get out of bed, and search the house for evidence of illegal activities. They found nothing, of course. My father was plenty scared. He just wanted to be a quiet little lamb from now on.

After his recovery, Mother sent a letter to the authorities, asking if Father could go back to his old job. They both knew it would help him keep going.

No, we were told, no more religious teaching. The state gave him a job as a street cleaner. The pay was even lower than what he got as a teacher and it exposed him to the public. People in the neighborhood would point at him and laugh loudly. "Look at the big teacher now!" they would shout.

I came home from school one day, all excited about an "Excellent" I had received on a history test. I was seven years old and in the second grade. I waved my test in the air as I ran home over the stones on the road in our town.

Father met me at the kitchen door. I was about to tell him about the "Excellent" when I saw he was crying. He never cried during his whole recovery time.

"We have to leave, Razvarr."

"Why?" I was crushed.

"It's not good here anymore. Pack your things. We leave tonight."

My mother and father didn't explain much, but in a way I understood that we had to leave quickly, without saying goodbye to family and friends. The religious police would find out. My uncle, Arak, the giant, was the only other close family member to come with us. (Other uncles, aunts, and cousins would come later.)

We took the most dangerous route physically, but the safest from the authorities. A guide helped us walk through the stone mountains to the west, to freedom.

I remember the wind the most. It cut through the middle of you. My father, who had been beaten to within inches of his death, didn't moan once, but the agony in his steps was plain to see. I cried at night during our journey, for him and for me. We were being forced from our home.

Part of me would always be in Kawidtodia. I was in exile from myself by being away from the land. I had never gone back. I knew I was a cynical and disaffected 20 year old man. And we were poor in Kawidtodia and the land was poor and the government was a corrupt monster. But the mountains, they had a hold on me. They were a part of me. And not living there, I felt a big piece of me was missing.

If Necu and I could blow up the Blue and White Temple, maybe we could start a revolution and get rid of the Pumn. And maybe, I thought, I might finally be able to go home.

So, I wanted to do this for my father, a little bit, but mostly I wanted to do it for myself. I had been taken away from the land. Visions of the land floated like the wind over to my head and enchanted and tormented me at the same time.

So, what do you have to say to that, Mr. Priest?

The Revelation

(Akeyde Kletser)

Vehktre and I got out of the subway at 77th Street and Lexington Avenue. We walked a few blocks over to Third Avenue. The sidewalks on Lexington were very tight. It was important to carve a physical box around Vehktre and me, but people kept bumping into me. A few times I got separated from Vehktre, but he always found his way back to my side.

The explosives seemed to feel heavier than ever. I tried to feel elated and engage with God. The sun was shining heartily. People were walking briskly to the subway, or to catch a bus. Beautiful young women in short dresses fought for cabs to get to their jobs downtown, working in advertising and public relations. They looked enticing even though I knew they were full of sin. Men in thousand-dollar suits got into their own private cars to go to their shaky empires in finance all over Wall Street.

Rich boys in shorts and "Che" tee-shirts skateboarded down sidewalks and on the streets, threatening everyone with bodily harm.

The Starbucks shops were thriving with customers. Spanish-speaking men behind fancy deli counters were handing out bagels and breakfasts as fast as they could make them. It was easy for me to feel contempt for them all, but I felt empty in my contempt. Where I looked for God, all I saw were people.

Then, for the third time in these few weeks, I stood across the street from the Kawidtodian Temple on 79th Street and Third Avenue, a little corner of Satan's House here on Earth, dedicated to the preaching of that dirty religion that has caused my people so much pain.

We watched as the Squids filed inside to attend their service of repentance. Why didn't they repent that they crushed us? A few stragglers still went in. Security had been beefed up since 10 days ago. Everybody had to put their backpacks or bags or briefcases on a table for the security guards to check. The bombing in the home country had put everyone on notice.

Stories of a man in Queens who had smashed in the glass front of a Kawidtodian store in Queens were circulating as well. That made the neighborhood papers, but not the big Manhattan dailies.

It was time for me to find my way into the Temple. Vehktre stopped me from crossing the street.

He pulled a small bottle from his pants pocket. It had a yellow film on it. Inside was a large pill, solid and strong.

"What is that?"

"Take this."

"Why?"

"It will make you feel good."

"Okay."

"Take the pill. Then I want to talk to you."

I took the bottle from him and lifted the lid. I put the cylinder to my mouth and let the pill slide in. It was hard to swallow. My mouth was as dry as a coffin before burial.

I swallowed it and waiting for something to happen. For a minute or two, nothing did. Then, slowly, mists of liquid indigo started to dance around me.

Vehktre said to me, "You'll now see through God's eyes, from the sky.

"You are Akeyde. You were Akeyde then, 5,800 years ago. And you are Akeyde now."

"I see that."

"Your father, Zan, founded a great religion based on your sacrifice. Zan told the people that he had gone up the mountain and learned what God wanted. God had chosen Zan's people to follow him and he had seen a vision of what God wanted from us. Zan was asked by God to sacrifice his only son, you, Akeyde, to prove his love and loyalty for God. Zan told the people he did so and that you were glad to give your life for God.

"There would be five precepts God taught. First, the Zans were to be loyal to God. In exchange, God said he would be loyal to us. Because we were the first tribe to find the one, true God, God listened to our prayers before he heard the prayers of others who might discover Him later. Second, we were to sacrifice ourselves for God and each other in battle, as you had been sacrificed to God. Third, God said that we would be asked to share our food and fields together. The tribe is like a family and we need to care for one another deeply, because outsiders will never help us. Sharing with the tribe is a form of worship of God. Fourth, we should read our holy books every day and revere them. Fifth, Akeyde will come back every one thousand years, to help the Zans and bless us."

I took a deep breath, in awe of the Zans' connection with God.

"God closed your eyes and you slept. Then God opened them again.

"It was one thousand years after you had sacrificed yourself so a great people could be born. God saw that the Zan people were starving. They had no food. The crops had been choked. There was no rain for many years. Zans by the hundreds were eating grass and dying because the grass was poison to their stomachs. God cried for his people and he asked you to help the Zans.

"So God sent you in spirit form to plant a flower the people could eat. You were branded on your right arm with a knife, the knife of the sacrifice.

"You put down a single seed and it blossomed unseen while the Zan people slept.

"When they woke up, the people found acres and acres of purple and yellow flowers surrounding their huts. In the middle of one field of flowers, there burned a single stalk and it sprayed seeds in every direction. The hearts of the people were strengthened.

"The tribe discovered that the seeds and the flowers could be eaten as they grew, and even cooked and brewed into a nourishing liquid. And so God and you saved the Zan.

"Then God closed your eyes again, for another thousand years.

"He opened them again, after the Zan people had grown into a strong people. Followers of God wrote down His words and shaped our Holy Book, the *Heylik Shetyn*.

"God said it was good to name the book for the mountain where we found Him. Mountains are sacred places. They can help the Zan people get closer to Him.

"The Zans had a King and he ruled with justice and goodness in his heart. The territory of the Zan tribe grew bigger. We encountered new people as our lands became larger. We called our lands Zandria.

"The King, Tog Mey, built a house to speak with God, the *Basmadrosh*. God told Tog Mey that when the Zans met other tribes, he should ask them to follow God. If they refused, God gave Tog Mey permission to slaughter them because they would never see the Truth.

"And so the house of Tog Mey grew larger.

"But after 40 years, Tog Mey died. The next generations ruled, but with each generation, the kings grew weaker.

"A man named Nechemat married a Zan princess and became king. He was not a true Zan. He was from Yek. Nechemat was corrupt. He stole food from the people for his own court. His taxes strained the very fiber out of the people.

"God sent you to Earth again to fight against Nechemat. You led a revolt against the king. The revolt went on for two years. You stormed the king's fortress with 12,000 men. You were killed inside the fortress by the King's elite guard, trying to help God correct the terrible sins of Nechemat. The king said you weren't really Akeyde. He cut off a slave's right arm and hung it upright on a pole to show the people that it had no knife imprinted on Akeyde.

"But it was you and you had fought well for God."

I ingested his words as if they were air.

"Then you came again, because the Yek king had come into the lands of our tribe, who were favored by God.

"Yek's people invaded the capital and the Yek king took thousands of our people away to make them slaves in his mines. You came to make the king die just after the invasion. You appeared to the king's advisor in a vision and told him to tell the new king to let the Zans go back home. The new king did and you were released back to heaven. Do you see it, Akeyde?"

"I see it."

He continued on.

"One thousand years later, many things were wrong. A new people had arisen in the midst of the Zans. There were many more of these people than Zans. They called themselves the Kawidtodians, after their king. All the barbarian Kawidtodians shaved their heads—both the men and women.

"The Kawidtodians wrote their own holy books. Kawidtod, the King, said the Zans were against God, that the Zans were filth. He said God told him this while he was making a pilgrimage to the Heylik Shetyn, the Zans' own sacred mountain.

"So now two peoples had claimed the same mountain as their own sacred place, with the same holy name. There would be a terrible war.

"The Kawidtodians attacked the Zans. They killed thousands. They killed hundreds of thousands. The king of the Zans was blinded and sent to live alone in a cave. Meat was thrown to him like he was a wild dog. The Kawidtodian soldiers who fed him laughed as they saw the blinded king pick up the food when he heard the meat fall to the ground.

"Our land was renamed. The land was no longer called Zandria. It was Kawidtodia.

"The Zan men were slaughtered, and many times, the boys were too. The women and the girls were carried off to become

Kawidtodians. If they did not submit, they were burned alive in front of all the other Zans taken prisoner.

"Soldiers would walk the streets and towns and corner Zans. If the Zan announced their allegiance to Kawidtod, the soldiers would leave them alone. If the Zan could not do it, the soldiers would shred the poor men with swords or knives, or beat them to death."

I cried out, "Where was God? Why did He stay away? Why did He not help His people?"

But there was no answer. Instead Vehktre continued his terrible story:

"After the Zans were decimated by Kawidtod's soldiers and the central *Basmadrosh* in Sed destroyed, the Zans who remained lived in small towns, away from the Kawidtodians. Their houses were built on top of one another. There was no food. Sickness was killing off the rest of our people.

"You were sent by God to lead an emigration of the strongest men and women of the tribe, the Nine Hundred, out of Kawidtodia, to a land in the north that had no people, just green grass and trees and a great river."

I saw it all in my mind.

"Yes."

"After you created the settlement, you were supposed to go back to Kawidtodia to try to help the remaining Zans live under the oppressive rule of Kawidtod.

"But you never arrived back. The holy books say you may have been killed by Kawidtodian soldiers on the frontier of the country."

I cried when I heard this. Even though I knew the story, with Vehktre's retelling it seemed like I was really living through it, for the first time.

"When you came back again, one thousand years later, there was a war between Kawidtodia and Yek. We fought with the Yeks. We thought they could help us throw off the yoke of the Kawidtodians. You led the Zans in battle. The Kawidtodians could not defeat the Yeks, but they set out against us and killed our tribesmen wherever they could find them. You were killed during the last battle, on the plains near the Heylik Shetyn mountains."

I sobbed and the bombs shook as my body heaved.

"Your pain was so great that you closed your spirit eyes. You could not look upon the suffering of the Zans, God's people. You fell into a deep sleep of the mists.

"God let you sleep. But then he awakened you to see new horrors, because he needed your help.

"The Kawidtodians were rulers of the land, and they continually grew larger. Every year they grew larger and the Zans shrank. The Zans who survived were ordered to wear purple and yellow jackets to identify themselves. They were not allowed to carry swords. In other words, they were no longer allowed to be men.

"Zans were allowed to practice their religion, but if they tried to convert a Kawidtodian to the Zan religion, they could be exiled and even killed. A Kawidtodian who read any Zan holy books could be blinded and killed.

"Many Zans were kept in a closed place at night. Every Zan had to go to this place in the big Kawidtodian cities. It was like a fort, but not for protection. It was more like a giant prison. The Zans went there at dusk and the door was closed and a key turned and the Zans were locked in, like animals. In such suffocating places, diseases ran rampant and more Zans died.

"At times, when food supplies ran low, the local Kawidtodian priests incited mobs to go after Zans. If a Kawidtodian child died, or the Kawidtodians just became restless, the priests, or the royal courts gathered mobs and encouraged them to attack Zans.

"The Kawidtodians burned Zan shops, chased them down in the streets. They went into Zan villages in the countryside and slaughtered as many of us as they could. Hundreds or thousands might be killed, raped or mutilated during these attacks. And so the Zans became ever smaller and less powerful. These were crimes against God, yet God was silent."

I was exhausted with sadness. But Vehktre kept talking.

"The centuries turned," Vehktre said.

"A great rock flew through the sky, sent by God, to punish the Kawidtodians. Finally, God had heard our cries and would help us. This rock came to Earth. It exploded in the air above the main Kawidtodian city, Shalhak. Many thousands of Kawidtodians were killed. Shalhak was set on fire. Many Zans were killed too, but nobody counted them.

"The surviving Kawidtodians blamed the Zans for the rock from the sky. The Kawidtodian ministers said the Zans must be punished. They herded the Zans together and drove them out of the Kawidtodian cities. The Kawidtodians forced the Zans to dig ditches in the countryside. Then they forced the Zans to jump in. If a Zan would not go in, the Kawidtodians would shoot them. When the Zans were in the ditch, the Kawidtodians buried them alive.

"Other Zans were hunted in the forests and shot. Kawidtodians threw Zan tribespeople from high bridges into rivers. Zan towns were put to the torch. Kawidtodians on horses would run through the streets and cut down Zans with bayonets as they tried to escape. The Kawidtodians laughed as they thrust their bayonets into our flesh.

"God was so troubled that he sent you back to Earth to learn first-hand about these terrors. You would be a witness this time, but not a savior."

I asked Vehktre, "Why?"

"God was not ready. He was preparing you for something else.

"Suddenly, you were no longer watching the slaughters from above but hurtling from the sky. You were a little boy, about seven years old, wearing a purple and yellow jacket. "You were running on the ground, with many others from our tribe. You were in a forest. People were shooting at you and the other Zans.

Our tribesmen were falling all around you, down onto the ground. They were bleeding and groaning. You were frightened for them, but you were scared for your life, so you kept running.

"You tried to go faster. Gunshots sounded out all around, shattering the air. They seemed like rain, but they brought death instead of life.

"A tree branch upended you and you fell. There was a part of you that wanted to lay there and just die. But you were Akeyde. You got up. A long gun stared at you.

"'Dirty Zan dog. Your perverted life is over,' the man with the long gun said to you.

"He marched you, with his gun in your back, to the edge of the forest. Other Zans had been captured and they were marching too, held in their paths by Kawidtodian men, all with shaved heads, a repugnant sight to us.

"You and the others came to a sandy field. The Kawidtodian men told you to shovel the dirt and make a ditch. Some of the Zans were given shovels, but the rest were told to use their hands to dig. Like many others, you got down on your knees and started clawing the sand with your hands. You threw scoops of dirt a few feet backwards.

"A few of the Zans refused. The Kawidtodians shot them. You and the others knew you were going to die, but you calculated that you could go on living for a few more hours if you dug this ditch. So you and the others did it.

"The ditch was carved out of the earth, about four feet deep. The Kawidtodian men held their guns at all of you and yelled at you to get in the ditch. A few Zans ran off. The Kawidtodian men shot them. Maybe a few got away. You were glad for them for a secret moment.

"The rest of the Zans slid into the ditch. Your head, Akeyde, barely rose above it. You saw the mounds of dirt you had made and not much else. You knew you were going to die. You looked sick.

"A few Kawidtodian men above you laughed. 'See how the Zan monkey is afraid!' you heard one man yell out.

"'The best Zan is a dead Zan,' you heard another say."

"So this is the final humiliation," I told Vehktre.

"Yes. You were being laughed at because you were afraid of being shot to death.

"The Kawidtodian men lined you all up in the ditch. They told you to put your hands over your heads and clasp them.

"You wondered about this. Were they afraid the Zans were going to hurt them? The Zans didn't have guns—they were not allowed to have any, by law. You were standing in a ditch, with the gunmen above. Why did they ask you to put your hands on your heads?"

I felt a deep ache in the knife burn on my arm.

"You could see the sand around you. You knew this is where you were going to be buried. You started to cry. You could not understand why you had to die because you were a Zan. You didn't understand why your life was worthless to them. You didn't know why the gunmen hated you so much.

"The shots started coming, fast. A gun blasted you in the shoulder. You fell in the ditch. There was blood rising up, spreading across your shirt. It was hard for you to breathe. Then you saw a piece of the sky, of God in the sky. The sky was so blue and beautiful. It was like water, a part of the essence of God.

"But then you couldn't look at God anymore, because the person next to you was shot and he fell on you. He was a man, very old, and now he was dead.

"His dead body smelled. You tried to move him off of you, but he was too heavy.

"The sounds of the gun shots were muffled then, because of the old man on top of you, but you heard the shots beat down on our people. You couldn't breathe. The old man was on top of your face. You tried to move him, but other people fell around him and they pushed down on you.

"Even as the people lay in the ditch, the Kawidtodians shot and shot and shot. It was like they were wild. This is the thing they had longed for. They would drink to their great success killing us and laugh about it later, in the local tavern.

"You were being crushed by all the bodies. Even though your body was wounded, you were trying to breathe, brave young Akeyde, just a boy. You tried to push the dead people off you, but you could only move them a little.

"The guns stopped. You were nauseated by the smell of death around you. Your lungs were bursting to breathe air. You could still see a tiny part of the sky, but you didn't care, you just wanted to breathe.

"You heard the sound of shovels digging sand and the dirt being thrown on you and the other dead Zans."

"If God sent the rock from the sky, why did He not protect us from the Kawidtodians when they attacked?" I asked Vehktre.

"We cannot know God's ways," he said.

"But we do know God wanted you to feel these terrors, so you would be ready to fight the Kawidtodians, when the right time came. You heard a Kawidtodian man say, 'These Zans are dogs. We are forced to dig sand to bury them.'

"You heard another Kawidtodian say, 'We can't just leave them there. They'll stink up the air. You don't want to smell their dirty bodies.'

"All the pictures, sounds, and smells started to fade for you. The sky was blotted out. Your ribs were being crushed under the weight of the dead people. The pain was great. You tried to squeeze out more breath, but it was too hard. Nothing made sense to you."

I shrank down on the sidewalk, on the concrete, overcome with my own death. People walking by stared at us.

"Is he okay?" I heard one woman ask another.

Vehktre picked me up.

"Slowly, Akeyde, everything turned black. You found yourself back above the sky, with God. But you were not happy.

Your physical pain was finished. But then God made you continue to watch and suffer the pain of our tribe.

"The Kawidtodian king said he did not know about what was happening in the country, but that when he learned of it, he put a stop to the killing. He asked the military to patrol the streets.

"Nobody knows how many Zans were killed. It happened more than 100 years ago. People didn't keep track.

"We know that from one to two million Zans were killed over a period of a year. The Kawidtodian government dismissed this as Zan propaganda. They said it never happened.

"The Kawidtodians said that about 200,000 Zans died that year because of disease or starvation or local ethnic fighting. The count of the dead was generally acknowledged as about one and a half million Zans, by authoritative historians. But in Kawidtodia, if you used the words, 'Zan genocide' in public, you could be arrested on the spot.

"This slaughter continues to shadow our tribe with sorrows too many to count."

I well knew what Vehktre was talking about to me on the street. Every year, on the day in December when the shooting supposedly started, we commemorated the death of those slaughtered, who were guilty of simply being alive and a Zan. It's called the Massacre of the Innocents—"The Oschargen."

Fortunately, my father did not create a pageant for that.

I was very tired by this time, but I knew Vehktre had more to say. Because the story hadn't ended.

"Another outpouring began, a great dispersal. Most of our tribe moved on and away to other nations. And most of us gave up our sacred religion."

The pictures flickered at me like an old black and white movie. The images filled me with grief so large I could not block it out. So many dead people, lying under the ground. Bullet-riddled bodies. Brains blown apart. People buried alive. Masses of them, piled together. All that flesh. Dead. My great-grandparents. Uncles. Cousins. My family. Whole people. People with families, with children. Cut down like little white mice, like nothing more than insects. My tribe. The Kawidtodians laughing about it all.

"Then, decades later, with maybe just five thousand Zans left in the country, the Midnight Murders. Kawidtodians smashing down doors, shooting a family of Zans in their beds. Setting Zan houses on fire with the people sleeping in them. Every week."

The strength of the images blew up my blood pressure. The knife brand on my arm flared with anger.

Vehktre did not let up: "Even in this country, we are not safe. The Kawidtodians have attacked us here. They slammed your head with a tire iron. You were just a boy. They put you in the hospital. Only your father rescued you."

God Himself, through Vehktre, said, "I have prepared you for this moment. Justice needs to be done."

Then God asked me a question, "Akeyde, what are you going to do?"

I shook off the pain in my head, breathed in, narrowed my eyes.

"Kill them all."

Vehktre looked at me, hugged me, then smiled and patted me on the shoulder.

I walked across the street to the Temple.

Worship

(Necu Brav)

The building manager took a liking to me. He asked me to come to the Cainta service with him.

I sat next to him in a front pew. The Blue and White Temple was suffering from a sea of worshippers. The bodies, thousands of them, were jammed together closely like tubes of glue. Worshipers in the first rows were bathed and perfumed. After the tenth row, there was a gradual rising of a poor odor. Water was scarce and many could not properly wash themselves, even for a day like this.

Some didn't wash because they had a superstition about water on Cainta. You were not even supposed to drink anything until after sundown. Some, many, were afraid that if they took a shower, they might accidentally take in some water. And what position would this put them in with God?

I showered.

Debyl's C4 bricks were sitting in a box placed under another box, covered by a massive blue and white prayer shawl, stored in a closet in my home. The prayer shawl belonged to my dead father.

I worried over the bricks of C4. I didn't want to be far away from them for too long. We had work to do on them. They had to be shaped and fitted with detonators. But I could not refuse the building manager.

I worried about the missing phones too. I wondered if the police were torturing Debyl and Mintal right at this very moment and if my name would come up in polite conversation.

I started to sweat with the rest of the crowd.

I called him Mr. Creder. He insisted I use his first name—Bava. But I was too shy to talk to him in such a familiar way. He elbowed me and smiled when he thought the priest had read an interesting passage from the prayer service. He seemed so old to me and I wondered where his family was. But I was afraid to ask.

Long white hairs stuck out of his ears and nose. That was the only hair on his shaved head. I looked over at him from time to time and he smiled at me. I wanted to pluck out the hairs growing like weeds out of his orifices and clean him up.

The priest told us to stand for the next section of the service. The sound of thousands of people standing up was deafening.

The priest led the prayer and we all said it together. We prayed to God to forgive us. Some people swayed in supplication. We were afraid we would be punished.

I didn't know why, but I thought about the Zans. I had never met one, but I saw them here and there, scurrying around the streets, talking desperately to each other, always looking nervous. They kept to themselves. Their beliefs were a little strange. They thought God sent a meteor to kill all the Kawidtodians way back in 1908. If that was the case, why did God fail?

Still, despite their different ways, their oddness, I wondered about them. I found myself not liking them but considered how they keep managing to survive. I knew a lot of them had left. I didn't think about those Zans. But the ones still here, they were interesting. They were buffeted on all sides by hatred, yet they kept on going, trying to live.

They wouldn't fight back against us. Some of them did things for the rich Kawidtodians. I had heard whispers of currency laundering, drug dealing and prostitution. But when I saw most of them on the street, they did not look like criminals. They looked like mice running away from us.

They were far too scared of the consequences to stand up to us. Every once in awhile, the Pumn ordered the police to string one up on a scaffold in a public square, just to keep them in their place. Any excuse would do. A Zan stole a piece of fruit from the market. There was an unsolved murder? Blame a Zan! A Zan looked at a Kawidtodian girl in a lustful way. (What's to lust after when the girl has a shaved head?)

The charges were usually ridiculous, but no one would stand up for them. We were afraid for ourselves too. They were trying to survive. We were down there in the muck with them too, even if we didn't want to admit it.

The priest read from our holy book. Kawidtod said survival is not enough. We had to find a way to rise above our petty needs and sins and pay constant homage to our creator for making us human. That was what set us apart from the animals. If we didn't, we would be in Zgmoto, the underworld.

In our religion, Zgmoto is never defined. It is left to the imagination.

Blind

(Akeyde Kletser)

The gate to the alley by the kitchen was locked this time. I decided to get as close to the Temple as possible. Even if the security guards stopped me at the front entrance, I should still have had time to press the detonator and take out at least two dozen Squids.

I made it to about 20 to 30 feet from the entrance. Somebody fell into me from behind.

"Sorry, sir. It's very crowded."

She giggled, embarrassed, not feeling the packs under the jacket.

"That's okay," I said, barely able to get out more than a whisper.

Her hair was jet-black. Parted in the middle, it dipped down to below her shoulders. I watched her as she went off to another part of the crowd. I had never seen hair so black. It was indigo. The hair, it was like velvet. I very much wanted to pet it.

"Malekhamoves."

I felt for the detonator.

Somebody walked into the vest from behind. My hand came off the detonator.

It was a kid. I glared at him. He was about 11 years old.

"I'm sorry, sir."

He slinked off. My hand found the detonator again. My finger was on the button. It was plastic and I could depress it the way you turn on a child's toy.

"Malekhamoves."

Anxiety coursed through my veins. It was hard to breathe. I wasn't paying attention. I got pushed to the head of the crowd somehow. A beefy security man in sunglasses saw me.

"Any bags, sir?"

"No."

"I don't have to check you. You can go in."

"Okay."

I took my finger off the button.

"Are you going in or not? I got hundreds of people here."

"Yes. Right."

I walked in with the scum all around me. It felt dirty. I was soiled by their presence.

I was in with a good crowd. I put my finger on the button again.

"Malekhamoves."

It's as if the dead air inside the Temple was talking to me. What did that word mean?

My index finger was riding over the button, caressing it. There was enough explosive in here to take half the foyer and turn it into atoms. I had nails, ball bearings, C4. I had fire. I was powerful. I was dangerous, a fighter for God. I was the chosen one, Akeyde, the sacrificial son.

My chest blew up. The pain was intense. Acid filled me from the upper GI tract. My head bowed a little. I was having a panic attack, with my finger still on the button.

I put my hand on my head and tried to stumble away from the crowd.

The progress of the crowd into the temple was agonizingly slow. I could push the detonator and hopefully kill hundreds of enemies of God.

"Malekhamoves."

A man walking by stopped.

"You alright, guy?"

I put my hands on my knees and looked up briefly.

"Just the heat."

"I can get you a cup of water."

"No, thank you. I'm okay."

An enemy of God walked off.

It was getting harder to breathe. The explosive pack felt like a thousand pounds of lead.

I pushed myself to a side hallway. That way was the kitchen, I knew, from my last visit.

There I would collect myself, then go into the auditorium and push the detonator.

My soul would finally be released to God.

Easy to do.

Except it wasn't.

I crawled into the empty kitchen. No caterer. No food would be served today. Cainta, day of repentance. A fasting day.

A word whispered to me through the garbage cans standing like hung-over soldiers, stinking with sweat in the sun at morning line-up. They should be out in the alley by now. Somebody hadn't done their job.

"Malekhamoves."

What was that word? I knew that word somehow, knew what it meant. Still, I couldn't place it.

But my legs seemed to be attached to the floor. Rivers of sweat drenched my face and chest and legs. My stomach felt as if it were blowing up inside me.

I couldn't move and I couldn't stand. So I slowly sat down next to the row of fetid garbage cans. The stink was overwhelming. It was as if I were sitting next to a rotting corpse. I felt bad for Tina.

The gun moved around in my left pocket, the detonator jangled in my right. I bumped up against something else.

A soft lump sat under my bottom. I lifted myself up off the ground a foot or so to see that I had been sitting on top of a dead rat. Its eyes were closed and its legs pulled up with rigor mortis. How could a rat die with this feast of garbage sitting all around? We could have called the health department and had the kitchen closed down.

"Malekhamoves."

What was that word?

My sneakers made no noise on the little red tiles. I walked through a passageway and remembered that someone had once killed a United States Senator in a kitchen. The senator was a good man. He cared about the poor. I don't know why, but knowing about the senator made me sad. Why was God telling me this now?

The passageway led to the garbage area. I had gone the wrong way. I took another path to try to find the main hall. My heart was getting bigger in my chest. The moment was here.

This path took me to the back door again. Okay. Retrace steps. Get back on track. I wanted to kill as many of these murdering dogs as possible.

I was in a maze. Except there was no way out. I kept running into white kitchen tiles or the ovens or the garbage area again. One time I found the refrigerator. Another time it was the large wood table for cutting vegetables and fruits. Then I came to the dishwashing room, with a huge industrial machine for cleaning plates and cups and silverware.

I started to panic. Some suicide bomber I was turning out to be.

"Malekhamoves."

There was a wooden chair sitting under a telephone. I sat in it, tried to collect myself, but I couldn't. A yawning hole of failure opened up before me. It was horrible to contemplate. My body started to shake. I couldn't stop vibrating. I was paralyzed by fear, yet I couldn't stop vibrating.

What to do?

Ahead, about 30 feet away was an archway that seemed to lead the way out. Beyond was blackness. I took it.

The Ceiling

(Razvarr Abatut)

The house priest was praying.

The priest asked the congregation to rise. He said a prayer in Kawidtodian to bless all believers in the coming year with prosperity. It was a call and response. He said a line and the congregation repeated the line. Many people swayed forward and backward. I swayed but didn't say the lines I knew so well. My mother shouted every word in the response. She was a real believer and I wondered how someone so cruel could be so devout.

I looked over at my father and I saw he was crying as he responded.

The priest asked the congregation to sit. Then he said a prayer to remember the four pillars of God. That I liked, because I was hoping to rock them.

The priest shouted out, "We must be humble before God!"

The congregation shouted back, "But that is not enough!"

The priest continued, "We must remember to help the poor. They need justice."

The congregation responded, "But that is not enough!"

The priest shouted, "Because God judges your thoughts and deeds. That is why you are here."

The congregation shouted back, "But that is not enough!"

The priest's voice strained against the microphone. "And we must fight the Zans unless they find God in Kawidtod!"

The congregation was brought to a full cry by the priest's anthem. "That would be enough!"

Then the priest asked the congregation to stand again. All this standing and sitting and swaying was making me hungry to read a good book. I found no great spiritual power in all this mumbo-jumbo.

The priest said a prayer. Then he raised a dried monkey's foreleg up off the podium. This is a symbol of sin and infidelity to our faith. Monkeys are offensive and considered unclean. Their tails and faces are thought of as ugly. They chatter and defecate wherever they feel like it.

In the Dreptat scripture, it is written that an ambassador from Yek (now Yekmonveldt) once brought twelve monkeys to Kawidtod as a tribute. Kawidtod observed their behavior at his court and disliked them so much that he had them slaughtered. Then he had Temple priests burn their bodies and break every single bone in each of their bodies.

An illegal trade in monkeys persisted throughout parts of the world in order to obtain monkey bones for Kawidtodian services. Protests by various conservation and wildlife groups for the priests to stop killing monkeys has had no effect on our religious authorities in our home state or anywhere we've emigrated.

The crowd looked at the bone with disgust and shouted out at the priest, "Break it!"

The priest stepped out from behind the podium with the dried foreleg and snapped the bone in two. Then he threw the pieces of the foreleg on the ground and stamped on them with his feet.

The crowd shouted, "Hablat is broken! We are in God! We are free of sin!"

Then people started shaking hands and hugging and kissing. This was an occasion for congratulation. We had been absolved of our sins for the year.

The priest broke the mood by starting to talk about our responsibility to the Kawidtodian government. He could have ended the service right here but obviously something about the situation there was compelling him to blather on. I wished I owned a BlackBerry or an iPhone. I would have texted Necu.

So much of life is boredom, waiting for something to happen.

I decided to stare at the ceiling. I prayed to God to levitate me above the crowd then have me rise to the ceiling and punch my way through it on the way to heaven. That would have given everybody something interesting to talk about it.

God said nothing doing. I was stuck in this chair for eternity.

A Lifetime on the Stage

(Akeyde Kletser)

Beyond the arch was a room, completely dark. I tried to find an opening. But I could only find walls. The only thing I had left was my sense of touch. I wondered if this would be what it's like when you are dead.

I heard a voice. The Kawidtodian priest was saying something into a microphone to the assembled crowd of worshippers of Gock, the king of the underworld. The devil's servants.

I had to kill them.

"Malekhamoves."

This word was a little bee buzzing around my head, trying to sting me.

I felt around the room again. A crack in the wall. I went through it. Twenty, maybe 30 feet in darkness.

A wooden step. I fell into it and hit my head. Where were the goddamn lights? Why was everything so dark?

I was bleeding and my head felt like it had been punched by my father. I sat down on the black steps and hugged myself. Of course Tina was in the way.

I should have given up and gotten on the subway. Something was terribly wrong. But the moment was so right.

"Malekhamoves."

I wanted to kill this word.

Get up, walk up the steps.

There were five steps and each plank of wood complained as I ascended.

Now I was on top of a platform. The space was big and dark. A knife edge of light finally came through to me from about twenty feet to my right, on the floor.

I stumbled toward the light. Before I got too far, something heavy blocked my way. I felt the heavy thing. It was a fabric.

When I pushed against it, the fabric folded against me, enclosed me. Tina dragged me down. Her weight against my weight. And I was losing.

I pushed against the fabric and it draped over me. Why was God doing this?

The priest was talking into a microphone, saying something about every Kawidtodian's individual responsibility to stand by the government. That while violence wasn't the answer to anything, we shouldn't question the government's actions in the homeland. Whatever they were doing, they were just trying to survive.

The people were silent.

I found an opening. I was standing in front of a curtain on a stage, behind the temple priest. The crowd gasped. I stumbled toward the podium. This was the moment.

The Gate Crasher

(Razvarr Abatut)

The priest was going on and on in his defense of the government and its mission to protect the people. We were about 6,000 miles from the country and we didn't know what it's like there. We could not be here in America and be disloyal to them. We needed to stand fast with the government and support their decisions. Whatever they were doing, it was in the best interests of our sacred religion and our people.

His arguments struck me as completely naïve, not to mention reckless. I would have liked to have thrown rotten tomatoes at him.

Suddenly there was a collective intake of breath from the crowd. A man wearing a blue and white jacket was stumbling behind the priest.

He was bleeding from the head, blood raining onto his thick black glasses. Of course I knew right away that it was Mr. Wood.

What the hell?

The priest turned around halfway, to see this horror show come at him. I wondered if this is a preacher's worst nightmare—somebody horning in on your time in the spotlight.

Mr. Wood started to fall, but he managed to get his arms out in front of him. He went toward the priest's ribs. The priest put his arms around Mr. Wood so he didn't crash to the floor.

I couldn't even believe Mr. Wood was here for a second time in 10 days.

Now he was back.

Did he think there was another catering job here today? In that, he was sorely mistaken. We had a fasting day and I was craving a cheeseburger.

Did he want to convert from Christianity to our religion, as unlikely as that might seem?

The priest asked the crowd for help, tried to guide Mr. Wood away, but even with his bad cut, Mr. Wood struggled forward, gestured toward the podium.

Everybody in the crowd was talking, pointing, taking pictures of the scene on their cell phones.

The priest was holding onto Mr. Wood, trying to get him to the side, but Mr. Wood, he was very persistent. He grabbed hold of both sides of the podium and we got a full view of his face now, bleeding, contorted, sweating and breathing heavily.

The priest called for the security guards, but nobody came. Were they all out having coffee?

People were unsure whether they should run up to the stage and help the bleeding man. This was a novel problem with no one quite sure what to do.

Mr. Wood wanted the microphone. The priest was equally adamant that he not have it. Mr. Wood said a few words to him, which no one could hear.

The priest backed off, snapped out a cell phone from the jacket of his suit.

Mr. Wood, now free, stumbled up to the microphone and pulled it down close to his mouth.

His breathing was unsteady and he arrived at the microphone as a hulk of a battle-scarred ship washing with the tides onto shore.

The air was now filled with deep and labored breaths. Blood had painted his forehead with streaks. The glasses were speckled with bright red drops.

Mr. Wood gathered himself up for a tremendous effort. The priest was talking fast into his cell phone, angry.

Mr. Wood turned to him and said something in a very calm voice. The priest ran off the stage. How appropriate, I thought. That was his true nature.

Now the assembly was in an uproar. What was going on?

A word, a whisper, came out of his lips. People were shouting, "What? What?"

My mother poked me in the side, asking, "What did he say?" My father was silent. I looked at him. He seemed to understand something about Mr. Wood in a way no one else did.

"He's trying to speak to us," Father said.

Mr. Wood sighed, then yelled out a word.

"Malekhamoves!"

The crowd was even more disturbed then. What the hell did this mean?

People started rushing to the stage. From the pocket of his blue and white windbreaker, terribly inappropriate for this time of year, Mr. Wood pulled out a big black gun. It was pointed to the ceiling. He shoots. He scores.

The sound was a Pavlovian trigger.

Everybody running toward the stage now started paddling in the other direction. We all started running. Running, pushing, stumbling to the back of the house, to the exits. A panicked crowd lets you know just how far we've advanced over the animals.

My mother was lost to us—not such a tragedy. She was swept up in a tsunami of fear. Father and I were the only ones who didn't move. We just stood in the middle of the auditorium and stared at Mr. Wood. Even though we didn't have the slightest idea about what he was trying to do, we couldn't move. I was fascinated by his behavior.

Mr. Wood put the steaming muzzle on the podium and looked over at the fast emptying auditorium.

He looked at my father and me, then smiled broadly and saluted us. We grimly saluted back.

Then, through all the pushing and yelling, a voice, a special kind of loud voice, with a shriek at its foundation, came at my father and me.

"Are you two crazy? Do you want to be killed?"

This is how all the fun times end. With your mother scolding you. She had fought back against the tides to try to save us. Except Dad and I knew we didn't need to be saved.

The Trigger Man

(Akeyde Kletser)

My sense of mission was strong, so I kept plodding forward, despite the injury to my head. My skull felt like it was being ground between two iron spikes.

It was all laid out. The situation was perfect for a bombing that would create maximum Squid casualties. I loved God. I loved the Zans. I hated Kawidtodians. They were enemies of God. I wanted to press the button.

Where was God?

"Malekhamoves."

Nothing felt right. Still I pressed on.

The crowd was hot and sweaty. The Kawidtodians in the crowd looking at me were starting to get ticked off, particularly the men. Many of them had shaved heads, but a lot didn't. Only a few of the women had shaved heads. This temple was pretty lax in its religious practices; this was the Upper East Side. The Kawidtodian population here was pretty affluent and less religious than the groups in Queens. They were still holding onto bits of their heritage, but only the traditions they liked.

This was the perfect moment. There were hundreds of people in front of me.

The priest looked back at me. He didn't want me to get to the podium. He tried to guide me away. I told him about the gun. He let me have the stage.

I was afraid of public speaking, so Tina would do the talking, like in my dream.

But Tina didn't talk. I wanted to yell out, "I am Akeyde! I am the sacrificial son!" then push the detonator.

Only that didn't come. Only one word could articulate itself in my mouth, just one word. I pulled the microphone to my mouth and let it out.

"Malekhamoves."

The audience shouted out that they couldn't hear. I gathered myself together, my head rough with blood.

"Malekhamoves!"

I yelled it out, as if I were unleashing the bomb itself. There, done.

The Squids didn't like what I said. Many started to rush the podium. The gun talked them out of it.

That gun had to go off. I didn't want to be surrounded by Squids again, get arrested. The priest was calling the police.

As the terrified Squids stumbled for the exits blindly, crashing into each other, pushing, running, screaming, panicking, creating a riot, I wondered where was their God now, to make them more than animals.

The only ones who stayed through all that tumult were that kid I saw 10 days ago,

Raz of all people, my long-ago student and friend and an older man who must have been his father.

I smiled at their courage, put the gun down on the podium, and saluted them. This was the truth of things. There were only a few real brave ones among us. The rest were sacks of shit.

They saluted back.

That made me smile again, despite the river of pain in my head.

I picked up the gun and put it in the pocket of my blue and white windbreaker, housing the vest, which held enough explosives to lay waste to this abomination, this House of Gock, this hell of hells. My little Tina.

As I made my way off the stage and through the dark hallway, then the kitchen, I got increasingly sicker in my mind. The only thing that came to me was to try to escape. I was just an animal too. I wasn't Akeyde, a warrior for God.

The kitchen was still and quiet and I wished I could stay there forever. But the police were coming for me. So I went into the alley.

The gate was there. But I knew there would be Squids outside close by, possibly still crashing into each other, the blind idiots. They would be following the New York rule—if you see something, say something. I was definitely something.

The alley had a high fence leading to a paved walkway, then a brownstone apartment house. The walkway led to the back of the brownstone. Possibly a good place to hide.

Despite the blood dripping onto my glasses, making little red clouds in front of me, I used whatever desperate strength I had to lift myself and Tina up, up, up.

The top of the fence had metal spikes. This might be a good way to die, to thrust my chest down on top of a spike and hang there. I would escape my persecutors.

I decided I couldn't kill myself. So I hauled myself slowly over the spikes and climbed down off the fence.

There was a garden along the walkway and through the back lot. Giant yellow lamps sprayed light onto them when the sun wasn't around, which was a lot of the time. Rich people could afford these things in the shadows of New York. Yellow roses and purple irises mixed with sunflowers and white carnations speckled with red.

I wondered if the owner of the brownstone was a Zan. Who would put such a combination of flowers together to make a small yellow and purple field, with red as a reminder of the blood of our tortured history?

The gardener was either a Zan or they had really bad taste in matching colors.

At the back of the house, the flowers gave way to thick hedges. I fell down into the soil bordering their roots and lay there, listening to echoes of police sirens and ambulances and people running and shouting, bouncing off the walls of the closed-in buildings.

If they found me in this garden, I would be arrested. I didn't know how I could possibly get out with the police scrambling around to find me. My head ached terribly. I removed my glasses and licked the blood off of them.

It was strangely quiet in the garden itself, as if this small, still space could create a bubble around itself.

And then I knew what the word was. It came from my Zan religious school.

Malekhamoves. The angel of death. That's who I was. Not Akeyde. Not a sacrificial son. Just a killer. Which is the worst thing a person can be. Lying in the mud, underneath a row of hedges, wearing a suicide vest, I felt terribly dirty.

And the question for me became, could I somehow make myself into a regular person, just like you?

The Networking Meeting

(Razvarr Abatut)

Necu traveled by bus to purchase a good, professional-looking camera from a vendor in Shalhak and he worked on training himself to use it in a basic way.

I decided that we couldn't afford to buy six new cell phones for communication purposes. In fact, talking on the cell phone might be tracked by the authorities. I hadn't figured on that before. My time in America had softened my paranoia.

Necu also had to recruit four new men for the plan. The rest of the first crew dropped out of sight after Debyl and Mintal were arrested. He found the new men in Sputten Dovil, the town where somebody blew up the restaurant that killed 27 people. The place is a viper's nest of tension. Their names were Mulnok, Perndo, Brigin, and Heshlu. We would have these four men and no more, to keep the group small and tight, unlike before.

Necu spent a few days studying the pillars with the help of the building manager.

Climbing up on a two-sided metal ladder after services had ended, Necu studied the lower details of the pillars, Creder approving and nodding.

Then Necu took Bava out to lunch. He purchased for the two of them a lovely bottle of imported French wine. They drained it and got another. The meal was lamb kebab painted with red hot spices and lots of bread. Dessert consisted of plums coated in sugared liquor, a traditional end to the meal.

Necu asked Bava if he could put up four floodlights in the central square to take pictures of the temple's pillars and walls with a camera. The lighting in the Temple Square was poor, he said, and he needed the flood lights to better illuminate the upper reaches of the pillars for quality photographs. He also asked to put up a webcam on one of the balconies, to stream video of his work to our believers on a Kawidtodian government Internet site.

Bava got very thoughtful, Necu said. He said Necu would have to write a proposal. Then Bava could take it to the director of the temple.

"Mr. Creder."

"Bava!"

"Okay, Bava. I want to take pictures of the balconies and the pillars, get good details of everything."

Bava laughed. "The pillars are sacred."

"You let me touch them, Bava."

"You are a Kawidtodian. You are a religious man—you want to be a priest. You have a connection to God. What does a camera or a webcam know about the Blue and White Temple? You are a Kawidtodian, not a machine. A camera is a machine."

"So, there's no way?"

"I didn't say that. The camera will have to be blessed and sanctified by a Temple priest. The floodlights and the tripods too."

"Okay, that shouldn't be a problem."

"No problem!" Bava had gotten quite happy.

"What's the timing on this?" Necu asked.

"Who knows? We'll have to get the Temple Authority to approve it. They're a big organization. Lots of committees to work with. Many people need to look at the proposal. It could take a lot of time."

"How much time?"

"Perhaps six weeks, perhaps three months. Depends. Don't look so worried. We will get the approval."

When Necu wrote me these words, my heart died a little. I didn't want to wait that long.

I thought about Mr. Wood. He didn't wait for anyone. I smiled when I thought of him, just whipping out that gun in front of everybody and firing off a shot.

In the aftermath of the incident, nobody really understood what he was trying to do. The papers and television stations and blogs were full of speculations.

They seemed to know a lot about him, except where he actually was at the moment. I found out from reading the articles that he was not a Christian, but actually a Zan. They said he resigned from being a public school teacher about eight or nine years ago to work in a Zan religious school. Perhaps he had been radicalized and was trying to kill Kawidtodians.

Was he a terrorist, a suicide bomber? Did his plan go awry?

The articles made me think about my relationship with him. Here was a dirty Zan teaching a Kawidtodian. Despite our mutual hatreds, he taught me. He helped me. He talked to me. I felt closer to him than my own parents sometimes.

I thought that I had actually, finally met a decent Zan in my life, but why did he go completely off the rails?

I wondered if he had become that lone crazy Zan I had envisioned trying to terrorize our Temple. But he didn't shoot anyone. You don't fire a gun into the ceiling unless you want to clear a room. He certainly did that. But what else he accomplished, nobody knew.

Crawling From the Wreckage

(Akeyde/Joe Wood)

I could not be Akeyde Kletser anymore. I had to be Joe Wood. Go back to my birth name. Or I would sink into the depths.

I wanted to stay in the garden, but I knew I could not. I could hear police officers talking and moving around on the street. I heard yelling too. Over the garden hedges I could see on Third Avenue at least five transmitters on those trucks that run around town looking for stories for television.

I wondered how I could leave. I was hunted and it focused me. I noticed a walkway in the back of the building. It led to a set of industrial steps that took you to another brownstone. I hadn't noticed it before.

I walked up the steps. It got me to the roof of a set of stores working out of the brownstone. Another set of steps to the south led to the entrance of the back of a common apartment building. As I walked down the steps, an orange cat that had been sitting on the railing yowled as if electrocuted and leaped into the bushes on the side.

A police officer said something.

"Hey Terry, you hear that sound?"

"The cat?"

"Yeah."

"Do you think he climbed this metal fence?"

"With the spikes? It's 10 feet high. He must be a good athlete."

"Or desperate. Let's call in somebody to let us in the front."

"No time."

"We'll have to scale the fence."

"Okay, but I'm calling it in first so Januszewski's guys can go in the front."

"Let's go!"

They were behind me by about two hundred feet. I scrambled out fast.

The glass door leading to the apartment building was open. Since this was the back of the apartment house, the landlord must have figured nobody needed a key for this door. You had already used a key to get in the front door. The management never considered that a failed suicide bomber might figure out a way to use it for his own purposes.

I walked through the back entranceway leading to yet another hallway and an elevator to take me to either the street side of the building or up to the apartments.

A woman wearing nothing but a piece of black lace lingerie for a top walked by me. Her brown hair shimmered in the greasy light.

"Hello."

"Hello."

She must have been a prostitute. What woman would say hello to a man with a bloodied forehead in the middle of two apartment buildings?

Still, I wanted to kiss her.

But I kept moving. The police were coming for me.

I took the elevator down to the basement. It let me out in a small laundry room.

When I came through the elevator, several rats sitting on the top of the washing machines and dryers sped off to holes in the walls. The walls of the basement were made of round stones patched together with concrete. It looked like the rats had eaten through the concrete to make the holes.

Off the laundry room was a corridor. I took it. I had nowhere else to go. I was afraid the police were closing in from behind me.

The building superintendent's apartment was down the corridor. I knocked on the door. No answer.

I knocked louder, just in case they hadn't heard me.

I didn't wait for an answer. I took out the gun and shot off the lock. The bullet slammed into the metal and made a loud announcement.

Inside the super's apartment, I went to the bathroom, took off the blue and white windbreaker and the bombs. I placed them in the shower and ran the water from the shower faucet over them. I kept the detonator, though, and slid it in my pants pocket. I thought I needed to keep the detonator and the vest far away from each other.

Then I looked around. On a shelf next to the mirror lay a package of razor blades and shaving cream. I shaved my head with four of the blades, and washed the hair out of the sink and down the drain.

I tried to find a bandage for the cut on my forehead. There wasn't much. I took a square piece of gauze and attached it to the cut with three band-aids. The gauze soaked up a lot of the blood, but not enough. I put another piece of gauze over the first square and attached that with band-aids.

Then I noticed a woman's make-up kit. I briefly wondered how the superintendent ever got a woman to live down here with all the rats nearby. But I gratefully took the kit and applied heavy black eye shadow to my eyelids and the space below my eyebrows.

Looking like a very sloppy, yet bald and cut-up transvestite, I rummaged through the lady's bureau, and found a long gray flannel skirt. I took off my dungarees and replaced them with the skirt. The detonator went into a pocket of the skirt. I took off my own soaked tee-shirt and put on a peach blouse. It was too small. It didn't cover the lower part of my belly and it was too tight around the shoulders.

So I threw the blouse back in the drawer of the bureau. I went to the man's part of the room and found button-down shirts hanging in the closet. They were of a thin polyester and had designs on them, like palm trees and sunsets. These were shirts you might find under a disco ball around 1977. I put on the palm tree shirt.

I briefly considered putting on the woman's high heels, but then thought I might need to run, so I kept on my sneakers.

The jacket and the bombs worried me. I couldn't leave them. And I figured I didn't have much time.

In the kitchen area I found a box of large black garbage bags. I put the jacket and the vest in a bag, then the gun, choked the air out of the bag, and closed the end off with a twist tie. I turtle-walked out of the apartment in the gray skirt, holding the garbage bag with its soaked contents close to my chest, looking exceptionally ridiculous and feeling terribly frightened.

An old, rough carpet, fraying on the sides, led me to an empty fountain in the front of the building.

I looked up the avenue. Several blocks were hived off with police officers barking into walkie-talkies, examining the Temple front and back, and talking to each other. Helicopters flew overhead, chopping the air like giant insects. A gauntlet of reporters was held back by police sawhorses. They yelled questions at the police, who tried to ignore them. Many of the reporters were doing minute-by-minute reports with their camera people. I had created a circus.

I walked very slowly away, trying to get to the river. Two cops ran by, close enough to grab me if they wanted. I wondered if they were the men who were behind me in the backyard garden.

I felt naked in the heat. It made me nauseous. I was determined to get into the East River Park, but had several blocks to go. With every step, the garbage bag felt heavier. It was like carrying 100 tons of dead weight.

My eyes were slits because of the sun and the buzz of the police and the reporters and the helicopters hammered my brain. The stink of the streets flooded my guts.

A block south of the park, everything exploded inside me. It had been many hours since I ate. But the fried eggs, butter, toast, orange juice, the three different kinds of cereal and the whole milk all erupted.

I splattered it all over the garbage bag and almost hit an old lady walking her dachshund.

"You goddamn dirty drunk."

I fell onto the sidewalk, let go of the bag, my head buried in the concrete.

"Malekhamoves."

My stomach burned. I vomited again. I didn't think I had anything left. This time it was worse—just gastric juices. I tasted a little of it—not good.

Lying on the sidewalk, I felt for the garbage bag with the bombs. It was the only thing firing me with the need to keep moving.

I couldn't do it, couldn't kill those Kawidtodians. Shame all over me.

"Malekhamoves."

I picked up the bag and crawled to an apartment building and leaned against it. I took the detonator out of the pocket of the skirt. The plastic felt good against my skin.

A few people walked by and saw a man with a shaved head, black eye shadow, a bandaged, bleeding cut on his forehead, wearing a skirt, holding a garbage bag blanched with vomit. Even in New York, this is a minor spectacle.

If I pushed down on the detonator, I wondered whether the bombs would go off. They had been soaked in water and in my stupidity and illness I really didn't know if they would ignite or not.

Go ahead. Push the button.

"Malekhamoves."

"All you have to do is press it down and then everything will be over. All your pain and loneliness and sadness will be gone. You will go to God."

"No, you won't."

"Who's talking to me?"

It was not God. It was another part of my mind.

The old woman with the dachshund passed by me again.

"I'm calling the cops."

I couldn't speak. I wanted to say, "I'm sick and I need help." But of course that would be impossible under the circumstances.

"Malekhamoves."

The woman and the dachshund disappeared into a building up the block. The sun was shining on the East River and the water glittered like millions of jewels.

"Malekhamoves."

I could press the button and end my suffering. Or not, if the bombs didn't work, because I had showered them with water.

But what if they did?

There was the lady and the dog. They probably would be killed. How many other people were in these apartments on this block? There were hundreds of old people on the block. And how many kids were here? They might all be dead. I would be one of the greatest mass murderers in national history, another Timothy McVeigh.

Their bodies would be split apart; heads would be separated from necks, arms from torsos. There would be blood, lots of it. And pain and suffering for the victims and their families. Just as if I had done this to the Kawidtodians.

I wanted to spend more time leaning against the wall, thinking about this, but if the old lady's threat was true, then I had to get moving. The cops weren't far away.

I got up, a little dizzy but no longer nauseous. I stumbled into East River Park with the heavy garbage bag. I passed some people sitting on benches trying to find in the river some escape from the heat. Some looked at me and shrugged. I was a sight.

I walked around the park. It did not have many secluded places. I had to fight off two impulses at once. I wanted to separate myself from the bag as soon as possible, yet I had to find a place where I would not be seen.

Gracie Mansion, the mayor's residence, sat on a slight rise in the park. It was a beautiful, stately home. A gate with a security guard was at the front of the house. A 10-foot-high wooden fence closed it off from the public, but you could see part of the second floor because of the small hill.

If you walk around to the side, it got very quiet. The area had no benches, just an asphalt walkway. There was almost no one walking there, because you couldn't see much. If a bomber wanted to try to blow up the mansion, this would be the best place to do it.

The asphalt from the walkway met up with the park's river promenade, which towered over the water. The promenade was at least 100 feet higher than the river, because the East Side in this area was like a small bluff. This was the most prized section of the park.

Benches were laid out facing the river. The sun was reflected in the water. This was a New York river. The current was very fast and the water black and dirty and murky. Oil barges cruised by. Police boats ripped through the water. It was a good place to kill yourself. If the plunge into the water didn't kill you, the current would.

I walked up to the black metal fence separating the promenade from the river. There were a few people sitting on benches near where I was standing, so I walked north to where the promenade curves to conform to the bend of the river.

It was quieter here. I looked around. No people. I walked again up to the fence.

I took the bag, with the gun, the windbreaker, the bombs and lifted it against the fence, like I was pushing a boulder up a steep cliff, hoping the twist tie would hold. If the bag fell back, I would have to push the boulder up the side of the fence again.

The bag ascended to the top of the fence, then rolled down the other side, gaining speed as it hit the rocks on the cliff tumbling down to the river. It hurtled into the river and sank. A hundred feet down, it made a small but satisfying splash. I hoped the bag was swallowed by the blackness.

A young man wearing loud plaid shorts and a white Ralph Lauren button-down shirt walked by as I stood behind the fence and looked at the bottom of the cliff and said, "You could dry clean that skirt, you know. The vomit will come out."

I looked down. Some of the contents of my stomach had streaked the gray lady's skirt.

I managed to squeeze out some words, to try to sound normal. I didn't want to be remembered here. I knew my appearance was working against me too.

"I'm tossing it. I don't want to remember this."

"So many things we don't want to keep."

"Right."

I thought about taking the subway. What if there were cops around the entrances? The safest thing to do might be to walk home and brave the looks of the denizens of the city, startled out of their daily fight for survival by a man with a shaved head, a bleeding cut, loads of black eye shadow, a gray skirt tainted with puke, white sweat socks and running shoes.

I walked down the spine of the East Side to the Queensboro Bridge, which connected Manhattan to my home borough, passing a few police officers standing around, looking for the Kawidtodian Temple shooter, drinking coffee, with my heart thumping in my throat the whole time.

The bridge had a walkway along the road. Cars blasted over the metal grated road. Taxis sped. Trucks rumbled. The bridge vibrated with noise.

I plodded on. Tina was gone.

The black, trash-laden river flowed beneath. A bicyclist almost ran me down, but I oozed out of the way in time.

Tech Talk

(Razvarr Abatut)

The bricks of C4 were fakes. All of them. I should have known. It was too easy to get them.

Necu was working in a warehouse in an industrial section of Shalhak sitting on wooden boxes with Brigin, our technician, to place the C4 inside the shells of the flood lights.

First they made the detonators, which they would then insert in the bricks.

Then Brigin picked up a block of the C4. A piece of it flaked off.

"This is not C4," he told Necu.

"Why?"

Brigin squeezed the brick. A piece crumbled.

"C4 is very stable. It doesn't flake. It doesn't crumble."

Necu was stunned. "What is this stuff?"

"It doesn't matter. But I think it might be modeling clay that's old."

Necu stared at the flaking brick.

"Can you help me find the real stuff?"

Brigin stood up.

"No. If somebody sold you fake C4, it could be the government. Some secret policeman could have conned you and is tracking you. I quit."

He threw down the brick and walked out of the warehouse. Necu watched him go. Then he picked up each brick and threw it against the warehouse walls. The stuff didn't even make a sound when it hit.

I was very angry, naturally. We needed new bombs, ones that actually worked.

I had been working with Necu to build a network to reach the C4 in the metal flood light shells and detonate it. He and I were building wires to carry commands from my computer, constructing a homemade communications system that meshed the Net with the wireless network in Kawidtodia, then to a wireless antenna on one of the tripods for the floodlights.

That way, I could push the detonator button remotely, from 6,000 miles away. Then no one in the country could be directly implicated in the bombing, except Necu, the only one among our group the Temple's building manager knew. And he would be on the way to Yekmonveldt.

When the time came, I would click my little mouse and the signal to detonate would travel through the Internet, jump to microwave relay stations, the tripod antenna, and then to the wires inside the C4 plugged into the floodlights, which we would place inside the Temple about 20 to 30 feet from the pillars. But we needed bombs, real explosives, C4—good, honest, and true.

I took out a new credit card in my father's name and borrowed cash against the card to pay for the bombs and the technician's work. I had been monitoring the mail to take my mother's new credit card bills out of the stacks of junk we got. It was not a big stretch to do the same with Dad's mail.

I wired the money to Necu. I loved America.

The Pigeon

(Akeyde/Joe Wood)

I made it back to the apartment, the one where Vehktre had set me up to help prepare me for the mission. He didn't want me around my parents.

I was too exhausted to try to find another place. A cheap hotel on the boulevard was another idea, but I had no credit cards or money and its rates ran on an hourly basis, which meant prostitution.

I suspected Vehktre might try to find me here, but my only real alternative was the train station, and I badly wanted to sleep in a bed.

I had given Vehktre the keys to the apartment. So I buzzed the building superintendent's apartment, hoping he would be there.

"Yeah?"

"This is apartment 2N. I forgot my keys."

There was cursing. "I'm watchin' TV."

"Please."

"Wait a fuckin' minute."

For a few uncomfortable minutes, I waited on the street for the super. People walked by me, laughing.

The super charged the door, unlocked it. He looked at me, shook his head.

We trudged up the stairs and through the dark hallway. He opened the door at 2N.

"Thank you," I said as I fell inside.

"Fuck you. Don't forget your keys again." He stomped off.

A few pigeons were on the ledge of the window, sleeping. I got down on my knees against the ledge to talk to one of them.

"Hello, Mr. Pigeon," I whispered. "How are you tonight?"

The ivory-white eyelid slid back and the pigeon's eye and mine were inches away from each other, separated only by the thin metal screen.

Its fiery red-orange eye stared at me, trying to figure out what sort of creature I was. The bird turned its head with something resembling curiosity. Mr. Pigeon had a gray crown with a purple and green collar around its neck, then more gray around the sides. Just a regular, ordinary urban bird.

That pigeon was suddenly very precious to me.

"Mr. Pigeon, you like living here? You can stay, always."

I cleaned up the gash on my forehead and put a white square bandage over it. I wondered if I should go to Parkway Hospital.

The skirt was nauseating to look at and to smell. I took it off. Then I remembered I had left the detonator in the skirt. I took the detonator out and laid it on a high shelf in the closet next to the bed.

The skirt went into a black garbage bag. I found a pair of jeans in a drawer and put on a tee-shirt. I took the trash down to the street.

I left my apartment door open and wedged open the front door of the building with the wooden broom handle from the closet of the apartment. I didn't want to roust the super again.

There were a dozen black garbage bags sitting on the street. I was lucky. The sanitation trucks would be coming early the next morning for pick-up. My bag joined the other bags and became anonymous.

I dragged myself back to the apartment.

The heaviness in my head overcame me. I crawled into bed and slept next to the pigeon. I didn't sleep well, though. I kept imagining that I hadn't gotten rid of the vest in the river, that it was sitting with all its bombs fully ready to blow, in the chair next to the kitchen table, just six feet away, and that it was silently judging me.

Later in the night, I had a fear that the vest wanted to suffocate me.

The night slid away fitfully. Around dawn, I was convinced the vest was back on the chair. I propped myself up on an elbow. I thought I saw a man sitting on the chair, but my head felt heavy and I went back down.

Ten o'clock in the morning and heat was boiling the apartment, despite the labored efforts of a window fan on the other side of the studio.

Groggy, I pushed the sheet away from me and sat up, rubbing both sides of my forehead. Through the slits between my fingers I could see the man.

"Hello, Akeyde." A voice of quiet hatreds.

I said nothing.

"Your suicide vest is gone."

My mouth opened. I had no words.

"Where did you put it?"

I recovered myself a little bit. "I think I put it in the river."

"You think you put it in the river?"

"Yeah."

He walked over to me in my single bed and hit my face with his open hand. The slap echoed in the room.

"These vests are expensive. This comes out of your father's budget.."

"I'm sorry."

"I don't think you are."

What could I say to that?

"You shaved your head. Now you look like a dirty little Squid."

I wanted to tell him that I shaved my head to escape, to get away. But I wasn't supposed to escape. He wouldn't care.

"You're going to be dead soon, so I suppose we'll just have to be satisfied with that."

I kind of knew this when I saw him, but it still took my breath.

"It's time to go."

"Where?"

"Your father's house. Get dressed."

"Can I take a shower, clean up?"

"You look terrible with that black mud around your eyes. I'm not even going to ask why you're wearing it. And you smell of sweat and vomit.

"I think you should stay this way. You're disgusting, a sick, pathetic Squid. That's the way your parents should see you, for what you really are."

I put on some jeans and a tee-shirt with an eagle on it. Also, I retrieved an old pair of purple high-top sneakers from the closet. I used to wear these at summer camp. I wouldn't let my mother throw them out. When Vehktre brought me here, they were one of the few items I took from my house. Even though they no longer fit, I put them on. The sneakers were mashed tight all around, but they provided some measure of comfort.

Bureaucracy

(Necu Brav)

Even with Razvarr's help, the proposal to take pictures of the pillars using floodlights for illumination, with the webcam posted on the balcony, took five days to write, 10 hours each day. We did nothing else on the project in that time. Despite all that work, we still didn't have explosives, so all this work felt like a sham and a waste anyway.

I submitted the proposal to the director of the Temple Authority, Mr. Adanko, and sent Razvarr an electronic copy by email. I did not get to see Mr. Adanko myself. I put the proposal in the inbox of the secretary to the great man.

After all that work, it was a little wrenching to see the proposal mingled with a neatly piled stack of papers a foot high.

I stood there for a moment and looked at the proposal, 22 pages long, with praise for Kawidtod, our religious heritage and appreciation for the construction of the Temple. Raz and I connected our religious devotion to the beauty and fidelity to Kawidtod with the Temple, the center of our faith. We praised the Temple Authority Director's mission to make the Temple available to all worshippers, and to explain the building's many murals and paintings and sculptures to visitors.

The secretary was writing a letter on his computer. He noticed that I was standing there.

"Can I help you with something?"

"No, no. It's just that I put a lot of work into this and I want to make sure the director will be able to read it in a timely manner."

"You think you are special? You must wait your turn, like everybody else. Now go."

I let myself be dismissed. What else could we do? We would have to wait.

After a week of doing very little but thinking about the proposal, I decided to ask Raz for more money to take the secretary out to lunch. Raz wired me the money.

The secretary agreed to go out to lunch in a heartbeat. We went out to a place of his choosing, which was quite expensive. I purchased three bottles of wine and let him drink most of them. The spicy lamb we ate was very delicate and easy to cut.

At a late point in the meal, after the third bottle had been consumed, I asked him, "Do you think you can help us get our proposal to the director?"

He wiped his mouth with a napkin and looked into the distance.

"No."

"No?"

The secretary laughed loudly and hit me in the arm. "Just kidding!"

I tried to laugh too.

"Maybe, to help the process along, you can help me?"

"Can you tell me more about that?"

"I'm thinking that a small contribution to my favorite charity would be appropriate."

"What's the charity?"

"It's the Temple Maintenance Fund. But don't trouble yourself about that. You give me a little payment and I will pass the money along to the Fund."

"Certainly, we can do that. How much do you need?"

"The Temple needs about 500 U.S. dollars. That would be most thoughtful and generous on your part."

I sat back. Five hundred dollars.

"I will see what I can do."

The secretary popped a chunk of bread into his mouth. "That would be good."

Dreaming About Death

(Razvarr Abatut)

After Necu's lunch with the secretary, I applied for another credit card in Dad's name. When I got the money, I wired it to Necu. This project was getting more expensive every day.

This depressed me, naturally. After wiring the money, I crawled into bed and suffered. Sleep took an hour to come. When I finally lost consciousness, there came a dream crawling around my brain.

Mr. Wood was walking by a tree. The tree changed into a giant man. The man fell and Mr. Wood was trapped under him. I saw all this and tried to get the man off Mr. Wood, who was trying to yell but couldn't get any sound out because the man was so big. I tried pushing the man off him. He turned to me and bit my wrist.

It was so very painful and I stepped back. Blood leaked out of my wrist.

I stood there and saw Mr. Wood struggle to get out from under the man. I could see his hands try to push the man's chest off his own, but the man would not get up. Eventually, Mr. Wood stopped moving. His hands became still. It was only then that the man got up and walked a few steps. He became a tree again. Mr. Wood and his thick black glasses lay on the grass, the eyes no longer open, the body no longer alive.

The Den Room

(Akeyde/Joe Wood)

I had been placed under arrest in my own house. My punishment when I was returned to the residence of my father was to sit in his very dark den.

Father allowed me to take a shower first, while Pilsiker (the Redwood Tree man, that was his name) stood in the small bathroom, looking as if he wanted to murder me. Very uncomfortable. Then I worked on getting rid of the black mud makeup around my eyes.

My father wasn't being charitable; I smelled like a homeless man in the beginning stages of dementia. I took the shower but I still felt unclean.

Then I was escorted into the den. The walls were some kind of cherry wood paneling. They closed in on you.

On one of the panels there was a photograph of my uncles and me, a black and white picture of us standing in front of their cabin at our summer camp. That was the only happy photo in the room, but it didn't make me feel good. I knew my uncles would be coming over to judge me. The thought of them condemning me, these men I looked up to, these men I grew up with, left me feeling as if I should be dead already.

The rest of the photos were devoted to subjects most people would rather not think about. There was a painting of people who lived thousands of years ago being slaughtered under a mud brown sky. The killers were armed with knives and swords and all had shaved heads.

The ones being impaled at the end of a sword or knife had blood spurting from their chests or abdomens. Their faces were engraved with the deepest of agonies. Their mouths were open, crying to God against this deepest of injustices, the dead stacked all around the sides of the painting, with slits for eyes and mouths.

Another painting in the gallery was a three-part mural. The first part depicted a meteor plunging to Earth, flying into a primitive city of a hundred years ago. The second section showed towns set on fire by rampaging mobs and people being shot in the central squares of the towns. The third part had a cemetery, with long rows of coffins ready to be placed in the ground. A few granite stones stood against the wind, all with a statue of a boy on the top, his arms raised up to the sky, reaching to God.

One of the worst pictures was an actual photo. I didn't know how my father obtained it. In black and white, a boy wearing an old, torn coat and short pants, perhaps seven or eight years old, stood in front of a ditch, his arms raised, surrounded by men with rifles. He was about to be shot and his body was supposed to fall into the ditch.

There were other black and white pictures too, of poor people with suitcases, standing on train platforms or the decks of ships, stunned. Some were slated to go to Europe, or Australia, or Bolivia, or the United States, to whatever country would take them. These were the refugees, kicked out of their homes, who knew they were never going to return. The genocides had made sure of that.

The vast majority would melt away into the general population of their new countries, trying to assimilate as quickly as they could.

If you asked the average Zan in Argentina today what they were, most would say, "I'm Argentinean." In America, most of us are American. Most of the Zans had given up on the ancient religion. It was an impediment to assimilating.

But there were still a number of pockets of fundamentalists left. Some tried to hold onto their faith when they moved, building assembly houses and observing the holidays and customs. Across the U.S. you could find one or two assembly houses in the big cities, from Chicago to Boston and San Francisco and a few other places. Most of the faithful were huddled in New York City, though, particularly in Queens.

Also nailed to the wall was my father's outdated OBEY God license plate. New OBEY GOD plates were on the car, just to make sure he was covered everywhere.

OBEY GOD.

What does that mean?

Anything you want it to mean.

The Director of the Temple

(Necu Brav)

After we bribed the secretary, he was friendlier. I called his office a few days after our lunch.

"The director would like to go out to lunch with you to discuss your proposal."

I knew I would have to ask Razvarr for more cash. When I emailed before, he wrote, "I am not made of money."

I wrote back: "Sorry, but this is what we need. You didn't think it would cost anything?"

A few days later, Razvarr sent the money and I set up the lunch date with the director, Vicat Adanko. The secretary came with us.

Mr. Adanko chose the place, one of the most expensive restaurants in the city, near the palace of the Pumn.

We three sat in a corner booth, with our backs to the restaurant. Mr. Adanko seated everyone. Mr. Adanko took the best spot in the booth. He made sure the secretary sat between him and me. This is what people in America call a power move.

There was a lot of discussion of women, with the director doing most of the talking and me nodding and laughing at all the crude jokes. After a number of bottles of wine, I thought I was getting somewhere.

Holding a glass of wine with one mouthful left, Mr. Adanko looked at me straight in the eye.

"I understand that your family has had some trouble with the regime."

First my eyes focused on the plate of bread and baked lamb's head in front of me. I was a little shocked, but I shouldn't have been. If they wanted to find out about you, they easily could. I felt the secretary's breath.

If I was not careful, we would destroy the whole deal right here. Staring at the plate, I said, "My mother made some mistakes. She was incorrect in her thinking."

I only looked up after finishing my statement. The director smiled, with a little hint of malice.

"Your mother was executed for her crimes," Mr. Adanko said with great conviction.

I swallowed, my mouth very dry. "My mother did not have sufficient faith in God. That was her mistake."

My hands trembled.

The director slapped his right hand on the white tablecloth. "Exactly! You are correct about the problem."

I was relieved, yet sad with myself. I wanted to cry, yet I dared not. I had betrayed my mother. If I could not stay faithful to her memory, what other crimes was I capable of? What was I becoming?

Mr. Adanko leaned in to get closer to me, sliding in front of the secretary's shoulder.

"My secretary says you are doing this photography project so you can apply to school to become a Kawidtodian priest."

"Yes, sir. This study will help show my scholarship skills and set me apart from the other applicants."

"Why not just use a camera with a zoom lens to photograph the pillars and central square of the building?"

Because I needed flood lights big enough to hold bricks of C4 and try to blow up the Temple Square.

"We need flood lights to better show the pillars. There are so many small paintings up so high that they're in shadow most of the time. There are many small details up there that I might not be able to see, even with a zoom function, because there isn't enough light. So we'll need scaffolds to stand up high enough to take photos of the paintings on the high ends of the pillars. The flood lights will help give me more light."

Mr. Adanko was very wary of this. It was a flimsy, babbling explanation, and I should have thought of a better one. But this was all I could come up with. It wasn't like I was one of those bluffing super spies you see in the movies, who can convince people they're telling the truth with a smile, big biceps and a tough-looking haircut.

So I said something else.

"You get better picture detail on each pillar with scaffolding and flood lights than from the floor of the Temple entrance."

"Why do you need these special photographs again?"

"Because I want to integrate the photographs with the paper I'm writing. The photos will be part of my study. The text will explain the religious significance of each artistic detail on the pillars, which we will show with the photographs. And I want to put up a webcam, a little video camera, on a balcony, to show me doing the work. It will be like a little TV show, to promote the faith."

The director looked bored by this.

"I don't understand all this technology."

Mr. Adanko looked exhausted for a moment and took a sip of wine.

Then he perked up. "We will need to read your paper before you send it to any religious authority."

"Okay. Sure."

"The scaffolds will need to be inspected and tested for safety. Our people will be providing ladders and spot you to get on the scaffolds."

"Yes. Of course. That's only proper."

"Also, you'll need to sign some documents explaining that you will reimburse the Temple for the cost of the scaffolds, the inspections, the testing, the ladders, the cost of labor and any reconstruction work if, God forbid, the pillars sustain even minor damage."

"Yes."

I shuddered to think I would need to ask Razvarr for more credit card monies. My stomach made complaining aches.

The secretary drank some more wine. Both men were silent for an uncomfortable few moments.

"We will require some additional demonstration of faith," Mr. Adanko said. "To make up for your mother's sins."

"What do you mean?"

"Your mother committed very grave blasphemy against God."

I wanted to shout at him, "Because she encouraged her students to think freely?" But of course I did not.

I looked down at my plate again, in shame. My appetite for the lamb's head had evaporated.

"I understand."

"You are trying to make up for your mother's lack of faith in God?"

"Yes, sir."

"Good boy."

The table was quiet again. I felt what Razvarr would say was a depression.

The director sliced off a piece of meat from his plate and chewed it slowly. When he swallowed, he said, "It is possible to do this project, but we need a real commitment from you about a few things."

"Okay."

"As you know, the Army is always looking for young men. It's a four-year contract and I think you will make a good soldier. We need to protect the homeland."

Protecting the homeland meant working with thugs with guns and breaking down people's doors late at night for various paranoid reasons, then dragging them to Divinnot Prison where they would be tortured, like my mother.

Despite myself, I raised my eyebrows and opened my mouth. I could not hide my fear. The Army!

"Oh, do not worry! It is a great honor to serve your religion and your country. Once you finish your service, you can go to religious school."

"Can I think about it?"

"Of course you can. I'll have my secretary get the signing papers from the military and present them to you."

Mr. Adanko leaned in toward me again, speaking softly, but firmly, "We also need 20,000 U.S. dollars for the Temple Maintenance Fund."

"I am poor, Mr. Adanko. I do not have this kind of money."

He smiled. "We haven't even totaled up the cost of the scaffolding you'll need for your photography work. We'll send you an estimate."

"I'm bringing in the floodlights myself."

"That's good. Anyway, I'm sure you'll think of something. Call on your relatives. Do you have some people in America?"

Razvarr and I had underestimated badly what we were up against. The lunch revealed us to be nothing more than amateurs. We were young and stupid. The cost of our little project had just gone up by exponents.

The Trial

(Akeyde/Joe Wood)

I stayed in the den for hours, locked up with my father's mausoleum of art. It felt as if the walls were moving in on me.

When night came, my mother visited.

"I can make you a turkey sandwich, Akeyde. We have wheat bread in the refrigerator."

My mother was very predictable in one specific way, as many mothers are—food comes first. She had come to visit me and my bald head in the den, because I was not allowed to go anywhere else in the house, where I might try to escape. The Redwood Tree man was standing outside the doors of the den. Little hairs were sprouting all over my skull to argue the point of my baldness.

Mom stood about five foot two inches tall. Her brown hair was going gray and she had strong arms, built by decades of lifting and handling and chopping and preparing foods. The middle of her body was like a solid stovepipe, but I didn't spend much time looking at her middle.

She was wearing a long brown dress, very plain, as many Zan women who still follow the faith do, even though it was summertime and hot, hot, hot. Her stockings were brown as well. The only concession to the heat was a blouse with sleeves that ended at the biceps. But she was inside. If she were outside, Mom might wear a sweater over the blouse, in 90 degree weather.

My mother's brown eyes were not really eyes; they're policemen. They were ever-watchful and they judge, harshly, if necessary. At this moment, she was quietly angry.

"Yeah, Mom. That would be great… Mom, are you mad at me?"

She had a butter knife in her hands for spreading mayonnaise on the turkey. She stopped and stared at me. I had to give her credit—she didn't say a word about my shaved skull or even look at me funny.

"I'm mad at you, yes, .but I'm more mad at them." She pointed her butter knife in the direction of the living room, where the elders had gathered for their meeting about me.

She went back to the kitchen, Mom put the sandwich on a plate, then put the plate on a large brown plastic tray taken from the lunchroom of the religious school and carried it through the living room to the den.

In the den, Mom put the food down on a tray stand in front of a hard-back wooden chair. She left immediately. I sat in the chair to contemplate my meal.

With the sandwich was an apple. My mother had set out two heavy cloth napkins, one sitting on top of the other. One I could understand. Why would I need two? Especially when I needed no cutlery to eat a sandwich.

I wished I had a cigarette to pass the time. Sitting in this grim museum, I was getting jangly from looking at all the death painted on the walls.

My parents lived in a house that's about a 10-minute subway ride from Uncle Cookie's strip club. It's an old brick home. The neighborhood was a little shabby. The shutters on many of the houses were losing their paint. The hedges in some of the front yards had grown out of their allotted places and taken over the lawn. The windows were dirty.

My uncles seemed rich to me, but my father was the responsible one. He could have made a lot more money, but as the Onfirer, my dad had to think about the tribe's members in the neighborhood. My father collected cash from my uncles and other wealthy tribesmen to pay for groceries for those coming over from our old country. He visited the old and the sick.

Dad organized the first assembly house in the neighborhood so our people would have a place to worship God. He organized the fund drives to build the prayer house, a *Basmadrosh*. He was the president of the congregation for 20 years and set up the religious school.

To avoid looking at the paintings and photos on the walls, I stared at my tray. The cloth napkins were odd. I picked up the top one and examined it. The stitching was very precise and tight. Beautiful, even.

The second one, the one underneath, had something in it. The outline of something that resembled a long ruler was profiled through the cloth.

I picked it up. The napkin was heavy. I teased the thing out of the napkin. A knife. Not just any knife. A sparkling new serrated knife, about seven inches long.

There was some talking in the living room. I quickly stuffed the knife, point down, into my sock, and covered the bulge with my khaki pants.

The redwood tree man opened the doors of the den and ushered me wordlessly into the bigger room. I tried to walk normally, but the knife pulled me down a bit.

Ten old men, the elder council, were sitting in my father's best chairs, with solid backs. Those who still had hair wore it long, combed straight back over their heads, and long gray beards, reaching to the top of their chests, because they thought this pleased God. They looked like Albert Einstein combined with the Unabomber.

Disagree with them and you might end up cleaning bedpans in a hospice. Or you would get assigned to stand in the middle of a swamp in summertime to see how many mosquitoes will bite you. Or there were other, worse things they contemplated.

The air in the room was stifling, humid with the breath of the elders. They were sitting in a semi-circle, around a long rectangular card table.

Many of the men were drinking an amber-colored liquid that is like a wheat beer. It was made from the Toyre plant.

My bare skull brought a spotlight of glares from the assembled men. A few cleared their throats. The permanent knife burn on my arm began to hurt.

My father was wearing a purple linen shirt with gold stripes racing from the shoulder toward the waist. For some reason, this reminded me of the Los Angeles Lakers.

My eyes swept the room. I forced myself. I wanted to run to my uncles sitting there, drinking, and hug them so tight.

Lhokem, Narish, and Dreykop. I looked at each of them in turn. They tried to stare through me, or look at me as if I were a stranger, as Tina did so many years ago when we broke up.

"Sit down, Akeyde," my father said, gesturing to a folding chair sitting on its own just outside the semi-circle. If my chair were moved a few feet closer it would be sitting as a part of the assembled chairs and complete a circle.

"Have some cookies." The card table in the middle of the room presented my mother's cookies. They were slightly arched and had the consistency of biscotti. The cookies contained nuts and chocolate chips. I don't know what my mother did to them, but they were incredibly tasty. These cookies could make you drunk with pleasure.

I knew this invitation was a method to get me to relax. I didn't want to relax, because I was afraid the elders were going to lower the boom on me. But when it came to my mother's cookies, I couldn't help myself.

I ate several cookies. The elders looked at me.

My father watched me. I looked at him.

I tried a joke.

"Hi, Dad."

"Shut up."

This was my father's way.

To find a way out of this confrontation, I looked up. The redwood tree man was looking at me like a piece of raw meat. His nostrils were flared. He hated me.

I expected something more from the elders, but there was just silence. If their eyes were lasers, my head would have been a fried crisp.

My father picked up a tabloid newspaper lying on the floor.

"You made it into the newspapers," he said with quiet anger. He turned a few pages. There was a picture of me shooting the gun from the podium of the Kawidtod Temple at 79th Street, badly defined, as many cell phone pictures were that had to cover a lot of distance.

"You're all over the television. The police are looking for you."

I had nothing to say to that.

"Two men in the temple told the police you were the shooter. They came over to the house. To ask where you were. I told them I didn't know. They had a search warrant."

I nodded.

"They looked through the house, Akeyde, went through my desk, my drawers. It was humiliating. My own house, combed through like I was a common criminal."

I nodded again.

"This is bad for the Zans."

"I don't see how blowing up all those people would have been good for anybody."

"After all they've done to you?"

"Yes."

"You are the reincarnation of Akeyde, the warrior. You are the sacrificial son."

My father said this with such steel and conviction that he almost talked me into believing it.

I looked at the purple carpet on the floor. I suddenly despised purple and wanted to rip off my purple hi-tops.

From looking down at the carpet, I brought my head up level with my father's for the first time in my life.

"I'm not Akeyde. I'm two hundred years early, remember? You violated the law, the scripture."

My uncles and cousins looked as if they were suddenly struck with a terrible muscular disease that paralyzed their facial muscles. Their mouths hung loose with terror. They could not conceive of a statement that would contradict their truths.

My father, to his credit, didn't flinch. He was always planning ahead for his next statement. He put the newspaper back on the floor.

"You have to be killed. That is your destiny. It's written in the scripture."

In a way, I had understood that he would say something like that as soon as I walked in the room. The orthodoxy of his religion demanded it. Even if he had brought an Akeyde into the world two hundred years before his time was due.

My mouth was very dry. I badly wanted a Toyre beer like the elders. Still, I managed to creak out, "So where are we going to do this?"

"Before we get to that, know this. We are going to go on with our plan, without you. We have a candidate to bomb the Temple on 79th Street."

"Who?"

"You don't have the right to know that, but I suppose it doesn't matter." He gestured at the redwood tree man.

"Pilsiker is going to be our man. After he kills you."

All the sorrows in me melted into the background. I was suddenly angry. They were going to keep trying the suicide bomb. The news changed me.

"If this is so important, why don't you do it? Why is it that old men always send young men off to war?"

The elders were shocked again. My father pulled his head backwards as if I had threatened him with a scissor, but he recovered quickly.

"We are like the generals. We plan strategy. Without us, the strategy could not be executed. And the community would be lost."

"Right. Leaving aside the fact that what you're planning is completely immoral, I thought the best generals always lead from the front, not the living room."

"You are against God," Narish said quietly.

"A disgrace," Dreykop told us.

Lhokem: "You're a crime against the community."

Each sentence was a bullet in my chest.

One of my cousins thundered, "You don't deserve to be Alter's son!"

"I wish I wasn't," I said coolly.

My father looked as if his anus was irritated.

"You little jutta," Narish said. That means pig.

My uncles had become so different from the men who raised me that I felt a great death from their words alone.

"Enough," my father said quietly. He stroked his beard.

"I don't think we explained to you adequately what's at stake for us," he said. "There are thousands more Kawidtodians moving into this country every month. Now they have more people here than us. They are going to make our lives very difficult."

"This is another country. This kind of stuff isn't supposed to matter anymore. In Kawidtodia, okay, I understand. But, here, no."

"It's called Zandria!" Lhokem yelled.

"I'm afraid I must disagree," Father said. "The Kawidtodian holy book calls the Zans, and I quote, 'sons of dogs and rats.' Their founding document says our very existence is against the will of God."

"You're talking about a book that was written almost 3,000 years ago, Dad."

"It still matters. As a teacher, you know, words matter. Books matter, what they say."

"They influence people," Lhokem said.

Dreykop weighed in: "They persuade people to do things."

"But they haven't done anything to us here!" I yelled in desperation, even though I knew I was wrong.

"Oh, there are little things here and there," Alter said. "Like bricks thrown into car windows and burglaries and smashing my son's head with a tire iron."

"That was a long time ago," I said.

"There are some other things too," Narish said. "Bad things."

"They shot and wounded a Zan kid in a car on the Manhattan Bridge," one of the elders said. "With an automatic weapon."

"Ten years ago," I said.

This started a chorus of memories.

"Remember that guy who attacked our *Basmadrosh* in San Francisco?" (The man threw a firebomb at the place in 2003, which started a fire that gutted the religious school. Fortunately, no one was seriously hurt.)

"How about the Zan daycare center in St. Louis?" (In 2005, two Zan women were shot and killed at the reception desk by a Kawidtodian man.)

"They knocked over five tombstones in the Zan cemetery on Long Island last month."

"That Squid priest in New Jersey wrote on the Internet, 'We will drink the blood of the dirty Zans.'"

"Six months ago, the police caught a Squid who was planning to blow himself up inside our Assembly House in Boston during Thursday services. A suicide bomber, who wanted to kill a dozen people. Think of it!"

"It makes me sick to hear this," Alter said.

"And you think if you bomb the Squids' temple in Manhattan that's going to help us?"

"It sends a message," Narish said. "We won't let you attack us whenever you want. We will fight back.

"And it tells the Squids who are thinking of coming over here that this country maybe isn't so great for them."

"We've been relying on our defense committee to protect us. The defense committee works well in this little neighborhood. But it's not enough," Lhokem explained. "They've gone national. We have to go national too. It's past time to do it. They've been shooting at us for too long."

By the time we had completed this round of emotional bloodletting, I was wilting. Still, I said in a low voice, "This won't solve anything. You can't fight this with bombs."

"How else then?" my father asked.

"I don't know."

For some unknown reason, I started bawling. Great sobs heaved out of me. My eyes blew out with gushers of tears. My body contorted in the chair. It was as if I were having a seizure.

The men, my uncles, my cousins, my family looked at me, this freak, this poor excuse of a man, in front of them.

After several minutes, when I was done, I wiped my nose on my shirt. I looked straight at my father.

"It's time," he said, nodding to the redwood tree. "Come get Akeyde."

When the redwood tree's massive hand pulled on my arm, I didn't resist, but I did say quietly, "My name is Joe Wood."

"Not here it isn't," Father said.

The Concerned Mother

(Razvarr Abatut)

When I received the news from Necu, I got really depressed. Depression is like a bitter, cold wind that you cannot escape. Your heart feels like it's being squeezed. You are in a narrow room with blazing lights and bare white walls. Your soul shrivels.

His email sat on the screen like a giant vampire bat, sucking the blood right out of me. I stared at it, not quite believing the entire account. We need $20,000 to bribe the director, another $20,000 for the scaffolding and manpower and inspections and Necu has to join the Army?

This was too high a price. What was I going to do? Get eight or nine more credit cards in Dad's name?

"Razvarr, what are you doing?"

"Mom!"

"What is all this, Razvarr?"

"Mom, you're not supposed to come in here. I'm working."

"On what? What is all this? Taking photographs of the pillars in the Blue and White Temple? Floodlights? Scaffolds? Somebody's joining the Army? Why do they need C4? What is C4? What is that supposed to do?"

"Get out, Mom!"

"Who needs all that money? Oh, this is big trouble. Raz, please stop."

"You have no right."

"I was worried about you, spending all your time in here with the computer. And I see I was right."

The bald, old woman had such a look of triumph that it made me sick.

"This is none of your business."

"My house! My roof over your head! I'm telling your father."

"Go tell him."

"I will. I will go to the store and tell him to take away your computer."

Right there I decided we would have to proceed as quickly as possible. I acquired the several credit cards we needed with online applications. The interest rates were exorbitant (25 percent? 32 percent?), but I didn't care by then.

The first installment of the money got to Necu in three days. The second would take a little longer because of some processing issues with the credit card company. I had to call them a number of times to get it to go through.

I could not take the haggling, the agony of having to negotiate for the money. It was horrible. After every nagging phone call and email with those idiots, I needed to retreat to my bed.

The Execution

(Akeyde/Joe Wood)

I was to be killed on the backyard lawn. The elders, my uncles, my cousins, my father had come to the picture window in the living room at the back of the house to watch it, like this was on television.

I looked at their faces, and that was the worst thing of all. After all the years together, they didn't know me. They didn't want to. They were going to treat me like a disease to be eliminated.

A sound of rushing came forward. I turned, but too late. Pilsiker tackled me and jammed my shoulder and ribs into the lawn. My glasses flew off into the air.

I twisted over to try to get up, but he threw himself on my midsection and punched me flat in the nose. Blood filled my nostrils. He hit me again, in the cheek.

Through the pain, I saw the hazy features of a man, with huge shoulders and a giant head. Without my glasses, I couldn't see his eyes or face very well.

"I'm going to kill you, you freaking coward. For your father."

The redwood tree hit me again right in the forehead. There was no way for me to win this kind of fight. So I threw myself forward into his crotch, grabbed his testicles and squeezed as hard as I could.

He immediately went for his crotch and screamed. I held on with all the desperation I could muster.

The redwood fell over. I punched him just to the right above the pubic bone, boom, boom, boom, three times, four times.

He groaned and tried to curl into a fetal position.

From the picture window, I could see stick figures of men, pointing like ghosts without faces. This wasn't the only problem.

Where could I cut the redwood tree to disable him and prevent him from trying to kill me?

I pulled the knife out of my sock. I made cuts over both of his eyelids, so blood would sting his retinas and make him think of little else. He was screaming now, holding his hands over his eyes.

I took off his boot and sock. His giant foot stuck straight up from the grass. I lifted it up about six inches.

The knife sawed through his Achilles tendon quite roughly. Without the proper care, the guy might limp for the rest of his life. Pilsiker's screams opened up a hole in the night. I thought about cutting into one of his biceps and twisting, but that might have overdone things.

I wanted to jump through the picture window to the living room, but without my glasses, I was greatly handicapped. I scrambled around the lawn with my fingers, as fast as possible, looking for my eyeglasses. Finding them was a great relief.

I felt much better until I heard a man whispering behind me.

"Die, Akeyde. Fulfill the prophecy!"

I didn't even have to turn around to know who it was. The fake policeman rushed and was on me in three quick steps.

He sliced up my right arm with his own. He had the ferocity of a pure believer. The knife fell to the ground. My father must have felt good. He was going to get his son's death. And he could watch it all from the comfort and safety of his den window.

I fell down on the grass, slippery with my own blood. One rip at my throat was all he needed to finish the job. The fake policeman came for my chest. It seemed he wanted to tear my heart out first. I dodged him just enough so the knife stabbed into my lung and not my heart. The pain was like electro-shock treatment.

I fell on the ground and groped for the knife with my bloody arm.

When I found it, the handle was slick with blood. The fake policeman kneeled over me and ripped into my already wounded shoulder. There wasn't much time. The muscle in my shoulder tore with pain around the nerve endings. My lung was screaming. Fear kept me going.

Gripping the knife tightly as if it might escape, I brought it up high and plunged Mother's blade right into his bicep.

That brought him up short. He let out an agonized complaint. Bleeding from the chest, arm, and nose (courtesy of the redwood tree), a big part of me just wanted to lie down and rest. But fear, desperation and adrenaline pulled me off the ground. I scrambled up to my feet and crouched down like a war-weary fighter in the 15th round, the knife like a boxing glove.

The fake policeman roared in pain and anger. He stood back then and ran at me with his bleeding knife arm raised up, screaming. I pointed the knife forward as he came at me. He was so crazed he didn't even seem to care that I was going to stab him as he was going to stab me.

He plunged into my left shoulder as I got him on his left. We were a matched set of killers.

I fell backwards with his knife in my shoulder. I had enough. I felt like I wanted to die. The fake policeman's shirt, crawling with blood, stuck to his body and he hit the ground too. He screamed with the new knowledge that knives can rip up your skin and muscles and vital organs.

Then, like an alarm being turned off, he went silent.

I realized something. I had his knife in my shoulder. But my knife was still in my hand.

I thought about killing him. Yes I did. How satisfying that would be, to plunge my mother's serrated knife into the center of his chest and rip his heart to shreds. To be an animal. To be part of nature.

But I didn't. I lay on the ground and saw puffs of breath escape from my mouth on this hot summer night. I dragged myself up. I withdrew the fake policeman's knife from my shoulder and dropped it on the ground. My body made banshee wails. I stabbed the fake policeman in his Achilles tendon and withdrew the knife, but I was too tired to cut through it. He was unconscious at the time, but I didn't want him getting up suddenly like some walking dead man to come after me again.

Pilsiker, the redwood tree man, lay on his side, near the back concrete walkway of the house, moaning in little gasps.

I walked over to him and looked at his agonies but didn't have the energy to even talk to him.

My father and my white-haired uncles and cousins in the picture window were looking on at the scene, in shock, but also fascinated. I wanted to say to them, "I am a real person. You stand there in comfort, exempting yourselves from the damage. This is what your war looks like. Flesh is ripped. Muscle is shredded. Blood pours. This isn't some TV show."

But I didn't say it. So I walked grimly up to the picture window, forcing the elders back, and thrust the bloody knife through the glass, shattering their TV screen into a thousand little pieces to spill onto all their heads.

The Set-Up

(Necu Brav)

We were in it, up to our necks. I signed the papers for the Army. And felt sick. My call-up date for training was in one month. If the police caught us, I would be dead anyway. If they didn't, I might be grateful for joining the Army and avoiding the noose. It had become very difficult for me to escape the country at this point. I would be an Army deserter. The law enforcement authorities would look for me.

I used Razvarr's money to give $20,000 to the director and told him I'd get the rest in about a week. He was happy with the payment, but asked if I was going to give him the final half sooner than that.

"You'll get it," I said.

The Hospital

(Otis B. Driftwood)

Have you ever been sick and far from home? You feel like you want to drop right where you are, but you don't dare because you're not in the right place. Your mind won't let your body rest.

That's how I felt after blowing out the Onfirer's window. Claws of fire tore at my shoulder, arm and lung. I couldn't lift my right arm and my hands seemed stuck on the knife.

After plodding for three blocks, I stumbled by a house and walked into the side yard. There I allowed myself to fall down on the grass. A few minutes later, a police car slowly cruised by on the street, not paying enough attention, thankfully.

The grass felt pleasant. It would be easy to fall asleep on the little sprigs. The muscles in my hand cramped tightly around the knife and woke me from the stupor.

I used my left hand to pry the fingers off the wooden handle. It was coated with blood. A lot of it was mine, and some of it was the fake policeman's, all mixed together. Lying down, I put the knife at my side.

God, I longed for sleep. But if I fell asleep, I might have bled to death. Or I might have awakened with the sunrise just three blocks from Father's house. And a police car possibly cruising the neighborhood.

Forcing my body up into a crouch, then a standing position, I thought about going to see Cookie. But after our last conversation, I felt I had cut off our relationship. I couldn't go to him for help again.

That left Parkway Hospital. I didn't want to go, but I couldn't avoid it. I needed medical attention.

But first I went to the train station a few blocks in the other direction from Father's house, walking to the edge of the east platform where it ends and the track takes over the rail bed completely. I tried to climb down off the platform to the rail bed, but with my head clouded by injuries, I fell about six feet onto the gravel of the bed. That brought some more blood out of my nose and arm. I placed the knife under the gravel, below the platform, where only rats searched. Again, exhaustion overtook me and I fought against the sleep creeping through my muscles.

The walk from the train station to Parkway Hospital would have ordinarily taken about 10 minutes. In my condition, it took twice that. I dragged myself through the night, silent except for the occasional screech of a young kid in a car out to thrill himself or his date, or both.

The emergency room doors, stark and white, were lit with red post lights. At the time, they looked as inviting as my old house when I was a kid.

Once inside the entrance, I saw a pretty young woman with enormous brown eyes and raven-black hair that seemed to dance in the air wearing green scrubs walk by with a clipboard in her hand. She was looking down the fluorescent hallway in the other direction. Her presence was all I needed to let my body collapse on the floor like a discarded puppet.

That redirected her attention. She ran over to me.

"What happened to you?"

It took a great deal of effort to open my eyes.

"Knife wounds."

"I know you. You shaved your head. You've had knife wounds before."

"Yeah."

"How do you keep getting stabbed?"

"Just lucky, I guess."

Then the cute lady in the scrubs started shouting for help.

I wanted to go to sleep, but there was one more thing to do.

"Don't take my shirt."

"Why, is there a bomb under it?"

I was too dumb to get the joke.

"No."

"It's full of blood. It's almost torn in half."

"It has an American flag on it. Don't throw it away."

"It's an eagle."

I gasped out the words: "Same thing!"

"Can you tell me your name?"

"Otis B. Driftwood," I said lazily.

"You're a Kletser. I don't remember your first name. Do you have insurance?"

"No." As a religious school teacher I had insurance, but using it with my real name would create all sorts of problems. Father's people would be able to find me easily.

"You're very pretty."

"Thank you."

"Your eyes are like pearls. Brown pearls."

"Mr. Kletser, you're very hurt. We're going to help you."

I felt lightheaded, drunk and therefore ready to channel Groucho Marx. "Would you hold it against me if I told you you had beautiful thighs?"

"Please try not to speak."

"Goodnight, beautiful thighs."

Dreaming of Opportunity

(Razvarr Abatut)

I dreamed the other night that I was walking and I met a wolf. The wolf opened its mouth to say hello. Its mouth was full of bombs.

The wolf said to me, "Come here."

So I walked over. The wolf opened its mouth and the bombs came spilling out onto the ground. The bombs were encased in little cylinders.

Then, from inside the wolf's mouth, I saw Mr. Wood. He was full-size, yet living inside the wolf. He looked happy.

"Hi, Raz."

"Hi, Mr. Wood."

"Do you have any news?"

"I'm going to pick up these bombs," I said. "I'm taking them home."

The Interview

(Otis B. Driftwood)

The Pillsbury Doughboy sat a few feet away from me, a gray tumor growing out of his neck.

An alien life form, shaped like a bag, sucked clear liquid from my arm.

A television was on somewhere, talking about term life insurance.

Yellow light burned through the windows.

A large bug with a black-humped back lay a few inches from my head.

"You asked us to save your shirt."

"Huh?"

"It's in the plastic bag on your table. Put on your glasses."

That was the black bug. I put the bug over my aching nose. I closed my hands over it, gently, as if that would make it feel better.

Beautiful Thighs had shown up in the room. "Your nose isn't broken, but it's bruised. Somebody punched you, very hard."

"Very true, Ma'am," I said slowly, still pretty hazy.

"My name is Karen Rogers."

"A good name."

"We've met before. You forgot. I don't know why you shaved your head, but I guess that's not too important considering the situation here."

I tried to speak, but tightness closed around my chest. It was somewhat difficult to breathe.

"Your chest hurts?"

I nodded.

"Your chest was cut up. Your arm and shoulder, too. You're very lucky, though. The knife only nicked your lung."

All I could manage was a whispery, "Yeah."

"You may be here for a while. So it would help if you would give us a first name, Mr. Kletser. If you don't have insurance or the money to pay for this stay, which you probably don't, I'm guessing, you can still get hospital coverage through Medicaid. But we need a Social Security number."

"Yeah." I struggled for breath. "Can we talk about this later?"

"Sure. Get some rest."

Come back later she did. It seemed like the afternoon. I was feeling a little brighter.

"I've seen you twice in one day."

"No. You slept all of yesterday after we talked. I'm following up on our conversation, you know, about your name?

"Holy crap. I didn't think the Homeland Security Department was that efficient."

Karen Rogers smiled broadly. Through all the body hurt and pain-killers, that smile affected me.

"I'm thinking about coffee."

"Mr. Kletser, you're in no condition."

"Call me Driftwood. I don't want coffee now. I want you and me and a coffee shop. Or a restaurant."

She turned her head aside, the long curls of her black hair sweeping left with her eyes away to a blank space on the opposite wall. "I don't date patients," she said curtly. "What's your name?"

"John Q. Public."

She got testy. "I'm an E.R. nurse and I just finished my shift. The only reason I'm here is to finish writing our file on you and get the paperwork going, for reimbursement. It would help me if you would give me your real name."

This speech made me feel honest. "I can't do that."

She looked at me as if I were an insect to be killed.

"There's also the police. The police would be very interested in a knife fight in the neighborhood. And there was a shooting in that Manhattan temple. That was you too, wasn't it?"

This is it, I thought. I'm going to be arrested. And if the police got me in an interrogation room, I would have spilled my guts. I wasn't the type to sit there and deny everything and ask for a lawyer. I wanted to tell everything, yet I didn't want to be arrested. I had to restrain myself from feeling euphoric about talking to the police. It's as if I wanted it, yet didn't want it.

"Are you going to call the police?"

"There's only person standing between you and the police."

That person walked in the room.

"His legal name is Joseph Wood. I have his Social."

I looked away from the beautiful nurse to the doorway.

I croaked out, "Cookie, you've blown my cover."

Karen Rogers hooked her head all the way to the door and flipped it back to me, then at Cookie.

"Thank you, Cookie. You have the insurance?"

Cookie drew my money clip from his fat pants pocket. He flipped through my bank card, past my subway transit pass and a Zan prayer card. Then he found my hospital insurance card. He handed it to Karen Rogers.

"Thank you, Cookie." She immediately headed out the door with the card, the memory of her smile hanging in the air like the Cheshire Cat from "Alice in Wonderland."

My pleasure upon seeing him was mixed with fear and not a little anger at losing the illusion of my secret identity.

"Cookie, why?"

Uncle came and sat by the side of my bed, like the father of a young boy might.

"What's the main objective here? We need to start getting at what's real."

I thought this was pretty odd coming from the owner of a strip club.

"Yes, but why start with me? Father's people will be able to find me like that," I said, snapping my fingers, not thinking it would sting my stitched-up arm.

"Oh, they already have. The tribe is all around you, ding-dong. You've been on television, in the newspapers, just like Karen knew. And that guy from television walking into the local hospital with wounds from a knife fight in the council leader's backyard, that's not going to stay underground for more than a few hours, know what I mean?"

"Then why am I still alive?"

"I've got my own people here. There's a big side of beef named Arak standing outside your door right now."

"Like that bartender who tried to kill me?"

"Yeah. We fired him. You know, I don't think he's ever going to walk right again. And he may lose a testicle. I didn't think you had that kind of fight in you, kid."

"Neither did I."

"Of course you walked around town with a suicide vest for weeks."

I felt sheepish about it.

"And you almost bombed a Squid Temple."

"Almost."

"Well, there's hope in that. You may be a fighter, but you're not a killer."

"I still have some time."

"To do what?"

"To kill."

Cookie squinted into the afternoon sun exploding through the window. He looked pale and not very happy.

"You lost some weight."

"Just a couple of pounds. The doc told me to cut out the cigarettes and doughnuts. And some other stuff. Or I'm on my way to a heart attack."

"Good. You doing the patch?"

"Yeah. But I miss the cigarettes like hell. I feel better and worse at the same time."

"Sorry."

He closed the cloth curtain at the window and sat down on the vinyl chair next to the bed.

"Don't worry about me. What I've got is small change compared to you."

"Like my father trying to have me killed in front of his den window? And the religious fanatic from hell who's after my head?"

"Yeah. And the police are going to figure this out. Soon."

He looked out the door of the room, beyond me, to the hallway. A nurse pushed an old man in a wheelchair who was breathing through an oxygen tube. He was gray and his skin was withered and he was slumped in the chair, his eyes seemingly struggling to stay open. He didn't look like he had much time left. Then again, I'm wasn't sure I did either.

I was starting to feel sleepy from all the exertions of talking and I suddenly wanted Cookie to go away.

But he wouldn't. He wanted to keep talking.

"This may be too much for you. I didn't want to say anything to you before. You've been getting chewed up like a piece of meat.

"But you gotta know. Your father arranged a hit on you, when you were 14. He told the Squids to slap you around and hit you with that tire iron."

I drawled out, "I don't see how this can be."

Cookie sighed.

"How do you know all this?"

"How else? Your mother. When I found out, I had a huge fight about it on the phone with your father. That's when we stopped talking"

"Why didn't she go to the police?"

"Jesus, Akeyde, don't you see it? Your father is too smart to leave any physical evidence. Your mom overheard some of his phone conversations. He left all the details to your uncles. There's nothing real to tie your father to the attack. Besides, it was more than 20 years ago."

"Why couldn't she stop them?"

"She knew something bad was going to happen, but she didn't know when or how. And even if she did, what could she do about it? Your father and your uncles are very bad people,

Akeyde. Nobody wants to go up against them, not your mother, not me."

I didn't want to see the bad thing in its real horror. So I diverted the conversation.

"You're not the greatest person, either, you know."

He blew up with rage. "Why does everybody bring that up all the time? I own a strip club. I'm not a killer!"

I chose not to take in that information at the time.

"Why would my father attack me?"

"To stop you from being friends with that Squid kid. To radicalize you. To hate the Squids so much that you'd want to kill them someday. Why do you think he got you involved in all those pageants after the tire iron? He was trying to program you, to set you up to do whatever he wanted. You're supposed to be the reincarnation of somebody who would do anything for God, to blow yourself up, to kill Squids, to kill yourself, if you believe all that crap."

I wasn't ready for what Cookie was saying. I didn't want to admit it. I wanted to crawl into a rabbit hole and stay there.

Cookie burst with rage again.

"Get your head out of your ass, kid!"

I understood it to be true, all of it, but it still took me down to a place I didn't want to go.

"It's too much, Cookie. Too much. I want to sleep. Let me sleep."

Cookie threw his hands in the air. "Okay, sleep. Sleep, you fucking moron. I'd hit you on the nose, you fucking idiot, if the guy I fired hadn't done it first."

Terror on Credit

(Razvarr Abatut)

I had begun working with Necu to build a network to reach the C4 in the metal containers of the flood lights and detonate it. He and I were constructing a homemade communications system that meshed the Net with the wireless network in Kawidtodia. One of the floodlights would have a wireless antenna attached to the pole in the tripod, which would give us the last jump the signal needed to make to explode the C4.

That way, I could push the detonator button remotely, from thousands of miles away. Then no one in the country would be directly implicated in the bombing, except Necu, the only one among our group the Temple's building manager knew. And he would be on the way to Yekmonveldt.

When the time came, I would click my little mouse and the signal to detonate would travel through the Internet, jump to microwave relay stations and then to the wireless network inside the country and finally the floodlight antenna placed inside the Temple.

I took out a few new credit cards in my father's name and borrowed cash against the card to pay for the technician's work and other assorted expenses.

Borrowing more money made me think again that maybe we could have taken another approach to this.

I went through an alternative plan again in my mind. We could have built a truck bomb and driven it straight into the front of the Temple. That would have certainly been cheaper than my plan.

But a truck requires a driver. And the driver could easily be shot driving right into the Temple gates. And if he succeeded in detonating, what damage could he really do to the pillars from the outside of the Temple?

No, I decided. I had the correct approach. Work it from the inside.

I monitored the mail to take my mother's new credit card bills out of the stacks of junk we get. It was not a big stretch to do the same with Dad's mail.

I wired the money to Necu. And had another burst of love for America.

Blue Ghosts of Night

(Necu Brav)

The streets of Shalhak were sleeping. The moon was hidden, the city dark. A crew of soldiers and a few lonely streetlights guarded the Pumn's palace and government ministries. The rest of the night was left undefended.

Millions of bald heads laid on pillows, doors shut against the wind and the grit that would come in at you. Sleep was one of the few times the state couldn't get to you.

The country was good at producing dirt, but not soil. Nothing good grew here. Wheat and oats were imported from Yekmonveldt and other nearby states. The government wanted to make sure we had enough to eat. A filled stomach diverted the mind from subversion. Any stray thoughts in that area were talked out of it by the overpowering strength of the Pumn.

The Army, the religious police, they were like giant arms raised at your throat. One move against those arms was enough to get the grubby little life you had rubbed out of you.

We were not brave. Most of us simply wanted to survive until the next day. Then do it again.

Night came as a relief to most. We made it. We earned our sleep. Except for those who sweated in their dreams, who couldn't escape the heat licking at our doorsteps and window frames.

The few men brave or crazy enough to challenge the state were dealt with efficiently. A bombing here or there got rubbed out in the public mind by the state. More people would get rounded up, then vanish as if they never existed.

Debyl and Mintal were almost certainly dead. We had not heard from them in weeks.

It was difficult for me to imagine. Death. I believed it was possible to be so weary of the life you led that you would welcome death to come in at you, but at the same time be so frightened of it you might try something desperate.

I was one of the unfortunate ones, a soldier in the legion of the lost, but I wanted to matter. I couldn't just go along like a sheep. I needed to feel I was human. That I could make decisions about my life that went above just survival.

And now, I had to go into the Pumn's Army for all my efforts. How was I going to get out of that?

So I risked the night to find a man who could sell me the explosives we needed. There were rough places in the city, as there were in any city, where you could be killed just for walking around.

I hesitated to call it a neighborhood. Tin shacks stood on hills, shoved together like crowds on the ragged morning bus going to the central market.

The walk up the steep hill felt like it would burst apart my chest. I had made it to the crest, relieved, when the end of the barrel of a gun poked me in the ribs.

I instinctively put my hands up.

"I'm looking for somebody." I didn't want to say his name. Even to say the name might get me killed.

The gun was shoved deeper into my ribs.

"You know him?"

"No. I would like to buy some packages from him."

Talk of money changed the gun's attitude. It came away from my body.

I was led to a man who was not in the business of directly challenging the state but simply wanted to make money. Lots of it. He had men with guns to help him make his money. Dozens of them. The state therefore left him alone. In exchange, he kept the hills around him quiet. The people here were sheep herding around his guiding arms, eating grass, not talking, not even whispering, just eating. This was a cold peace.

From the outside the shack was like any other. The man did not live here. He worked here, at night. His home was somewhere else in the hills, inconspicuous. He did not live in a palace but a modest little home. He did not want to stick out. This was part of the deal he had with the state.

The shack was small and stuffy. Three women were lying in a row, on cots, asleep in the back of the room, glossy lipstick smudged, thick eyeliner crumbling and raining onto their cheeks. They were barely dressed in a rainbow of lingerie, yellow, purple lace, red strings. Their bosoms fell this way and that, an abundance I could only dream about. They all had full heads of hair, mussed up but luxuriant. This was wealth I had never seen.

"Don't worry," the gunman said to me, friendly now that he had me under control. "They're wigs."

"What?"

"Mr. Somebody likes girls with hair. When they go back home, they can take off the wigs and live their lives."

I began to understand that these girls might be prostitutes.

A small gray curtain stirred at the back wall of the shack.

"Stinger, who is it?"

Stinger yelled out. "A man here says he wants to buy some packages from you."

"What kind of packages?"

"He didn't say."

I was afraid to speak out without being directly summoned.

"What do you want?"

"Explosives."

The curtain seemed to get suddenly quiet. There was a pause of some seconds, but it could have been minutes. I was starting to feel wobbly.

"Tell him to come. Stay outside."

"Okay, boss."

Mr. Somebody sat at a wooden table, calmly separating dollars, euros, and rubles. The piles weren't very high, but the amounts of each bill were.

When he saw me separating the two pieces of curtain, he barely looked up before going back to playing solitaire with his money.

"Do I know you?" he said, addressing the money.

"No."

"What is your name?"

"Necu Brav."

"So, what of it?"

I thought he was insulting me, but I was afraid and would not rise to the challenge.

I tried to speak calmly, but I felt my meager dinner start bouncing around inside me.

"That is my name."

He became a little heated with me.

"No, what of it? What brings you here?"

I had thought I made this clear before, but I felt as if I were in unfamiliar terrain and I tried to follow his instructions as best I could.

My voice came out like a squeaking mouse.

"I want to buy explosives."

The man cocked his head at me.

"We call it product."

"Okay."

"You are not serious."

"I am."

He shook his head.

"I look at you."

"Yes. You are looking at me."

Mr. Somebody laughed. "I can see inside you."

This terrified me.

"You are a boy. I don't know, maybe 19 or 20. Easily led. You are not a bull. I am a bull."

"Yes."

"Why do you want this product?"

"I cannot tell you."

He laughed again.

"So, you do have some guts."

He took a gun out from a bag under the table and pointed it at me, his elbow resting on thousands of euros.

"You have any guts left now, little boy? Why do you want my product?"

If my life had to end, at least let it be with defiance. I was not a sheep.

"I am not going to tell you. Now, go ahead and shoot."

Mr. Somebody smiled broadly. "Maybe I will, later. Show me your money."

I took the pack off my shoulders. I opened up the bag.

Mr. Somebody raised his eyebrows.

"This isn't enough. I want more."

"I'll see what I can do. I have access to an American credit card."

"Very good. I may or may not give you what you want. First, I tell you this. I hope you are not one of these crazy revolutionaries trying to blow up marketplaces. It's stupid business and I don't want to be involved."

"Well, who do you sell to then?"

"Why should I tell you, you little bugger?

I tried to figure out an answer that wouldn't be disrespectful. I looked at him with a slightly open mouth, like an idiot. When Mr. Somebody saw that the transaction had come to a dead end, he lit the fuse again.

"Alright, I'll tell you, little bugger. I sell to construction companies. They don't have to pay taxes on what I sell."

"Okay."

"You didn't thank me."

"I'm sorry?"

"You didn't thank me for volunteering that information. You must be courteous or society will crumble."

"Thank you."

"We have gotten off track. I shall repeat. Are you in the blowing up marketplaces business?

"I understand. It's not that kind of business."

He leveled his eyes at me. "So, what kind of business is it?"

"We are shipping product to another country, to Yekmonveldt, then onto somewhere else."

It was a ridiculous lie to me, but it was the best I could come up with on short notice.

"You are in the shipping business."

"Yes."

"Fire in the hole!"

I jumped back in my chair as if shot.

A six-year-old boy had suddenly materialized from the shadows of the room.

He had a round moon face and demented eyes and he was running toward me. He was wearing a tee-shirt of a boy smiling a sick smile and urinating on a baseball cap, with the logo of an American team. It was the New York Yankees, I believe.

The boy ran right into my stomach and shouted, "Fire in the hole!"

Why was I being attacked by a six-year-old?

I backed away and out of the chair. The boy jumped up as high as he could and spat in my face, "Fire in the hole!"

Mr. Somebody smiled.

"That's my son, the douchebag. Hey douchebag, lay off my customer."

The dealer turned back to me and explained, "He likes explosives."

The boy turned from me and ran straight at the tin shack wall in an effort to run up it. I supposed he was satisfied with the one-two slap that his sneakers made on the metal because he shouted, "Fire in the hole!"

"This is how it's going to be. You give me this money. I give you a little product. You bring back more money in a few days, I give you the rest of the product."

"Okay."

"Stinger!"

Stinger came through the curtain.

"Come, give this man three packs of product. No, not those. Give him some good stuff."

Stinger complained. "Why?"

Mr. Somebody grabbed my chin with his hand, dug his long, dirty fingernails into my flesh and said, "Because he's a good boy. Aren't you?"

"Yes."

"Say it!"

"I'm a good boy."

Stinger took the money from my backpack, shoveled it onto the table of euros, then quickly loaded three packs of what I hoped was high-grade explosive into my bag, then zipped it shut.

"Stinger will walk you home."

"Then you'll know where I live."

Mr. Somebody laughed and slapped my chin with the full cup of his hand, where he had left five rips of red blood.

"You are a smart boy. Stinger will take you home."

"No. If he comes, the deal is off. I won't bring you any more money."

"Stinger, should we kill this little boy?"

"For sure, boss."

"Then do it."

Stinger put his gun to the back of my head.

My heart was sick with panic. But I had a feeling this was an old routine the men were pulling, and I tried to stand my ground.

"If you kill me, the police will come."

Mr. Somebody dismissed that pretty quickly. "People get killed on this little mound of shit here all the time and no one comes. No one."

"Shoot him!" the little boy demanded.

"I want to study to become a priest. I have friends at the Blue and White Temple who are trying to help me. If you kill me, they will wonder what's happened to me."

"You have connections. If they're so great, why are you here?"

"My parents are dead. I have to make money. It's expensive to study."

Mr. Somebody laughed a little. "I wish I was in that business! The religious authorities always ask for more money than anyone else. What a great racket."

Stinger still had the gun pointed at the back of my skull.

"Can I go now?"

"Stinger, should we let him live?"

"For sure, boss."

Before I could turn around, Mr. Somebody wagged his finger at me.

"Schoolboy, you don't come back tomorrow with the rest of the money, Stinger will find you. He will ask around at the Temple and he will find you."

I threw on my backpack.

"Yes, sir. Cash from an American credit card. I promise."

"You are going to give me an anxiety attack while I'm waiting for you."

I nodded and got out of there as quickly as I could.

A Question of Insurance

(Akeyde/Joe Wood)

I was kissing a girl with black hair and brown eyes. But I also wanted to see her face. So the kissing would stop every few seconds in order for me to look at the beautiful girl I had in my arms. Then we would kiss again and commune with a mutual delight.

"Mr. Kletser, hey, I need to talk to you about your insurance."

Karen Rogers sat on my bed.

"Uh, yeah?"

"There's a problem. Your insurance card has you with one name and your Social has another."

The sun was full up in the sky outside my window and I couldn't stand it. There were no dark corners in the room.

"What day is it?"

"Tuesday. You've been sleeping a lot."

"Right."

"You need to start getting up and walking around. It will help you heal faster."

"Okay."

All I wanted to do was stare at Karen Rogers, but she was quite intent on getting me to focus on her problem.

"Your Social says your name is Joseph Wood. But your insurance card says you are Akeyde Kletser. That's a problem."

"Right."

"Can you explain this?"

"I need my glasses to talk."

Karen Rogers quickly handed me my glasses from the set of drawers next to the bed, then promptly started firing questions at me as I struggled to put them on.

"How do you have two names?"

I cleared my throat. "My father did this."

"Okay."

"When I was born, my father was in his assimilation phase. He thought I should have an American name when dealing with the government."

"So, why is your insurance card different?"

I had a lot on my chest, besides the scars, as always. And I wanted to get rid of the burdens. I sat up further on the cheap hospital mattress.

"I have tried to move between being a Zan and being an American. It's not working out very well. My father has had quite a bit of trouble with it as well.'

"You haven't answered the question."

"I don't know if I can."

"Please give me something so I can explain this to the insurance company."

She was very beautiful to me and I wanted to simply kiss her, even while various parts of my body were bandaged as heavily as a mummy.

"I work for a religious school. I'm a teacher there. The secretary insisted that I use my tribal name on the card."

"Why didn't you argue with her? You knew your Social had a different name."

I shrugged.

Karen Rogers was getting exasperated with me, and I sensed that perhaps this conversation wasn't all business. She was very close to me and I very much wanted to take her firm bicep and hold it.

"You need to work harder here. Why Joe Wood? What kind of name is that?"

"Akeyde Kletser means 'bound to wood.' My father wanted to Americanize my name, but keep some of the meaning of my tribal name."

"I don't get it."

I was starting to get impatient, despite her beauty and my wanting to please her.

"My father wanted me to always carry around the fact that I was sacrificed by my original father on a cross of wood."

"What?"

"I'm supposed to be the sixth reincarnation of the original Akeyde, who was slain by his father."

She let the part about a child being killed by his father slide to ask this: "The Zans believe in reincarnation?"

"For one person—me."

"Wow."

"Most Zans are secular."

"But not you?"

"No."

Karen Rogers looked at me, her head slanted to one side. I thought she was judging me poorly. There was a glint of steel in her eyes and I saw how strong she was, much stronger than me. Along with that, I could see the exhaustion in her face. She was stressed out. I felt defensive.

"So, why Joe?"

"Excuse me?"

"Why did your father name you Joe as a first name? What does that mean?"

"Nothing. He just thought it sounded very ordinary. Regular."

She looked away for a moment, then returned her brown pearls to me. I couldn't get over her raven hair, the way it curled like rose petals around her face.

"Who the hell are you?"

I lifted my hands up off the bed to fend her off.

"I don't know."

I wanted to change the subject.

"What are you going to tell the insurance company?"

She got up from the bed and stood over me. She talked to me in a firm, professional voice.

"To go with the name on your Social and change it for their records. That way everything's consistent."

She turned to the door, her white nurse's shoes plunging into the hallway.

The Visitor

(Razvarr Abatut)

My dad came to visit me in my room. The computer was off and I was lying in bed at the end of the afternoon with the lights on.

He sat on the edge of the bed. Little gray sprouts of hair laced the sides of his scalp. He hadn't shaved his skull for a few days. The skin under his eyes looked as if it were trying to crawl into his mouth.

I felt so moved by his appearance that I sat up and hugged him. He was surprised, but hugged me back. Then I fell back on the bed.

"What is all this your mother is telling me?"

"It's nothing, Dad."

"You shouldn't be talking to people in Kawidtodia. They can get in a lot of trouble."

"Don't worry about it."

"I am going to worry. You don't remember what they've done to us."

"I remember. That's why I'm getting involved."

"You could be endangering someone's life over there."

"Somebody has to stand up and do something. You did." That was a slip I would regret, but my father seemed to understand what was happening on a deeper level, even though I had trouble admitting that at the time.

"It shouldn't be you. You are safe and comfortable here in Queens."

"I spend half my day in bed! You think that's safe and comfortable?"

"I was going to get to that in a minute. Think about what it means for someone to be able to lie in bed without anybody monitoring your thoughts and your actions."

"But I do have that. Mom is like the secret police here."

"You don't really know what the secret police is. Stop pulling the covers over your head."

I came out from the covers and yelled, "You were a religious teacher. And they tortured you. How can you sit by and let them run things?"

Father's chest rose up in a deep breath and then he sank down again until his head was almost even with mine on the bed.

"I challenged them, which was very foolish. They didn't have the right to shut down newspapers. They cited Dreptat scripture to do it. I thought they were wrong. But it didn't matter. They can read the holy books however they want. You must have, what do they say, a calculation in your head about their power and your power. I did not have that."

"I think you did the right thing."

"I'm not so sure. Anyway, we are here to talk about you."

"What about?"

"Maybe you should think about going to the four-year school again. I don't want you talking to people in Kawidtodia. Maybe we should get rid of this computer. That's how you talk to people there, right, with the computer?"

He pointed to the back-up system.

"And that thing, that is some kind of alternative power supply."

"Yeah."

"To keep the computer running, in case the power goes out."

"Yeah."

"And you also have a generator. Which runs on gasoline. In case the power really goes out. For hours."

"Yeah."

"You must have some serious business to have that around."

"I'm thinking of starting a business. I need power in case the electricity fails."

My father breathed deeply.

"I wish I could believe you. Please give the generator and all the other equipment you borrowed back to Amic. Maybe I will have Arak come and disconnect the computer. He's good with technology."

"You can't take my computer. It's mine. It was a gift."

"I work very hard."

"This is going to be bad," I thought.

"I try to make a good life for you here."

"You think this is a good life?"

"We got you to community college. You can continue your studies at the local school here, get a good job, get married, have a family."

"It doesn't seem real."

"What do you mean?"

"Out of reach."

"You are so smart, but you know so little."

I pulled the covers over my head again.

"I will talk to Uncle Arak. Maybe he can help."

"The perv? He's a real moral authority!"

Dad got up and shut the door.

He shuffled down the stairs, every creak on the steps a hammer to my forehead.

I heard arguing downstairs. How typical.

"Binele, what did he say?"

"He said he is out of reach."

"I will go upstairs and talk to him."

"What are you going to do? Hit him? That won't do anything."

"It will do something. It will show him we don't approve of this."

"He already knows. Don't do it, Matca."

"Don't you hold me back. You never hold me back!"

Then there was scuffling and shouting and the throwing of dishes. That surprised me.

It ended with this: "I will try to talk to him again. If you go up there, there will be hitting. And that will make things worse."

The old feet creaked up the stairs again. *He's coming for me.*

The door opened slowly, the hinges protesting.

There was the rustle of light summer clothing sitting on a chair. The thing in the room edged the chair near the desk, near the ages-old rock from the homeland.

From under the covers, I mocked him. "Are you going to hit me?"

He didn't say anything.

I didn't know how to respond to the silence.

He just sat there.

I moved the sheet off my head, made a little opening near my mouth to get some air. I could have turned to see him, but would not. I stared at the ceiling, trying not to breathe too deeply. I didn't want to give the old man any hope.

"I have considered your problem from a spiritual perspective."

My reflex was to say, "Yeah?" But I caught myself. I didn't want to get drawn into another discussion.

"You are in Zgmoto, even though you are not dead."

My chest became constricted. I didn't think that kind of religious talk could still reach me.

"I did not see it before. But now I understand. You are in a very painful place."

This strategy was working on me. I felt a great heaviness. In those moments I wanted to be dead.

He came over to the bed and hugged me and kissed me on the forehead. He hugged me in such a way that my arms were pinned down to the bed. I could not fight him off.

This hug was not just a loving hug. He squeezed me around the shoulders as if he were trying to exorcise a demon from my body. I pushed back against him, but more than a decade of lifting newspapers, soda bottles, stacks of pornographic magazines, and garbage had restored strength to his arms, and he was more than a match for my community college biceps.

"I am going to help you."

Then he released me and walked out, with an even more ponderous shuffle than usual. I knew what he had done. It's a Kawidtodian religious technique. He was taking my burdens unto himself.

I was a little upset. I didn't want anyone else to share the weight. Especially him.

My parents feelings, my father's love, the pressure was tightening around me. I had to fight it off. I decided that early the next morning we would blow up the Blue and White Temple.

Exit Strategy

(Akeyde/Joe Wood)

"Akeyde, I think I've figured out a way to help you get out of this thing with your father."

I sat up in the hospital bed, even though it was 10:30 at night, when the nurses turn off the lights and tell you to go to sleep. My bandages were off, the tubes out. The stitches were bare on my arms at the time, but I was starting to feel physically good. My discharge was planned for after breakfast in the morning.

Visiting hours were clearly over but Cookie was allowed many privileges with Karen Rogers. He had come to see me even though the strip club was just starting to come alive with men walking in the door.

Cookie didn't look so good. He was pale again and breathing heavily.

"How?"

"The police are looking for you in the neighborhood, you know. It's only a matter of time, hours maybe, before they end up here."

"What am I supposed to do, Cookie? I can't think about it."

Cookie took several deep breaths.

"Well, that's you, Akeyde. You're book smart, but you don't think too deeply."

He looked at me and pushed my dirty hair away from my eyes, something he hadn't done since I was about 7 years old.

"We're going to have to go to the police. You need some more muscle on your side. That's the main objective here. I can't protect you forever. Your father has too many people. Besides, I can't worry about you all the time. I have businesses to take care of."

"I'll get indicted. I'll go to jail. I don't see the sense in it."

"Just listen, I've figured out how to do this with minimal damage to you."

"I don't want to go to the police."

Cookie's head moved back and forth as if he were praying. He breathed in and out as if he had just run a race and needed more air.

"Your father is still trying to kill you! The only reason he hasn't is me. I've got guys all over this hospital. And Arak. He's a dome-head, but he's alright. I sold him a piece of the club, gave him a leg up."

Arak was on his cell phone at the time and he didn't seem too concerned about my health. His voice was rising in volume with each exchange from the person on the other end. I tried to ignore him.

"He wants to do what? How?" That was Arak beginning to lose his composure.

"Dome-head?"

"A Squid, but that doesn't matter. He's one of the best men I know. Now look, here's how you can get out from under this rock…"

Arak was shouting loudly now. "I can't leave the hospital! I've got business here."

"Your bodyguard has a problem."

"They have their own little troubles. I'm sure it's nothing."

The dome-head came bursting into the room. I noticed he had a very big gun underneath his shirt, near the belt line. Vehktre had taught me to notice things like that.

"We have to go!"

I thought Cookie was going to have a heart attack.

"What?"

"My nephew. He's going to do something terrible!"

Cookie was confused, which didn't happen often.

"Please. Come. We must go."

"We can't leave Akeyde here. He hasn't been discharged."

"I want him to come. He was my nephew's teacher. He might be able to help."

Cookie looked at me. "What the fuck?"

I raised my arms.

"I don't know what he's talking about."

Cookie looked at Arak with an aggravated face.

I asked Arak, "What's his name?"

"Razvarr."

Cookie looked at me.

"It's true."

"Just, let's go, please."

"Arak, what is this shit?"

"We need to go to my brother's house."

My uncle swung his head from side to side.

"You can't leave the door."

Arak brought his face close to Cookie's and grabbed his shoulders. He eyes burned with fear and anger.

"This is very bad. Trust me."

"Okay, okay!"

Cookie rose up with some difficulty. He took his car keys out of his pocket, handed them to Arak.

"You drive the Escalade. I don't feel so good."

"Can you get Akeyde's things?" Arak asked.

Cookie slowly shuffled to the locker in my room and piled my clothes into a plastic bag stored there by the hospital.

"Quickly! Quickly!"

The side of beef picked me up out of the bed like I was a little kid. Cookie got my stuff and looked at us, his eyes starting to wander. Suddenly, he wasn't in charge. Arak hustled me through the hallway to the elevator, Cookie trailing behind us.

We brushed by Karen Rogers, who yelled, "What the hell is going on?"

Arak yelled back, "Sorry, so sorry, we'll bring him back!"

The last words I heard her say, before the elevator doors closed were, "Cookie, he hasn't been discharged! What are you doing?"

The Brink of Disaster

(Razvarr Abatut)

My mattress was flat against the door, with a heavy bureau pushed against the mattress. It was the best protection I could manage.

The wait for Necu's work to be done was agonizing. I had wired him all the funds the Temple Director and the little hill thug with the explosives asked for, using new credit cards I took out in Dad's name. All the extortionate bribes were paid, finally.

As part of the plan, Necu also attached to the central part of the square balcony a webcam to show video of the Temple as he did his work and to podcast the results of the click of my mouse, to make the wireless connection across 6,000 miles to an antenna on a floodlight tripod to explode the bombs.

We had to go through a scaffold inspection, which took up a lot of time. I was impatient with it. I just wanted to press the button. Finally.

One of the minor Temple priests blessed and sanctified the scaffolds and floodlight tripods and Necu's camera in the early morning at the Temple, before it opened for prayers, one of the requirements of the Temple Director. Since they were 10 hours ahead of New York time, I was working at 11 o'clock in the evening to wait for the signal from Necu that he was ready. The Temple opened at 10:00 AM in Kawidtodia, midnight here in Queens.

In the little staff cafeteria Necu set up a hearty, elaborate breakfast with imported wine for the Temple maintenance men and the six security guards who covered the main square.

Necu's two men, Perno and Heshlu, brought in four floodlights, with a portable generator for electricity to power the lamps, through a ramp in the back of the Temple, built for deliveries. They were loaded with the bricks of C4, molded into the shells of the lights themselves, each one with a detonator ready for a wireless connection.

The two plugged the lights in to a generator and the floodlights came on. They set up the webcam on a balcony.

These bricks were not duds. Necu had cut off a small piece of the brick and attached a detonator to it. The piece was no bigger than a child's wood block toy. He conducted this little experiment in a dusty old field, far away from any roads or houses, with Perno and Heshlu helping out. The three of them walked 300 yards away from the block, then Necu set off the detonator with a cell phone. The block flashed and exploded as if it were opening up the ground. We had good stuff.

The maintenance men and security guards were happily absent for the sanctification ceremony and the placement and activation of the floodlights.

After this work was accomplished Perno and Heshlu disappeared. The security guards came back from the breakfast, as did the maintenance men. The guards walked to the front of the Temple to sit at a desk and provide security for the front of the Temple.

A few of the priests came by the look at the work Necu was doing. He ascended and descended a ladder while one of the maintenance men held the bottom. On the scaffolds he made a good show of taking pictures of each of the four the pillars from various angles while the priests looked on from the floor and pointed out details he should photograph.

After about ten minutes on the scaffold next to a pillar, Necu came down from the pillar. He brought out two bottles of wine from his backpack for the priests and the maintenance men.

"Here is a token of my gratitude."

The leader of the maintenance men took the bottle and saluted Necu. One of the priests grabbed the other bottle like he was a child snatching a chocolate bar.

"Let's bless the wine," Necu said.

"Yes! A good idea."

So the priest who had grabbed the wine said the blessing over the bottles.

The men all stood there with their heads bowed.

When the prayer was finished, Necu said, "Why not give yourselves a break? Enjoy your bottle of wine for a few minutes."

The leader of the work crew agreed. "There will be plenty of time for work later."

"Right!" Necu said. "It is a sacred act to drink wine in the Temple. I put extra cups in the cafeteria.

"And here are cups for you two gentlemen," he said, indicating the priests. He brought out cups for the priests.

"Very thoughtful," one of the priests said.

The maintenance men walked back to the cafeteria for the cups. The two priests stayed. They uncorked the wine with a corkscrew supplied by the resourceful Necu and drank a few cups while watching Necu climb the other ladders to the scaffolds and photograph the pillars.

"I'm going to take a little break and eat something, then come back and take more photographs," he announced and the priests shook his hand and went through the doors into the main chapel.

The Temple was due to open to worshippers in 15 minutes. Necu left the building and walked several blocks away to text his news to me from a phone outside. He was going to catch a bus to get moving as far away from the Temple as possible.

When he called to let me know he was on the bus, I knew it was finally time.

My index finger was itchy to click the signal to detonate, but my bladder was full. It had been some hours since I could go to the toilet. I started to urinate in a giant beer glass a friend from community college gave me, and which stood on my desk unused this whole summer.

In the middle of evacuating my bladder, the sound of a fierce knocking on the bedroom door startled me and I almost dropped the beer glass out of my left hand.

"Raz, open the door!"

It was Uncle Arak. I didn't respond and he didn't wait for me to open up. He tried to bust in the door. The wood started to bend as he bashed at it repeatedly.

I didn't know how much time would be left to me, so I finished up with the beer glass, set it down quickly on the carpet, zipped up fast and ran to the computer.

One click of the mouse and I could bring down a pillar, a wall and maybe more in the central square of the Blue and White Temple, the holiest site in the Kawidtodian religion. I was out of minutes.

I went to grab the mouse.

My bedroom window shattered. Glass fragments flew at me when I looked at the explosion. The bottom of a pair of purple basketball sneakers swung through the blaze of diamonds, screaming out of the night, and landed on the beer glass, throwing my horse load of urine up and onto the computer keyboard.

The sound of a power saw cutting through the wooden bedroom door threw my attention away from the purple sneakers.

The man wearing the sneakers dove for my power strip. His face landed in a puddle of urine. Even if he had gotten to the strip, I had my UPS and generator running with backup power. The computer stayed on.

The power saw had almost cut the door in half. I went for the mouse.

From underneath me came a hand, which grabbed my right wrist so I couldn't reach the mouse.

"Don't do it, Raz!"

"Who the fuck? Mr. Wood?"

Blood spurted from his right arm and shoulder, through a cross-weave of stitches. Urine ran down his cheeks.

I went for the mouse with my left hand. Mr. Wood pinched my wrist with his little paw. We wrestled and then he put his head into my chest and plunged us down onto the floor. The mouse flew off the desk and the wire connecting it to the screen dangled in the air.

I heard the power saw take out my beloved mattress and bureau.

Mr. Wood held on with an animal fierceness that shocked me. But I lifted my arm upward and hit him in his bloody stitches.

He released me and I reached for the dangling mouse again. I got it in my hand. My index finger was poised to click on the connection to detonate the bombs.

Teeth—human teeth—sunk into my wrist as deep as they could go.

I screamed as my flesh was punctured by his canines, but I held onto the mouse.

The elusive mouse click finally arrived through my finger, even though Mr. Wood's jaw locked on my wrist. I looked forward to seeing pieces of the Temple fall in front of my eyes. But my satisfaction was short-lived.

Uncle Arak's power saw sliced through the wire connecting the mouse to the screen. The thin cable flew through the air like a flying snake.

I screamed out: "Zgmoto!"

The Temple's central square froze. The webcam picture went black.

The Aftermath of Revolution

(Necu Brav)

I approached the mountains as fast as I could.

The winds were omnipresent and overwhelming and knifed through me at this height. There wasn't much snow left up here. It was summer, for one. Warmer weather was vaporizing whatever moisture we had. This dusty land, already so deprived of natural blessings, will probably grow even more arid in the coming years.

Some define tragedy as a disastrous event, especially one involving distressing loss or injury to life (source: thefreedictionary.com).

How do you define tragedy when the damage you have done to your target is not what you hoped it would be?

I suggest another definition. I will not take credit for this thought. I read it in a book, but cannot remember where I saw it first. Here it is: Tragedy is the inability to change the past.

When Razvarr contacted me, I did not realize how much my involvement would cost. As I plunged into the work, I began to understand. But, being young, I thought my committing to this cause would be sufficient to make everything work. We were revolutionaries. We would change things.

What a cruel joke that thought is to me now. Oh, what I would give to be a poor boy without a means of advancement, to live alone in a destitute flat, to wander the streets of the garbage-strewn city of Shalhak, with the goats and pigs foraging about for food.

When I got on the bus to leave the Temple area, I thought everything was going well.

But when the bus arrived in one town in the foothills of the mountains, stopping so passengers could get some food, the store I visited had a small television on. That's where I heard that someone had bombed the Blue and White Temple. A piece of a limestone wall in the central Temple square had come down, and the pillars were scratched and cut, but still stood.

The country was put on high alert. My name was broadcast on the national television. My chest burned with panic.

The Army regiments sped out of their barracks. The religious police were out on the streets, all units looking for "conspirators."

I knew I could not get back on the bus. The Army would stop it somewhere on the road and search the people.

I have written this journal and I am leaving it with a local contact I made on the underground railroad, in the hopes that it will find its way to Razvarr, so he obtains an understanding about what I have given.

Razvarr put almost nothing at risk. I want him to remember that.

I have a lot more to say, but I must stop. The Army trucks are coming. I can hear the roars of their engines. I am going to go into the harsh mountains on foot. Raz, wish me every drop of luck.

The Sacrifice

(Akeyde/Joe Wood)

I walked by an empty lot filled with discarded plastic bottles and cans of Gatorade, Red Bull and various energy drinks and vitamin waters. My outfit consisted of jeans, my torn and bloody eagle tee-shirt, and a yellow and purple windbreaker over that, hiding a special package.

I was on my way to my local assembly house, fully armed with a new suicide vest, which I put together pretty easily, to walk in on my father and the elders and blow myself up, and them, especially them, and rid the world of the sickness of the blood sacrifice of Akeyde.

After the lot came a small cemetery with a tall wire-metal fence.

Some of the tombstones were 200 years old, thin and weak. A number were cracked in two. The names on many had been rubbed out by wind and rain and time. Weeds grew among the graves. Trees had grown up right on top of the buried coffins. All denominations were here and they were all treated the same—badly.

The city owned the land and either willfully neglected it or just couldn't afford the upkeep. The city government was overwhelmed with financial trouble, so most people around here were willing to cut them slack on the cemetery. They were more worried about making the rent, paying for gas and putting food in the bellies of their children.

I had been out of the hospital for two weeks. The hair on my head was growing back. The religious school year would be starting up again in a week, after Labor Day.

"So, how did you spend your summer vacation?" I could imagine the other teachers asking me, and I laughed to myself.

I knew I wouldn't be going back, and I did feel a tinge of regret. I had been teaching there for almost a decade. In a way, it was like a second home. When I taught in public school all those years ago, I never had the same feeling about it.

The principal of the public school used to say, "You're part of our family here." But I never felt that. There was no family. All the principal's talk was hollow public relations.

But teaching in a Zan school, with my mother in the office, my uncles dropping around every once in awhile and the little Zan kids around me, treating me with respect (mostly) because of my knowledge of our tribe's history, I felt good. That was where I belonged.

Well, I needed to say goodbye to all that.

I had spent some time talking to Cookie about our strategy for tonight. He was letting me stay at his place, with Arak and his people always about, patrolling the property with guns hidden underneath their shirts or socks. (But I couldn't stay with him too long, as Cookie was loudly complaining just about every hour that I was distracting him from his businesses.)

I had talked to Cookie about running off, to not put on another suicide vest, ever.

Everything I knew was in Queens. If I belonged anywhere, it was here. What if I ran off? Where would I go? Where would I be safe? South Dakota, maybe. But the winters were frozen-awful and I heard somewhere that they put Cheez-Whiz on their hamburgers.

The stitches had more or less healed on my chest, shoulder and arm. My nicked lung was doing okay. Breaking through that kid's window a few weeks ago wasn't the ideal therapy for my body, but it had been great for my spiritual development.

It was Arak's idea. We didn't really have a plan. The trip from the hospital to the kid's house in Cookie's giant Escalade, with a truck bed in the back, only took about 15 minutes. Big, broad Arak, his bald head shiny with sweat, drove like a madman through the humid streets, babbling with panic. I sat in the front passenger seat. Cookie had fallen asleep in the back and I was worried about him. He was slumping under his seat belt.

"Akeyde, maybe you can talk to him. At the very least, it may shock Raz to hear your voice. You can distract him. Maybe, I don't know. Talk to him, yes. But, no. It won't work. He won't even listen to his parents. Let's think this thing through. Think, think, think!"

This wasn't helping me. I felt a little rush in my stomach. Only a quarter of an hour earlier, I had been sitting comfortably in a hospital bed, protected by Cookie's people. Now I was riding in a car with a giant, bald-headed man who was telling me that his nephew was planning on blowing up the central Temple in a country several thousand miles away and that we had to stop him.

"No, no, he's beyond talk. What's the main objective? What's the main objective? What's the main objective?" Arak screamed into the dashboard.

All the screaming woke up Cookie.

"Stop him," he whispered in a labored voice from the back seat.

Fortified by Cookie, Arak shouted, "Stop the kid from doing it!"

"Binele told me he has a back-up generator. Cutting the house's power won't work. We must get the kid out of the room. Kill the computer."

The truck tore around a corner and we braked in front of a small house. Arak left the truck lights on and the motor running.

"Wait here. I have to get something."

He put the truck in park and ran to a garage. He unlocked it, threw open the door, attacked a wall, ran out with a power saw and threw it in the bed of the Escalade. Then he went back and got a metal extension ladder and tossed it in the truck too.

"You don't want to lock the door to the garage?"

"There's no time! Think of the main objective!'

We ripped out of the driveway. "You feel okay?" he shouted at me.

"I'm healing."

"Heal faster! I need you to get on the roof."

"Why?"

"Two fronts. We need two fronts! Redundancy. Redundancy! You break through the boy's window. I'll get through his bedroom door."

"You're kidding."

"No! Do it! Just do what I tell you!"

"Arak, I don't know."

"You're good at breaking windows! I know this. Pretend your father is in there!"

When we parked, Arak threw the ladder up against the little two-story house and yelled at me, "Climb! Fast! Fast! Fast!"

I did it, my wounds clenching. Somehow, there was little pain. Arak had hyped me up and I scrambled up the ladder. Then I had the problem of having to get in the window. So I reached up for the gutter and flew into the glass. It seemed right and wrong at the same time.

As for the rest, I found it useful to pretend this kid who was one of my students when I was a public school teacher so long ago was really my father. That helped, especially when I bit into the kid's wrist.

When Arak had ripped through the computer's mouse cable with the power saw, we left the kid there, stunned and bleeding, while his parents squeezed through the door to tend to him.

I heard a little exchange before we left.

"Raz, are you okay?" That was the father.

"I will kill you, you little piece of horse pookie!" the mom said.

"Get away from me!" the kid shouted at them. "Now I really am in Zgmoto!"

I was glad to leave. We drove back to the hospital slowly. I limped in through the E.R. door, urine soaking through my clothes and bandages and drying on my face. Arak carried Cookie. He was admitted. Apparently, he had a clogged artery, but fortunately, no heart attack.

The hospital people ballooned out the artery and Cookie was ready to be discharged a few days later.

The beautiful Karen Rogers, her poetic black curls shaking with anger, stripped off my bandages, cleaned me up, and placed me back in my hospital bed for the night, as if I had never left.

"I don't even want to know what you did. Just sign these papers acknowledging that you left the building without authorization. You may have some trouble with the insurance company. You'll have to talk to them about leaving without authorization."

"Don't you need to know too?"

"I'll ask my supervisor to come and record your story. I don't want to hear it. I'm done with you and Cookie."

I wondered what she would think about me walking by a cemetery to a Zan assembly house, fully armed with a suicide vest.

Alter, Narish, Dreykop, and Lhokem and the other long-haired elders were meeting in the basement chapel of the *Basmadrosh*, the assembly house . They didn't think my father's house was safe for meetings anymore. Cookie had found out about the meeting through his network of people—namely, my mother—and told me to go.

Lost in thought, I had almost cleared the cemetery when a man in a purple and yellow windbreaker, seemingly out of nowhere, crept up from behind and tackled me at the midsection, driving both of us into the fence of the cemetery. The Zan assembly house, my objective, was about 200 yards away.

My wounds complained, as did my head, which had banged against the fence. I was a little dazed, but I knew who it was. The fake policeman. The fanatic.

This time he had a gun. Which he placed against my skull.

"Move."

"Where?"

He pushed me up to the front gate of the cemetery. He shot off the lock with the gun. The noise made my head hurt as if it had been laid open. He seemed undisturbed.

The lock thoroughly shot through, the gate swung open, as if it wanted us inside.

The fanatic pushed me into the graveyard.

We walked on a small gravel path, past the old tombstones. The man still had a bit of a limp where I had cut him with my mother's serrated knife. At the back of the cemetery, where a fence blocked off the cemetery from a stand of trees, he stopped me.

"Get on the ground."

I silently complied. I thought of the Squids ordering Zans to get on the ground before they shot them, the massacres of more than one hundred years ago.

He holstered the gun in the front of his jeans and I hoped it would go off and shoot his private parts.

"If you try to get up, I've got the gun right here for you."

He opened up his windbreaker, which had a long python of rope inside.

The fanatic tied me up, with my arms tied behind me and my calves tucked under my thighs. It was all too familiar. This was how my father used to tie me up for our pageants, except he used the rope to tie me to strips of wood, just like the original Akeyde. Who was me. Or not me. I was thinking not.

Then the fanatic drew a long knife from a leather holster across his chest. He put it up high in the air.

"Now you need to say, 'Will it please God that I die?'"

"I'm really tired of this. Just kill me already."

He brought down the knife. It hit the bricks of explosives.

"What is this?"

"This is a suicide vest."

"Where is the detonator?"

I laughed.

"You'll need to untie me to get to it."

So the man turned me over and unknotted the ropes tying my arms together.

When he finished with that, he attended to the ropes around my legs. After he had freed me, I stood up and considered running. There were dozens of gravestones though, and I wouldn't have a clear path.

He reached down on the ground for his gun and put it in his right hand.

"Now, where is the detonator?"

The fanatic limped toward me and went to search my pockets with his left hand.

I punched him in the throat.

It wasn't a very good punch. My fist didn't have a lot of space to gather speed. But it stunned the fanatic enough to stagger him backwards away from my pockets.

"Okay," he whispered out hoarsely, "I'll just shoot you. Die, Akeyde. Fulfill the prophecy."

He didn't say it with much conviction. His voice had a dead quality to it, whether from the punch to the throat or something else, I don't know. Maybe exhaustion.

I was so sick of people telling me I had to die. The fanatic shot the gun, looking like a man frozen on a page, a stick figure from a comic book.

Loaded with the bombs, I jumped and crouched behind a gravestone. The bullet hit a marker and dug into the stone.

He limped after me and shot the gun again. I dove for the shelter of another grave. The fanatic shot the top off a 200-year-old piece of stone. It was thin from age. I picked it up and threw it at him with two hands.

I missed his head and he shot at me again. This bullet hit another marker. I dug up a clod of earth and threw it at him. I hit him in the forehead with a piece of dirt and grass.

That infuriated him and he shot the gun again, this time wildly. Another gravestone took a bullet.

I moved up his right flank and threw a second clutch of grass and dirt at his head and got him in the eye.

He shook it off and tried to find me. I tried to get around behind him.

A voice rumbled through the darkness of the cemetery.

"Stop shooting or I'll blow your head off."

I heard the click of a gun. A very big gun.

"Drop it."

A gun fell to the ground. I stood up from behind a grave. The giant Arak had the fanatic's head in front of a gray gun, the color matching the gravestones. The barrel had a long tunnel. The fanatic looked terrified.

"I owe you," I told him.

He ignored that. "What are we going to do with this monkey?"

"Let's make him an example."

The Reckoning

(Akeyde/Joe Wood)

Alter, Narish, Dreykop, and Lhokem and the other long-haired elders were talking when I walked down the steps and into the basement, with my vest. Three muscle men with large handguns guarded the elders as they sat at a long table in the children's chapel. Fine ceramic plates were set for a post-meeting snack of yellow cake and coffee. Their world was crashing down around them, but they still made time for cake and coffee.

Behind me was the fanatic, slumped over and spent, with Arak at his back with the giant gun.

"How are we going to deal with this situation?" Dreykop asked.

"Akeyde has to be removed," Narish said.

Panic was spreading through the room like a virus. The elders started shouting at each other.

"Shut up!" Father yelled. "Shut up!"

Everybody got quiet fast.

"We may not be able to kill him now. Everything is too public," said another elder named Yenooz Pakhed. "We can put him on trial in front of the Zan assembly house. The whole congregation can hear about his crimes."

"No, no," Alter said. "A congregational trial is crazy. This business has already gotten far out of hand. Besides, the police are looking for him. If they catch him, there will be lots of trouble for all of us."

"We can wait six months or so, let everything calm down," said Lhokem. "Then, we catch him and he disappears. Somebody drives him out to the swamps around Kennedy Airport and one of these men takes care of him. He will never be found. That gives us deniability."

The men guarding the elders stayed silent, looking forward, not showing any emotion.

"The grasslands at Kennedy may not be far enough away," Alter mused. "We will have to disappear him, but we need to do it now," my father said. "Every day he's alive he mocks our faith, mocks God."

I chose this moment to make our entrance.

My wounds burned, but I ignored them.

"Hi, Dad. I brought you a present!"

Arak swept over to my side, with the fanatic in front of him

He stayed in his seat and looked at me as if I were crazy, his mouth open, stunned.

The guards pulled out their very big guns. Two aimed for somewhere around my ears. The other one pointed his barrel at Arak. That made me a little nervous, but I pressed on.

"You bring a dirty Squid in here? You're going to straight to hell," Narish said.

"You'll be there with me, old man."

That shocked Narish. I had never spoken to him like that. He picked up his cup of coffee and threw the contents at me. He missed, but got the fanatic, burning his ear. The fanatic screamed and jerked. Arak righted him and pressed the gun more tightly to his skull.

"You have no right to be here," Lhokem said. "You're an infidel and a criminal."

My head bowed at that. My family, these men, who tried to send me to my death, could still hurt me with their words. How is it that they could have changed so much from the men I knew when I was young?

My father stopped Lhokem with an upraised hand.

"We need to talk. You get the fanatic back, I don't even know his name, don't want to know his name, and don't tell me he's my cousin, I'm sick of cousins. Arak walks out of here unharmed. That's the deal."

My father squinted at me, then said in a low voice, "Okay." I kind of knew he was lying. He was the type of person who would agree to what you were saying, then when you turned your back, he would do whatever he wanted to do. I could easily see him appointing one of the muscle men to try to hunt down Arak and kill him.

I proceeded with my speech.

"Before you kill me, I just want to make sure I've got everything clear. I'm not that bright, as I've repeatedly demonstrated."

Father relaxed a little. I had conceded my own death at his hands, so this helped him trust me.

I gestured at the fanatic. "Why did you send this crazy son of a bitch after me?"

"Don't tell him, he doesn't deserve to know," Dreykop said.

My father ignored him.

"He was just a tool to persuade you to do the job."

"He could have killed me. He almost did."

"It was a gamble, but we needed to motivate you, after your first failure. If you fought off Doy here—he has a name and he is one of your cousins—I thought you would have the necessary spiritual strength to blow up the Squid Temple."

"And if I didn't?"

"You would be dead and we would have fulfilled the prophecy and found someone else to blow up the Temple. It was a test. You fought off Doy, but you still failed it."

"Did I fail?"

"Completely."

We were talking about two different ideas and I knew engaging my fundamentalist father in a conversation about morals wouldn't go anywhere.

"Why do you keep trying to hurt me? You hired some Squid goons to hit me with a tire iron 21 years ago. You trained me to become a killer. All this pain and death. For what?"

"You need to follow the rules, Akeyde. You are the sacrificial son."

"You wanted to punish me?"

"I wanted to make you angry, son, like me. You were such a little nothing before that."

"I'm not so sure I'm your son anymore."

"You will always be my son."

"Only technically."

With that, Father motioned to the three gunmen to approach me. I ripped open the windbreaker to expose the bombs, then pulled the plastic detonator out of my pocket and raised it into the air.

Many of the elders screamed like young children.

My father drew back a little in fear. But he was also still scrutinizing.

"How did you get a new vest?"

"I built a new one. It's so easy to make these things. Your man Vehktre taught me that."

Then I gestured to the men with the guns.

"Move back behind the table where I can see you," I told the thugs. They held their hands, with the guns, in the air and walked backwards to behind my father's chair.

"If I hear one click of a gun, we all go boom."

"What do you want?" Narish asked, with fear and steel in his voice at the same time.

"First, let Arak, my man here, go."

"Alright."

Arak knocked the fanatic on the head with his gun and sent him to the floor. Then he aimed his gun at the long table of elders and backed out of the hall, finally walking backwards up the staircase, his gun still pointed at the table.

"Now, let's talk."

Lhokem piped up. "About what, infidel?"

I held the detonator a little higher. "If you keep insulting me, maybe we'll all just explode together."

The elders' faces were drawn in horror.

"I was there at the Kawidtodian Temple, with dozens of people I could have killed. Why would you all want me to do this terrible thing?"

Alter breathed deeply. "We talked about this before, Akeyde. We are in a war with the Kawidtodians. They are attacking us. We need to fight back."

"They can't be all bad. I met a nice one tonight. He saved my life."

"They're all the same."

"So they all deserve to die."

Father sucked in his breath.

"Yes."

"I need to hear you say it, clearly. You programmed me to kill the Squids."

He finally lost his old temper with me. "Why do you ask me what you already know?"

"For the record."

"What record? You'll be dead and we will try again with somebody else."

"You programmed me to kill the Kawidtodians. Say it."

The temper went boom.

"Yes! I wanted you to kill as many Squids as possible! We gave you the rage. But you didn't have the guts!"

The old man could still bring me low.

"I'm ashamed of the rage now, Alter. But I'm not ashamed of failing to kill those people."

"You're not allowed to call me that. I'm your Onfirer."

"Alter."

My father laughed, his skull more a death's-head visage than ever. "You can't kill us now, Akeyde. You couldn't kill anybody before. You won't do it here."

"Old man, I'm looking at death anyway. Your men are going to kill me, so why not take all of you down to hell with me? You want to wage war from the safety of your living room couches. Now you'll see what a suicide bomb is really like."

"You cannot. You are too soft."

I fingered the detonator. "I'm going to count down from three, and when I reach zero, it's all over."

The elders scrambled out of their chairs and started running. Their seats shot out from them. Some fell on the floor. Some limped to the exit.

Alter shouted at the gunmen: "Shoot!"

The men raised their guns and pointed them at my chest, ready to fire.

We heard the front door of the assembly house blown apart. Fevered steps of shoe leather running downstairs brought the blue shirts of the New York City Department to the basement to face the elders.

The gunmen were stunned and reflexively pulled their heads and guns backward.

"Gun!"

Half a dozen cops were frozen like statues next to me, their Glocks aimed at the foreheads of the gunmen. The lead guy, a detective in sharp clothes, about six foot three inches and with football lineman shoulders, edged up behind me. Keeping a gun on my father's thugs, he quickly wedged his feet behind mine, then threw his knees into the back of my legs and brought me face down onto the floor.

The detective shouted at me, "Stay down!"

The thugs recovered their aim, but now pointed at the detective.

"You wanna shoot somebody, schmucks? Now you're gonna have to shoot me."

I looked up but still didn't see much from the floor.

There was a long moment where nothing seemed to happen.

"Put the guns down, assholes," Lt. Rosten shouted. He was the one who had knocked me to the floor.

I heard a sound of somebody getting ready to fire a weapon, from about six feet away.

Then another gun opened up just once. The blast came from the police lieutenant.

I couldn't help myself. I tried to stand up. The lieutenant punched me in the back of the head with his free hand.

One of the gunmen had fallen backwards. I saw him from the floor. He appeared to be bleeding from the shoulder.

Coming on from the shadows of the assembly house's back entrance, a cop placed his gun on the neck of one of the thugs still standing, as did the other officer with him—a Lt. Braff. A Lt. Heck, a lady detective and a Lt. Martinez, another lady, put their guns up against the neck of the other thug. They were dressed crisply in suits too—a New York City detective tradition.

"God, I hate shooting people!" yelled Lt. Rosten. "There's too much goddamn paperwork."

The two gunmen put their hands up. The cops ordered the men to lie on the floor, where they got quickly cuffed.

I was allowed to get up. The third gunman's shoulder was blasted into mangled tissue. He was moaning on the floor. Lt. Rosten kicked him in the ribs. "You fucking idiot. Why couldn't you just put your fucking gun down?"

I was glad that somebody else was being called an idiot.

"You can't do this," shouted Uncle Dreykop as he was recovered from the back of the hall and brought over in handcuffs to go up the stairs to a police van. "This is a house of God."

"You planned a mass murder here," Lt. Braff told them.

Lt. Heck said to the elders, "Hands behind your backs."

"You don't know what you're doing," Uncle Narish said. "We're religious men."

"You're under arrest for terrorist activity. We have recordings of you people admitting conspiracy to kill dozens of people at the Kawidtodian Temple in Manhattan," Lt. Braff explained. "We also have you on tape planning to kill this young man," he said, pointing at me. "We've placed microphones all over this place."

"Akeyde, you have betrayed the Zan people!" Lhokem yelled wildly as they carried him off to the police van upstairs.

I yelled back. "My name is Joe Wood! It says so on my Social!"

I took my finger off the detonator. The suicide vest was a fake anyway.

Debts Come Due

(Razvarr Abatut)

I received Necu's journal, mailed in the middle of October, by somebody on the Kawidtodian underground railroad, without a return address, so I didn't know where he was. That might have been for the best.

It was difficult for me to respond to what Necu wrote. I asked him to make a big commitment to the cause. Maybe he just wasn't strong enough for the job. And we did knock down a piece of the Temple wall. We staggered the government, even if only for a few moments.

I made commitments of my own, which were significant. I gave the credit card bills I had hidden in a drawer to my parents, with my father's and mother's names on them. I was mad at them for what they'd done to stop me, so I unloaded on them however I could.

Predictably, my bald-headed parents panicked.

"What is all this?" Father asked.

"The cost of revolution," was all I could say.

"How much money did you borrow in my name?" he demanded.

"I'm not sure."

Mother swooned when she saw the bills. There is nothing like debt to concentrate the mind.

After days of hysteria and recrimination (which was a terrible persecution to my brain and body), I was pressed into service at my father's store. I will work as a cashier, stock boy, and janitor, all rolled into one. Father will supervise my work. I am exhilarated by this arrangement.

Father is also going to take a second job with a cousin to help pay off the debt. My mother tried to use this to create all kinds of guilt in me. It was beginning to work, but I still resented the hell out of her.

"We can lose the house, lose the business, everything, because of you," Mother said.

I could not concede the point to her, but I made no counterargument. Father talked to Arak about all his worries and Arak asked Cookie Kletser for a loan. He could not go to our cousins because they would ask us for a reason why we needed the money. Arak would not be able to explain the truth without the cousins going completely crazy. And Arak did not feel he could make up a lie that would make sense to anybody.

When Arak explained why he needed the money, Cookie paid off all the card debt immediately, so the interest on the loans would not grow to poisonously high levels. There was plenty of principal and interest to pay, don't get me wrong, but at least we would not increase it horribly every month.

"You can't screw around with these credit card companies," Cookie said to us in his unique way. "They're like the Mafia. They'll choke the life out of you."

But now we owed all the money to Cookie. He was better than the credit card companies, I suppose, but he was still a Zan.

Based on Cookie's seat-of-the-pants analysis, I may have to work for my father for the next seven years.

My mother told me that I needed to have my buttocks kicked. Well, now they will be. For seven years.

So, while I have not paid the same price as Necu for our little project, I feel oppressed by the very considerable cost of my own commitment.

On a lesser, yet still profound level, I am still in some shock at having my old second-grade teacher crash through the bedroom window and bite me on the wrist to try to stop me from going through with the Blue and White Temple project. Which didn't quite work. I blew out part of the limestone wall and did some damage despite his efforts. The pillars of the Temple were lined with scratches and dust, but remained standing.

I did a study of the situation as to why we didn't get a bigger explosion. Amic came over the house again, completely ignorant of what I'd done. He wanted to show me his new iPad. I used it to quickly investigate what happened at the Temple.

C4 is very destructive, but we just didn't have enough of it. The shells of the floodlights didn't contain enough space for more C4. We didn't have enough power packed into the floodlight shells to do maximum damage.

I should have seen this before. I made a huge mistake and I can't reverse it now.

A few weeks after Mr. Wood attacked me, Arak asked that I meet with him and his uncle at a secret location on Long Island.

I did so quite reluctantly, but my mother made me go. Arak also worked on me, said Mr. Wood's attorney had gone to some trouble to negotiate this meeting. He told me how hard it was to get me to see Mr. Wood. He nagged and nagged me. I had been coerced again, as I had been strong-armed into going to Temple with my mother.

We drove to a town filled with cemeteries. Arak stopped the car in front of a national military cemetery. So many tombstones, arranged in neat rows that ran on and on.

Arak made a call on his phone.

A few minutes later, a van with no windows met us. A man wearing sunglasses and an F.B.I. windbreaker directed us into the back of the van.

The van had seats lined against the walls. A steel partition separated us from the driver, so we couldn't see out the front of the vehicle.

This was all very interesting and not a little scary. But the ride was short. A few minutes later, we arrived in a small city of warehouses, three to four stories high, all beige brick and completely undistinguished. You could not tell one from the other.

The F.B.I. agent was met by other agents in blue windbreakers, and soldiers in full combat uniforms, holding very big automatic weapons.

I was quite jealous. I wished I had that kind of firepower at my disposal to help bring down the Kawidtodian government.

We were escorted inside. The warehouse itself was empty. There was a concrete slab for a floor. Guided by the agents and soldiers, we walked to a small windowed office in the back of the building.

In the office was the biter. Mr. Wood. With him was an older man, with a belly the size of Rhode Island. This was the famed "savior" of our family – Cookie Kletser. They were sitting on metal-backed folder chairs at a flimsy card table in the middle of the room, next to a thick oak desk that looked to be from the 1930s.

Two soldiers were placed inside the room. The agents directed us to sit at the card table with Mr. Wood and Cookie.

I understood that Mr. Wood must have been in a great deal of serious trouble, but I didn't know why.

He shot up a Kawidtodian temple. One bullet fired. What did he do to deserve this? Breaking my bedroom window and biting me on the wrist didn't earn him national security protection.

Two soldiers were placed in the room with us, no trace of emotion on their faces. The F.B.I. agent, still wearing his sunglasses barked out, "You have 10 minutes." He closed the door.

Mr. Wood wasn't particularly happy to see me. He looked at me and nodded hello with a grimace. I realized that Mr. Wood and his attorney didn't even necessarily want this meeting.

I sat down, didn't say hello, tried to avoid looking at the man who bit me. Turning to Arak, I said, "You wanted this meeting, didn't you?"

"He," I said, gesturing at Mr. Wood, "doesn't even want to be here."

"He was your teacher. You looked up to him. I hoped you two could be friends again."

I smiled. "You want us to make up?"

Arak didn't get my sarcasm. "Yes!"

My uncle then gestured at Mr. Wood. "You better start talking or we'll run out of time."

Cookie, his fat forehead sweating, elbowed Mr. Wood in the arm. He grimaced.

Mr. Wood hunched his shoulders forward and smashed his jaws together as if he didn't want to speak. Then came a torrent of mealy-mouthed words. .

"I'm sorry I crashed through your window. I'm sorry I bit you. Your uncle asked me for help. We wanted to make sure you didn't do something crazy."

I looked at the soldiers. I didn't like this conversation in front of them.

"You had no right," I said, spitting out the words.

"My uncle is deducting the cost of the window and the cost of treating your wound from what your parents owe him for taking on their debts."

"Don't you mean my debts?"

He sighed heavily.

"You're ignoring the main issue," I said. You're not making things better."

Mr. Wood shook his head.

I was careful with my words around the two soldiers. If they hadn't been there, I would have been far more poisonous.

"I made a statement. My webcam video made it onto YouTube and I've gotten a couple thousand views so far. And you tried to stop me."

Amic told me about the video of the bombing, on one of his oppressive visits to my room. He didn't know I planned the whole thing. He was very agitated that somebody would have the violence in him to try to blow up the Temple Square. I nodded my head and made a grim face as if to agree with him.

I almost couldn't brag to Mr. Wood about what I had done. In the end, it wasn't really much.

"You can't go around doing stuff like this," he said to me.

The soldiers made me nervous. I didn't want Mr. Wood to go into any details. So I turned the focus back on him.

"You should talk. You shot a gun in our temple. What the hell were you trying to do?"

"I had some problems I needed to work out."

"You've got an interesting method of solving your issues."

"So do you."

My anger with him made me temporarily incautious around the soldiers. I worried about that after we had left.

"You are a counter-revolutionary."

Cookie was dozing into an upraised hand propped on the card table and he suddenly came fully awake.

"What? What'd he say?" Cookie shouted. "Listen, ding-dong, your own tribesmen might kill you if they find out you did this. Joe and Arak were trying to save your life!'

I gave him two squinty eyes. "I was trying to save my own life. I didn't need anybody to help."

"I am sorry," Arak said. "He is not ready to listen."

I stood up. I wanted out of there. The soldiers, the F.B.I. agents, the anonymous warehouse, the conversation, Mr. Wood's circumstances, all creeped me out. Mr. Wood looked at me with a pained expression.

I pointed at him and yelled, "Who do you think you are?"

Mr. Wood took off his thick glasses, bowed his head and leaned into his right hand.

I walked out on them. The F.B.I. men escorted us to the door, then drove us in their van to Arak's S.U.V. He and I drove home in silence.

Where I've Got Some More Explaining to Do

(Akeyde/Joe Wood)

My physical wounds were healing.

Father, the elders, and Pilsiker (the redwood tree man), were locked up, their braying requests for bail denied. Mother had not tried to contact me and I didn't call her either. I wanted to keep her serrated knife in Cookie's house, but I had to give it up to the investigators on the case for possible use in the trial, or trials.

Vehktre was nowhere to be found, and I suspect he never will be.

I am being prosecuted for breaking a shop window on Queens Boulevard, burglary in the Manhattan apartment where I first took refuge, the knife fights with the redwood tree man and the fanatic in my backyard, the shooting in the Kawidtodian temple and of course the aborted suicide bombing attempts, but the U.S. Attorney for the southern district of New York is not quite sure how to approach my case, because Cookie and I went to the police. I turned myself in and I agreed to trap my father and the elders.

Nobody thought about the possibility of a fanatic attacking me in the graveyard near the *Basmadrosh* and disrupting the entrapment scheme.

Except for Cookie. He asked Arak to shadow me, just in case. The police were embarrassed about that little gap in their plan, so Arak wasn't charged with carrying a concealed weapon.

The police had released me from a black van two blocks away from the graveyard for my trip to the assembly house, to see my father. They wanted to create the illusion that I was alone. They succeeded. Arak and Cookie got us all out of the ultimate screw-up in the whole plan. (The fanatic is still shouting for my head in solitary confinement at Riker's Island.)

We dealt with the threat from one Zan fundamentalist. Now I have to deal with the other fundamentalists in my tribe, as well as the one still lurking inside me.

I agreed to testify in open court against Alter and the other hairy lunatic elders, including my uncles, whom I loved like older brothers, and who turned on me, a source of continuing pain for me.

I have talked to the F.B.I. and the New York City Police Department about what I know of my uncles' criminal activities from since I was a boy, and from my information about them and their family connections, the police have been able to get to work on dismantling their drug dealing and money laundering networks and protection rackets.

As a result, I have been told I might receive a relatively short sentence that could range from 15 to 20 years. As an incentive to get me to talk even more, the U.S. Attorney's people seem to hint that they might ask the judge for a lighter sentence than that.

I don't necessarily trust them when they try to sweet-talk me. I've been talking because I need to talk. I didn't need incentives. I wanted to get rid of all the history of the Zans rocketing around inside me. I could still feel terrible agonies when I recalled atrocities I've read about from centuries ago, from the conquests of the Zans by the Kawidtodians to the genocides of 1908. I can't contain it all.

I have had plenty of time to think about these tragedies. It was impossible to get bail. The U.S. Attorney originally wanted to put me in prison outside the state for my own protection. But my lawyer argued that this might have an extremely negative effect on my mental state and my ability to testify clearly.

I told my lawyer, Seymour Glickstein, that I could handle being in prison, that I deserved to be in prison, but when he heard that, Glickstein started gesturing wildly and angrily shouted me down.

Glickstein yelled, "You have the mental stability of a porcupine!"

I didn't know why he was so mad.

The two sides made a compromise. During the week I am held in an undisclosed location, where I am deposed and I give material to the U.S. attorney's staff to help them build a case against the elders. F.B.I. agents play cards and watch television with me and bring me books to read. On random varying weekends, Cookie is occasionally allowed to stay with me overnight, with federal agents and police officers guarding us at all times.

After negotiations with Glickstein and consulting with a team of government psychiatrists, the U.S. Attorney determined that seeing Cookie every once in awhile would help keep me somewhat sane.

The police hunted the East River for my suicide vest and they found it, after weeks of intensive searching. They were very lucky. The black plastic bag holding the vest had gotten wrapped around a small rock about a mile downstream from where I threw it over the fence. Despite the whipsaw currents of the river, the bag held fast to the stone. The police investigators separated the wet nails, ball bearings and explosives into pieces, and bagged them for court.

It is a general rule of Chekhov's that if a weapon is introduced it must be used. Well, he never considered a suicide vest.

The federal trial is currently scheduled for January. Also, the U.S. attorney is considering filing charges against the elders for attempted violation of the Kawidtodians' civil rights. A hate crime, in other words.

The newspapers, the TV, and the Net have been busted wide open in talking about the case.

The publicity made me extremely uncomfortable. The bloggers were particularly hard to digest. A guy on a liberal web site wrote that I was "a sick, violently disturbed man who should be locked up forever." A news anchor from the WHIP network condemned me as well. "First Wood wanted to bomb the

Kawidtodian Temple," he said. "Then he changed his mind and didn't bomb the temple. He's just another liberal flip-flopper."

The New York Times editorialized that "Mr. Wood is a confused young man who actually ended up doing the right thing. However, he needs psychiatric support services immediately."

My own tribe had been pretty tough too. A number of Zan bloggers ripped into me for refusing to go through with the bombing.

The Kawidtodian people here and overseas have cursed me. First, I am a Zan, which is a strike against me right there. And my attempt to do the bombing aroused Kawidtodian hatred to new levels of vitriol, even though I aborted. Only a few Kawidtodians came to my defense by saying that by refusing to push the detonator in the temple I showed that I am a friend of their people.

The nation of Kawidtodia responded to the news of the case by cracking down even harder on their own people. Also, the country's government put the two bombing plots—mine and Razvarr's—together in the public mind.

The Pumn brought the population to a boil by denouncing both the Manhattan and Blue and White Temple bomb plots as a "Zan conspiracy to destroy us."

The Blue and White Temple was closed until further notice. The nation's leading architects were consulting on how to fix the wall and the pillars. There was much crying and shouting and fist-shaking about the damage to a temple that was almost 3,000 years old.

The Temple's entire security team and janitorial staffs were fired. An investigation into how Razvarr (who was of course directed by me, according to the Kawidtodian press) and his people penetrated the Temple's defenses so easily was being led by the nation's chief of secret police.

Thousands of people with shaved heads were on the streets of Shalhak every day, carrying signs about the Zan monkeys and dogs. Dozens of the four to five thousand of Zans left in the country have been beaten. Many have been harassed. Three Zans were murdered in their little shops.

At the demonstrations, my photograph was displayed in black and white on posters with a red hole in my forehead. I got hanged and burned in effigy too. It's all pretty upsetting. Razvarr is not even a factor to the Kawidtodians. I am the only villain, the corrupt Zan who developed the twin plots against the temples in the U.S. and in Kawidtodia and controlled the small group of Kawidtodians henchman so thoroughly to do exactly what I wanted.

Worldwide, Zans were taking hits left and right. My father, the elders, me: we all brought new shame to the Zan people. Zan assembly houses in France and Russia were torched. A Spaama in Uzbekistan was attacked by thugs outside his assembly house. They broke his spine. He is paralyzed for life.

The TV shows, newspapers and blogs gushed with confessions by members of my tribe, where they said they were ashamed of being a Zan. That didn't help either, but I understood their pain. I felt it every day.

My job was lost, of course. The religious school sent me a notice that I'd been fired, delivered by the U.S. Postal Service to Cookie's house. I heard from Cookie that my mother lost her job with the Spaama too.

Cookie was looking for a job for her in the neighborhood, with his many business contacts. Something clean, like working as an appointments secretary in a medical office. He had a friend who owned an MRI clinic on Austin Street, one of the main streets in the neighborhood.

Razvarr threatened to press charges against me for breaking his bedroom window and biting him. Cookie told me about it, laughing, because his parents and Arak told him if he did that, he'd have some bigger problems explaining to the police what he was doing to cause us to break into his room. Arak also pointed out that credit card fraud was only the most minor of his crimes.

A few weekends ago I ran into Karen Rogers. I was on suburban Long Island, in one of the bedroom communities, wandering around a book store on the one outside trip Glickstein had negotiated on my behalf. The U.S. Attorney and Glickstein had a shouting match about it, but Glickstein was good. He brought up saving what was left of my sanity. (Even though I'm totally sane.)

I wanted to breathe in the air of a book store. Ordering books online just isn't enough sometimes.

I was allowed out into the world for one hour. As soon as we were outside of the safe house, I knew this trip was a mistake. But I had to go through with it, or Glickstein might get upset. He had fought so hard for this.

The reason the trip was a mistake: I was enclosed in a fluid human box, with two F.B.I. agents and four soldiers from the United States Marine Corps holding machine guns, their faces nervous and twitchy. We were only slightly less conspicuous than the circus coming to town. I looked at the stacks of books, trying to duck and weave around the bodies and gun barrels of my escorts, shopping for a good read.

"Sorry," I said to one Marine," could you move your gun a little to the left? I can't see the titles on the middle shelf."

He glared at me, but he did it. For about two seconds.

But then I saw Karen Rogers and her tight black curls at the end of an impossibly narrow aisle of books. I charged down the aisle. I didn't let anyone stop me.

When I got closer to her, I half-smiled and put my hand up to wave. At first she didn't know who I was. A few moments later she remembered. I walked up to her, with my escorts all around, rushing to keep pace with me and keep me surrounded among all the books.

"Is there any chance I can get you to come out for dinner with me?"

She lowered her eyes and smiled in a parental sort of way.

"You are a very interesting person. I think deep inside you is something romantic. But you've got too many scars for me, Akeyde. Too much damage."

She swept her hand at the soldiers as evidence.

"Call me Joe."

"See, I don't even know what name to call you. You're really screwed up."

I looked back at the soldiers. They had raised eyebrows.

After that trip, the U.S. Attorney called Glickstein and they had another shouting match. We had to move to a new undisclosed location. And I would not be permitted to go outside again.

It's been a pretty ugly education in human behavior. You know you're in trouble when federal agents, New York City Police Department detectives, and the U.S. Attorney are your best friends. Federal agents and several men armed with very large automatic weapons watched dozens of romantic comedies with me on DVDs in a plain white room at my undisclosed location.

I couldn't see action movies. The agents asked me. I wasn't able to bring myself to watch that stuff. I disappointed them on a daily basis.

Lt. Braff, Lt. Heck, and Lt. Rosten sometimes visited me and brought me scones with Toyre seeds baked into them.

Cookie, bless his damaged heart, has stood by me as solidly as any human being can. When he comes to see me, I get a human connection outside all the cops and agents.

Cookie lost 20 pounds altogether, but he was somewhat miserable. He couldn't smoke, drink coffee, or eat chocolate. His love of pornography was undiminished, but he had to cut down on his entertainment time by going for walks in the neighborhood on his surgeon's advice. He was also sleeping more.

I think about escaping constantly. However, Akeyde/Joseph Wood is essentially a ward of the U.S. Attorney until the trials are over and I fulfill the terms of whatever sentence I get from the court. I can't possibly leave.

I have a dream of teaching in a town in northern Vermont, after my trial, and the elders' trials, and the required prison time for me. This may not be realistic, considering my history. But the F.B.I. has been talking to me about the possibility of putting me in a witness protection program after I have served my sentence. I could start fresh somewhere.

Burlington is one place I've been thinking about. According to the town's official web site, the place has a great university, an interesting downtown, and a beautiful lake. Whenever the trials and my incarceration are over, I think I would like to go. Even though Queens is my home, I don't think I will be able to come back and keep my sanity. Too many people are angry with me. Under the witness protection program, I can change my name again, maybe to something even more anonymous than Joe Wood, like Steve Jones. Also, it may be a good idea to convert to Christianity, to blend in better.

I wish for happy endings, so I'm sorry I can't end with me getting a date with the beautiful Karen Rogers or a great joke. I'm not a dark kind of person, not really. I'm just screwed up, like everybody else. Okay, I guess not like everybody else. How many people let themselves get pulled into fundamentalist religious nightmares based on a founding myth requiring human sacrifice?

There is a religious saying I've heard around our Queens neighborhood in years past, from some other minor tribe that moved to America (I think it was the Jews – they're always hanging around), but it goes like this: "To life!" That's one religious ethic I feel is safe and positive. That means no one gets killed for who they are or what they believe or don't believe.

Philip Roth once wrote, "Oh, to be a center fielder, a center fielder—and nothing more."

I hope I know what Roth was getting at, so I want to offer a thought of my own as to my identity:

Oh, to be an American and nothing more!

Perhaps that's not enough for some, even for many. But it may be for me.

Cookie suggested that I write down all this stuff. It would help explain the story to the public and help with the trial, he said.

Arak confiscated Razvarr's computer at the point of his power saw and we were able to retrieve all his Word and email files to include them here. Arak also stripped Razvarr's room for any other evidence about the plot. He found a journal from some kid named Necu, in Kawidtodia. He didn't know exactly what it was, but he gave it to Cookie anyway. The story would not be complete without Razvarr's account of things, as well as Necu's little journal.

Razvarr's family had terrible misgivings about including all this damning information here, but Cookie insisted, and they are quite literally in debt to him. The family is concerned about retribution from other Kawidtodians, naturally, and the possibility of a federal investigation into his attempt to bomb the Blue and White Temple.

They have a right to be paranoid. Arak told Cookie that Razvarr's mother and father have already decided if they get trouble from the publication of these materials that they will consider changing their names and moving to some very quiet place far away. Even if the Justice Department doesn't come after Raz, they've thought of moving to Australia. I know what that kind of trouble feels like.

I am sure Razvarr will be quite angry about the use of his computer files, but at this point, I'm trying to salvage something of a life. I have a lot of work to do. I still don't like the Squids (Except for Arak and Raz and Raz's father. And all the Kawidtodian students I had when I was a public school teacher. And their parents. And the guy who kissed my head at the train station.), but I can't kill them. Glickstein advised me not to write that here, but I have to admit the truth of my feelings. I must try to find a way to go beyond the old books, the ancient myths, the bitter roots of my need to hate.

Afterword

"...no man shall be compelled to frequent or support any religious worship or ministry or shall otherwise suffer on account of his religious belief..."

—Thomas Jefferson

I would like to believe in God, a wise, loving, kind God. But then I see Kim Kardashian, star of such fine cultural fare as "Keeping Up With the Kardashians," walking across a red carpet accompanied by hundreds of flashbulbs and I have my doubts.

But for those of us who still believe unequivocally in the Deity, let's consider the possibilities of humility.

A Catholic monk, John Dominic Crossan, once wrote, "God is even more radical than we can imagine." With this in mind, there are a number of people who think they have a real understanding of what God wants. (I wish I could share their confidence.) Some even believe that God wants them to kill other people who don't share their particular beliefs.

In a way, this book was inspired by a visit to my brother-in-law's house. He lives in Washington, D.C. My wife released me for a day from my family responsibilities so I could go pay my respects to our soldiers at Arlington and visit with a few Presidents, namely Mr. Lincoln and Mr. Jefferson.

I had never visited the Jefferson Memorial, so I really wanted to do that. The least inspiring thing about it is the huge statue of Jefferson standing in the middle of the rotunda. What grabbed me were the words on the arched walls. Many of the quotations etched in the marble are about religion. In the light of suicide bombings and terrorist attacks from around the world that scream out from the pages of the daily newspapers, I thought about Jefferson's words. Aside from straight-on mass murder, what are suicide bombings but a form of compulsion to worship a particular religion or die?

So to try to tell a story about this problem, I have created a fantasy world, with two made-up tribes from the same land, and two different made-up religions, who have survived from ancient times to the modern age, who both carry old traditions and neuroses and who both hate each other intensely.

This story was written to address a simple ethical question—does God want us to kill other people who don't believe as we do? As with the case of Kim Kardashian, I have my doubts.

After the Afterword—
Some Final Thoughts to Consider

"...the government of the United States... gives to bigotry no sanction, to persecution no assistance..."

—George Washington

"Violence is the last refuge of the incompetent."

—Isaac Asimov

"As I walk through this wicked world searchin' for light in the darkness of insanity, I ask myself, is all hope lost, is there only pain and hatred and misery? And each time I feel like this inside, there's one thing I wanna know, what's so funny about peace, love and understanding?"

—Nick Lowe

"Re 'Romney's Faith, Silent but Deep; Applying Mormonism's Lessons in Life and Campaign" ('The Long Run' series, front page, May 20): Ann Romney is quoted as saying of running for president that the Romneys both 'felt it was what God wanted them to do.'...That perception always reminds me of Susan B. Anthony's comment: 'I distrust those people who know so well what God wants them to do because I notice it always coincides with their own desires."

—Claire Cafaro, letter to the New York Times, May 24, 2012

ACKNOWLEDGEMENTS

I want to thank Paul Hughes and Mark Brand for their insights and advice to improve this story. Their help was invaluable.

I also want to thank my brother, Mark Gold, for providing technical advice.

ABOUT THE AUTHOR

Michael Gold has written for newspapers and magazines in Florida (The Palm Beach Post, The Stuart News, and the Jupiter Courier), New York (The Manhattan Times, The Queens Ledger, The Queens Examiner, Fund Raising Management and Direct Marketing magazines), and Oregon (The Eugene Daily Emerald, The Cottage Grove Sentinel and Willamette Valley Observer). He has also published work in Management Accounting and Pre-magazines.

He worked as a business writer for 17 years. He has written newsletters, promotional articles, brochures, and ghost-written pieces for corporate clients.

He published *Horror House Detective*, a novel in stories, with Silverthought in 2009, as well as a short essay, "The Heat Is Always On," with Penguin Books' climate change anthology, *Thoreau's Legacy*. He has also published nine fiction pieces with Silverthought Online, the last of which was "Mr. Head Finds Love" in October, 2009.

Michael lives in New York City with his family.

www.ingramcontent.com/pod-product-compliance
Lightning Source LLC
LaVergne TN
LVHW050922080826
845145LV00001B/173

* 9 7 8 0 9 8 4 1 7 3 8 8 4 *